The First Lady Escapes

FLOTUS Flees the White House

What people are saying about

The First Lady Escapes

"Just what we need in these dark times: A hilarious and wildly imaginative story about FLOTUS fleeing from the White House and her grotesque husband. And yet it is also strangely plausible—leading to the question, could it all be true?"
Jon Weiner, host of *Trump Watch*, KPFK 90.7 FM Los Angeles

"The First Lady escapes the White House with the help of a lively troupe of characters who stand for everything the President despises. This fantastical tale spins into a hilarious contest of power, willfulness, and cunning."
Maureen Muldaur, Award-winning Documentary Filmmaker

"This hugely entertaining tale resonates with the hitherto unimaginable absurdities of current affairs. Never was a book more engaging nor more timely. I chuckled all the way through it."
Lionel Friedberg, Author of *New York Times* bestseller *Full Service*

"What a page turner! The engrossing, racy, and humorous writing speeds you along. The best literary/political escape of the year!"
Ivor Davis, Author of *The Beatles and Me on Tour*

"A rippingly funny and surreal lampoon, the comic relief we so desperately need from the twisted absurdity of our current political horrors. It will leave you gasping with laughter and Trumpetized at the same time."
Jennifer Evans, Author of *Bitchin' in the Kitchen*

"I can't stop laughing! I'm buying a hundred copies to pass out at the next Women's March!"
Robin Leavitt, Loyal participant in the Women's March, Ketchum, Idaho

"Exactly what I need to get through the horrors of our current state of affairs. I constantly catch myself cracking up while reading chapters aloud to others."
Woosterlad, Disheartened Liberal from the Bay Area

The First Lady Escapes

FLOTUS Flees the White House

Verity Speeks

Winchester, UK
Washington, USA

First published by Roundfire Books, 2019
Roundfire Books is an imprint of John Hunt Publishing Ltd., No. 3 East St., Alresford,
Hampshire SO24 9EE, UK
office1@jhpbooks.net
www.johnhuntpublishing.com
www.roundfire-books.com

For distributor details and how to order please visit the 'Ordering' section on our website.

Text copyright: Verity Speeks 2018

ISBN: 978 1 78904 208 5
978 1 78904 209 2 (ebook)
Library of Congress Control Number: 2018952030

A CIP catalogue record for this book is available from the British Library.

Design: Stuart Davies

This is a work of fiction. Names, characters, places, and incidents
either are products of the author's imagination or are used fictitiously.
Any resemblance to actual events or locales or persons, living or dead,
is entirely coincidental.

UK: Printed and bound by CPI Group (UK) Ltd, Croydon, CR0 4YY
US: Printed and bound by Thomson Shore, 7300 West Joy Road, Dexter, MI 48130

We operate a distinctive and ethical publishing philosophy in
all areas of our business, from our global network of authors to
production and worldwide distribution.

Contents

To my beloved husband, and to all who share my belief that it's time to restore the values of freedom, decency, and tolerance in America.

"America is great because she is good. If America ceases to be good, America will cease to be great."
— Alexis de Tocqueville

Prologue

The White House

December 15, 11:31 p.m.

"Mr. Speaker; Mr. Vice President; my good friends in Congress; beautiful First Lady of the United States; and my fabulous fellow Americans..."

Natalia could hear her husband's first State of the Union Address blasting from the TV inside his bedroom. President Rex Funck had delivered the speech nearly three years ago, but he could never get enough of it. She knew that watching it tonight was especially important for the success of his latest scheme. She tightened the belt on her white-silk Prada bathrobe, fighting the urge to turn and flee. But as FLOTUS, she was expected to be an essential part of it.

Pricker, a hulking Secret Service special agent, held out a box of sanitary gloves. She plucked out two and pulled them on, checking to see that the 15-karat diamond on her ring didn't poke a hole in the latex. He touched the coiled-plastic tubing on his radio earpiece and said, "Trophy is ready, Mr. President." He opened the door and she walked in.

"Thank you for making me your leader in the biggest, huuuugest landslide of any Presidential election in American history..."

Natalia was always startled by the glittering crystal chandeliers and gilded antique furniture in her husband's bedroom, as extravagant as those she once saw in the Palace of Versailles. Engrossed in his speech, Rex was slumped on a high-backed, gold-trimmed red armchair as imposing as a throne. Years ago, when they had started dating, he told her he had a recurring dream that he was the reincarnation of Louis XIV, France's Sun King. Tonight, wrapped in a terrycloth bathrobe and eating a Big Mac, his eyes glued to his image on the 88-inch-wide TV screen, Rex looks more like a deranged, pot-bellied pasha than a king, she thought.

3

"Now the work begins. We face terrible, tremendous trials that I've got to say I warned you about, and dangers that even I never could have imagined..."

Gretchen Funck sat barefoot at Rex's feet, her skintight white Armani sheath hiked up above her knees, her black Louboutin stiletto heels lying topsy-turvy on the carpet, their red soles lolling like dog's tongues. She seemed as rapt in her father's speech as he was.

"Each day, from now on, we will march forward with a tough vision and a righteous task: to make this country fantastic again for each and every — but you better believe 100 percent legitimate — American — "

"Alllllright!" Rex toasted his TV image with a Diet Coke. "Is this guy a god or *what?*" He polished off his burger and handed the grease-stained wrapper to Gretchen.

She took it with a latex-gloved hand. "Yes, Daddy!"

Even the First Daughter now wears sanitary gloves in his presence, Natalia thought. She wondered how long it would take for his germ phobia to get so bad it killed him, or at least affected his ratings. She walked toward them.

"FLOTUS is here," Gretchen said with an edge in her voice. Natalia knew it was to remind her that she was the *real* First Lady in POTUS's eyes. Gretchen wiggled into her stilettos. "G'night, Daddy," she called on her way out of the bedroom.

"Yes, this is the most amazing time in the history of mankind for us — and by 'us' I mean only legally-within-our-borders citizens — to live the American dream..."

Without looking up from the TV, Rex motioned to Natalia. "Get your pussy over here!"

She stiffened. He had never used vulgar words with her before he was President. He had treated her with respect and he had admired her with intent, loving eyes. Now he spoke to her as coarsely as he did to his political opponents and he rarely glanced at her. My husband has become such a *hlupák*, she thought, using the word for "asshole" from her native Slovakia.

4

"It's going to happen, starting right now! I've told you what's important: being smart and strong and following me and the tremendous minds I have assembled to help me lead..."

She kneeled at Rex's feet, slid a rosewood box from under his chair, and opened it. Inside were dozens of "penis sleeves" and "penis extenders," silicone devices designed to add length and/or rigidity to a man's *vták,* the Slovak word that Natalia preferred using for "penis."

"I want every toddler, every tyke, and every teenager to be safe in their households at night..."

"What's your pleasure, Rex?"

"I want every man to keep what he earns from a hard day's labor; women too of course..."

"Whatever's biggest," he said, riveted by his image on the TV screen.

"And don't believe the stupid fake news you hear about global warming. Every U.S. citizen should be proud of this pure, unpolluted, and perfect land that we cherish..."

She selected the silicone sleeve that was the smallest and hastily attached it to his vták. In the unlikely event Rex took his eyes off the TV, she didn't want him to see that it was the perfect fit. She knew he would scream, "It's a fake measurement! Fake!"

"As long as Americans believe in smart but tough values, in God, and in me as your leader, we will not be losers..."

Natalia stood up and untied her bathrobe. As it fell to the floor, the flutter of silk caught his attention. He gazed at her body. "Why do wives have to get old?"

Pretending she didn't hear that—she was eager to get tonight over with—she sat down on his lap, facing him. She delicately wedged his silicone-enhanced vták inside her.

"You're in the fucking way!" He shoved her head to the left so that he could see the TV screen.

"My government will not tolerate morons. Our people must thrive. Our people must be safe. Our people must trust in me. I'm

tremendously smart—we're talking 'genius'—and our people can count on me to save their you-know-whats..."

Natalia could feel Rex's vták growing firmer. She closed her eyes so that she wouldn't be staring at his dyed-orange comb-over.

"With me as your President, our nation will be secure and strong and proud and mighty and free and amazing..."

Rex started to thrust, grunting.

Natalia's last thought before she turned off her mind: The only way the President of the United States can get it up is facing a mega-TV screen filled with his own image.

"Thank you, and God bless America!"

Part I

Two Weeks Earlier

Chapter 1

New York City

December 1, 2:00 p.m.

Natalia peered out of the smoked bulletproof window of the black Escalade as it crept through snow-day traffic on Madison Avenue. The SUV stopped at a red light on Fifty-Ninth street. She glanced at the holiday decorations in a window of Barney's. Four white plastic robots in sequined party dresses formed an awkward chorus line, their sleek white plastic legs thrusting into the air, their shiny white plastic heads wagging from side to side. Their faces lacked eyes, ears, and noses. The only indication that the robots were feminine was their exaggeratedly plumped red lips, each pursed in a pout. Natalia touched her own Juvederm-swollen lips and realized that they were tightly pressed together, like theirs. Nothing to smile about, she thought. Like the plastic robots, I'm just going through the motions. She hoped that her visit today in New York would motivate her to get off her Slovak *zadok*.

The light turned green and the SUV continued up Madison Avenue, past Celine, Givenchy, and Valentino. She sighed wistfully. Before she became the First Lady, she could pop into any one of these designer boutiques without causing pandemonium among the hedge-fund wives and brand-crazy Chinese shoppers who worshipped there. The female store managers welcomed her with double air kisses. The gay male store managers kissed her hand, admiring the 15-karat emerald-cut diamond engagement ring that hugged her diamond wedding band.

Fourteen years ago, the opulent De Beers diamond ring hadn't been a surprise. Rex didn't like surprises, but he loved publicity. So before giving her the engagement ring, he flashed it to the press. "It's worth $3 million," he bragged. "But I got a great deal!

9

Just like I got a great deal on Natalia!" Everyone knew that he was referring to the ironclad prenup that she was forced to sign before their wedding.

Natalia glanced down at the diamond. It glinted in the light from the backseat TV screen that was tuned to *The Ellen DeGeneres Show*, the sound muted. She stroked the stone with her index finger, imagining that she was rubbing a magic lantern and a genie would pop out. She pictured the genie looking like Ellen: boyish, perky, eager to grant her every wish. She only had one: to disappear from the White House and from President Rex Funck's life. She would happily give the genie her ring if her wish were granted.

Not that Ellen needs a 15-karat diamond ring, she thought. And not that I can get it off my finger. She twisted the platinum band, but it was too tight. She couldn't work the engagement ring or the wedding band up over her swollen knuckle. It was as if she were shackled to the multi-million-dollar rings, like she was shackled to Rex Funck.

Natalia shuddered, remembering the morning a few weeks ago when Rex had summoned Dr. Abraham Steinberg, Ob-Gyn, to the White House. "He's a Jew," Rex said, as if that added to his reputation as America's leading fertility expert. "When it comes to medicine and money, Jews work miracles." She had no choice but to meet with the aged, hunched-over doctor. She knew that President Rex Funck only heard the word "no" when it came out of his own mouth.

The White House butlers had wheeled an examining table, complete with stirrups, into her bedroom. Without saying a word, the doctor examined her inside and out and then signaled for her to turn onto her side. "You have a mole on your right buttock," he muttered as he positioned himself behind her. "Very odd, but it is heart-shaped, like on a Valentine's Day card." He recommended that it be surgically removed.

She quickly set him straight. "That mole is part of my body.

It stays."

Dr. Steinberg swabbed alcohol on her left buttock, then pinched her flesh longer and harder than she thought necessary. "What are you doing?" she asked.

"I am going to pump you with FSH to cause your eggs to ripen and LH to trigger their release," he wheezed into her ear. He stabbed in the needle. "And for good measure, Clomiphene citrate to block the effect of o-estrogen in your brain and trick your body into bumping up its natural levels of FSH and LH." He slapped a bandage on Natalia's throbbing sore spot. "Since you are a woman with overdeveloped female characteristics to begin with, this ought to do the trick."

Natalia had tolerated Dr. Steinberg's injections for ten days straight. She reviled the hormones' effects on her: Her body swelled up until she felt like the goose that was fattened all year on her grandmother's farm in Slovakia for Christmas dinner. Since her modeling days, she had weighed herself daily. If she gained even two pounds she went on a leek-juice fast to quickly shed them. Last week, she looked down at her bathroom scale in horror: She had put on seven pounds overnight. Not just from the estrogen bloating. Dr. Steinberg's hormones gave her night cravings.

Natalia was in control during the day. She ate as if she were still a model: delicately skating the food around her plate with a fork but putting only one-fourth of it into her mouth. When she and Rex had lived in New York, she "did" lunch at chic restaurants three times a week with her ex-model friends. They all had the same "eating habit" and took their leftovers home in eco-friendly doggie bags. She guessed that the minute they were alone in their hedge-fund husbands' (or lovers') $20-million TriBeCa condos, they scarfed down the scraps. Natalia was proud that she had the willpower to hand over her doggie bag to her doorman.

At official White House dinners, she was under strict orders from Rex to speak politely to guests, but never to express a personal or political opinion. "Michelle Obama, Laura Bush, and other First Ladies may have had their 'causes,'" he said. "But you have only one: to make me look fucking great!" Natalia barely touched her food, but not thanks to her willpower. Being First Lady to Rex's President had killed her appetite.

Until Dr. Steinberg began shooting hormones into her zadok. Now, in the middle of the night, she awoke ravenous. Her willpower morphed into an overwhelming compulsion to pig out. Last week, at 3:00 a.m., she had snuck down a back stairway in the White House to the staff-cafeteria kitchen in the basement. There she discovered a lanky young African-American baker mixing 50 pounds of batter in a bowl big enough to bathe a St. Bernard. "The folks that work at the White House can't get enough of my buttermilk biscuits," Stella Brown said. "They love down-home Southern cooking." She explained that most of the ushers, butlers, and maids at the White House were African-American. "Generations of the same black families have been working here since before the Civil War, including mine." Natalia knew that "before the Civil War" was code for "when they were slaves." She adored Stella's buttermilk biscuits, especially hot from the oven and smothered in butter. As the Escalade took a right on Eighty-Seventh Street, she wished she could stuff one into her mouth right now.

The SUV turned left on Park Avenue, continuing uptown. A few more blocks to go.

The reason Natalia had come to New York today was because of Dr. Steinberg's hormone shots. The mega-doses of estrogen that made her hungry also had caused havoc with her emotions. Before getting the daily injections, she had been able to suppress the disgust she felt increasingly for her husband. Now, one look at Rex makes me want to slit my wrists, she thought, or his.

To shake the thought from her mind, she slid open the vanity mirror on the back of the front seat and checked her makeup.

She could use a touch more mascara and some blusher, but she knew that the person she was visiting today wouldn't care. She wiped a smudge of liner from the corner of her eye. Men had always found her long-lashed, emerald-green eyes, with their slight Asian slant, exotic. "The slant's because some barbarian Tartar invader had his way with my beautiful Slovak great-great-grandmother," her mother liked to say. Today, her eyes didn't look exotic or beautiful. They've lost their sparkle, she thought.

She sank deeper into the soft leather. On TV, Ellen was handing out $100 bills to screaming members of the audience. Natalia realized that there was no point in making a wish to genie/Ellen. Even if her wish were granted, and even if she could wrench the 15-karat diamond engagement ring off her swollen finger, she couldn't give it away. Thanks to the prenup, Rex owned all her jewelry.

Chapter 2

New York City

December 1, 2:30 p.m.

"*Hovno,*" Natalia muttered as the Escalade pulled up to the brass-trimmed portico of a Park Avenue high-rise.

In the front seat, the African-American bodyguard asked, "Ma'am?"

"*Hovno* is Slovak for 'shit,' Ken. You should know that by now."

"Yes, ma'am," he replied. "I meant, should we abort?"

She dipped into the Gucci leather tote bag at her feet and pulled out a black wig. Fitting it over her ash-blonde hair, she tucked a few stray hairs underneath and slipped on oversized Dior sunglasses. "No, there's only one clown on my zadok today, and it's just Phil."

She glanced out the window at the slight young man in a well-worn jacket who was wearing crooked eyeglasses and a dingy blue L.A. Dodgers baseball cap. He was hunched behind the potted mini-Christmas tree at the building entrance, shivering in the cold. She was both annoyed and amazed that Phil was here. Her visit in New York today had not been included on her official FLOTUS schedule. How could he have known that she was coming?

Last year, Natalia seemed to spot Phil's face in the crowd of paparazzi at the perimeter fence every time she left the White House. Something about the disheveled young man with the blank stare had made her feel vulnerable. She asked Sally-Ann, her thirty-something social secretary, to have him checked out by White House security. Natalia hoped that he was in the country illegally and that they could deport him, or on probation or parole from prison and that they could slap an injunction on him to keep him away from her.

Sally-Ann had come back with a clean report. Phil Smith was as ordinary as his name. He grew up in Pasadena, dropped out of college, and delivered pizzas until he made enough money to buy his first camera. He joined the cadre of paparazzi who hung around outside Los Angeles restaurants, hotels, and hair salons favored by Hollywood celebrities. Apparently, Phil was good enough to snap photos of stars like Jennifer Aniston, George Clooney, and Beyoncé that sold for thousands of dollars to the tabloids. The report said that after Funck was elected President, Phil moved from L.A. to Washington, D.C., and switched his focus from superstars to the First Lady. Natalia hoped that Phil's reason for moving was because there were fewer paparazzi in the nation's capital than in Hollywood and therefore less competition, not because he was obsessed with her.

As Ken climbed out of the Escalade, she grabbed the mink coat on the seat and slipped into it, then pulled an ivory Bottega Veneta cashmere scarf from her tote. She wrapped the scarf around her neck and pulled it over her chin, all the way up to her nose. She relished its downy warmth—she had read that it was made with the soft undercoat of Mongolian goats—and the sense of security it gave her. She knew it would be fleeting.

Ken tapped on the window of the Escalade, indicating that he was ready to open her door at her signal. Ken had been her favorite Secret Service agent since Rex became President-elect. The day when the President referred to African nations as "shithole countries," she had felt compelled to apologize to Ken for what her husband said. But within minutes Rex tweeted that he never uttered those words, that it was "fake news." And as her husband and the First Daughter always reminded Natalia, FLOTUS was forbidden to comment on whatever POTUS deemed "fake news."

She grabbed a pair of kidskin gloves from her tote and pulled them on. Then, ever the high-fashion model checking for flaws before stepping onto the runway, she checked that the clasp on her Chanel clutch was secure, and glanced down at her black Louboutin stiletto boots. A faint blemish marred the left toe. She licked her finger and rubbed the spot to the count of ten, as she had learned in Paris, until it disappeared.

Outside the smoked window, she saw that Phil had emerged from behind the mini-Christmas tree. Hunched against the cold in his ragged jacket, the paparazzo was wearing threadbare sneakers that were drenched from the slush. For a moment, she felt sorry for him. But should she? Phil was a loser who devoted his life to trying to take a photo of her for the *National Enquirer*, a photo that could make her life more of a living hell than it already was.

She tapped on the window. Ken opened the back door of the SUV. Phil snapped a barrage of photos as the bodyguard blocked her cashmere-scarf-wrapped face with his burly body and swept her into the building. Sorry, Phil, she thought, no million-dollar shot for you today.

Chapter 3

New York City

December 1, 2:45 p.m.

"You look fat!" said Ingrid in her gravelly smoker's voice. "Like a Slovak pig."

"Thanks, *Mamina*!" Natalia tossed her mink coat and purse onto the bed, where her mother was propped up against a heap of pillows watching *The Ellen DeGeneres Show* on a TV hanging from the ceiling. Natalia glanced at the room's peach walls, gossamer peach curtains, and softly lit crystal chandelier. They created a warm, even luxurious, ambience in what was essentially a hospital room at this recovery center for women who had plastic surgery more often than their teeth cleaned. She remembered the day in Paris when she had modeled for a fashion shoot in a similarly peach-hued suite at the Paris Ritz Hotel. The photographer explained that hotel founder Caesar Ritz once said that even the ugliest woman looks better against the color peach. That certainly didn't hold true today for her mother. "Mamina, you look like hovno," she said.

As if incensed by the insult, the toy Pomeranian on her mother's lap yipped.

"Vladimir, shush!" Ingrid shoved the tiny dog under the peach-colored covers, aimed the remote at the TV screen, and zapped it off. She tossed the remote onto the nightstand, beside her iPhone. "Better to look like shit than fat. What will Rex say?"

"Do I care?" Natalia yanked off her scarf, sunglasses, and black wig, and tossed them onto the heap of fur. She sat down on the bed and examined the bruises around her mother's eyes, the stitches tracing a pink zigzag along her hairline and throat. "*Seriously*? You needed a third facelift?"

"My daughter is FLOTUS, First Lady of the United States,"

19

said Ingrid, exaggerating her thick Slovak accent. "I deserve it."

Natalia touched a surgical thread poking out of the swollen flesh under her mother's right ear. "You look like a scarecrow on *Babika's* farm."

Ingrid slapped Natalia's hand away. "Why aren't you at the White House? I watch CNN. There is a state dinner tonight with the Prime Minister of Cambodia." She primped her thinning reddish hair, as if offended that she hadn't been invited.

"Not Cambodia, Malaysia." Natalia stood up, walked over to the window, and cautiously pulled aside an inch of the gossamer peach curtains. As she had feared, Phil was stationed on the sidewalk below, tapping on his iPhone. Was he tweeting? The tweet flashed before her eyes: *"FLOTUS gets plastic surgery!"* She scrambled for a plan: "Mamina, you've got to see this," she said. "A lady is walking a dog on the street that looks like Vladimir. Oh my God, the dog could be Vladimir's twin!"

At the sound of its name, Ingrid's toy Pomeranian struggled out from under the covers. Yipping plaintively, it pawed at Ingrid's chest, its tiny nails snagging her peach silk nightgown. She melted. "You want to see your twin?" She cradled the dog in her arms and carefully swung her legs over the side of the bed. Natalia helped her over to the window. Standing behind her, she yanked open the curtains.

Ingrid held her Pomeranian up to the window. "Do you see your twin?" The dog whimpered, trembling, its nails pattering on the window like raindrops. She scanned the sidewalk. "I don't see a dog, just a homeless man with a camera."

"Look closer." Natalia gently pushed her mother nearer to the window. From below, she heard the barrage of clicks from Phil's camera. Vladimir jumped out of Ingrid's arms, yipping.

"*Suka!*" Ingrid hissed at Natalia.

"I'm not a bitch! People in America cannot think FLOTUS is getting work done!"

"So now they will know *I* did." Unsteady on her feet, Ingrid started back toward her bed.

"Let me help you."

Ingrid reluctantly took her daughter's arm. "Suka," she grumbled.

Natalia jiggled her arm, the musical clink drawing attention to the three gold Cartier LOVE bracelets on her wrist, each studded with tiny screws and precious jewels. Natalia's mother studied the bracelets and tapped one glittering with diamonds and sapphires. "How much?"

She knew where this was leading. "$20,000?"

Ingrid tapped another Cartier LOVE bracelet, this one encrusted with mini rubies. *"And?"*

It was an exaggeration, but why not? "$27,000," Natalia said.

Her mother tapped the bracelet twice.

"It's yours!" Natalia grabbed her purse and pulled out a black-velvet drawstring jewelry bag. Inside it was a delicate rose-gold screwdriver. She twisted the tiny screwdriver into a screw on the selected Cartier bracelet and turned it gently, until the bracelet unlatched. She slipped the bracelet off her own arm and onto her mother's, and clamped it shut. She placed the screwdriver back into the velvet bag and handed it to her. "In case you ever want to take it off."

"Ďakujem, thank you." Ingrid smiled, satisfied, just as she did the last time Natalia bestowed one of her Cartier LOVE Bracelets on her, the perfect remedy for a mother-daughter tiff. Ingrid placed the jewelry bag next to her iPhone on the nightstand and climbed back into bed.

Rex had given Natalia dozens of Cartier LOVE bracelets, so many that she didn't worry he would notice some were missing. She suspected that he gave them to her whenever he felt a twinge of what passed for guilt after cheating on her. How ironic that Rex's usual "guilt gift" smacks of "enslavement," she thought. The Cartier LOVE bracelet is the only bracelet in the world that requires a screwdriver to remove it.

Ingrid's toy Pomeranian yipped at her feet. She gently picked it up and settled it onto her mother's lap. Ingrid kissed the dog on its tiny wet nose and turned to her daughter. "Why are you here?"

"News update," she said, testing the waters.

"Real or fake news?"

"Both."

Ingrid slid over on the bed and she sat down beside her. She took a deep breath and then let it out slowly, as if she were in yoga class.

Her mother squirmed, impatient. "*So?*"

"Rex wants me to have a baby."

Ingrid's jaw dropped. "But 'no children' is part of your prenup!"

"Correct."

"He didn't want more *deti* because he hates the children he has."

"Except the First Daughter."

"And his deti get worse each time he has one, like prime ministers in Slovakia! Why did Rex change his mind so now he wants more children?"

Natalia blurted it out: "The Presidential election is less than a year away, Mamina. Rex will be seventy-five years old. He says if he gets me pregnant and I have a baby bump at the Republican Convention, the American people will think he's a macho stud. They will elect him to a second term."

Ingrid applauded joyfully. "Brilliant!" She stopped clapping. A frown pinched her bruised forehead. "Natalia, you're almost fifty—"

"If I'm almost fifty, you're almost seventy."

"I'm still sixty-eight for another month! But forty-nine, forty-eight, the chances of your getting pregnant are hovno." Moving only her eyes so as not to disturb her stitches, she looked Natalia up and down. "Aha!"

"What?"

"I know why you're fat. You're getting hormone shots to stimulate eggs to make a baby!"

She nodded. Ingrid gripped her hand, caressing the 15-karat diamond with her thumb as she spoke. "Natalia, my darling daughter, my darling *FLOTUS* daughter, this is big news! Wonderful news! You always wanted a baby. It broke your heart when Rex made 'no *dieťa*' a condition of your marriage."

Natalia paused, knowing that her mother would not be happy with her decision. "I do not want to have Rex's baby."

"*What? Why?* You did fourteen years ago!"

"I don't now!"

"But you will get four more years in the White House!"

"I hate the White House!

"You will get four more years of hot-stone massages and collagen facials at Beau Rivage in Palm Beach, near me and Papa..." Her eyes suddenly brimmed with tears. She touched her iPhone on the nightstand. "I wish I could call Papa right now with the good news."

Natalia took Ingrid's hand, knowing that she missed her husband, who had died of a heart attack a year ago—even though he was in bed with his Slovak mistress at the time. Ingrid had made it through forty-nine years of marriage to Natalia's handsome, but womanizing, father by adhering to an old Slovak saying that she tried to instill in her: "*What eyes don't see, heart doesn't hurt.*"

"Mamina, I know it's hard for you without Papa."

"A baby would give me something to do! I could move into the White House and help with the baby!"

How typical of my mother to make this about herself, she thought. If she *did* have a baby, the last thing she wanted was her mother in her face. But that was beside the point right now. "I do not want a baby with Rex," she said. "I hate Rex!"

"No, darling, you love Rex. It's only the hormones talking."

"He makes me a laughing stock!"

"Don't be stupid. What they say about Rex and that woman—"

"*Women!*"

"It's all fake news."

She wondered if Ingrid actually believed that. "Mamina, *seriously*?"

"Men have needs, Natalia. Especially powerful, rich men. You must work harder to keep them interested. Even your father—"

"Papa wasn't rich until Rex bought him ten Slovak Audi dealerships!"

"May Papa rest in peace!" Ingrid made the sign of the cross. "Be grateful those Audi dealerships gave your baby brother a job. You want Franc back in jail?"

"Rex owns Franc and you and me!"

"Rex doesn't own us. He is a loving man, a generous man. A *great* man! He is POTUS, the greatest leader on the planet!"

"Rex is a *bad* leader! He is *zlý*, bad, period! Weekends at Beau Rivage, I sit through long, boring dinners with him in the dining room. Businessmen, friends, come over to our table, groveling and seeking favors. Rex is eating Funck steak dripping with ketchup. He's talking to them with his mouth full, specks of meat spewing out with his spit. What are they talking about? Feeding starving migrant children at the Mexican border? I don't think so!"

Ingrid snorted. "Name me one government official in Slovakia who doesn't stuff his own pocket! Name me one in Russia, in China!"

"Rex calls immigrants 'animals' and takes their babies away," she said, ignoring her. "His company makes business deals with foreign governments. He refuses to admit the world is being devastated by global warming!"

"Rex is POTUS. You must trust he's doing the right thing."

"I *must*? In citizenship class, they taught me America is a democracy. A free country where the President is honest and thinks of the people first, not himself." It sounded strange to her as she said the words, as if it were all a scam.

"Democracy is a *bájka*," said Ingrid. "A folktale, like the folktales Babika told you when you were a little *halusky*." She pinched Natalia's cheek.

Natalia pulled away, remembering how when she was a little girl, her grandmother would tell her stories by the fireplace in her farmhouse, a pile of potatoes on the floor. Her babika never washed her hands after digging up potatoes. She always smelled like dirt.

"Natalia, darling, when you met Rex, you said you felt loved, safe, worshipped." Ingrid's suddenly sweet tone warned her that she was launching into a sell mode. "You felt you found your *Zlatorog*!"

"*Zlatorog?*" Natalia shook her head. "The Slovak mountain-goat god who owns all the treasures in the world? The story says the god is a monster until he marries a beautiful woman. Then he becomes good. '*Good*?' That's the bájka about Rex!"

"I remember Babika told me that story when I was little girl." Ingrid smiled wistfully, ignoring Natalia's point. "She said Zlatorog was guarded by a dragon."

"A dragon with a hundred heads. Now when I think of Rex, he's not Zlatorog, the god. He's the dragon!"

"Natalia, you are the luckiest woman on the planet," said Ingrid, her voice hardening.

"I am a prisoner."

"Stop this craziness!" She grabbed her by the shoulders. "Listen to me. Don't I know what's best for you?" When Natalia averted her eyes, Ingrid shook her. "Didn't I stop you from making the biggest mistake in your life?" She shook her again, harder. "*Didn't I?*"

"Yes."

Suddenly Natalia was fifteen years old, admitting that her mother's suspicions were correct. She was pregnant. That day her mother convinced her to have the baby in secret and give it away to an orphanage. "You must do this. You are young and beautiful, and you will be an internationally famous fashion model." She remembered how Ingrid repeated it over and over, hammering away as if it were dream for herself. "You must not give that up!"

"Maybe you knew what was best for me when I was fifteen," she said, squirming out of her mother's grasp. "But not now. Not this time." She stood up from the bed.

"Natalia, you gave birth to a baby in sin," hissed Ingrid. She clutched the gold crucifix around her neck. "This is your chance to make up for it in the eyes of God."

Natalia flinched, stung in her most vulnerable spot.

* * *

Natalia had been burdened with guilt since the baby's birth. She prayed nightly to the Virgin Mary to forgive her. The memory flashed in her mind: screaming in pain as she lay in bed by the fireplace in her grandmother's farmhouse, her babika squeezing her hand as Natalia pushed a child out into the world. In the flickering firelight, she saw it was a boy. She wished she could tell the baby's father, her one true love, but she had been forbidden to ever see him again.

Before the midwife could wipe off the bloody afterbirth, her mother snatched the baby and wrapped it in a blanket. Natalia hadn't expected to feel maternal instincts, but they suddenly overwhelmed her. "Mamina," she cried, reaching for the baby. Ingrid ignored her, carrying the child out the door. Natalia glimpsed a withered Catholic nun hovering on the threshold. Her mother put the baby in the nun's arms and shoved cash into the pocket of her frayed habit. The nun vanished into the snowy night.

Natalia remembered wailing in grief. Ingrid had no patience

for her tears. "Put today out of your mind," she had said, as if it were a command. "Forget all about it. Focus on the future!" She cringed, remembering the old Slovak saying that her mother then repeated and had been repeating ever since: *"What eyes don't see, heart doesn't hurt."*

Natalia had to admit that as her modeling career took off, she did forget about the baby. But the guilt never disappeared. Years later, she came up with a way to assuage it. She had been dating Rex and had moved to New York when he confessed that he was in love with her. "As soon as I get you a ring, I might just propose," he joked. She called her mother in Slovakia.

"Say yes!" Ingrid screamed into the phone.

"But I don't know if love him," Natalia admitted.

"You love him!"

"How can I be sure?"

"How can you *not* love a billionaire with palaces, limos, yachts, jet planes, and hotels?"

Natalia hung up on Ingrid—she wanted to make her own decision—but her mother's words had echoed in her mind. After a few days, despite her doubts, she came up with a persuasive reason—okay, it was a rationalization, she admitted—to marry Rex. It hit her one afternoon when she was in Serendipity Café pigging out on a hot-fudge sundae because she was so depressed that she didn't even have the desire to go shopping. She called this reason for marrying Rex the "cherry on top," like the maraschino cherry on top of her hot-fudge sundae. It was small, but so sweet and such a happy color, that she saved it for last.

Natalia remembered how she spun a fantasy of finding her long-lost son; she even hired a detective to scour Slovakia looking for him. After she and Rex got married, she imagined bringing the young man—he would be grown by now—to live with them in America. She convinced herself that if Rex loved her enough to marry her, he would accept her child. She pictured Rex taking him into his family and his business. It seemed the perfect happy ending: She would not only right the wrong she had done in the eyes of God, but her son would become a millionaire.

She recalled the night that Rex had proposed to her on his yacht, the shimmering lights of the New York skyline behind them. She was touched to see tears in his eyes when he said, "I feel I've been waiting for you my entire life," and presented her with the 15-karat diamond engagement ring that he had already flashed to reporters. "I promise to do everything in my power to make you happy." She felt so loved, so confident that Rex would do anything to please her, that after they returned to his penthouse in Funck Tower and were slipping into bed, she confessed that she had given up a baby when she was young. "If I find him, I hope you will accept him as part of our family."

Instead of agreeing to her request, he had lashed out at her. "Are you out of your fucking mind? You think I want another bastard child to support? No fucking way! This one's not even mine!" He kicked her out of bed. "Come back when you're ready to play by my rules!"

She remembered wandering, dazed, through the penthouse condo, realizing that she had nowhere else to go. In the palatial living room, she flicked on the lights and gazed at the gold-framed eighteenth-century French landscapes and gilded furniture. "Talk about antiques!" Rex had bragged the first time he brought her here. "These priceless beauties once belonged to King Louis XIV of France. The fucking Sun King! They were in the fucking Palace of Versailles!"

Natalia knew that King Louis XIV's furniture was still in Versailles. She had seen it there when she trooped through the palace with hundreds of other tourists after moving to Paris from Slovakia. This was just one more of Rex's... She didn't think of them as lies in those days, just innocent exaggerations. But so what if his "antiques" were replicas? They glowed in the radiance of massive chandeliers dripping with crystal. When she toured Versailles, she had dreamed of one day living in a palace. Now she had the chance. Would she ever have another one? Could she turn all this down because of a son she might never find? She crept over to the phone and called her mother in Slovakia for advice.

"You told Rex about the *dieťa*, the baby? You are *bláznivý*!" Ingrid screamed.

"I'm not crazy, Mamina! I thought he loved me enough to—"

"Do not think, Natalia! Thinking is what got you in deep *hovno*!" Her mother's voice was faint—the phone connection with Slovakia was weak—but her panic was loud and clear. "Do whatever you must to make him forget you ever said it! Rex will not just be your husband. He will be your boss, your master, and your savior! Without Rex, you will end up a dirty-legs *prostitútka* in Bratislava!"

Natalia angrily hung up the phone, but she was terrified that her mother was right. She crept back into Rex's bedroom. He was lying in bed watching FOX News, a Diet Coke in his hand. He didn't look up from the screen when she apologized and begged for his forgiveness. Instead, he snatched a thick document from the nightstand and tossed it at her: the prenuptial agreement. She didn't bother to read it. She signed it, climbed into bed, and slid down the straps of the black-silk La Perla nightgown that he had given her to wear tonight.

"That black-ass Muslim motherfucker!" yelled Rex. Natalia glimpsed the TV screen. He was referring to Barak Obama, who at the time was being mentioned as a potential future candidate for President. She licked her lips and ducked under the covers. She knew that it was crucial right now to give Rex the blowjob to blow away all blowjobs, or she would be history.

* * *

"Natalia!" Her mother's voice startled her back to the glorified hospital room. "Look at your ring!"

"What?"

"It's like the headlight on a locomotive." Ingrid grabbed Natalia's left hand and wrenched it close to her face. "How many women in the world have a ring like this?"

"I don't care."

"You are royalty!"

"I would rather be a *roľník,* a peasant!" A wave of guilt, as sour as bile, surged in Natalia's gut. She remembered back to the day before her wedding to Rex, when the Slovak detective she had hired to find her son reported that the boy died of rheumatic fever at the age of five. She considered the news a bad omen for her marriage, but her mother convinced her that it was too late to back out. She wished now that she had. What her mother said was wrong: Having Rex's child wouldn't make up for the guilt she still felt for having a baby in sin. It would make her feel guiltier.

"I will not have Rex's baby, Mamina. Rex is the *diabol!*" She grabbed her coat, scarf, and purse from the bed.

"Natalia, do not do something stupid!"

Sensing Ingrid's panic, her dog jumped off the bed and peed on the floor. "*Ach!* Vladimir! *Zlý pes!* Bad dog!" She rummaged in the bed covers for the buzzer to summon a nurse.

In that instant, when her back was turned, Natalia snatched her mother's iPhone from the nightstand and pocketed it. "Love you, Mamina!" She donned her black wig and sunglasses, blew her an air kiss, and headed toward the door.

Still rummaging for the buzzer, Ingrid called after her, "Promise you will not do something *bláznivý,* crazy!"

Natalia waved to her mother and walked out the door. In the hall, she pulled the iPhone from her pocket and stowed it in her purse.

Sorry, Mamina, she thought. Right now, I need this phone more than you do.

Chapter 4

New York City

December 1, 4:00 p.m.

Bristling from the visit with her mother, Natalia sank into the back seat of the Escalade. Ken eased the door shut and hopped in front. The driver pulled into Park Avenue traffic. Sliding into a corner that Ken and the driver couldn't see in the rearview mirror, she took her mother's iPhone out of her purse and pressed the start button. Nothing.

"Hovno!" She should have known that her mother would forget to charge it.

She slid open a panel on the back of the driver's seat, revealing a mini fridge and a tray holding crystal glasses etched with the Presidential seal. Beside it, iPhone cords dangled from two data ports. She grabbed one and plugged in the iPhone. While waiting for it to charge, she surveyed the contents of the fridge. In addition to Rex's regulation cans of Diet Coke, it was stocked with bottles of Evian, Perrier, and San Pellegrino, her three mineral waters of choice. She usually drank Evian because it was flat water, calming when she needed to stay calm. Right now, she craved bubbles.

She opened a bottle of Perrier and poured the fizzing water into a crystal glass. She took a sip and closed her eyes. Savoring the tickle on her tongue, she pretended it was champagne. She had something to celebrate: She had convinced Rex to allow her to visit her mother in New York today so that she could secretly snatch her iPhone. Now she possessed a phone that was not monitored by the White House, as her FLOTUS phone was. Rex and Gretchen would never know whom she called—or what she searched for online—with it. Natalia reverently placed her fingers on the phone, as if it were a religious relic. May you

31

charge quickly, she thought, and yield Google information that will change my life.

They were pulling onto the East River Highway. She knew that she had to access the iPhone before the SUV arrived at the East River Heliport. Once she climbed aboard the helicopter that was waiting there to whisk her back to the White House, she would have no privacy. Her fingers itched to tap on Slovak Google, Slovak Facebook, and the dozens of Slovak apps that she knew her mother had on her phone. They were crucial to locating the man that she was desperate to find.

She remembered that a few years ago her mother had said she used the same password for all her online accounts: "At my age, it's hard enough to remember *one* password!" She asked Natalia to remember it, just in case she forgot: "*Haluski 1724.*" "*Haluskis* are my favorite Slovak potato dumplings," she said to Natalia. "When you were a little girl, I used to feed you haluskis by hand! I even nicknamed you 'haluski'!"

Natalia remembered the morning of her fourteenth birthday. She was naked, rummaging in a drawer for something to wear in the bedroom she shared with her brother in the family's Communist-era, high-rise apartment. Her mother had barged in. "Happy Birthday, my little *haluski!*" She looked Natalia up and down and crossed herself. "*Mami Maria!* You are the tallest, slimmest, and most beautiful girl in Žilina Catholic School! With the smallest waist and the biggest *haluskis!*"

"Mamina, you're embarrassing me!"

"For such beauty, you have God, and me, to thank!" Ingrid lifted her enormous, but now-sagging, breasts, and gave them a shake. Laughing, she hugged Natalia.

After her fourteenth birthday, her mother continued to call her "haluski," but she no longer hand-fed her dumplings, or allowed her to eat them. "Soon you will be a famous model! You cannot be fat!"

"No more haluskis!" was her mother's mantra.

In the back of the Escalade, Natalia checked the charging iPhone. Not enough power yet. She focused back on the password. Her mother had told her that she chose the number "1724" to go with "haluskis" because 1724 was the address of the little four-room house on Čierny Mor Street in Žilina that Natalia bought her parents after she became a successful model in Paris, when she was nineteen. "Papa and I are so proud of you," Ingrid had said. "Our little haluski is now rich and famous!"

Natalia thought back to that time. The truth? Her modeling career wasn't all that successful, and she was a long way from being "rich and famous." She recalled her first months working in Paris. It was winter and bitterly cold, and she and her roommate Yvonne, a stunning young Belgian model, could barely pay for heating. Her mother encouraged her to do what Natalia admitted some of their model friends did: get paid to go on dates with wealthy men. "A rich man wants a gold watch on his wrist and a beautiful woman on his arm," Ingrid nagged on her daily call from Slovakia. "Makes the man look powerful and makes other powerful men envy him. You will wear beautiful clothes and meet handsome men. You must be very nice to the richest." She recommended that Natalia encourage Yvonne to become an escort too, to keep her company. "You will have a girlfriend to gossip about men with. It will be fun!"

Ingrid sent her money so that she could buy sexy, secondhand clothes for her new side hustle. Soon Natalia made more money from the escort service than from modeling; so did Yvonne. The two roommates gossiped about their dates, but it wasn't "fun." Most of the men they "escorted" were rich, but they were also either old or ugly—or both. Natalia had sex with the few that she liked, but it wasn't a turn-on to sleep with men who regarded her as a sex object, not a some*one*, but a some*thing* that they could conquer, whether or not they paid for the privilege. She could fake an orgasm as well as the next model/escort, but real orgasms with them were nonexistent. Her worse pet peeve:

They felt entitled to forego foreplay, the soft, sweet kisses on the lips and neck, and the gentle caresses, that make a woman feel desired. The oafs cut right to the chase: First they stuck their tongues down her throat; then they stuck in something else. When she met Rex, he forced his tongue down her throat too, but somehow she hadn't found it as offensive. Maybe because his tongue is not all that long, she thought, like another part of his anatomy.

She remembered the night that she met Rex. Pierre, her gay model/escort agent, had nabbed her an invitation to a VIP reception for Funck's international beauty pageant at the Funck International Hotel on the Champs-Élysées. "Rex Funck is a *sac de sleaze*, but he has *un appétit* for Slavic women," Pierre said. "He married three. *Jouez bien tous les cartes*," which she knew from the French she had learned since moving to Paris meant, "play your cards right, and he'll marry you!"

Natalia was sick in bed with a bad cold the day of the reception. She called Ingrid for some motherly sympathy. "Get out of bed right now and get your Slovak zadok to that party!" she shouted over the phone. "And stick it in Rex Funck's face!"

Natalia forced herself to follow her mother's advice. She wore a form-clinging, black-sequined gown that Pierre borrowed from Dolce and Gabbana, promising the boutique a photo in the newspapers of Natalia wearing it with Rex Funck at her side. When Pierre escorted her into the hotel ballroom, Rex was greeting guests with his arm possessively around a sultry Brazilian wearing the beauty-pageant crown. Within minutes, his arm was around Natalia instead of the Brazilian "Miss Whatever." Their picture ended up in *Le Monde*.

Natalia tried to visualize what Rex looked like back then. He had a lot more hair and he was semi-naturally blond. He was trim and relatively fit. No flabby gut to hide under baggy suits with pants so large, that they flapped in the wind when he walked. Back then he didn't have that "I don't trust anyone but myself" look that pinched his face now, or that thrust-out jaw that jutted out even more when he nervously ground his teeth. He even smiled occasionally. Natalia couldn't remember the last time she saw her husband smile, except for the camera.

In the back of the Escalade, the iPhone lit up: 30 percent charged. Natalia placed the glass of Perrier on the tray and positioned her index finger over the iPhone keyboard, focusing on what she hoped was still her mother's password: *"Haluski1724."* She flexed her right index finger to tap in the letters; she found finger-tapping more accurate than thumb-tapping. Besides, thumb-tapping was a Rex thing. She pictured him at his worst: cursing as he thumb-tapped a vicious, hurtful, and lie-filled tweet. Natalia despised him for calling people names in his tweets: *"crooked," "phony," "crazy," "cheatin'," "stupid," "hypocrite," "sleazy."* They sounded like evil dwarves in a fairytale. She wondered if it ever occurred to him that the labels he used most were words that best described himself.

She shook her head, scolding herself for getting so angry thinking about Rex. It had made her forget her mother's possible iPhone password. She took a deep yoga breath, concentrated, and it came back to her. She tapped in: *"Haluski1724."* She counted: *"One one thousand, two one thousand..."*

A message flashed on-screen: *"Forget Password? Change Password."*

"Hovno!"

The SUV veered onto the highway skirting the East River, its waves gilded in the sunset. In a few minutes, they would arrive at the East River Heliport.

Frantic, she typed in *"1724Haluski."*

"Forget Password? Change Password."

Put yourself in Mamina's head, she told herself. Maybe she changed her password to something she loves in her life now, in America. From what she had observed today, Ingrid was nuts for her incessantly yipping toy Pomeranian. *Vladimir.*

As for numbers, Natalia guessed that Ingrid used the address of the faux Mediterranean villa that Rex had bought her and Papa in Palm Beach, near Beau Rivage: 20045 Coconut Palm Drive. She remembered how surprised Ingrid had been at Rex's generosity when he handed her the keys. "First you get us green cards. Now this mansion," she said, tears in her eyes. "A husband who treasures his in-laws is a great man!" Natalia guessed that Rex had shelled out $5 million for her parents' house for another reason than treasuring his in-laws. He knew that Ingrid would do anything to keep her daughter from leaving him, no matter how many times, or ways, he broke their wedding vows.

She tapped in *"Vladimir20045."*

One one thousand, two one thousand, three one thou…

The iPhone home screen lit up.

"Yesss!" She typed in "www.google.sk."

Before the Slovak website could open, FACETIME bleeped on. Her mother's bruised and bandaged face filled the iPhone screen.

"Suka!" Ingrid hissed.

"Mamina!"

"You stole my—"

"I *borrowed*—"

"I emailed Gretchen that you stole my phone!"

"You *what*?"

"I gave the First Daughter my phone number!"

"How *could* you?"

"If you use my phone to google any hovno, Gretchen will monitor it! She will know every search and every call you make on my phone!"

Natalia gasped. Flushing with anger at her mother's betrayal, she plunged the iPhone into the glass of Perrier. The lighted screen fizzled out.

She sank back against the soft leather seat of the Escalade, on the verge of tears. She had been so close…

She forced herself to take deep, calming yoga breaths. There had to be a way to locate the man she had hoped to find today on Google. Since being pumped with female hormones, his face had been appearing to her in dreams, *erotic* dreams: her one true love and the father of the only child she ever had.

Vaclav Szabo.

The image of fifteen-year-old Vaclav sharpened into focus in her mind. His brown hair was long and shaggy; he was always brushing it out of his eyes. And his eyes... His eyes were so dark that they were almost black, fringed with long dark eyelashes. In Slovak *Cosmo,* she had read that such eyes were considered sexy and called "bedroom eyes." She remembered how, soon after her fourteenth birthday, she selected Vaclav for her first kiss. Not just because she and her girlfriends considered him the hottest boy in their school. Now that she had grown to nearly six feet tall, he was the only boy who was taller than she was.

She thought back to the first time Vaclav kissed her. To be fair, she thought, I was the one who kissed *him*. It was after he led the school basketball team to victory in the regional finals. She had read in Slovak *Cosmo* how to kiss a boy: to teasingly probe the tip of your tongue between his lips. In the sweltering gymnasium, she ran over to Vaclav, threw her arms around his sweaty neck, and did what *Cosmo* said.

She wasn't prepared for his response: He shoved his tongue down her throat. Gagging, she pulled away from him. For a moment, the two of them stared at each other; then she turned and ran. She couldn't get the image of him out of her mind: standing there, a look of surprise on his face, an erection straining against his sweat-soaked basketball shorts.

Vaclav followed her home from school the next day. She started to run, but he caught up with her. "I love you!" he blurted out. "I've loved you forever!" She admitted that she loved him too, except for one thing: "If you ever stick your tongue down my throat again, we're finished!"

In the weeks that followed, after school they would meet in the equipment shed behind the school soccer field. Despite the cold, they pulled off their heavy jackets, but there wasn't room enough in the cramped space for anything more than embracing while leaning against the rotting wooden wall that gave them splinters. Both of them were virgins, too insecure about what to do to have real sex.

In the Escalade, Natalia smiled, remembering the day in the shed when they rubbed against each other, doing what she'd read in Slovak *Cosmo* was called "dry humping." She was suddenly anything but dry. She unzipped Vaclav's fly, begging him to make love to her. Too late. He came in his pants.

After church the following Sunday, Natalia's parents planned to take her to babika's farm for supper. During Mass, she prayed to the Virgin Mary to forgive her for losing her virginity later that day. "Please make it not hurt," she whispered. Suddenly, she bent over, dramatically clutched her stomach and groaned. Sitting beside her in the church pew, her mother grabbed her arm. "Haluski? What's wrong?"

"My period!" she said. "I'm bleeding to death! Papa, Mamina, let me go home!"

People were staring.

"Go!" her father said.

Natalia hustled out of the church and raced back to their apartment, excited yet nervous. She didn't worry that her twelve-year-old brother Franc would spoil the afternoon alone with Vaclav that she had planned. She knew Franc spent his Sundays smoking dope with his friends on the riverbank near the Váh River railroad bridge.

In the back of the Escalade, Natalia felt her body growing warm. She remembered how as she waited for Vaclav to arrive that afternoon, she took off her bra and rolled over the waistband of her gray school-uniform skirt to pull the hem up to mid-thigh. Then she cut the arms off of her tightest black T-shirt and pinched her nipples until they pressed against the cotton from inside, like mini erections. But her white panties were a sickly gray from too many washings, the elastic around the leg holes so worn that they drooped down and flapped against her thighs. She slipped into her parents' bedroom and rummaged in her mother's drawers. Underneath a pile of white underpants, even grayer and droopier than her own, she discovered black panties with a patch of black mesh in the shape of a valentine over the crotch. Just as the doorbell rang, she put them on.

She remembered feeling disappointed that Vaclav showed up in a threadbare Batman T-shirt and the torn Levis he wore to school every day. He smelled like the gym locker room. But within minutes she found his sweat smell intoxicating, more dizzying than the Fanta-and-wine "Mish Mash" drink he had brought along for them to sip after sex, instead of smoking a cigarette.

In her darkened bedroom, they pulled off their clothes and explored each other's bodies. He had remarkably big hands and long fingers, she remembered. Perfect for tossing a basketball, playing guitar, and making her body tingle. Rex was taller than Vaclav, but his fingers were short, like pencil stubs. Despite Rex's boasts to the press, every woman in America knew that for a man with short fingers, another part of his anatomy was short, too.

Vaclav had a long, beautiful vták. One look at her naked body that day and it grew rigid, its smooth pink head jutting upward. And when it slid into her body, as if her prayers had been answered, she felt no pain. Only pleasure.

Lingering on the memory in the back seat of the Escalade, she twisted the 15-karat diamond ring on her swollen finger. It was on so tight, that her finger throbbed as she maneuvered it around until the diamond was on the palm side of her hand. She thrust her hand through an opening between the buttons of her mink coat, then pressed the hard stone against what she called her *pubičné* mound and rubbed. At least this monster ring is good for something, she thought.

Tap, tap.

Her eyes popped open. She glimpsed Ken's linebacker body through the smoked Escalade window, heard the whirring of the White House helicopter blades. She subtly withdrew her hand from inside her fur coat and sighed. It is definitely time to pray to the Virgin Mary to bring Vaclav back into my life, she thought.

Part II

Two Weeks Later

(Continuous with Prologue)

Chapter 5

The White House

December 16, 12:25 a.m.

Natalia tied the belt of her white-silk Prada bathrobe, walked out of Rex's bedroom, and closed the door behind her. Thank God *that's* over, she thought.

From inside the bedroom, she heard Rex applauding over: *"Mr. Speaker; Mr. Vice President; my good friends in Congress; the beautiful First Lady of the United States; and my fabulous fellow Americans..."*

She realized that he had restarted the DVR of the State of the Union Address he watched while having sex with her tonight. She wondered if Rex obsessively replayed his speech to reassure himself that he was still President.

"Thank you for making me your leader in the biggest, huuuugest landslide of any Presidential election in American history..."

Tuning out what she knew was a lie, she grabbed her mink coat from where she had dropped it on a chair and draped it over her bathrobe. Special Agent Pricker, who was stationed nearby, hunched over his laptop, didn't even blink.

She hustled down the back stairs of the White House. It had taken her weeks to learn her way around the vast building. After she moved in, Sally-Ann had given her a White House tour in the Alabama drawl that she since had come to loathe. She suspected that Sally-Ann secretly taped all of her conversations in the First Lady's bedroom and played them back for the First Daughter.

On the tour, Sally-Ann spouted off facts about the White House: "There are 132 rooms, 147 windows, 28 fireplaces, eight staircases, and three elevators spread across six floors, plus two hidden mezzanine levels, all tucked within what appears to be only a three-story building." The information went into one ear and out the other. If Natalia had her way, she would stay put in her private bedroom.

She stepped out of the stairwell on the main floor. In the daytime, these stately halls lined with Presidential portraits were bustling with White House staff. During visiting hours, people from all over the world waited in line for hours to take tours. Natalia remembered the first week she lived in the White House, she mistakenly stepped into this hall and stumbled upon a group of Chinese tourists. They screamed her name and rushed her, snapping selfies. She was proud of herself for calmly smiling for their cameras. She loathed being surrounded by staring strangers.

An antique grandfather clock chimed one o'clock. At this time of night, she was relieved to see only a few Uniformed Division Officers as she swept down the hall in her slippers. Not one of the U.D. guards glanced at her. They had been instructed to give her privacy, something she begged Rex for, when she made a middle-of-the-night pilgrimage to the one room in the White House that she considered sacred.

She couldn't remember the last time she had been in a Catholic church or gone to confession. She missed it. Rex paid lip service to religion, but she knew he didn't take it seriously. "Jewish, Christian, Muslim; it's all bullshit," he had said to her after a photo op in the National Cathedral on Inauguration Day.

She stepped into the Vermeil Room, its arched windows draped with olive-and-gold-striped panels, their sashes trimmed in tassels. Sally-Ann had explained that the room was named for its collection of nineteenth-century English and French silver-gilt tableware. She glanced at the ornate gilded bowls and serving utensils that gleamed in velvet-lined vitrines, but she had not come here tonight to see the vermeil collection.

The walls were hung with half-a-dozen portraits of First Ladies, including Eleanor Roosevelt, Lady Bird Johnson, and Nancy Reagan. She walked across the Turkish carpet, the ancient floorboards creaking, toward a rose-and-gold damask sofa. Above it hung a full-length portrait of Jacqueline Kennedy. She gazed up at the oil painting. Sally-Ann had mentioned that Jackie's official First Lady portrait was controversial. "Some critics said that Jackie's filmy peach gown and the brown background make her look unreal and downright eerie."

Natalia studied the portrait of Jackie. She thought the former First Lady looked angelic, even saintly. Long sleeves covered her arms, a ruffled collar hid her neck, and a spray of white flowers formed a halo behind her head. Natalia sought solace here with Jackie whenever she felt troubled, as she did tonight.

She knelt down, as if she were in a church, and clasped her hands together. Just as she had once prayed to the Virgin Mary, she closed her eyes and pictured Jackie's serene, beatific face. "Please help me, Jackie," she murmured. "I have a dreadful sin from my youth to atone for. I have wicked thoughts about my husband. Please help me make the right choice and do the right thing." She crossed herself. "And please help me find Vaclav." She crossed herself again. She stared up at Jackie's face in the portrait and held her breath, waiting for a sign. All she heard was the faint ticking of the antique grandfather clock in the hall.

Chapter 6

The White House

December 16, 7:00 a.m.

Aboard Air Force One, Natalia could hear the final brass chords of "Hail to the Chief" from the Marine Corps band on the tarmac at Pearl Harbor–Hickam Air Force Base, then applause. She gazed at her image in the mirror: Hair and makeup. Check. Blue Dior dress. Check. Red stiletto-heeled Ferragamo sandals. Check.

Sally-Ann stuck her head into the First Lady's cabin. "Ma'am, the President has arrived."

"I can't wait to see him!" Her husband had been away for two weeks, way too long. She missed him while he was on state visits to China, Japan, and Korea. She was glad that the First Daughter had come up with the idea of Natalia joining him for a romantic weekend in Honolulu before he returned to Washington. "We want the world to see you're a happily married couple," Gretchen said. "That you are very much in love." Natalia was happy to give Gretchen and the world what they wanted.

Sally-Ann led Natalia down the aisle of the plane and then stepped aside. Natalia knew that a horde of photographers on the tarmac was waiting to get the perfect shot: the First Lady walking gracefully down the jet stairs and into the embrace of the President.

She paused at the top of the jet stairs, scanning the crowd. A line of traditional Hawaiian hula dancers swayed to the music of ukulele players that she couldn't hear over the roar of the applause. The usual U.S. dignitaries wore muumuus and Aloha shirts, rather than suits, she noted. But where was the President?

"Ma'am?" Sally-Ann nodded toward the jet stairs. "They're waiting for you."

Natalia spotted a man making his way through the throng below. The crowd parted for him, applauding as he broke into a run toward the aircraft.

Finally, she could see him clearly. He was dribbling a basketball...

Fifteen-year-old Vaclav Szabo, his sweaty basketball uniform stuck to his body revealing his rock-hard erection.

She broke into a smile and hurried down the jet stairs.

Below, he tossed her the basketball.

She reached out to catch it, but lost her balance.

"Mrs. Funck?"

She felt herself falling.

"Mrs. Funck?" The soft feminine voice spoke again, softly, lovingly.

She opened her eyes and found herself peering into the face of Jackie Kennedy, the Jackie from the official portrait: beatific smile, ruffled high-necked collar, eyes that looked into her soul. She reached out a hand to Natalia, to help her up.

"Jackie..."

* * *

"Jackie?"

Startled, Natalia opened her eyes. She was lying in bed in her White House bedroom, looking up into the round, overly made-up face of Sally-Ann. As usual, her social secretary was wearing a prim black pantsuit and carrying an iPad, a black-leather tote bag emblazoned with a Tory Burch logo slung over her shoulder. "Who's *Jackie*?" she asked.

"I was dreaming."

Sally-Ann winked knowingly. "About last night with POTUS?"

Natalia winced at her memory of make-a-baby sex with Rex last night. After leaving his bedroom and praying to Jackie, she had taken a quick detour to the staff-cafeteria kitchen in the basement for a buttermilk biscuit snack and a friendly chat with Stella. Then she had returned to her bedroom, climbed into bed, and pulled the covers over her head. Usually snuggling under her white Frette comforter relaxed her: there was something about its delicate cover made from 1000-thread Egyptian cotton and its filling of 850-loft white goose down from Hungary, just across the border from her native Slovakia. Not last night. The question had tormented her: Should she have Rex's baby or leave him? Finally, she fell asleep and had that dream.

The images from the dream careened back into her mind. She sat up in bed. "It was a sign!"

"Ma'am, your yoga instructor is here in ten minutes," said Sally-Ann, reading from the FLOTUS daily schedule on her iPad. "After that, you've got a Shiatsu massage. Then makeup and Angel."

Natalia threw back the covers and climbed out of bed. "Jackie heard me!"

"Who's Jackie?"

"Cancel my morning appointments!" She hurried across the thick white carpet toward the bathroom.

"All of them?"

"Except Angel."

"What about Hilda? Ma'am, Hilda's here to get you bathed and dressed!"

Natalia glimpsed the white-uniformed Slovak maid walking into the bedroom with a stack of towels. The First Daughter had hired Hilda. "To make you feel at home," Gretchen had explained. "You'll have someone to talk Slovak with. Hilda doesn't speak English."

Natalia hadn't bonded with Hilda. She found the muscle-bound woman with whiskers on her chin creepy, like the gym teachers who lurked in the locker room of Žilina Catholic School when she and her girlfriends took showers. She didn't believe for a minute that Hilda spoke no English. She bet that Gretchen had hired Hilda to spy on her.

"I can take a bath and get dressed by myself."

She closed the bathroom door and walked across the white-marble floor to one of the three white-marble sinks with gold-plated, swan-shaped faucets. She studied her face in the mirror. Her cheeks were puffy and the dark circles around her almond-shaped, deep-set green eyes made her look as if someone had punched her. "You look like hovno," she said, then broke into a grin. "But for the first time in months you have something to smile about!"

She walked past the Jacuzzi bathtub to the steam shower. She turned on the faucets for all six showerheads: two on the ceiling and two on each wall. She had found the shower a welcome retreat since the hormone shots started making her feel sexually aroused. Surrounded by swirling steam, with the gentle pulse of warm shower spray caressing her private spots, she fantasized about making love with Vaclav. She hoped that soon the orgasms she enjoyed as a result wouldn't be stimulated by fantasies, but by Vaclav in the flesh. For now, they would have to do.

She pushed an intercom button on the bathroom wall. "Hilda, I'm taking a shower," she said in Slovak. "Don't bother me."

Chapter 7

The White House

December 16, 8:00 a.m.

Natalia sipped from a bottle of Evian and wrapped her wet hair in a towel. She slipped into her terrycloth robe and studied her face in the bathroom mirror. Three orgasms and you *still* look like hovno, she thought.

"Madame Funck," said Sally-Ann over the intercom. "Your mother is on the phone."

"Tell her I'm busy."

"She says it's urgent."

"Tell her I don't believe her."

"Madame Funck, I don't really think I can—"

"Tell her I'll call her later."

Natalia opened a door from the bathroom that led into her own personal salon and spa. The vast room was wrapped in mirrors and held a styling chair surrounded by makeup lights; a massage table; and a station for facials, complete with high frequency, galvanic and ultrasonic wands, an ozone steamer and a UV sterilizer. She felt calmer here than in any other room in the White House. The reason was simple: It made her completely forget that she was in the White House.

Across the room, his back to her, a twenty-something Latino was standing at the counter by the styling chair. Angel was wearing a red-sequined "Frida Kahlo" T-shirt, tight black jeans, and red-alligator cowboy boots with silver heels. She suspected that he put elevator insoles in his boots to add three inches to his five-foot-four-inch height. At five-foot eleven plus, she still towered over him. His White House ID hung from a beaded red cord, a touch he had added to match his outfit. Angel loved flashy. Once, when she had teased him about it, he grinned and said: "It's not 'flashy,' it's 'colorful.' Us Mexicans love bright colors cuz they make us feel happy, even when we're facing sad things and hard times." Too bad Slovaks aren't like that, she thought. Black, gray, and brown are our favorite colors.

"Hola!" she called to him.

Angel spun around to face her. "Hola, mi amor!" He winked at her, so quickly that it looked like his eye had twitched. Angel always winked like that, she knew, as if a gnat had flown into his eye.

"I gotta lay out my bag of tricks." He broke into a lively Mexican song, gracefully moving to a salsa beat as he pulled scissors, combs, hairbrushes, and a hair dryer from his red-leather Gucci satchel and laid them on the counter.

The satchel had been a Christmas gift from her. She realized that last year, she had gotten more pleasure from buying Christmas presents for Angel than for Rex. As she headed toward the walk-in closet, she stopped behind him and wrapped her arms around him.

"Yo, *chica*, you're goosing me!" he said.

She rested her chin on top of his head. "I need to talk to you."

"*'Perame!* Give me a minute!"

She ducked into the walk-in closet and dressed in the form-fitting Lululemon Wunder-Under yoga pants and scooped-neck shirt that Hilda had laid out for her. She could hear Angel singing in the salon, his voice sweet and gentle. She thought back to when she met him, a little more than five years ago. In those days, she was just the wife of a billionaire who owned hotels and real estate all over the world, as well as Beau Rivage Resort and Club in Miami. Angel was a five-dollar-an-hour-plus-tips hair washer in the Beau Rivage beauty salon. The first time he washed her hair, he massaged her scalp with a touch that was strong yet sensual. She found the experience remarkably intense, even bordering on orgasmic, and gave him a $100 tip.

The next time Angel washed her hair, she urged him to open

up about himself. "I grew up in *pinche* TJ, where the *pinches* macho assholes beat up *maricóns*, gays, like me," he said. At first Natalia thought the word *pinche* was Spanish for "pinch me." She didn't understand why Angel used it so much. "Would you rather I said 'fucking?'" he said. Natalia agreed that *pinche*, or *pinches* if describing a plural noun, was a much nicer-sounding adjective than the F-word that Rex used to an obnoxious degree. But she teased Angel that she might just pinch him the next time he said it.

"So, Tania, my aunt, got me a job washing hair on Saturdays at the salon in TJ where she worked," he went on. "Pretty soon I was totally into cutting and styling hair and realized *que estaba que chido*, it's awesome. I decided to, like, make doing hair my art. I saved enough money to get the hell out of TJ, out of Mexico. I chose Miami cuz I read there are lots of gays in Miami, especially in South Beach, and like, everyone speaks Spanish."

"How did you get into the U.S.?"

"On my *estómago*, my pinche stomach!"

She pinched him playfully.

"I crawled through a pinche tunnel that was, like, two miles long."

"Seriously?"

"There were rats, dead bodies. It totally sucked!"

Natalia was so touched by Angel's story, that she asked the salon manager to give him an opportunity to prove his talent as a hair stylist. She would be his blank canvas. The next time she visited Beau Rivage, Angel softened her hair style and added nuance to her ash-blonde color. Even Rex complimented her on the change. Soon Angel was styling hair regularly for her and all the Palm Beach billionaires' trophy-wives at Beau Rivage. It didn't take long for his fee to rise to $1500 a pop.

When Rex announced his run for President, Natalia invited Angel to travel on the campaign trail with them. She admitted to Rex that Angel was in the United States illegally, that his papers were fake. 'I'm campaigning to build a fucking border wall and you've got a fucking homo wetback cutting your hair?" he screamed. "I'll deport his ass!" She threatened to ditch the campaign if he did. Rex caved. Through his scuzzy lawyer, he paid thousands to fast-track Angel for an EB-1 visa. Known as the Einstein Visa, it was offered only to immigrants who proved they had "genius" or other superior and unique qualities invaluable to the United States.

She remembered how, a few months ago, the press ridiculed her when they discovered that years earlier, when she and Rex were dating, he had paid big bucks through the same scuzzy lawyer to get her an Einstein Visa. She knew that being a *Sports Illustrated* swimsuit model didn't require genius, just good looks and big tits. Angel has the "genius" to make women look beautiful, she thought. He deserved the EB-1.

She recalled the hours that she and Angel spent alone together aboard the Funck 757 as Rex campaigned for President around the country. During each flight, Rex hunkered down with his advisors; she could hear him shouting at them through the cabin walls. While Angel washed and blow-dried her hair, or when they were just sitting together, gazing out at the clouds, she shared her dread with him about how her life would change if Rex were elected President. He had made his decision to run on a whim, the way he made most of his decisions, she thought. When she had expressed her reluctance to be First Lady, he said, "I'm doing this for the fun of it. No way in hell can I really win." But what if he *did* win? "How can I be the First Lady of a country I barely know?" she asked Angel. "I have no education, no skills for it."

"You are smart. You will learn quickly," he reassured her. "You will be the most beautiful, elegant, and gracious First Lady this country has ever had!"

She also confided in Angel about the anger she felt at the press for playing up the revelations about his sordid affairs.

"I'm sure everything they say is true, but it makes me look like a gold-digger to stay with him," she said.

Angel's response was never, "Rex is rich and he takes care of you. Don't knock it," like her mother repeated constantly. He would nestle closer to her and lay his head on her shoulder. "I feel your pain," he would say. "But you're a *mujer fuerte*, a strong woman. You will figure out the right thing to do."

Natalia recalled how soon after she married Rex, when she suspected that he was having flings behind her back, she considered going to a therapist, like her ex-model friends who had married billionaire adulterers. Rex refused to pay for it. "Psychology is a pile of shit," he said. "You go to a shrink, he'll just tell you fake news about your feelings." She was grateful for Angel. Angel was better than a therapist.

She walked back into the salon and grabbed a bottle of Evian from the counter. Across the room, Angel looked to her more like eighteen years old than twenty-four. She was certain that gay men found him attractive, but he never discussed his love life with her. "It's too pinche nasty for your beautiful ears," he said. With his carefully clipped stubble, bushy eyebrows over sparkling amber eyes, and neatly trimmed black hair, he looked like a modern-day Mexican angel. If I were a gay man, she thought, I'd jump his bones.

Smiling at the image, she plopped down on the styling chair. She swigged from the Evian bottle, then put it down on the counter with a bang. "Buenos dias!"

"What're you so pinche cheerful about?" he asked. She pinched him playfully. "Wait! I know! You fell back in love with Rex last night!"

She made the finger-down-throat barf gesture, then whispered, "Turn it on!"

Angel scooped up the sleek aluminum Dyson Supersonic hairdryer from the counter, like it was a 357 Magnum. He clicked the "On" switch to high. The dryer's metallic racket filled the room. Natalia knew that the noise would drown out any conversation that she and Angel had if, as she suspected, the room was bugged. He stepped behind her chair and unwound the towel from her head.

"Did you bring it?"

He did one of his twitch winks, raised his right leg, and rested his foot on the edge of the counter, the silver heel of his red-alligator cowboy boot glimmering under the makeup lights. With a flick of his wrist, he parted the blades of a scissors, and poked one sharp tip into a slot on the side of his silver heel. He gently pried open a secret compartment and pulled out a tiny plastic bag.

"Levonorgestrel," he said. "The morning-after pill."

She reached for the bag, but he drew back his hand. "Chica, are you sure?"

"Positive!" She snatched the bag away from him, drew out a yellow tablet, and gulped it down before he could hand her the bottle of Evian.

"You got one more pill in there for tomorrow."

"I can't believe I have to do it with Rex again tonight." She shoved the plastic bag into the depths of her cleavage. "But after that..." She raised a hand to high-five Angel.

"What're we high-fiving?"

"Freedom!" She saw that he was toying with the arc of silver studs on his left ear, a telltale sign that he was skeptical. "Jackie came to me in a dream last night," she said. "So did Vaclav!"

"Yo, I know about Saint Jackie, but, like, who's Vaclav?"

"My first true love. My *only* true love."

Angel slipped a plastic hair-salon cape over her clothes and snapped it closed at the back of her neck. "Go on."

"We were fifteen. Okay, I was fourteen and a half. Anyway, we had sex whenever and wherever we could. Six months of great sex. Then I got pregnant."

He covered his mouth in mock horror. *"Dios mio!"* He

unwrapped the towel from her head and ran a comb through her wet hair.

"My parents made me give the baby away. Then they sent me to live with Aunt Zorina in Bratislava and finish school. They didn't know she was not just a waitress. She had 'boyfriends' who came to the flat at night. Some were hitting on me. Her solution was to kick me out. For days, I was living on the street. Lucky for me, Pierre, this French modeling agent, was in Bratislava looking for Slovak women. He saw me and said, 'The hot new model for Guess, Eva Herzigová, is Slovak. You can be famous like Eva if you dye your hair platinum blonde and come to Paris with me. I'm gay. I don't want to fuck you, just get rich off you.'"

"What did you do?" He picked up the scissors and trimmed her hair.

"I didn't want to end up like Aunt Zorina in Bratislava. I dyed my hair platinum blonde and went to Paris with Pierre."

"What happened to Vaclav?"

"Papa was a welder at the Škoda factory where Vaclav's father worked. There are many car factories in Slovakia. When I got pregnant, Papa told Vaclav if he tried to see me again, his papa would have a deadly run-in with a five-ton machine on the assembly line."

"Did you ever see Vaclav again?" He snipped at her hair.

"Once, four or five years later. I was in Paris, starting to make it in modeling. One day, Vaclav shows up at my flat. He says he bribed Franc, my baby brother, to tell him where I lived. I swear, Vaclav's wearing the same jeans he wore in high school. It didn't matter. We made love. All night, all the next day. He was a better lover than any man before or since. Then we hear a horn honking on the street below. I ignore it. Pierre, my agent, calls me on my cell. He says, 'What the fuck! You have a date! He's waiting outside!' Pierre's yelling so loud, Vaclav hears him. He looks out the window. He sees my date is this old guy driving a

57

shiny new silver Porsche. He says, 'I work on an assembly line to make Porsches. You date dudes who *drive* Porsches! Go, live a good life, Natalia. I cannot give you that life.' And he walks out. I never saw him again."

"Chica, how come this is, like, the first time you're telling me all this. About the baby, about Vaclav? How come now?"

"The hormone shots."

"Huh?"

"All the fertility hormones made me start thinking and dreaming about Vaclav. It's like my body is calling to him."

He winked/twitched at her. "Are you saying FLOTUS is *horny*?"

"Like when I was fourteen!" She laughed. "So, then, in this amazing dream I had last night, Vaclav threw me a basketball!"

"A *basketball*?"

"I made a decision this morning. I will leave Rex and be with Vaclav!"

Angel tugged at the diamond studs on his ear. "Whoa, chica, this is, like, *wow*!"

"I know, right?"

"No, I mean, it's very romantic, but, like, you're married to the President of the United States. You're the First Lady of the land. You can't just—"

"Why not?"

"And anyway, how will you ever find the dude?"

"I don't have a phone, an iPad, or a computer that's not bugged."

As if he knew what was coming next, he said, "You expect me to find Vaclav?"

"Why *not*?"

"Chica, I don't speak Slovak. I don't even know where pinche Slovakia is!"

"It's just south of the Czech Republic. You see, until 1993 the Czech Republic and Slovakia were one country, called

Czechoslovakia. Then—"

"Chica, this is loco!"

She swiveled the salon chair around to face him. "Please! You're my angel!"

"But—"

"You've got a safe phone. The White House can't monitor you—"

"Mi amor—"

"...Go to Slovak Google, Google.sk. Go to Slovak Facebook. Slovaks love Facebook. Please find him. Vaclav is my *Zlatorog*!"

"Your *what*?"

"Zlatorog is an old mythical Slovak god that looks like a mountain goat." She cupped Angel's face with her hands. "But in Vaclav's case he's a mountain goat who becomes a good man."

"*Huh?*"

"Never mind. Find Vaclav!" She opened a drawer below the counter. It held a scramble of mascara wands, eyebrow pencils, and lipsticks. She rummaged around and located a ballpoint pen. She grabbed Angel's hand and wrote the name on his palm: *Vaclav Szabo.*

Chapter 8

The White House

December 16, 11:00 a.m.

James Conner, officer of the White House Secret Service Uniformed Division, checked his watch. *Only two hours until my shit-ass shift ends,* he thought. He could almost taste the doobie he would light the minute he walked into his shit-ass apartment, kicked off his regulation thick-soled U.D. shoes, and turned on FOX News.

Killing time, he chewed off a hangnail and spit it on the floor of the staff-entrance security checkpoint. "I wonder which cabinet guy POTUS is gonna *'You're fired!'* tonight?" he said, though he knew that U.D. Officer Tallisha Jones wouldn't answer, that she wouldn't even look up at him from her Galaxy. She had that sullen "poor me/fuck you" black-lesbo attitude that he had hated since he was a beat cop in Baltimore, breaking up gang fights. He longed to tell her, but he didn't want her branding him a *me-too* dupe, like the clueless black janitor in the staff cafeteria who got canned last week for calling her an "African Bush Mama." Conner grunted. He bet Tallisha's huge Afro was a sign that she didn't shave her pubes, but so what? He liked bush more than a furry arrow pointing to a ho's pussy. Take the one on the bitch he hooked up with last weekend. He grunted again. He couldn't remember the bitch's name, or her face. Just that goddamned furry arrow.

Tallisha smiled when she saw Angel walking out of the tunnel from the White House and over to their security checkpoint. "How's it goin', bro?" she called to him. Conner didn't get why she thought the pint-sized wetback faggot with the red-alligator cowboy boots was cool.

"Yo, Tallisha, when are you gonna let me do your hair?"

asked Angel. "I'll make you look like FLOTUS." He reached up to pat her Afro, but she playfully swatted his hand away.

"I don't wanna look like no Natalia," she said. "But how 'bout Michelle?"

"You're on!" He slapped her a high-five.

Conner turned to the shelves holding staff personal items and rooted around. He came up with Angel's iPhone and keys and slapped them down on the counter. "You got a Chihuahua?" He pointed to the tiny plastic dog on Angel's key ring. "Perfect mutt for a runt."

"Yo, it's a *xoloitzcuintle*, mascot of the Xolos, TJ's soccer team." Angel pocketed his keys. "These dogs been around since the Aztecs. They're small, but they'd rip your balls off!" As he slipped his iPhone into his red Gucci satchel, he nodded toward Conner's high-and-tight haircut. "Too bad they make you U.D.s shave your heads. If you were a Secret Service special agent, you'd get to keep your hair and wear a boss suit and Ray-Bans." He stepped away from the counter. "But I hear you gotta have a brain to be promoted to special agent."

Conner was about to shout, "Fuck you!" He noticed that Tallisha was evil-eyeing him. He grunted instead.

* * *

Angel hustled out of the security checkpoint, toward the gate to the street.

"Hey, Angel!" A man waved to him from among the crowd of tourists and paparazzi glued to the White House perimeter fence.

Angel recognized the slight young man in the frayed jacket and blue L.A. Dodgers baseball cap: Phil Smith. The paparazzo was so persistent, that Natalia called him her shadow.

Phil pushed his smudged eyeglasses up on his nose. "Angel, you and Natalia are besties. I read it in *People*. How about you get me a photo op with her?"

"Dude, that's what you always ask me. You know the answer: I wish a could, but—"

"You *do*?" Phil asked in earnest.

"Maybe next time!" Angel shot him a thumbs-up, then jogged two blocks to the Willard Parking Garage, his silver cowboy-boot heels clicking on the icy pavement. Seeing a line for the elevator, he pulled open the stairwell door and tore up the steps, two at a time. A homeless man was slumped on the landing of the third floor. Barely a teenager, he had dark, Latino features and was shivering in his threadbare hoodie, his grimy toes poking out of worn-through sneakers. The kid held out his hand. *"Por favor, señor,"* he said in a weak voice.

Angel had seen more than his share of homeless people when he was growing up in Tijuana. "I know where you're at man," he said in Spanish. He pulled out his wallet and came up with $100 in ten-dollar bills. He handed five to him. The boy's mouth fell open in astonishment. "It's Alexander Hamilton," explained Angel in Spanish, pointing to the face on the ten-dollar bill. "He was an immigrant, like you and me. He got rich and famous. He did good things for this country. He was a good man."

The teenager's eyes filled with tears. *"Gracias, señor! Gracias!"*

Angel walked through the parking structure toward a shiny red Mustang and pressed the button on his car keys. The car's interior lights flicked on and he heard the click of the locks. He licked his finger and wiped a smudge from the windshield, then opened the door and slipped behind the wheel. Angel looked around the interior, as he did every time he climbed in, as if to remind himself that it was really his car. Thanks to his success, which he owed all to Natalia, he could have afforded to buy a BMW or a Range Rover when he passed his driver's test and went car shopping. But a red Mustang had been his dream car since he was a kid. It was the car that UCLA frat boys and Marines from Camp Pendleton drove when they came down to

Tijuana to party.

He started the motor; the radio blasted Mexican salsa music. He was about to back out of his parking space, but decided he had something more important to do right now. He pulled his iPhone from his satchel and turned it on. When the screen lit up, he tapped in the address for Slovak Google. The Google search box appeared, but the words under it had strange accents.

"Slovak! *Puta madre*," he muttered. "Shit."

Then he noticed a line: "*Google sa ponúka aj v jazyku* English." He highlighted "English" and clicked "Enter."

* * *

Excited by the discovery he had made on Google, Angel ran the two blocks back from the Willard Parking Garage to the White House. Camera in hand, Phil was still among the crowd outside the perimeter fence. "Hey, Angel," he called to him. "Don't forget me!"

Another thumbs-up. "No worries!"

Angel slowed to a walk as he approached the staff entrance. He could see that U.D. Officer Conner still was on duty at the security checkpoint. He knew the pinche redneck would love nothing more than to fuck over a maricón. Eager to share his news with Natalia, he didn't want to give him any reason. He caught his breath and walked in.

Tallisha smiled at him. "Yo!"

Conner grunted. "Back so soon?"

"I, like, forgot my, uh, blow dryer," Angel said.

Conner snickered. "Right. Can't give blow jobs if you don't gotta blow dryer." He scanned his computer. "Sorry. You're not on FLOTUS's guest list."

"Please call and let them know I'm here."

"How 'bout I call and have them send your blow jobber down. I don't want POTUS distracted by a midget in red cowboy boots running around the White House. They might think you're some kind of weirdo-spic-leprechaun spy."

Tallisha stuck her face into Conner's. "Shut up, fool!" She turned to Angel and scanned the ID around his neck. "I'll let 'em know you're coming up."

"Thank you."

Conner held out a metal collection bin for Angel's possessions. He tossed in his keys. "Phone?"

"Left it in the car," said Angel.

Tallisha motioned for him to walk through the metal detector. As he passed through it and headed into the White House, he fought the urge to break into a run.

Chapter 9

The White House

December 16, 12:00 p.m.

Natalia sucked in her breath. Standing behind her in the First Lady's mirrored dressing room, Hilda strained to zip up her gown. The Slovak maid frowned. *"Nebude."*

"You're right. No damn good!" Natalia exhaled, frustrated. Thanks to the bloating from the hormone shots—and, okay, the midnight snacks too—she couldn't squeeze into this exquisite red tulle-and-silk Valentino evening gown. What would she wear for the Presidential Family Christmas photo session tomorrow? She ran her hand over the bosom of the $15,000 dress, admiring how beautifully it was decorated with hand-beaded, red-and-black satin butterflies. Last week, when a Valentino stylist sent it to her, she worried that it was too bold. "It's so...*red*," she said to Angel, who was doing her hair at the time.

"Go for it, chica! You're gonna upstage the First Daughter," he whispered.

Natalia nodded for Hilda to unzip the gown. She stepped out of it, kicked off her matching red-satin Manolos, and jumped down from the fitting platform. In her scarlet Prada thong panties and bra, she padded into the cavernous walk-in closet. She punched a button on the wall and the motorized racks of clothes began to move, zigzagging around her like a garment carousel in a dry-cleaning shop. As she scanned the clothes moving by, each carefully cocooned in tissue paper and plastic, she recalled how she fell in love with fashion when she was a little girl. Her babika had taught her how to stitch dresses out of rags for her dolls. She remembered the time she promised her little brother that if he watched her doll fashion show, she would give him her one leftover candy cane from Christmas. Franc sat through the fashion show, but he made nasty faces and told her, "Ugly clothes, for witches!" To punish him, she ate the candy cane in front of him, enjoying every crunchy bite. In revenge, Franc ripped her doll dresses into pieces. Papa took the strap to him, but he didn't cry. She knew then that her baby brother would end up in jail. If it wasn't for Rex, she thought, Franc would still be in a Slovak cell that stank of urine.

"Need help finding something to wear?" Angel stepped into the closet behind her.

"Hovno, what are you—"

"*Shhh!*" He closed the door behind him, then punched the button on the garment rack. It launched into high speed; the hum of the motor and the swooshing of the tissue paper and plastic grew louder. He grabbed her hand and they ducked under the first row of moving clothes, so that they were surrounded by them. Natalia knew that here they couldn't be heard by prying ears.

She read the excitement on Angel's face. "You found Vaclav?"

"Chica, do you know how many Vaclav Szabos there are on Slovak Facebook?"

"You *didn't* find him?"

"*Your* Vaclav Szabo isn't on Facebook."

"How can you be sure?"

"The Vaclav Szabos on Facebook are either old farts, or teenage boys with *pinches espinillas,* pimples!"

"Oh no!"

"So I didn't find your Vaclav." He grinned. "But I found his rock band!"

"*Rock band?*"

"Vaclav plays guitar in a band called that other name you mentioned."

"What name?"

"The god that's, like, a mountain goat? Starts with a 'Z'?"

"*Zlatorog?*"

"Zlatorog and the Dragons! That's the name of his *pinche*

rock band in Prague."

"Zlatorog and the Dragons! That's another sign!" Natalia crossed herself, put her hands together in prayer and squeezed her eyes shut. "Ďakujem, Mother Maria! Thank you, Saint Jackie!" She embraced Angel. "Vaclav played guitar in high school. I knew he had talent!"

"I found the band's website. It was in Slovak. The Google translation was pinche weird, but I got Vaclav's email address."

"You did? Thank you *soooo, soooo* much! I've got to figure out a way to email him!" She paused, thinking, then blurted out, "How about we meet for lunch tomorrow at that vegan restaurant in Georgetown I like. I'll sneak your iPhone into the ladies—"

"Chica, I'm way ahead of you."

"What?"

"In Mexico, there's a saying, *Camarón que se duerme se lo lleva la corriente.*"

"What does *that* mean?"

"'The shrimp that falls asleep is swept away by the current.' In other words, 'You snooze, you lose.' I emailed Vaclav ASAP."

"But *I* wanted to email Vaclav!"

He threw up his hands in exasperation. "Chica, I did my best!"

She grabbed his hand. "Of course you did! I'm sorry, Angel. I'm glad you emailed him. What did you say?"

"I said, 'Yo, Vaclav, like, this is top secret, but I am writing for…' I realized I don't know your maiden name, but I figured he'd know 'Natalia Funck.'"

"Gosovic."

"What's that?"

"My maiden name. What else did you say in the email?"

"That you want to see him and be with him, like, forever, right?"

"Absolutely!"

"So, I put it to him: 'Dude, are you cool with this or not?'"

"That's perfect!" She hugged him. "I can't wait to see what he emails back!" She frowned. "*If* he emails back!"

"He already did!"

"*Seriously*?"

"It was in sort of half Slovak, half English."

Natalia sucked in her breath, eyes wide. "What did he say?"

"I think what he said was, like, 'Go fuck yourself.'"

"No!"

"He thought I was conning him. He said, 'Fuck you! You insult most beautiful woman in world!'"

"Vaclav *said that*?"

"There's more. He said, 'Love me life!'"

"Love me life?"

"I think he meant, like, 'love *of my* life.'"

Natalia shook her hands excitedly. "Vaclav still loves me!"

"I had to convince him we're BFFs before he'd believe me."

"How did you do that?"

"The valentine on your ass."

It took a moment for that to sink in. "How did you know I have a mole shaped like a heart on my zadok?"

"Natalia, you can never make up your pinche mind what to wear! Do you know how many times I see you get dressed, then undressed, then dressed again, then undressed? Like, look at you right now!"

Natalia glanced down and realized that she was wearing only her red bra and thong undies. "Oh!"

"Chica, you wear a pinche thong. I see your heart-shaped mole mucho." He turned her around and pointed to her right butt cheek.

She craned her neck around and tried to spot it. Without a mirror, it was impossible.

"No worries. It's still there."

"I didn't know I had that mole until Vaclav kissed it. He

loved it. When Rex saw it, he said I should get it cut off. So did Dr. Hormone."

"Vaclav still loves it."

"He *said* that?"

"Not exactly, but he said he's ready to risk his job, his *life*, for you."

"*Seriously?*"

"Natalia, this is me, your angel!"

"Yes, I know! Of course!" She grabbed his hand. "What do we do now?"

"Yo, don't I always take care of you?"

"Yes! Yes! But how? *Where?*"

"You gotta authorize a White House pass tomorrow for 'Moon Kusnetzov.'"

"Who's Moon Kusnetzov?"

"You'll find out tomorrow, when I come to do your hair. But to make this work, I need something else from you."

"Anything."

"Do you have any *compas,* pals, in the White House kitchen?"

"No, but I do in the staff-cafeteria kitchen. In the basement."

"Where you told me you go at night to pig out?"

"One biscuit is not 'pigging out'!"

"Whatever."

Her eyes brightened. "Biscuits. It's *osud!*"

"What's *osud?*"

"'Fate!' Biscuits are another sign that Vaclav and I are meant to be together!"

"A *sign*? Like, how?"

"Last night, Stella, the baker, pointed to these two Vietnamese girls who work in the kitchen. They're shy. Stella said, 'Them sisters don't talk much, but I always say what's on my mind.' She hopes that's okay with me. Since I'm eating her biscuits, it better be."

"What's on Stella's mind?"

"The ghost in the kitchen."

"A *ghost*?"

"She says she's sure it's the ghost of Abraham Lincoln, who freed the slaves. Then she blurts out, 'I don't think President Lincoln likes your husband!' She leans closer and says, 'From what I see on TV, and from what I see in your eyes when you come down here hungry in the middle of the night, like you hope food's gonna make everything all right, or like maybe you can sneak outta here or somethin', I don't think you like your husband either!'"

"She *said* that?"

"Yes!"

"In Spanish, this is, like, pinche *destino,* destiny! This is just what we—"

"Madame Funck? Are you in there?" Sally-Ann called from the entrance to the closet.

"Uh...Angel's helping me select something to wear," said Natalia.

"Your mother's on the phone! She says you promised to call!"

"Tell her—"

"She was crying."

Natalia rolled her eyes. "I'll be right there!" She grabbed Angel's hand and they made their way out from among the moving racks of clothes.

"Remember, 'Moon Kusnetzov,'" he whispered.

"Moon Kusnetzov."

"I need a pass for Moon Kusnetzov tomorrow, when I come do your hair."

"You are my Zlatorog, Angel." She stopped and embraced him, resting her chin on his head.

"I thought Vaclav was your Zlatorog."

"Vaclav is my Slovak Zlatorog. You are my *Mexican* Zlatorog."

"Do I become a good man?"

"You *are* a good man!"

Chapter 10

The White House

December 17, 1:30 a.m.

Natalia closed the door to Rex's bedroom behind her and tightened the sash on her antique-silk kimono, a gift from the Japanese Prime Minister. She breathed a sigh of relief. She had managed to survive the second horrid night of make-a-baby sex with Rex, just like Dr. Steinberg ordered. If Angel helps me escape from the White House tomorrow, she thought, it will be my last. Making certain that the Secret Service guard wasn't watching, she dug in her kimono pocket for the morning-after pill that Angel had given her this morning. She gulped it down.

She peeled off her latex sanitary gloves and dumped them in the wastebasket. She also dumped another germ-avoidance item. Tonight was the first time Rex had made her wear one: an ASTM Level 3, fluid-resistant medical face mask. She wondered if he made his daughter wear one too. Probably not. Sanitary gloves were one thing. Though Rex was growing increasingly germ phobic, when he looked at Gretchen she knew that he saw a reflection of himself. He wouldn't want that hidden behind a face mask.

The sound of Rex addressing the NRA convention on the TV in his bedroom faded into the distance as Natalia hurried down the back staircase of the White House. She felt moistness on her neck and wiped it away with her kimono sleeve. She put the fabric to her nose and took a whiff of the damp, foul-smelling spot: definitely Rex's slobber. Before the age of seventy, Rex never drooled on her neck when he climaxed. She snickered. It was almost as if now that he was too old to produce more than a few drops of semen, his oral excretion while having sex made up for it.

The make-a-baby sex had taken longer tonight than last night. She remembered realizing that she would be in for a long haul when she entered his bedroom and found him watching CNN instead of FOX News. On TV, Christian Anderson was interviewing three prominent psychiatrists. They were discussing the "dangerous psychological implications" of the President's latest cabinet-member-firing-by-hate-filled tweet. "Faggot, I'm not a power-hungry maniac," Rex shouted at Anderson's image on TV. "They should make me fucking king! I'll send you all to fucking Siberia!"

Fuming, Rex had clicked the remote to FOX News and motioned for her to approach his throne/chair. He took a sip of Diet Coke, as if to fortify himself. "Got to show the world I'm a stud," he muttered. "Got to knock you up." He raised his hooded eyes and looked her up and down with obvious disgust. "How about it, FLOTUS?"

"How about what?" she said, trying to stay calm.

"How about, for once, you make me want to fuck you?"

She untied her kimono and let it drop to the floor. "This used to do it for you," she said, forcing herself to sound alluring. She kneeled before him, leaned closer, and placed her hands under her ample breasts. Then she pressed them into his face. He grabbed her right breast, latched onto the nipple, and sucked. When she first dated Rex, sucking boob had been an instant turn-on for him. Not tonight. One slurp, and he shoved her breast away and spit. "Shit! You're dripping sour fucking milk!" She couldn't suppress a chuckle. "Must be the hormone shots," she said, wiping off the drop of clear liquid on her breast.

She had then walked over to a cabinet that held porn DVDs. "What's your pleasure?" He pointed to a DVD on the floor.

What happened next still galled her. Talk about a new low. The DVD Rex requested was one starring Windy Darling, the porn star who bragged to the press that she had an affair with him during the Presidential campaign. Natalia fought the urge to hurl the DVD at his head. She slipped it into the DVD player instead. Anything to get tonight over with.

Rex had denied his affair with Windy Darling, of course, but his reaction to the tape convinced her that he was lying. His face turned crimson, spittle oozing from the corners of his mouth, as he watched Windy's size-EEEE breasts swaying like oversized coconuts on the DVD while she was humped from behind. As much as he loves fake news, Natalia thought, he loves fake breasts even more. Then the camera angle widened to reveal who was humping Windy: a jock wearing a Rex Funck Halloween mask. She almost burst out laughing. Not Rex. It pumped him up to pump away faster.

After fifteen minutes, even the Windy Darling DVD hadn't done it for him. He grabbed the remote and resorted to a visual stimulation guaranteed to make him come: a DVR of himself, in this case addressing the NRA Convention in Dallas.

"Democrats are stupid losers; they're morons! They want to disarm law-abiding Americans at the same time they release dangerous criminal animals and savage gang members onto our streets! Well, no way! Not on my watch!"

At least I didn't have to listen to his State of the Union Address again, she thought.

* * *

Natalia descended the back staircase to the first floor of the White House and hustled down the hall to the Vermeil Room. In the glare from the lights on the White House lawn that filtered through the curtains, she walked over to the melancholy portrait of Jackie Kennedy. She kneeled in prayer. "You are my patron saint," she whispered, staring up at the wistful smile on Jackie's face. "Even though I won't see you again after tomorrow, I hope and pray, you will be in my heart." She left the Vermeil Room and took the service elevator down to the White House basement. Now comes the moment of truth, she thought.

A U.D. officer was posted outside the swinging doors to the staff-cafeteria kitchen. He didn't glance up at her as she walked inside. It was empty except for the petite young Vietnamese cooks cutting onions and peeling potatoes in a far corner. She checked her watch: 1:30 a.m. If she was going to escape from the White House through here tomorrow night, this would be an ideal time.

She looked around for Stella. Usually she found the baker up to her elbows in biscuit dough, but the 50-gallon bowl of the sticky mixture sat on a counter, untouched. She heard giggles from the walk-in refrigerator and noticed the heavy door was ajar. She stepped closer. What she spotted inside surprised her: Stella was leaning against a shelf lined with milk cartons, sticks of butter, and boxes of eggs. Her arms were around a young black female uniformed U.D. officer. They were kissing tenderly.

Natalia backed away, but Stella spotted her.

"Madame First Lady!"

"Sorry to interrupt."

"No worries," said Stella. "This is U.D. Officer Tallisha Jones. She works the staff-entrance security checkpoint."

Tallisha lowered her eyes in embarrassment. "Pleased to meet you, ma'am."

Stella squeezed her hand, as if to reassure her that she was among friends. "Tallisha and me met at the staff party last Christmas. We've been together almost a year. In fact, I just asked her to marry me!"

"How nice!" Natalia smiled at Tallisha. "Stella's the best! I hope you said yes."

She laughed, relaxing. "I did!"

Stella reached behind the milk bottles and grabbed a magnum of Veuve Clicquot that was stashed there. A White House napkin was stuffed into the open top. "I saved this champagne from the last state dinner. There oughta be enough left for three glasses.

Can't promise it's still bubbly, but wanna join us in a toast?"

Natalia stepped over to the women. "It will be my pleasure!"

Ladies, I have a good feeling you are going to be my Zlatorogs too, she thought. My good African-American Zlatorogs.

Chapter 11

The White House

December 17, 8:00 a.m.

"What the fuck?"

U.D. Officer James Conner gaped out the window at the tall figure towering over Angel. The two were waiting their turn to enter the security checkpoint.

Spotting them, Tallisha waved a White House usher in line ahead of them through the metal detector. "Say, what?" she whispered under her breath.

"Yo, Tallisha," Angel said with a smile as he walked in. He threw his red Gucci satchel, jacket, and cowboy boots into the X-ray bin, and then motioned for the person behind him to do the same with her metal-studded motorcycle boots and bulging black garment bag. He turned to Conner and his smile faded. "Dude, you got an ID badge for my friend here, Moon Kusnetzov?" He handed his keys and cell phone to the officer, along with Moon's.

Conner stored them under the counter, then hitched up his pants, put his hand on his crotch, and hastily rearranged his balls, a gesture Angel had seen him do whenever he was about to play macho-asshole cop. "You got passports?"

"Sure thing." Angel flashed his passport.

Ignoring it, Conner grabbed Moon's passport out of her hand it and studied it. "Says here Moon Kusnetzov is a twenty-eight-year-old man, but your friend don't exactly *look* like one, Angel." He took in Moon's pink-streaked, bob-and-bangs black wig; garish makeup; "wife-beater" T-shirt that revealed substantial cleavage; and bulge at Moon's crotch. "Not unless you call a person with tits and a dick a man."

Moon grabbed her crotch. "Dude," she said in a low, but

definitely feminine voice, "you call a person with tits and a dick a *trans* woman."

Angel glared at Conner. "And you call a person who gives a trans woman shit a motherfucking, sexist, pig-ignorant redneck asswipe!"

"Is that right?" Conner turned to Moon. "I need you to remove your wig and throw it in the bin. Gotta make sure you're not hiding nothing."

Stone-faced, she removed her wig, revealing her shaved head.

He grimaced. "Sorry I asked."

Suddenly, Tallisha was in Conner's face. "Give Moon *Whatever* her ID badge, fool, or I'll call HR on you!" She waved Angel and Moon through the metal detector.

Conner punched a button on his computer. An ID with "Moon Kusnetsov" spit out of the printer. Tallisha tucked it into a plastic holder attached to a necklace cord. As Moon repositioned her wig, Tallisha handed her the ID. "Welcome to the White House."

Conner eyed the X-ray screen as Moon's garment bag glided along the X-ray machine belt. "Looks like you got a bunch of dresses in there."

"They're for FLOTUS," said Angel.

"I bet," said Conner. He winked at Moon. "Ask nicely, maybe she'll let you wear one!"

Chapter 12

The White House

December 17, 8:30 a.m.

"Ohmygod, ohmygod, ohmygod!"

Natalia looked up from the daily schedule that Sally-Ann was reviewing with her on her iPad to see who was squealing excitedly at the bedroom door. Sally-Ann looked too. "Oh my God is right," she murmured.

Angel nudged Moon into the room, but she wavered, seemingly spellbound by the posh surroundings.

"Ohmygod, ohmygod, ohmygod!"

"Natalia, Sally-Ann, meet Moon, my intern," said Angel. "Moon's, like, helping me out today."

Moon gazed at Natalia, who was still in her bathrobe, her hair askew; she had just climbed out of bed. *"Ohmygod, ohmygod, even without makeup, Madame FLOTUS, you are so stunning!"*

Natalia wasn't sure what Angel was up to, but she knew it wouldn't include nosy Sally-Ann, or maid/spy Hilda, who was clipping the stems of white roses in a service alcove. "Sally-Ann, Hilda, you may go."

Sally-Ann balked: "I don't know what you're wearing for the—"

"Angel will help me decide. OUT!"

Sally-Ann grabbed her tote bag from a chair, stuffed in her iPad, and headed for the door. Oblivious, Hilda continued clipping the rose stems.

"Odložte nožnice a chod'te," Natalia shouted.

In the service alcove, Hilda dropped the clippers on the counter and scurried out after Sally-Ann, closing the bedroom door behind her.

Natalia led Angel and Moon into the salon and flicked on

a noisy hair dryer. She then opened the closet door wide and clicked the garment carousel into deafening high gear.

Moon knelt down on one knee and bowed her head. "Madame FLOTUS, I am so, *so, SO* honored and excited to meet you! Like, *ohmygod, ohmygod*, this is my dream come true!" She grabbed Natalia's hand and kissed it, tears streaming down her face.

Natalia turned to Angel. "Who *is* this person?"

"Moon's transitioning from male to female, so please refer to her as 'she,' not 'he.' She's been on HRT for, like, a year. Y'know, estrogen. Makes her super emotional."

"Forgive me." Moon sniffled.

"It's okay, Moon, I know all about estrogen." She helped her up, then pulled a Kleenex from a box on the makeup counter and handed it to her. Moon wiped her eyes and blew her nose.

Angel motioned to Moon. "Yo, show her."

Moon he laid the garment bag on the counter and unzipped it, then reached under a sea-blue sequined evening gown and pulled out a folder. She opened it gingerly, as if it were filled with rare manuscripts, then spread out its dozen 8x10 glossy color photos on the counter.

Natalia couldn't believe her eyes as she gazed at the photos: There she was, the First Lady, in the sea-blue sequined gown from the garment bag; in a purple sheath she didn't recognize; and in a pink-tulle ball gown fit for Cinderella that she had never worn. In each photo, she was wearing a tight neck bandana of a matching color, an item of clothing that she also had never worn.

She looked at Moon suspiciously. "How is this possible? Photoshop?"

Angel chuckled. "Mi amor, these photos aren't *you,* they're *Moon!* On weekends, Moon *is* you!"

"*Me?*"

"Moon stars as FLOTUS in a show at Cross Queen, a female impersonator club in South Beach."

Natalia looked up from the photos to study the "she" with

breasts and a bulging crotch. "Wow! But...how do you *do* it?"

Moon put her hand over her heart. "You can't imagine how much this means to me, Madame FLOTUS. *Ohmygod*, I try so hard to impersonate you faithfully in every way, like with my makeup, my hair—"

"I styled Moon's 'Natalia wig' and gave her makeup tips back in Miami," said Angel. "That's how we met."

"I can even *talk* like you," said Moon in a voice that was suddenly higher and dripping with Natalia's Slovak accent. "Like, *ohmygod*, you're my idol, Madame FLOTUS!" Her eyes brimmed with tears. "I will do anything for you. *Anything!* Just tell me how I can help you escape from that vulgar, foul-mouthed beast you're shackled to!"

"*Escape*?" Natalia turned to Angel. "I thought you wanted me to go to the staff kitchen tonight and that Stella and her friend, Tallisha—"

"Stella's friends with Tallisha?"

"They're getting married."

"No shit!" Angel grinned. "I knew Tallisha was *lesbiana!* Bravo!"

"Stella said they would sneak me out. It will make the ghost happy."

"What ghost?"

"President Lincoln! I told you, Lincoln's ghost haunts the White House because it hates Rex. Stella hates Rex too. That's why she'll help. Like in the movies. She and Tallisha will hide me in a laundry bin full of dirty towels and load me into the laundry truck that comes at 5 a.m. The truck driver is a Somali immigrant; he's Muslim. ICE won't let his wife and kids into the country. The Muslim truck driver hates Rex most of all."

"So great, everyone hates Rex," said Angel. "Only it's not you your pals in the kitchen are gonna smuggle outta there tonight. It's Moon, acting and looking *like* you!"

"Where will *I* be?"

"Long gone."

"*What?*"

"Escaping from the staff kitchen's too risky. You can only try it in the middle of the night. That means in the morning, when Sally-Ann walks into your bedroom to wake you up and finds you've split, President Asshole will send the Secret Service after you. He's such a drama queen, he could call out the National Guard, or the army. By tomorrow morning, you already gotta be, like, halfway across the country."

"What about Moon? What if they catch *her*?"

"I'll tell the truth," Moon said. "I've got no clue where you went. Angel isn't paying me for this. It's my privilege to help you, my idol, the muse for my art, escape a monster!"

Natalia turned to Angel. "Where *am* I going? Where am I meeting Vaclav?"

"No names! You didn't hear that name, Moon!"

She put her fingers in her ears. "It's scrubbed from my memory forever."

"I'll tell you the plan when we're outta here," Angel said to Natalia. "What time's the family Christmas card photo shoot today?"

"11 a.m."

He checked his watch. "We've got, like, ninety minutes to prep! Let's pinche do this!"

Chapter 13

The White House

December 17, 9:00 a.m.

Natalia sat nervously in the styling chair, her back to the mirror, the whine of the electric razor in her ears. Ten minutes ago, Angel had said, "I'm not letting you watch. If you see what I'm doing, you'll totally lose it." Now he clicked off the razor. "Muy bien!"

She shut her eyes as he spun her chair around to face the mirror. She opened one, then the other. Her jaw dropped in horror. "I can't believe I let you do this!" Angel had rouged her cheeks and applied false eyelashes, bright red lipstick, and glittery purple eye shadow, so that her makeup was identical to Moon's. But that's not what freaked her out right now.

"I'm *bald*! Hovno!"

Moon walked over and met Natalia's eyes in the mirror.

"On you, dear FLOTUS, even a bald head is beautiful."

"Hovno," she said quietly. "It better not be forever."

"And it's perfect for beautiful wigs." Moon reached into the garment bag and pulled out a shoulder-length ash-blonde wig. "Especially this one." She positioned it on Natalia's bald head. Natalia realized that the wig was the exact shade and style of her own hair, before...

"Or we could swap," said Moon, removing Natalia's "FLOTUS wig." Moon took off her own pink-streaked black wig, revealing her own bald head. She put on the FLOTUS wig, then positioned the pink-streaked black wig on Natalia's bald head. "See?" She straightened the wig's bangs until Natalia looked exactly like Moon had looked moments ago.

In shock, Natalia studied her weirdo-trans image in the mirror. What the hell have I done? she thought. She looked down wistfully at the pile of her shorn locks on the floor. "Hovno," she whispered.

"Yo, never do that!" Angel hastily swept up the hair with a broom. "Never look at what *was*." He swept the pile of hair clippings into a dustpan and emptied it into a plastic garbage bag. "Focus on what will be."

She nervously bit her lip. "But...what *will* be?"

"Your freedom!"

Unconvinced, she gnawed at a red-polished nail. The acrylic was too tough to crack.

He pushed her hand away from her mouth. "You wanna break a tooth?"

She folded her hands in her lap. "I haven't bitten my nails since I was fourteen!"

"No *problemo*. They're coming off next." He opened a drawer below the counter and grabbed a bottle of a polish remover and nail clippers. "I'm gonna make them look like Moon's."

"*I'll* do it!" Moon barged in and took Natalia's right hand. She held out her own right hand—short nails, no polish—and compared it to Natalia's. "Girlfriend, it will be my pleasure!"

"You wear eye shadow and rouge," said Natalia. "Why no nail polish?"

"When I'm not being *you*, I'm a hospice nurse."

"*Seriously?*"

"You're surprised I'm an RN, or surprised I work with dying patients?" Moon set to clipping Natalia's nails.

"Both, I guess," she said. "I'm sorry. I mean, I never thought—"

"Hospice patients are very accepting. They love me for who I am, not *what* I am." Moon nodded toward the pink-streaked black wig on Natalia's head. "They love my crazy, out-there style. It cheers them up!" She finished trimming the nails on Natalia's right hand and started on her left. "Anyway, at the hospital I live in latex gloves."

"What do latex gloves have to with fingernails?"

"*Acrylic* fingernails. Latex and acrylic nails don't mix."

"They don't?"

"You wear latex gloves over acrylic nails, girlfriend, your nails break."

"So *that's* why mine break when I have sex with Rex," she said. She saw the confusion on Moon and Angel's faces. "Long story."

Angel swept up the fingernail clippings on the floor and added them to the garbage bag. "We gotta dispose of the evidence." He removed a few of the dresses from the garment bag and shoved the plastic bag of hair and nail clippings into it. "This comes with us."

* * *

Natalia stared at herself in the mirror. She had metal studs on her ears and nose, like Moon's. They looked like they were piercing her skin, but Moon had glued them on. "I can't have permanent holes on my body if I'm going to play *you* on weekends," Moon explained, gluing on the last stud. "It would be an insult to your perfection."

"What about *that*?" Natalia nodded toward the red-gold-and-black Buddha tattoo on Moon's arm.

"Also fake." Moon laughed. "Like every word out of your two-faced husband's mouth." She dabbed cleansing cream on her "tattoo" and wiped it off with Kleenex. "Anyway, I could never have a *real* tattoo. A Jewish person with a tattoo cannot be buried in a Jewish cemetery."

"You're *Jewish*?"

"My mother was Jewish. From Russia. She named me 'Sasha.' It means 'protector of mankind.' Maybe that's why I became a nurse. Anyway, after we emigrated to the U.S. when I was eight, I started getting this urge to dress up in girls' clothes. Other Jewish mothers would have freaked out, but not mine. She was totally cool with it. She took me shopping for dresses."

"You were lucky to have a mother who let you do what you felt was right."

"At my high-school graduation, I gave this awesome valedictorian speech. My mom didn't blink an eye when I announced that from now on I wanted to be called 'Moon.'"

"Why 'Moon?'"

"Throughout history, many cultures have considered the moon feminine, maybe because it's associated with women's monthly menstrual cycles. But if you think about it, the moon is a planetary satellite that orbits the earth. Why should an astronomical body made of rocks and minerals be considered masculine *or* feminine? No reason, right? But it is. So, I figured, why can't a person who was born male be considered female if that's what he/she wants?"

"You're absolutely right."

Moon reached into the file of photos and brought out a sheet of plastic with a Buddha tattoo like hers. "A damp rag, and your arm will look just like mine." She positioned the plastic design on Natalia's arm. She pressed it with a damp washcloth, then rubbed gently and counted to ten.

"*Ta da!*" Moon peeled off the plastic, revealing the Buddha tattoo on Natalia's arm. "Buddha is part of my heritage too."

"What do you mean?"

"Look at my eyes, girlfriend. They're almond-shaped, like yours. That's why I can impersonate you so perfectly."

Natalia compared their similarly slanted eyes in the mirror. "Mine came from a Tartar barbarian who porked one of my mother's great-great-or-whatever grandmas."

"Mine came from a Japanese businessman my mother met in Moscow," said Moon. "At least that's what she told me. It's hard to picture. She was almost six feet tall, like me, a real ball-buster. I can't imagine her with a tiny Japanese dude."

"Were they married?"

Moon shook her head. "Once, when she was drunk—my mom

had that Russian thing for vodka—she admitted that before I was born she was a model-slash-hooker. Maybe that's why I got so obsessed with you."

Natalia gasped. *"What?"*

"Not the hooker part," Moon added hastily. "But, like, you were a model, like my mom. And Slavic, like her, right?"

"Slovak."

"Slovak, Slavic. Same thing, right?"

"Uh...kind of."

"My mom died when she was about your age. Breast cancer."

"I'm sorry."

"She blamed it on the tacky Soviet-era implants she got in Volgograd, before she moved to Moscow to become a model-slash—"

"Escort."

"Right." Moon put the fake Buddha tattoo scraps in the garbage bag, sealed it, and stuffed it among the dresses in the garment bag. "I made my nose like yours last year."

"Your *nose?*"

Moon put her face next to Natalia's and pointed at their two noses in the mirror. "Look."

"At what?"

"Our noses. They're identical."

Natalia studied their reflections, amazed. "They are! How's that possible?"

Moon ran her finger down Natalia's perfect nose. "I brought your photo to the plastic surgeon. I told him, 'Dude, make mine look just like Natalia Funck's nose job.'"

"Hey, did I say I got a *nose job?*"

"Girlfriend, we're twins now! No secrets! The plastic surgeon did my chin reduction, cheek implants, and tits and ass jobs just like yours too." Moon pulled back her shoulders and thrust out her breasts.

"Okay, no secrets! Now what?"

"Something else to make you look like Moon." Angel walked over with a hypodermic needle. "And this one's not fake." He squirted excess liquid from the needle.

Natalia's eyes widened. "What *is* that?"

Moon placed her face beside Natalia's and pointed to her own brow. "See how my forehead is kinda heavy and low over my eyes? That's natural for men. Some scientists say it's because back in caveman days, guys needed strong foreheads to hold up jaws big enough to chomp on tough mastodon meat. Women didn't need big jaws because their cavemen sweeties chewed the meat into tiny pieces and then gave it to them and the kids to eat. That's why women's foreheads are flatter, like yours. Anyway, when I get the big bucks, I'm gonna have my forehead smoothed down. They call it 'facial feminization.' Y'see, first the doc cuts near the hairline and peels back the skin, kind of like removing a mask. Then he buffs down the brow-ridge bone with this electric sander thing —"

"TMI! Too much info!" Angel nudged her aside.

She pulled off the yellow bandana wrapped around her neck. "I'll have him sand down my Adam's-fucking-apple too." She pointed to the bony protuberance on her throat. "I'm sick of hiding my golf ball."

"Moon, okay, like, dude, she gets it! It's tough being trans!" Angel removed Natalia's pink-streaked black wig. "You trust me to do better Botox than a plastic surgeon?"

"I trust you not to hurt me," she said. "Plastic surgeons are closet sadists."

"Tell me about it," said Moon.

Angel positioned the needle over Natalia's forehead, just above the center spot between her eyebrows. "So, y'know how when I do your forehead, I, like, give you just enough to smooth the wrinkles? And I joke that if I inject too much, you'll look like a pinche caveman?"

Natalia grimaced. "It's caveman time?"

Angel nodded. "Frown," he commanded her. She frowned. "Now relax." She relaxed. "You'll feel a little pinch." He smiled. "A *pinche* pinch!"

Angel moved the needle closer to her forehead. Natalia shut her eyes and thought of Vaclav.

Chapter 14

The White House

December 17, 10:30 a.m.

Natalia stared at herself in the mirror: She was wearing Moon's wife-beater T-shirt with the yellow bandana around her neck, along with her tight jeans and studded motorcycle boots. She sized up her pink-streaked, bob-and-bangs black wig; Buddha arm tattoo; nose and ear studs; outrageous makeup job; and her new caveman forehead. After injecting the Botox, Angel had pressed his fingers down on her eyebrows to the count of 1000 to help the drug make them drop. To her amazement, it had worked.

Except for her 15-karat diamond engagement ring, matching diamond wedding band, and two Cartier LOVE bracelets, she had to admit that she looked strikingly like the trans woman who had walked into her bedroom with Angel only a few hours earlier. She threw on Moon's pink parka and patted her bulging crotch, proud of her creative ingenuity: She had used a wadded-up Frette Egyptian-cotton washcloth to create what Moon dubbed "the illusion of a hidden purple-headed warrior."

"Ready or not, here I come!" Moon swept in from the walk-in closet, with Angel in tow.

Natalia felt as if she were looking into a mirror: Moon's ash-blonde wig and makeup were identical to what she considered her best First Lady image. She was wearing the red tulle-and-satin Valentino gown with the beaded butterflies and Natalia's red-satin Manolo stilettos. Her long acrylic fingernails were painted a matching red. Natalia's eyes fell on her red-satin choker. "Adam's apple concealer?"

"If anyone asks, I saw it in *Vogue*," said Moon. "How's this?" She evocatively narrowed her eyes, combined a fish-gape pout with a smile, and gracefully brushed her hair from her face.

Natalia squirmed, recognizing the mannerism that photographers had captured in her public appearances. "Do I look like *that*?"

"Only when you're having fun!" Angel joked.

Moon twirled around, to give Natalia the whole 360-degree view.

"The Valentino fits you better than it fits me!"

"I wear a corset from hell to create feminine curves."

"How do you hide your...uh...masculine bump?" She nodded toward the smooth spot at Moon's crotch.

"A tucking gaff."

"A *what*?"

"A tucking gaff. Think 'thong from hell,'" said Moon. "But I'm a perfectionist. I do the whole taping thing first."

"Taping?"

Moon hesitated. "Girlfriend, you really want to know?"

"Unless it's a trade secret."

"Okay, like, first you coax your acorns up into your nut sack," she said, pointing to her private parts. "Works best if you're lying down. Then you pull 'Mr. Happy' down and around between your legs, tuck him into your ass crack, and secure him in place with what looks like duct tape. Mr. Happy's not very happy, but it works."

"Definitely more info than *I* wanna know," said Angel. "Chica, give Moon your bling."

Natalia tugged at her diamond rings, but they wouldn't come off.

"Hormone bloat. It's the worst." Moon grabbed Natalia's ring finger and sucked on it.

Natalia grimaced. *"Gross!"*

"Almost got it," Moon mumbled, her mouth full. She sucked noisily, then stopped suddenly, her eyes bulging. She pulled Natalia's ring-less finger out of her mouth. "Shit! I swallowed them!"

"You *what*?" gasped Natalia.

Angel ran over. "Dude, stick your finger down your throat! Puke them out! Or...I'll get MiraLAX to shit them out!"

Moon winked. "Just kidding!" She spit the rings into her hand.

Natalia breathed a sigh of relief.

"Smart ass!" Angel playfully punched Moon.

Moon pushed the rings onto her own finger and admired them. "*Ohmygod, ohmygod, ohmygod!*"

"Leave them here on the counter before you split tonight," said Angel. "If you're caught with them, they'll bust you for theft." He tapped Natalia's Cartier LOVE bracelets. "Next."

"Uh-oh. I gave my mother the screwdriver that unlocks them."

"Anything in here that'll do the job?"

Natalia scanned the room. She spotted the white roses in the service alcove. "Hilda was clipping roses..." She walked into the service alcove and returned with the clippers.

"That'll get the bracelets off you," said Angel. "But, like, we can't put them back together for Moon."

"No worries. I've got plenty more." She handed the rose clippers to Angel. He cut first one, then the second Cartier LOVE bracelet off her wrist. They tumbled to the floor.

She impulsively grabbed the clippers and picked up the bracelets. Using all her strength, she cut the bejeweled bands into little pieces.

"What are you pinche doing, chica?"

"Imagining these are Rex's pinche balls!"

Angel gathered the scraps of gold and pavé diamonds from the floor. "Where can we hide these?"

She headed toward the walk-in closet, motioning for Moon and Angel to follow her. Inside, she slid back a full-length wall mirror. Behind it was a tall ebony jewelry safe. She pressed her right index finger on a small fingerprint-scanning screen on the door. The lock clicked open. Inside the safe were rows of drawers, each with an ornate rose-gold handle.

Moon shook her head, disbelieving. *"Seriously?"*

"Custom-made in Italy," said Natalia. "Rex wanted a jewelry safe like the one he saw at the house…make that the *mansion*…of one of his Russian oligarch golf buddies."

She slid open the bottom drawer. It was filled with dozens of Cartier LOVE Bracelets.

"Obscene!" said Moon.

"Guilt gifts," she said. "$10,000 to $40,000 apiece, depending on how much guilt Rex was feeling that day, or *pretending* to feel." She burrowed the scraps of the ruined Cartier bracelets underneath the pile.

Angel spotted a couple of gold mini-screwdrivers in the drawer. "You could have used these to get off the bracelets."

"Cutting them off was a lot more fun." She motioned to Moon. "Go ahead, choose a couple."

While Moon sifted through the bracelets, she pulled open a jewelry drawer near the top of the safe and another just below it. Their contents quickly diverted Moon's attention. One was filled with diamond earrings and matching necklaces, the other with ruby-and-diamond earrings and necklaces, each glittering treasure nestled in its own blue-velvet-lined compartment.

"I would wear only diamonds with the red Valentino, but since you're FLOTUS today, you decide."

"Wow, wow, *wow!*" Humming "Diamonds are a Girl's Best Friend," Moon studied the jewelry in both drawers, gently picking up each item and fondling it, before returning it to its compartment.

"Yo, dude, c'mon!" said Angel, checking his Rolex.

Moon stopped humming, as if annoyed that she didn't have all day. She settled on a pair of ruby-and-diamond earrings and a matching pendant. "Rubies will make the red pop and take eyes off the choker." She scooped up the earrings and noticed that they were pierced. "Got a clean hypodermic, Angel?"

"I forgot," said Natalia. "You don't have pierced ears."

"Not yet." Moon handed the jewelry to her. "Don't drop them."

Angel walked into the salon and rummaged in his satchel under the counter. He returned with an alcohol pad and a plastic-wrapped hypodermic needle. "Want me to do it?"

"Who's the RN around here?" Moon wiped her ear lobes with the alcohol pad, unwrapped the needle, looked at herself in the mirror, and took aim. Stone-faced, she pierced first one, then the other ear lobe.

"Didn't that *hurt*?" Natalia said in amazement.

"RNs are trained to have nerves of steel." She wiped away the few traces of blood. "Earrings please?" Natalia slipped them into Moon's palm. Moon expertly inserted them.

Natalia sized up Moon in the mirror. "The rubies *do* make the red pop!" She attached the matching pendant around Moon's neck. "And you hardly notice the choker."

"Told ya, girlfriend!"

Natalia turned to Angel. "Shall we take some jewelry along? It's not like I have a credit card or checkbook. We can pawn them for cash."

"They don't usually X-ray stuff going *out* of the White House, only going in. But if they do," he said, "and we get caught with FLOTUS's jewelry, we're fucked." He braced one cowboy-booted foot against the wall. "But I have a little space in here." Using the tip of the hypodermic needle, he pried open the secret compartment in his silver boot heel.

Natalia opened a small jewelry drawer filled with unset diamonds. "These belonged to Rex's first, second, and third wives," she said. "When they got divorced, he reclaimed their jewelry, trashed the settings, and the put the stones in here. He said they have bad karma."

Angel examined the diamonds, picked out six of the smallest ones—Natalia figured they were from one to three karats each—and fit them into the boot-heel compartment. "Bad karma's bullshit," he said.

Moon looked up from the drawer full of Cartier LOVE bracelets. "I'll pass on the bracelets. I don't do guilt gifts." She closed the drawer and peeked into random drawers, searching for something. When she found what she was looking for, she opened the drawer wide. It held dozens of expensive watches. "I need to know when it's Cinderella time tonight." She selected a Cartier tank watch with a pavé-diamond face and slipped it on.

"Leave that here too when you split tonight," said Angel. "Vamanos!"

Natalia closed the jewelry safe and locked it. She followed Angel and Moon out of the closet.

Moon primped nervously in front of the salon mirror. "*Ohmygod, ohmygod*, I'm getting stage fright! Girlfriend, you've got to tell me what to say to the fucking Funck fuckers at the photo shoot. They've got to believe I'm *you*!"

"Say nothing," she said. "Funck family members never talk to me. When they're together, I'm a piece of furniture. All you have to do is smile."

"One more time?" Moon struck the pose she showed Natalia earlier, her eyes evocatively narrowed, a bland fish-gape smile. She gracefully brushed her hair from her face.

"Perfect!"

Moon took her hands. "Natalia, beautiful, sweet Natalia! Thank you for giving me this chance to live my dream today." She gave her air kisses on both cheeks. "Girlfriend, I will do everything in my power not to screw it up."

"Thank you for giving me this chance for my freedom." She saw tears brimming in Moon's eyes. "Sorry, Moon, but First Ladies don't cry," she said gently.

Chapter 15

The White House

December 17, 10:45 a.m.

"Here comes the faggot-patrol again," said Conner.

Tallisha saw that he was looking at the black-and-white image of Angel and Moon on the security screens. They were walking toward them through the tunnel from the White House basement. "Trans folks aren't gay," she said. "It's just they feel they were born in the wrong body."

Conner nodded toward the trans woman in the pink-streaked black wig on the screen. "So, it's not that this dude hates his wanker cuz it's not big enough, or cuz it points kinda sideways. He wishes he had a pussy instead?"

"Uh-huh. It's a matter of nature."

"Like it's nature you're a bull dyke?"

"Maybe," she said, unfazed. "Or maybe like it's nature you're dumb as dog shit."

* * *

In the tunnel, Angel shot Natalia a warning look that she knew meant, "Are you ready?" She took a deep breath and nodded. Then she made the gesture that Rex always made before he walked into a room, the move she'd seen men make her entire life anytime they needed to reassure themselves that they were men. She put her hand on her "crotch" and "rearranged" what was underneath.

Angel snickered. "You got that part right!"

They walked into the security checkpoint.

As if he couldn't help it, Conner hitched up his pants and made a similar gesture. He grunted at Moon. "So, did FLOTUS let you wear her silk undies?"

"Just give the lady her stuff," Angel said.

Natalia felt a wave of relief that he answered before she could put her trans-woman voice to the test. Moon had rehearsed it with her, but she didn't feel confident. Conner kept staring at her. Was it contempt or suspicion?

Tallisha handed Moon's passport and iPhone to Natalia. For a moment, their fingers touched. Tallisha glanced up at her. Natalia worried that her hands had given her away. She turned quickly to leave.

"Throw it on the X-ray belt." Conner pointed to her garment bag. "Gotta make sure you didn't steal nothing."

Natalia glanced at Angel, hoping he would say something to prevent the X-ray scan. She didn't want the nasty guard sorting through her shorn hair and nail clippings inside. She saw beads of sweat on Angel's forehead.

Conner nodded to Natalia's wig. "Head bush too!"

"Ignore the dumbass," said Tallisha. "He sucks shit." She waved Natalia and Angel through the exit gate, bags and all. "Y'all have a nice day now."

"Hovno," Natalia whispered once they were outside and heading toward the White House grounds exit. "I thought we were screwed."

"C'mon, piece of cake," Angel joked.

Ahead, the usual horde of tourists and paparazzi were milling around outside the perimeter fence, hoping to spot VIPs exiting the White House.

"Hey, Angel!" a voice called from the crowd. "Did you get me that photo op with FLOTUS?"

Natalia recognized the man pushing his way closer to the fence: Phil Smith, the paparazzo who creeped her out. "He'll know it's me!" she whispered to Angel.

"Chill." He waved to Phil. "Not yet, dude, but hang in there. It's gonna happen!"

Natalia focused on the turnstile exit ahead. The finish line; fifteen feet to go. Ten feet. Her stomach clenched in cold terror. She remembered feeling this way the first time she walked down a runway in Paris. You felt this way on your first date with Rex, she reminded herself. Look where that got you!

She glanced over her shoulder at the gleaming white mansion that had been her prison. Praying it would be her last look at it, she murmured, "Goodbye and fuck you."

In that instant, out of the corner of her eye, she spotted Phil behind the perimeter fence. Like a hunter with his prey in his crosshairs, he was snapping photos of her. "My shadow!" she whispered to Angel. "He's taking pictures of me!"

He turned to see. "It's all in your head."

She glanced back at the fence: no sign of Phil. "He was there! I saw him!"

"You're uptight. Your mind, like, fucks you over when you're uptight."

She nodded, but she wasn't convinced.

Angel nudged her ahead of him, to push her through the turnstile first. "Welcome to the real world, chica!"

Part III

Chapter 16

The White House

December 17, 11:15 a.m.

Perspiration soaked Moon's armpits, threatening to drip down the sides of her red Valentino gown. *Ohmygod, ohmygod,* she thought, as Sally-Ann escorted her down the sweeping staircase of the White House. What if I show up at the photo op with ginormous sweat stains on this $15,000 dress? What if my makeup runs? They'll know I'm an imposter! Wait, I'll blame it on the hormone shots. Moon repeated the excuse in her mind to reassure herself, but it only made her sweat more profusely.

She had stayed cool when Natalia's tight-ass social secretary bustled into FLOTUS's bedroom five minutes ago. "Wow! You look fantastic!" Sally-Ann gushed, taking in the gown, shoes, and jewelry. "And red is perfect for Christmas!" Moon had caught the moment when Sally-Ann spotted her red choker: Her mouth tightened, as if she were hiding her disapproval, afraid to offend FLOTUS. "Chokers are hot this season," Moon had said in her best Natalia voice. "I saw it in *Vogue.*" She wasn't sure the zaftig blonde with the Alabama drawl believed her, but so what? I'm fucking *FLOTUS,* she thought. She works for *me.*

To make small talk as they walked down the staircase, Moon was about to ask Sally-Ann if she'd had her social-secretary job long. Then she realized that Natalia would know the answer to that. She had hired Sally-Ann. On second thought, it was more likely that President Funck gave Sally-Ann her dream job. Moon imagined that Sally-Ann's father was a filthy-rich, hardcore Republican who donated the big bucks to Funck's campaign coffers. No doubt, Sally-Ann's Alabama ancestors owned a cotton plantation right out of *Gone with the Wind,* with thousands of slaves, and fought for Dixie in the Civil War. For sure her family owned an arsenal of shotguns and hunted deer, quail, and pheasants, anything with fur or feathers and a heartbeat. She bet that her father went big-game hunting in Africa with one of President Funck's sons. Maybe Sally-Ann tagged along. She imagined fleshy Sally-Ann in a Ralph Lauren safari shirt, pants, and pith helmet, flanking her pot-bellied father in the same attire, posing with their rifles next to a dead elephant. Not a pretty picture, she thought.

Enough with the fantasies, Moon told herself. You know the reason why your imagination is having diarrhea right now: You are scared shitless about meeting President Funck and his family face-to-face.

They reached the bottom of the grand staircase. "Have a wonderful time, ma'am," said Sally-Ann, turning to walk back upstairs.

"Aren't you...?" Moon was about to say, "coming with me," but realized that it might give her away. FLOTUS doesn't have her social secretary by her side 24/7, she thought. She can't stand Sally-Ann; she thinks she spies on her. "Thank you, Sally-Ann."

One strapping Marine guard was posted on each side of the staircase. They stared straight ahead as she walked past them into the grand foyer, its marble floors shimmering like ice. She spotted the Funck children and grandchildren at the other end of the room. No sign of the President. Good, she thought. I can try out my FLOTUS impersonation on "my" stepchildren and grandchildren before facing "my" husband.

She approached the grandchildren first. They sat primly on antique high-backed chairs along one wall, lined up by ages that she judged were from about two to fifteen. The boys wore dark Brooks Brothers suits and red ties; the girls wore red party dresses. At least I match, she thought. But will they find me out? As she stepped toward them, not one glanced up. All the children, even the two-year-olds, were bent over iPads nestled in their laps, earbud wires dangling from their ears like marionette strings. The boys were playing blood-splattered video-combat games. The girls were watching insipid girl-band music videos, humming along. At least they're not watching FOX News, Moon thought. Not yet.

Funck's three sons and their wives were positioned around an oversized Christmas tree that reached up to the crystal chandeliers dangling from the ceiling and rivaled them for bling. Enveloped in twinkling lights and gold ornaments, each shaped like a different Funck international hotel, the tree should have looked spectacular. To Moon's eyes, it looked tacky, unnatural. As tacky and unnatural as the Funck offspring, she thought. She judged that hundreds of thousands of dollars had been spent on plastic surgery for the blonde Funck Barbie wives: tits, asses, noses, cheekbones, chins. The President's sons looked like clones of their father when he was a young playboy, with carefully plucked eyebrows, chiseled features that she guessed resulted from gel-dermal filler, and maybe plastic surgery as well. Their slicked-back hair gleamed in the light from the chandeliers, like furniture with too much polish. They wore obscenely large Rex Funck watches and absurdly long ties, just like their dad.

Natalia had said that the President's children never spoke to her at family gatherings, that she felt like a piece of furniture among them. I get it, thought Moon. But right now she didn't feel like one of the antique side tables that no doubt belonged to George Washington. She felt like a sagging, secondhand sofa with rusted springs that someone had dumped in an alley.

She walked past a black-clad goateed photographer and his slim female assistant. They were setting up lights and camera equipment. She caught up with an African-American butler carrying a silver tray. The butler bowed obsequiously as he passed out glasses of champagne to the Funck litter. Moon snagged one, nodding "thanks." The butler's eyes widened. Before she could take a sip, she stopped, her glass poised in midair. She realized that everyone in the room was staring at her.

Shit. Natalia doesn't drink, she thought. Like her husband. The motherfucker probably forbids it. As much as she was dying to drain her glass, she placed it back on the serving tray. Within seconds, Moon was a piece of furniture again.

"Are we pregnant yet?"

She turned to face a blonde in a skin-tight white dress whose tits seemed way too inflated for her anorexic body. Her overly filler-pumped lips attempted to curl into a smile. They reminded Moon of the lips on the koi at the park in Miami where she played when she was a little boy. There was no doubt in her mind that this was Gretchen, the First Daughter.

Gretchen pointed to the red-ribbon choker around Moon's neck. "Nice touch."

"I saw it in *Vogue*," she said in her best Natalia voice. "It's the new hot thing."

"Perfect for hiding a turkey-neck, right?" Gretchen said it as a statement, not a question.

Moon felt her face flush. Natalia had warned her not to speak to family members, but she couldn't resist. "Y'know what, Gretchen? White's just not your color. Makes you look like a stiff." She turned on her heel and walked away.

But where could she go? She was surrounded. Trapped.

"Listen up!"

James, Funck's oldest son, branded by the press as the most pompous, motioned for his siblings to gather around him. "I just got word that Daddy had to bail on the photo shoot today. Some shit came up. Maybe North Korea. Maybe Iran. I don't know, cuz *damn*, I lost my fucking security clearance! Thanks a lot, Pops!" He wiped away a pretend tear. The others laughed.

"Shall we adjourn to the bar at the Funck?" Conrad, Funck's second son, whom the press dubbed the sleaziest, smirked. There were murmurs of approval. Moon knew that when the Funck offspring were in Washington, but not at the White House, they hung out on the government's dime at the family's posh Funck hotel a block away. "No wives. No brother-in-laws," said Conrad. "Just brothers!"

"And Gretchen," added Rex Jr., son number three, named the dimmest by the press.

"Sorry," Gretchen said. "Daddy needs me with the Joint Chiefs in the Situation Room." She strutted over to a tall, slender young man with pallid skin and a blank expression. He was standing alone in a corner holding a half-empty glass of champagne. Moon hadn't noticed him before. She assumed that this was Jacob Cohn, Gretchen's husband. It looked as if he felt as much like a piece of furniture here as she did.

"Jacob," Gretchen said in a tone that Moon found soft, yet haughty. He raised his eyes to his wife, but said nothing, as if waiting for her command. "I may be hours with Daddy, so make sure the children have a healthy dinner. No yogurt with additives, no beef that isn't grass-fed. Also figure out which of the nannies scared the shit out of them last night with her bedtime story."

"It was Marianne, the French girl your celebrity-divorcée friend Whitney pawned off on us."

"Remind me to put Whitney on my shit list, fire Marianne's ass, and get one of the other nannies to do bedtime." She walked away. "And make sure Elizabeth wears her night guard."

"It's Amanda who wears a night guard," Jacob said in a voice so subdued, he reminded Moon of a squashed bug.

"I knew that," Gretchen snapped at him. "And Frederick gets a tablespoon of Robitussin."

"It's Samuel who gets Robitussin, but only *one* teaspoon."

Gretchen walked back to Jacob, stopping when she was nose to nose with him. "Do you think I don't know the needs of my own *children*?"

"How about, 'Do I think you don't know the *names* of your own children?'"

Eyes flashing, Gretchen stormed away from Jacob. Moon was standing close enough to hear her hiss, "Shithead!"

Moon wondered if the "fake news" was true that Gretchen and Jacob only stayed together to keep up a "happy family" facade. It was common knowledge that Rex had opposed his daughter's marriage to the Orthodox Jew, but that with Rex Funck, money talked. *The New York Times* reported that Jacob's father, a developer with a larger net worth than his, offered him a lucrative partnership in a Chelsea real-estate project. The next day, Rex approved the union.

Now, six years and four children later, Gretchen spent more time at her father's side than at her husband's. The press hinted that it was because she realized she had more to gain from allying with President Funck than with a junior real-estate mogul who could end up doing time, like his father.

She also wondered how true the "fake news" was that since her father's election, Gretchen was considering running for President herself someday, that she pictured herself becoming the female version of President George Bush Jr. I sure as hell hope not, thought Moon. The father and son President Bushes fucked over America enough. We don't need the father and daughter President Funcks finishing it off.

She grabbed a smoked-salmon canapé from a silver tray. As she savored it, she watched Gretchen furiously punching the button to call the elevator.

"Wait!"

The photographer ran over, trailed by his assistant lugging an umbrella-hooded light stand. "How about we at least get a few shots of the family without the President?"

The Funck boys rolled their eyes.

Gretchen said, "Absolutely!" She corralled her reluctant brothers. "Even without Daddy, we need Funcks in the public eye daily."

James slipped his arm around her. "Helps promote your 2024

Presidential bid, right, Sis?" Gretchen jabbed him with an elbow.

Like father, like daughter, thought Moon.

The photographer motioned for everyone to line up in front of the Christmas tree. The Funck sons' wives and Jacob wrestled the iPads from their children and walked them over. Moon wasn't sure where to stand and none of the Funck offspring glanced her way. I'm not a piece of furniture, she thought. I'm invisible.

"Madame First Lady?" The photographer motioned for Moon to flank Gretchen, who stood beside her brother James. Moon took her place. She noticed that Jacob, Gretchen's husband, was standing at the end of the line with his children, like an unwanted dinner guest banished to the kids' table.

The photographer tugged on his goatee as he peered through the lens of his Canon. "Closer please, everybody! Move closer together. You're a loving family, remember?"

"Gretchen, do you love me?" teased James as he pressed closer to her. "Gretchen only loves Daddy."

"And herself," said Conrad.

"Go to hell." Gretchen edged away from James, closer to Moon. Gretchen's toned arm brushed against hers. As the photographer clicked away, she felt perspiration dribbling down her sides.

"Oh dear, are we nervous?" whispered Gretchen through her fake-for-the-camera smile.

"It's not nerves," Moon whispered back. "I'm wearing your new Gretchen Funck deodorant." She knew that Gretchen was taking heat from the press for selling her line of beauty products in China while acting as a Presidential advisor. She couldn't resist adding, "Guess it's as fake as its namesake."

Suddenly, the photo shoot was over. The family scattered. Moon found herself alone in the grand foyer. She started up the staircase, but then realized that she didn't know her way back to Natalia's bedroom and there was no sign of Sally-Ann. She called to the Marine guards posted at the bottom of the stairs. "Excuse me," she said in her Natalia voice. "I seem to have twisted my ankle. Can one of you please escort me back to my room?"

"Yes, ma'am," said one. He started up the stairs toward her. She studied the other guard. He was taller and more handsome than her escort, in a young Brad Pitt-ish way. It doesn't matter that I'm stuck with the ugly one, she thought. I passed the "First Lady test" today and tonight I'm outta here. I sure as hell get why Natalia wanted to blow this joint.

Chapter 17

Highway West of Washington, D.C.

December 17, 12:00 p.m.

"*Tijuana*?" Natalia wriggled in the passenger seat of Angel's red Mustang as they inched along in bumper-to-bumper traffic out of Washington. "We're going to *Mexico*?"

"Mi amor, I smuggled myself from Mexico into the U.S. five years ago," he said. "It'll be a lot easier to smuggle you out of the U.S. into Mexico."

"What about Vaclav? Where am I meeting him? When?"

"In three days. I emailed him to go to this little hotel, El Paraiso. It's on the beach in Rosarito, just outside of TJ. My family used to go have lunch on Sundays in Rosarito." He kissed the tips of his fingers. "You won't believe the fish tacos!"

Natalia didn't answer. She wasn't thinking about tacos. She was picturing herself running barefoot on a windswept beach, the waves crashing, the sun setting fire to the horizon, into Vaclav's arms.

Suddenly, they heard sirens, lots of them, racing closer from behind.

Natalia looked through the rear window and saw the flashing red lights on what seemed like hundreds of police cars. Vehicles were veering out of their way. "It's over!" she gasped.

"*What?*"

"They're coming for me!"

"No way!"

But as Angel checked the rear-view mirror, she saw that he was toying with the arc of silver studs on his left ear, a sign that he was skeptical. "Get down on the floor," he said. "Just in case."

Natalia struggled to wedge her tall body into the narrow space between the passenger seat and the dashboard. Impossible.

"Hovno, why do you have such a little car?"

"A Mustang's not a little car. It's a pinche sports car."

She realized that she was too large to squeeze her body below the dashboard. Feeling a stab of pain in her neck, she raised her head to peer out the passenger-side window. "It's no use. People can see me." She met the gaze of the driver in the Chevy beside them. He was staring suspiciously at her. "He knows who I am!"

"Trust me. He thinks you're a trans weirdo, not the First Lady."

The sirens screamed closer. In the rear-view mirror, Natalia and Angel watched as a column of police motorcycles pulled out from behind the police cars and roared toward them. Cars were forced to swerve into the left and right lanes of the freeway to let them pass. Angel spotted an off-ramp up ahead. He cut in front of a pickup truck and raced toward it.

One, two, and then three motorcycles whizzed past them. Half a dozen more followed, all flying American flags. Natalia realized that the motorcycles were leading the way for a phalanx of police cars. Behind them, she could make out half a dozen hulking black SUVs: Escalades with smoked-bulletproof windows. "It's the President's motorcade!"

"It's the pinche President?" Angel checked the rear-view mirror. "Which limo is he in?"

"It's always the one in middle. They call it the 'Beast.'"

"The car's not the beast. President Funck's the 'Beast!'"

As the limos whizzed past the Mustang, he slapped Natalia a victorious high-five. "And he has no pinche idea you ditched him!"

She said a silent prayer to Jackie as the motorcade passed. When the sirens faded away and Angel cut back into the fast lane, she turned to him. "That was a sign. It was another good omen!"

"A good omen?"

"It means that I did the right thing, that it's all going to work out!" She crossed herself.

"Yo, chica, here's to *el destino*!" He raised his palm for another high-five.

"Destiny!" She slapped his sweaty palm with her own.

Chapter 18

Washington, D.C.

December 17, 1:00 p.m.

Phil climbed the narrow staircase in his rundown apartment building. He was breathless by the time he reached the fourth floor. The super hadn't replaced the bulb that blew out six months ago, but it was just as well. He lived in NoMa, the worst part of Washington. The dim lighting hid the gang graffiti that covered the walls. Some people called graffiti "poor-man's art." Phil called it "wall garbage."

He pulled a key from the pocket of his worn jeans and unlocked the door. Nudging it open, he kicked off his threadbare sneakers and padded into the studio apartment in his mismatched socks.

An empty container of "Hot & Spicy Cup of Noodles" that he had microwaved for breakfast sat on the scarred Formica-topped table, one dried noodle stuck to the Styrofoam like a shriveled worm. He tossed the cup into a wastebasket and made room for the old Dell laptop he spotted on the sofa that doubled as his bed. He walked over and picked it up. A fluffy tabby cat curled up next to it awoke with a start. "Sorry, Oscar," he said, running his hand over its natty fur. The cat opened its mouth, emitted a squeak that he recognized as "Hello," then dropped its head back on its paws and closed its eyes.

Phil slid the laptop onto the table, plugged it in, and removed the Nikon slung around his neck. He gently removed the digital chip from the camera. While he waited for the computer to fire up, he walked over to the refrigerator, its door plastered with celebrity photos that he had taken over the years. He proudly straightened the photos of Jennifer Aniston, Beyoncé, and George Clooney, the only three photos that had earned him the big bucks. Below them were dozens of celebrity photos that hadn't sold. Too often, the celebrity had covered his or her face with a hand, a purse, or a hat at the last minute, or flipped him the bird.

Among what Phil called his "turkey photos" were a few of FLOTUS. In one, the First Lady was more sunglasses than face. In another, she was so bundled up in a white cashmere scarf, that her only recognizable feature was her nose. Phil had stalked Natalia Funck for months and come up empty. He wondered if she had put a Slovak curse on him. He had read that they still believed in witches in Slovakia. Whether or not she had cursed him, she certainly had bewitched him. He spent hours poring over everything he could find out about her online. The First Lady remained a mystery to him, an obsession, a riddle he felt compelled to solve.

Some of Phil's paparazzi buddies on FLOTUS watch, guys who viewed Natalia through telephoto lenses so powerful that they revealed the dark roots at her widow's peak two weeks before her next dye job, said that there was nothing behind her dazzling almond-shaped eyes. "She's just a vapid, empty-headed bitch," said Ralph, who had been a paparazzo since before Michael Jackson died. "She's a gold-digger who is so beautiful and so lucky that she nabbed a billionaire husband who just happened to become the most powerful man in the world."

Phil didn't agree with Ralph. Even though his telephoto wasn't as powerful as Ralph's, he had taken pictures of Natalia that revealed the vulnerability, pain, and helplessness in her exotic green eyes. He felt for her, even pitied her.

Maybe that's why, a few weeks ago, when a paparazzo friend had texted him that he spotted Natalia's mother getting out of a taxi in front of Mount Sinai in New York, Phil took the next Amtrak to Penn Station. He hung around the hospital until the next day, when he saw her emerge in a wheelchair, her face bandaged, and bundled into an Uber. He tailed the car to a Park Avenue surgery-recovery center. After a day and a half of lurking near the entrance, he got the photo of Natalia's nose peeking out of the white scarf, along with one of her mother's freshly lifted face framed in a window, looking like the one in Munch's painting, *The Scream*.

This morning, Phil had taken the Metro to the White House. Somehow he felt certain — *was it a dream? a wish?* — that today he would score a Natalia sighting. He vowed that if he got a great shot of her, he would send a box of See's candy to his mother in Pasadena and buy himself a longer telephoto lens.

There had been no Natalia sighting this morning. The only person-of-interest Phil saw leaving the White House was Angel, her Mexican-American hairdresser, with a freak wearing a pink-streaked black wig. Phil wasn't sure if the person was a man or a woman. The face was one he hadn't seen before. But there had been something about it...

The computer screen lit up. He inserted the digital camera chip into his laptop. As he waited for the photos to upload, he grabbed a carton of almond milk from the fridge and gulped from it.

His laptop pinged: It was a Google Alert for FLOTUS, a CNN piece about the Presidential Family Christmas photo session at the White House this morning. The President had bowed out at the last minute for reasons unknown, but there was a photo of the First Family, minus President Funck, standing in front of the White House Christmas tree.

In it, FLOTUS was standing next to Gretchen, her dazzling red-beaded gown making the First Daughter's white sheath look frumpy. Gretchen was flashing her usual fake smile. Natalia's face was pasted with what he called her "grin-and-bear-it" smile, but it looked a little tighter than usual. He wondered if that was because she was nervous around her stepchildren and step-grandchildren when her husband wasn't there, or because she was upset that another one of his sordid affairs had been revealed in the press. He downloaded the photo to his laptop.

Phil was convinced that he could trace Natalia Funck's emotional arc as First Lady by comparing old photos of her with the newest. He decided to compare today's photo with one he took last summer. He pulled it up: Natalia crossing the lawn with the President, about to step aboard Marine One. At the last moment, she had defiantly pulled ahead of him. The press speculated that it was because she was furious that a Victoria's Secret model had revealed she slept with Funck the day before their wedding.

Phil cut and pasted last summer's photo of Natalia next to today's White House Christmas photo. Something wasn't right. Was it because she was wearing a light-blue dress and pink lipstick in the first photo, and a red gown and red lipstick in today's photo? He looked from one to the other, trying to discern the difference. In today's photo, she looked unhappy, but she looked unhappy in the photo taken last summer too. And yet what was it? There was something more to the difference between the two photos, he felt certain.

The images from his camera finished uploading. There were only a few, mostly shots of Angel and his weirdo companion leaving the White House. Who was she, or *he*? Something about the person with Angel intrigued him. He enlarged it. Now he could see that she had breasts as well as a bulge at "her" crotch. Was she a *trans* woman?

Phil had been buddies with a paparazzo in L.A. who was a trans. Her name was Harriet, but before she took female hormones and got breast implants, he was Harry. "Being trans is the worst," Harriet explained one day as they waited outside the Chateau Marmont for a Jennifer Lawrence sighting. "It's not that you hate your thighs, but that it feels like they're on the wrong person." Phil was bombarded with so many thoughts and feelings he couldn't account for that he often wondered if he was born with the wrong brain. Maybe that's why Harriet and I got along so well, he thought. We're both misfits.

He cropped the photo and zoomed in closer, moving in on the trans-woman's eyes. They were slightly slanted, as if he/she had Asian blood. Exotic, like Natalia's. On his laptop, he moved the photo of the trans woman next to the photo of the First Lady at the White House today. He studied them both. The trans woman's eyes and the First Lady's eyes looked strikingly similar. Was it just an illusion? Was his mind screwing around with him because he was obsessed with FLOTUS?

Phil moved the photo of Natalia on the White House lawn last summer, so that it was on the left side of the photo of the trans woman. He moved today's White House Christmas photo to the right side of it. He enlarged the three photos. Something about the eyes... *What was it?*

He switched the positions of the three photos on his laptop screen. Now the lineup was:

1.) FLOTUS on the White House lawn last summer.
2.) FLOTUS at today's White House Christmas photo shoot.
3.) The trans woman with Angel outside the White House this morning.

Studying them, Phil realized that the eyes in the first and third photos looked more similar than those in the first and second. How can that be? he thought.

He felt a nudge against his leg. It was Oscar, eager for lunch. He scooped up the cat and held it up to the laptop screen. "Oscar, am I losing it, or what?"

Chapter 19

The White House

December 17, 3:00 p.m.

A cup of squash-and-broccoli soup; a kale, radish and quinoa salad; and an antioxidant-protein smoothie the hue of the fresh-mown White House lawn. This is what FLOTUS eats for lunch when she is alone in her bedroom? thought Moon. Oh, well. It beats a formal luncheon in the Blue Room with a contingent of apple-polishing ambassadors' wives from South America.

Per Natalia's instructions, after the family photo session this morning, Moon had complained of a headache and instructed Sally-Ann to offer the First Lady's regrets for bowing out of the lunch. She also asked her to bar visitors and staff from the First Lady's quarters for the rest of the day. "No worries. I will ask Hilda to give you her special Slovak anti-headache spa ritual," Sally-Ann said.

"Please refresh my memory about it," Moon replied because she was a secret spa whore at heart and couldn't resist.

"It includes a sauna, a scrub using birch branches, rock salt, and dry-ice cubes, plus a massage and a body mask made of clay from the Morava River, a tributary of the Danube," explained Sally-Ann. It sounded awesome to Moon, but obviously she could not allow Hilda's hands on her body. She declined in favor of what passed for lunch and a siesta. Staring at the barely touched soup and salad, Moon took a sip of the grass-green smoothie. She grimaced from the nasty flavor, wishing she were on a massage table getting scrubbed with birch branches instead.

As she stood up from the table, she glimpsed her reflection in the expansive mirror on the wall. It had been a bitch unzipping the Valentino without Hilda's help, which she also had refused for obvious reasons, but when she finally liberated her body, she had snuggled into Natalia's peach terrycloth bathrobe. She noticed that the peach color made her cheeks look rosier. She padded, barefoot, over to Natalia's canopied bed, and dove in.

Natalia had mentioned that the bed's mahogany frame was an antique; it once belonged to Dolley Madison, wife of James Madison, the fourth President of the United States. "I hate Dolley Madison," she had said. Moon asked why and learned that Dolley Madison was the first powerhouse First Lady, always at the President's side. "It boosted Madison's popularity, so since then, First Ladies are expected to be in the public eye." Natalia repeated, "I hate her."

Moon stretched out her long legs in Dolley Madison's bed, remembering the time she watched Martha Stewart make a Dolley Madison cake on her TV show, for the Fourth of July. Moon loved to bake and tried making one at home. A White House favorite during Dolley's time, the cake looked okay until Moon frosted it. The chocolate icing never quite stiffened. It dripped down the sides of the cake and pooled around it on the plate, like a mud puddle.

Luxuriating in the softness of what she deemed to be at least 1,000-count Egyptian cotton sheets, Moon picked up a remote control on the nightstand and tried to figure out the buttons. She tapped one. The floor-to-ceiling bookcase across the room sank into the floor, revealing an expansive flat-screen TV. She punched another button and the screen lit up: *The Ellen DeGeneres Show*.

It must be one of Natalia's favorites, she thought. Mine too.

Ellen had done wonders for the LGBTQ cause, Moon knew. But thanks to bigots like President Funck, this country had a long way to go. She pressed another button on the remote. Without a hint of a mechanical hum, the mattress glided up into an ideal position for watching TV: her head and back raised to a not-quite sitting position, a slight lift under her knees. All I need now is a margarita, she thought.

Moon wondered if Natalia was really an abstainer, like

the *teetotalitarian* President, or if she kept a bottle stashed somewhere. Perhaps Funck Vodka. There must have been hundreds of leftover cases after the brand tanked a few years back. The reason it failed was obvious: Funck told everyone he met not to drink. "Alcohol will kill you like it killed my brother Billy when he was only twenty-five years old," he always said. Moon didn't know which was worse: That Rex Funck put his family's name on vodka and sold it even though his brother drank himself to death, or that Americans elected a President who was so clueless, that he torpedoed his own brand of booze.

She climbed out of bed and walked over to Natalia's desk. The antique was so highly polished that she was startled to glimpse her "Natalia face" in the burnished walnut. She rummaged through the drawers. Lipsticks, mascara wands, and a handful of white acrylic nails, like caterpillar cocoons, filled one drawer. A stack of *Vogue, Harper's Bazaar,* and *Town & Country* magazines filled another. In the bottom drawer, behind a box of embossed FLOTUS stationery that looked untouched, she noticed a sliding panel. She imagined that whoever once owned this desk, maybe Dolley Madison, kept a pistol hidden here, or, she hoped, liquor. She slid the panel aside and discovered•a half-empty bottle. She read the label: "Slivovika."

Moon unscrewed the cap and took a whiff. The potent fermented-plum scent evoked memories of her mother. She had drowned herself in Bulgarian Slivovitz, a plum brandy like this Slovak one, when she was dying of breast cancer. At 150 proof, nearly twice as strong as 80-proof Russian vodka, Slivovitz was her go-to pain reliever. "Better than morphine," she had claimed.

Moon cradled the bottle of Slivovika against her terrycloth bathrobe and climbed back into bed. She muted the TV volume; she didn't need to hear Ellen to know what she was saying. She took a gulp of Slivovika. It burned, but in an invigorating way, as it slid down her throat.

* * *

Moon dreamed of her mother, young and beautiful. Moon was a little boy pretending to be a little girl. They were playing hide-and-seek in their favorite park in Miami. Her eyes were closed; it was her mother's turn to hide. Suddenly she heard the wail of a siren, hurtling closer. Her heart beat faster as she ran to find her mother. She was nowhere. Gone. She noticed the play structures that had been filled with screaming children moments before were empty, and that the picnickers had disappeared from the grass. The only living things in the park were the fleshy orange-and-white-spotted koi in the fishpond. They floated in the water, motionless except for their obscenely plump lips, which opened and closed, as if to the beat of a ticking clock. The siren grew louder. Deafening.

* * *

Moon gasped and opened her eyes. She was lying in Dolley Madison's bed; the phone on the nightstand beside her was ringing. Shaken from her dream, she reached over and picked up the receiver slowly, reminding herself to answer in Natalia's voice. "Hello?"

"Madame Funck, your mother is calling," said Sally-Ann on the phone.

"My mother?" Natalia had not given Moon instructions about how to deal with her mother. Moon didn't even know her name.

"She says it's urgent."

"Urgent?" Moon paused, torn. If she spoke to Natalia's mother, the woman would realize she was a fraud. Mothers know their own daughters.

"She says she's got to talk to you. She's worried about you."

"Worried about me?"

"You want me to kiss her off? I can give her the headache excuse, or the food poisoning."

Moon wondered why Natalia avoided talking to her mother. If it were her own mother, *olav ha-sholom*, she would talk to her for hours. "Tell her I'm resting. I'll call her later. And tell her I love her."

A long silence on the other end of the phone. "*Seriously?*" said Sally-Ann.

"Yes." As she hung up the phone, Moon pictured her own mother's young face, caring and worried. Whatever was going on between Natalia and her mother, she hoped her loving response would soothe things. That poor woman is going to go ballistic tomorrow when she learns her daughter escaped from the White House, she thought.

Moon checked the gilded antique clock on the nightstand. It was after 6:00 p.m. She had slept for three hours. She hoped that she could fall back to sleep for six more hours and dream about her mother again. Only this dream will end happily, with my mother at my side, she thought. It will be a good omen for my escape later tonight.

Chapter 20

Washington, D.C.

December 17, 5:00 p.m.

Phil Smith tucked his Nikon into his backpack and climbed the marble steps to the Funck International Hotel. He admired the four sets of double Doric columns that graced the facade of what was once the original Patent Office. Phil knew a lot about historic buildings. He photographed them when there was a dearth of celebrities at which to aim his camera. But he had no time for that now, he realized. Paparazzi were a definite no-no here.

A burly doorman in a green uniform tipped his bowler hat to the well-dressed men and women moving into and out of the brass-trimmed revolving door. The doorman glanced at Phil's cheap jacket, worn-out jeans and sneakers, and blocked his way. "Sorry, buddy," he growled softly so others couldn't hear. "This is private property. No homeless allowed."

"I'm not homeless. I live in NoMa."

The doorman snickered. "You're better off homeless." He shot a thumb toward Pennsylvania Avenue. "Beat it!"

As Phil reluctantly turned to go, a team of Secret Service agents in black suits, Ray-Bans, and coiled-tube radio earpieces, exploded out of the hotel's side doors. They took position on the landing, jaws set and legs wide, hands clasped over their crotches. The doorman rushed over to the revolving door as three men burst outside.

Phil recognized the President's sons. Their ties loosened and laughing loudly, they were unsteady on their feet, as if they had spent the afternoon boozing it up in the Funck Hotel bar. Their Escalade awaited them below. Noticing that they were tipsy, the doorman guided them down the marble steps. As the doorman helped load the Funck brothers into the SUV, Phil had his opening to slip into the hotel.

He knew that he had no time to size up the carved ceilings and chandeliers in the marble-wrapped lobby. Fighting an urge to pull out his Nikon and snap photos, he walked down a hall, following a sign to the hair salon.

The receptionist at the desk was a twenty-something blonde Gretchen-Funck wannabe. "Excuse me, miss?"

She flashed a smile before she looked up. It faded the moment she laid eyes on him. "Can I help you?"

"Is Angel Garcia here? FLOTUS's hairdresser? I need to see him."

"He's not here today."

"Where is he?"

"I have no idea."

Phil could see that the receptionist was rattled by his urgency. He spoke as calmly as he could. "I've got to see him." He saw her hand move below the reception counter. No doubt she was pushing a button to summon security.

He recognized a slender young black woman with braided hair at a styling station. She was trimming the hair of an elderly female client, seemingly deaf to the client's incessant chatter. He noticed the gold nameplate on her counter: "Jazz." He had seen Jazz enter and leave the White House staff entrance a few times on days when he hadn't seen Angel there. He figured that Jazz filled in as the First Lady's hairdresser when Angel was out sick.

Phil spotted a hefty security guard striding toward the salon. He hurried over to Jazz. "Please! Angel is my friend! You must tell me where Angel is!"

Jazz looked him up and down and shrugged her shoulders. "I don't know, sorry."

"*I* know."

To his surprise, it was the client in Jazz's styling chair. He estimated that she was in her late seventies, but that a plastic surgeon had attempted to lock her face at sixty-five. He'd blown it. "Please, tell me where Angel is," he said.

"Well, Angel does my hair every Wednesday at four. We've had a standing appointment since just before President Funck moved into the White House." She paused, thinking. "Or maybe it was after he moved in."

Out of the corner of his eye, Phil saw the security guard chatting with the receptionist. She pointed to him. "Where is Angel?" he asked the client.

"So, he calls me this morning and cancels," she said. "I mean, he's canceled before. That's the downside of getting my hair done by FLOTUS's hairdresser."

"Do you know where he is?"

Ignoring him, she continued, "Usually he cancels because he's flying off somewhere with her on Air Force One. But this time he said he had to leave town on personal business." The client glanced in the mirror at the job Jazz was doing on her hair and scowled. "He damn well better be back at work next week, like he promised."

"Thank you." Phil turned to face the approaching security guard, knowing it was no use resisting him.

"You're coming with me." The guard grabbed his arm and led him out of the salon, down a long vitrine-filled hallway, and through the kitchen to a staff exit.

Thirty minutes later, Phil was back in his apartment on his laptop, reading an online *People* article about Angel Garcia that had run last year. *FLOTUS Is Besties with Her Barber* was the cutesy headline. Phil had read the piece when it came out. Now he planned to study every word and every picture in it, and anything else he could google about Angel. His mind was flooded with bizarre, perhaps preposterous, scenarios about the First Lady, her hairdresser, and the trans woman with Angel this morning, each one more impossible than the last. Either my brain is in meltdown, he thought, or I'm onto something amazing.

Chapter 21

Knoxville, TN

December 17, 10:00 p.m.

"Here ya go, hon!" An ungainly waitress in her sixties, with a TGIF nametag that said "Charlene," set down an armful of plates on the table where Angel sat across from Natalia.

"Thanks," he said. "Better bring us coffee too. Long night ahead."

"You got it." Charlene cracked her gum and walked away.

Natalia leaned forward in the red-plastic-upholstered booth and took in the pungent feast: barbequed pork ribs dripping with sauce; a mountain of coleslaw; deep-fried onion rings. She scooped a spoonful of coleslaw onto her plate.

Angel dug into the ribs. "Not as good as in Baja," he mumbled with his mouth full. "But here we got Wi-Fi." He checked his iPhone, which was recharging on a cord from a wall socket.

Natalia picked at the duct tape covering a rip in her seat. "I'm too nervous to eat."

"Leaves more for me." He hoisted a golden onion ring and admired it. "This thing's got more bling than your so-called LOVE bracelets." He could see that she wasn't listening. She bit her lip. "Chica, chill! Vaclav will call from Prague any minute. It's *que chido*, all cool!" He devoured the onion ring.

The waitress returned with two cups of coffee. "I don't feel sorry for her, do you?"

"Who?" said Angel.

Charlene plunked down the cups and nodded to the TV over the bar. The photo of the unsmiling First Lady with the Funck children at the Presidential Christmas-card shoot was on FOX News. Under it, a chyron read: *"Why did POTUS bow out?"* She cracked her gum. "I mean, she looks like she wants to blow her brains out. All that money, all them clothes, and she's got a fly up her ass? Lots of husbands are shits!" She walked off.

Natalia folded her hands on the table. "Angel, the truth. Was I crazy to leave Rex?"

"*Un poco,* a little," he teased. Seeing her eyes widen, he quickly added, "No, you did the right thing."

She nervously rubbed her thumbs together. "You're sure?"

To distract her, Angel nodded at the photo on the TV screen. "Check out Moon. She's crushing it!"

Natalia looked up at the photo on TV. "She looks depressed, like the waitress said."

"Moon is just being *you.*"

"Poor Moon."

"Yo, this has gotta be a real high for her to pull *you* off in front of those fucking Funck fuckers." He sipped his coffee, grimacing from the bitter taste. "Maybe it's better Rex didn't show up today. You'd think, like, a husband would know his wife from a fake."

"If he looked into her eyes, maybe," she said. "But Rex doesn't spend a lot of time looking into anyone's eyes but his own." FOX News cut away to commercial. "I hope Moon manages to escape tonight, so she won't have to risk meeting him tomorrow."

"She'll be outta there by, like, 2:00 a.m." He knocked on the Formica-topped table. "*Toco madera.*"

Natalia knocked on the table. "*Klopať na drevo.*"

Angel's iPhone shimmied on the table, playing *La Cucaracha.* She grabbed his hand. "*Ohmygod, ohmygod!*"

"You sound like you-know-who!" He scooped up his phone. "Hola!" He listened, then said, "She's right here." He held out the phone to her. "*Tu amor.*" As she cautiously took it, he started to slide out of the booth. "I'll give you privacy."

She wrenched him back down onto his seat. "Stay with me! Please!"

He shrugged his shoulders, then grabbed another barbequed

rib.

Natalia spoke softly in English. "Hello?" She listened, then launched into excited, loud Slovak. "Vaclav, Vaclav!" was all Angel understood. She wept with joy as the words tumbled out. He felt a rush of tenderness for her, like he did the day she cried on his shoulder when the *National Enquirer* ran a story about a Pilates teacher at the Puerto Rico Funck International Hotel who confessed she slept with Rex while Rex and Natalia were there on their honeymoon.

Ten minutes later, as he polished off his umpteenth onion ring, he heard smooching sounds and looked up. Natalia was kissing his cell phone, tears streaming down her face. "Vaclav, Vaclav, *L'úbim t'a! L'úbim t'a!*" She hung up, then buried her face in her hands.

"Yo, earth to Natalia?"

Natalia shook her head, as if forcing herself to return to reality. "I can't believe it. Vaclav still loves me! And I love him!"

"Beautiful!"

"He said he married a Slovak woman he thought looked like me, but he couldn't love her the way she needed. He got a divorce and moved to Prague. That's when he joined a band. He said if I could live my dream and become a model, he wanted to live his dream and play music."

"Que chido! You inspired him."

"Then he saw in the news I married Rex. It killed him." She fought back tears. "And then I became First Lady. He was sure I forgot about him."

"Yo, it's all good, chica!" He handed her a paper napkin. She dabbed at her eyes with it.

"Vaclav is flying to San Diego tomorrow. He's renting a car and driving across the border. He said he'll meet us at that hotel you told him about in Rosarito Beach."

"Hotel Paraiso. It means 'paradise.'"

Natalia blew her nose into the napkin and laughed. "He

wanted to Facetime with me, but I said no way." In the mirrored wall behind Angel, she glimpsed her pink-streaked black wig and drooping forehead. "If he saw me like this, he'd stay home!"

"No worries! Before you meet, I promise to turn you back into Natalia." He patted the red Gucci satchel on the seat beside him. "I got my bag of tricks." He pushed the plate of ribs toward her. "Eat."

She hungrily eyed the ribs and onion rings, then put her hands on her stomach and frowned. "I haven't worked out or taken a yoga class in two days. Angel, tell me the truth. Do I look fat?"

"Chica, you're outta the White House, outta the public eye. You don't have to look pinche perfect anymore!"

"I *DO* look fat!" She pressed her fingers into her stomach. "Hovno!"

"This is the real world! You gotta get over your food hang-up!"

"What food hang-up?"

"C'mon, Natalia. You feel, like, guilty about every scrap of food you pop in your mouth."

"For models, that's not a hang-up. That's reality!"

"Chica, today you had the *cajones* to walk out on a life where you gotta look like a supermodel for your husband, and for, like, millions of people who know you for *what* you are, not who you are."

"Who *am* I?"

"That's for you to find out. In your new life, you can look any way you want, be anything you want, and pinche eat anything you want!" He picked up the last onion ring and held it out to her.

She eyed it hungrily. "Will Vaclav still love me if I get fat?"

"He's loved you since you were fourteen."

"I was innocent when I was fourteen, plus I had a firm zadok."

"And I bet you ate, like, whatever you wanted, right?"

"My mother told me halushkies would make me fat, but I ate them anyway."

"What's *halushkies?*"

"Slovak potato dumplings. They come in this sauce made with fried cabbage, fried onions, and bacon. I pigged out on halushkies whenever I went to Babika's farm, just to spite Mamina."

"Did you get fat?"

"No."

"Was that when you were fucking Vaclav?"

"Every day, sometimes twice a day." Her eyes gleamed. "We met at secret places." She leaned closer to him. "Sometimes we did it in Babika's barn!"

"So eat whatever you want. In two days, you and Vaclav will be going at it like crazed Chihuahuas!"

A smile spread on her face, as if she were picturing the image. Angel pushed the plate of ribs closer to her. She dug in. "My babika made the best ribs," she said, her mouth full. "She cooked them for hours in a sauce with tons of paprika. Slovaks love paprika."

Angel felt that tenderness-for-Natalia twinge again. She was eating real food for a change. He decided to make small talk to keep her eating. "Wait 'til you taste the ribs in Baja. Best in the world."

She discarded a chewed-over bone, licked the sauce from her fingers, and started in on a meaty one. "You really think Vaclav and I will like living in Baja?"

"Money-back! It takes, like, a day to drive down the coast of Baja from TJ to Cabo. From there, you drive past where all the gringo tourists hang. There's this village that's half Mexican farmers and fishermen, half artsy ex-pats from all over. They grow their own food, grow their own weed, and chill. No one gives a shit who you are or where you came from."

She reached for an onion ring with her free hand. "I'll have goats," she said dreamily.

"Goats?"

"My babika had three little goats. In winter, when it was too cold outside, she let them spend the night in the farmhouse. They'd jump on my bed and sleep with me."

"You slept with *goats*?"

"It was cozy." Suddenly, her eyes widened. "I know what I can do in Baja!"

"What?"

"Start a goat-cheese business."

"Goat cheese?"

"Babika made goat cheese. She taught me how. Vaclav can surf and play in a band. I'll make goat cheese and have babies." She frowned. "Unless I'm too old, for babies, I mean."

"Yo, all those hormones that doctor shot you up with for Rex's baby… There oughta be enough left over to kickstart you and Vaclav."

She crossed herself with the onion ring, murmured a prayer, and ate it.

Angel held up the last juicy rib. Her eyes sparkling with hope, she tossed down the rib she had finished and snatched it. "Thank you, my angel!"

Chapter 22

Washington, D.C.

December 17, 11:00 p.m.

Phil winced from a sharp prick on his right thigh. He glanced down at Oscar. The tabby cat was curled up on his lap, sound asleep, its claws—which he never bothered to trim—flexing in and out. He wondered if Oscar was dreaming about catching a rat. For the past six hours, he had felt as if he were on the trail of a rat himself.

He had read and reread the online *People* article, *FLOTUS Is Besties with Her Barber*. The story told how Natalia discovered Angel Garcia, an illegal Mexican immigrant, when he was a humble hair-washer at Funck's Beau Rivage Resort in Miami. "Thanks to the encouragement of Natalia Funck, Angel quickly became their top hairdresser," the article said. The "happy ending" was Angel becoming the official FLOTUS hairdresser, with a lucrative side hustle as a stylist at Washington's Funck International Hotel. "Angel is more than my hair stylist," Natalia was quoted as saying. "He's my dear, dear friend." Phil wondered if Natalia had persuaded her friend to do something unthinkable, or if it had been Angel's idea. He was determined to find out, even if it took all night.

Phil nudged the cat off of his lap. He stretched his legs, which were propped up on the discarded Amazon cartons that passed as a coffee table, and turned back to the laptop balanced on his knees. He clicked on the photo gallery with the *People* story. One picture showed Angel styling Natalia's hair in her private salon at the White House. The next was of Angel blow-drying her hair aboard Air Force One. He clicked on another photo: Angel walking across the White House lawn with Natalia to the Marine One helicopter. The photo was so full of energy and emotion—

you could see they adored each other—that Phil wished he'd taken it.

An hour earlier, while studying these photos, he had focused on the fact that they made an odd couple: the tall, elegant First Lady towering over the flamboyantly dressed young Mexican. It had struck him that the difference in their heights was about the same as between Angel and the trans woman in the photo he took this morning. Was it possible that the trans woman was Natalia in disguise? To check out his hunch, he had pulled up that photo and compared it to the one on People.com. Unfortunately, he'd discovered that the trans woman was taller than Angel in the photo he took, but in the *People* photo, Natalia had an additional three inches on Angel.

Though discouraged, Phil decided to study both photos again. Looking more closely this time, he noticed that in the photo on the White House lawn, Natalia was wearing five-inch stiletto heels, while in the photo he took this morning, the trans woman was wearing motorcycle boots with what looked like two-inch heels. That could explain the extra three inches, he thought. If so, the trans woman could be Natalia in disguise.

A rush of excitement motivated his next thought: If the trans woman was Natalia in disguise, then perhaps Angel entered the White House earlier with a *real* trans woman whom Natalia was now impersonating, and that trans woman was now impersonating Natalia. If that was so, the "Natalia" in the Christmas card photo taken at the White House this morning could be the trans woman in drag.

Phil hastily googled "Drag-queen clubs Washington, D.C." He discovered half a dozen clubs that featured impersonators of celebrities like Cher, Bette Midler, and Barbra Streisand. They looked somewhat like the women they were imitating, but in a garish, over-the-top way. Not one could be mistaken as the real celebrity. He supposed that the exaggeration, the theatricality, was what audiences paid for.

Phil next typed in "First Lady female impersonator" and came up with a handful. Several were featured in YouTube videos, one with a not-very-convincing "Natalia" performance against a shaky Oval Office backdrop. But none of them looked like the real FLOTUS. He clicked on more First Lady female impersonators, determined to do his due diligence.

An hour later, Phil was still at it. He reached into his camera bag and rummaged around until his fingers seized on a plastic baggie. It held half a ragged joint that he'd been saving for a long paparazzi stakeout. A couple of puffs always zoned him out enough to hang in a little while longer. He needed it now.

Phil slid his laptop onto the sofa, next to the cat, and walked over to the gas stove. He knew it was dangerous, that he could set his hair on fire, but he clicked on the front burner, stuck the joint tip in the flame and sucked. What he called "happy fog" was creeping over his brain by the time he sat back down on the sofa and repositioned the laptop on his knees.

He took another toke and pulled up more images of First Lady female impersonators. Maybe it was the weed, but soon Phil discovered what he had hoped for: a Natalia impersonator in South Beach who looked so much like the *real* Natalia, that maybe the public, but not he, could be fooled.

Chapter 23

The White House

December 18, 1:30 a.m.

Moon hugged Natalia's long Frette terrycloth bathrobe close to her body. As she walked through the halls of the White House, she noticed that the guards on night duty averted their eyes respectfully as she passed. Underneath the bathrobe she wore a pair of Natalia's $10,000 black Escada jeans, rolled up, and Natalia's' $2,000 black Bottega Veneta cashmere sweater, its long sleeves rolled up too. Natalia had said that she could keep them. "A White House souvenir," she had joked.

Moon felt in the bathrobe pocket for Natalia's $1,700 black Moncler puffer coat, another White House souvenir. Before she and Angel left this morning, Natalia had stuffed it into its tiny nylon pouch, a feat Moon found magical. Natalia had assured her that once she escaped the White House hidden in the laundry truck and climbed out, all she had to do was pull the material out of its pocket and it would puff up into a warm coat. Moon glanced down at her feet. Too bad Natalia's Frette terrycloth slippers wouldn't puff up into Ugg sheepskin boots. Through the White House windows, she saw that snow was falling.

Following the map that Natalia had forced her to memorize, Moon ducked into the Vermeil Room. The guards knew that on her way down to the kitchen for a midnight snack, the First Lady always took a quick detour through here. Moon wondered if they ever peeked when Natalia prayed to the Jackie Kennedy portrait. She spotted it on the far wall, between a pair of primly draped arched windows. Just in case, she walked over to it, kneeled down, and clasped her hands together the way she'd seen Ingrid Bergman do it in the old black-and-white movie *Joan of Arc* on TCM.

She looked up at the portrait. Natalia was right: Jackie looked serene, wistful, almost holy. She knew, of course, that Jewish people don't pray to saints. They don't have saints, like Catholics do. But since she was on her knees anyway, to satisfy any prying eyes, Moon figured that she would give it try.

"Dear Jackie, even though I'm Jewish and a trans," she murmured, "I hope you'll find it in your heart to help me get out of here tonight in one piece." She was about to stand up, but stopped herself. "P.S., I think you are *the* most beautiful First Lady in all of American history. Until Natalia, that is." Feeling a flutter of guilt and fear of jinxing it, she quickly added, "It's actually pretty much a tie between you and Natalia, plus my mother, olav ha sholom, worshiped you, so I really hope you'll help me."

She slipped out of the Vermeil Room and followed her memorized map to a back staircase, which took her down to the White House basement. The guard near the swinging doors to the staff kitchen opened them, as if he'd been expecting her.

Inside, a lanky young African-American woman was busy mixing dough in a huge bowl. This must be Stella, thought Moon. Beside her was the U.D. officer that she figured was Tallisha. At first, she thought that Tallisha was reading Stella a recipe from a cookbook. But as she stepped closer, she saw that the book Tallisha held was *Becoming*, Michelle Obama's memoir.

Stella broke into a smile when she noticed Moon. "Madame First Lady!" She beckoned her over. "I got a batch of biscuits piping hot from the oven!"

"Sounds yummy," she said in her Natalia voice in case anyone else was listening. One whiff of the fresh-baked biscuits and she realized that she was starving. The dinner that had been sent up to Natalia's bedroom earlier had seemed like starvation rations: a paper-thin filet of broiled salmon; three meager sprigs of raw broccoli; and six, count 'em, six, fresh strawberries. Plus a sewage-brown smoothie of dozens of fruits and vegetables that managed to taste like none of them.

"Here ya go!" Stella slid a basket filled with plump, flaky biscuits onto a counter. Their golden crusts glistened with melted butter. Moon reached for one and raised it to her mouth.

"Madame Funck!" said a man's voice behind her.

Moon turned around, the biscuit poised midair. A brawny Secret Service agent approached, the kitchen doors swinging behind him. "The President wants you." She read his nametag: "Pricker." This must be the man Natalia described as Rex's favorite bodyguard with an obscene-sounding name, she thought. He adjusted the coiled plastic wire on his radio earpiece. "I got Trophy," he said into it. She guessed that "Trophy" must be the Secret Service code name for FLOTUS. With a sigh of defeat, she put the biscuit back into the basket. So much for praying to Saint Jackie, she thought.

Chapter 24

Between Nashville and Jackson, TN

December 18, 2:00 a.m.

Angel checked the speedometer: The Mustang was pushing 80. He eased off the pedal. He knew the highway patrol in the South would not take kindly to a gay Mexican and a tattooed trans woman trashing the speed limit. He had been driving for more than six hours and found himself starting to drift off, but they were six hours behind schedule. No time to stop at a motel for the night if they were going to make it to TJ and meet Vaclav in two-and-a-half days.

Natalia was slumped against the window, fast asleep. Even with her caveman forehead, wig, and faux ear and nose studs, she looked beautiful. More than that, she is a *mujer valiente*, a brave woman, thought Angel. How many women could walk away from everything the way she did, to follow her heart?

Natalia stirred in her sleep.

"Chica?"

Her eyes fluttered open. For an instant, she looked at him as if she didn't know who he was, or where they were. Then he saw the realization kick in. She eyed the dashboard clock. "Moon better be hidden under a pile of dirty kitchen towels by now."

"She'll be fine. Yo, it's me I'm worried about. If I don't, like, *hecharme un sueño*, take a nap, we're gonna end up in a ditch."

Natalia turned on the radio. Garth Brooks was singing, "*I got tears in my ears from cryin' in my bed —* "

"Does this help?"

"Country and western's for Funck-loving gringos."

"How about this?" She sang a lovely, slow song in Slovak.

"Sweet, but you're, like, putting me to sleep."

"All I know is lullabies my babika sang to me." She thought

for a moment. "I know. Talk to me. That will keep you awake. Tell me what happens after we get to Tijuana and I leave with Vaclav. Are you going back to D.C. to work at the Funck Hotel salon? Style the hair of the woman Rex finds to replace me?"

"Gretchen?"

"Right! Of course! The First Daughter will become FLOTUS. They'll make the perfect First Couple." She laughed. "Seriously, what are you going to do?"

"That's what I wanted to ask you."

"Ask me?"

"Y'know that, like, village in Baja near Cabo, where you and Vaclav are gonna live? It's called Todos Santos, by the way."

"Todos Santos? I love the name! What does it mean?"

"All Saints."

"Perfect. I'll go to church every Sunday!"

"What if I lived in Todos Santos too?"

"Seriously?"

"Except for the go-to-church-on-Sunday part."

"I'd love it, but I don't get it!

"Long story, but this dude, Raphael, he was, like, my first love. Kinda like you and Vaclav, only we were maricóns and one of us didn't get *embarazada*."

"Embarrassed?"

"In Spanish, *embarazada* means 'pregnant.'"

"You're making fun of me?"

"Sorry! Anyway, Raphael's father was, like, el *Jefe Segundo*, deputy mayor, in TJ. Super macho. Super *pendejo*, an asshole. When he discovered Raphael's a maricón, he kicked him out of the house."

"No!"

"Raphael disappeared. Poof! No more Raphael! I tried to find him, but it's, like, he didn't want me to. A couple of years later, I got the hell out of Mexico, went to Miami, blah, blah, blah. Then, when I found Vaclav for you on Google the other day, I figured, why not see if I can track down Raphael too?"

"Did you?"

Angel nodded. "He's head chef at the Four Seasons Hotel in Cabo. Worked his way up from pinche dishwasher."

"Wow! He must be an amazing cook."

"When he was a kid, he'd hang out with my mom when she was making tacos. He was really into it. Food was always Raphael's thing, like mine's hair. Anyway, a couple of days ago we Facetimed. Raphael looks like he always looked. *Guapo*, handsome dude. He said I looked pretty good too."

"You are muy guapo!"

"Yo, I've had lots of, like, boyfriends since Raphael, but he was always in my heart."

"Like with me and Vaclav."

"Right. So, Raphael has this little beach house in Todos Santos. He commutes about an hour to work at the Four Seasons Hotel in Cabo. He asked me to come down and stay with him for a while. We'll see how it goes. If it works out for us, he's gonna get me a job doing hair at the hotel."

"I'm happy for you," she said. "And for me." Tears filled her eyes. "Vaclav and I won't be all alone in Baja. You and Raphael will be our family."

"Que chido! So since we're family, how about you help me out right now."

"What?"

"Take a turn at the wheel?"

"You mean, drive?"

"Please? I'm a *camarón*, a shrimp," said Angel. "I can, like, curl up on the back seat and take a *siesta*."

"I don't drive."

"*What?*"

"I've never driven a car."

"Dude, how's that possible? What forty-eight-year-old woman can't drive, except in pinche Saudi Arabia?"

"It's not my fault! In Slovakia you have to be seventeen to drive. I was fifteen when I got—" She stopped herself. "I wasn't old enough to drive when my parents sent me to Bratislava. Then I moved to Paris, where you take the Metro—"

"And then you moved to the U.S., where Rex Funck is driven around in a pinche limo! Hey, does Rex even *know* how to drive?"

She thought for a moment. "I've seen him drive a golf cart."

He pulled over to the side of the highway. Leaving the motor running, he climbed out of the car. Natalia climbed out on her side. "What are we doing?"

In the distance, a coyote howled. "I love that sound," he said.

"What is it?"

"A coyote. The slums in TJ had lots of coyotes. They competed with the people for the garbage."

"What are we doing in the middle of nowhere, listening to coyotes?"

He walked around to Natalia's side of the car, grabbed her hand, and led her to the driver's seat. "Get in."

"What?"

"Chica, you're about to change your life. This is a perfect time to learn something new." He nudged her. Natalia guardedly slid behind the wheel. She was so much taller than Angel, that her knees were crammed up against the steering wheel.

"There's a bar thing beneath the seat." He pointed down. "Give it a yank and push yourself back."

She adjusted the seat and put her hands on the steering wheel. By the time Angel sat down in the passenger seat and closed the door, her face had spread into a smile. "I'm ready! Yo, dude, I'm pinche ready!"

"Okay, so first thing you gotta know about driving in Mexico: You drive with your *cojones*, your balls!"

She grabbed her washcloth-bulged crotch and laughed. "I can do that!"

Chapter 25

The White House

December 18, 2:15 a.m.

Moon picked up Natalia's 15-karat diamond engagement ring and slipped it on her finger, then the matching diamond wedding band. She had been scrupulous about leaving them in plain sight here on the counter in the First Lady's bathroom before sneaking down to the staff-cafeteria kitchen, so that she wouldn't be accused of stealing them after she fled tonight. She had never expected to see them again. Now it felt like the diamond rings were burning a hole in her finger.

Ten minutes earlier, on their way upstairs, Pricker had handed her his cell phone. President Funck was on the line. "Where the fuck are you?" He shouted so loudly that Pricker flinched. Before she could answer, he barked, "The Jew doctor says your 'ripe' period could still be a go tonight. We've got to fuck again! He stabbed my butt with a mega-dose of testosterone to get my sperm off their asses. So get yours up here!"

Moon had needed to buy some time. "I've been down in the kitchen," she said in her Natalia voice. "*The staff-cafeteria* kitchen." Natalia had mentioned that the President never went to the staff cafeteria or the staff-cafeteria kitchen because the staff was mostly African-American. "You know I hate that. Makes you smell like fucking Africa!" Rex shouted over the phone. "Take a shower. You've got twenty fucking minutes!"

Moon's life flashed before her eyes as she stepped into Natalia's closet. She unrolled the cuffs on the First Lady's $10,000 black Escada jeans, peeled them off, and carried them over to the motorized garment rack. On the rack's control pad, she punched in the number she located on an inside-back label of the jeans: "402." The motor hummed as the rack started to move, the hundreds of plastic-and-tissue-wrapped designer clothes gliding by. It stopped at position "402." "Goodbye beautiful, precious, ridiculously overpriced jeans that could have been mine," she said, and hung the jeans on the waiting hanger.

Next, she took off Natalia's $2,000 black Bottega Veneta cashmere sweater. She stroked it, as if it were a Persian cat. "Thank you for being the softest sweater I've ever worn in my entire life." She carried it into a mahogany-lined closet-within-a-closet; it smelled like Chanel Number 5, not mothballs. She neatly folded it and added it to a pile of cashmere sweaters on one of a dozen shelves.

Finally, Moon stepped over to a corner of the closet that Natalia called the "lingerie alcove." Here, flanking a three-way, full-length mirror were row after row of drawers. She opened one at a time, trying not to gasp at the multitude of exquisite silk and satin designer underwear, brassieres, and nightgowns they held. Her hands trembling, she carefully sorted through a selection of neatly folded nighties. They came in only three colors: white, peach, and black. Too bad Natalia doesn't have a red nightgown I can wear when I climb into the President's bed tonight, she thought. It will hide the blood when he shoots me.

As she removed Natalia's bra and tucked it into its proper drawer, she felt the tingle of her nipples hardening. Not from the cold—it was a good 72 degrees in here—but from fear. She wondered if Joan of Arc's tits hardened like this when she felt the heat of the flames around her stake.

She pulled a gossamer peach Prada nightgown over her head, careful not to muss her Natalia wig, then reached down to remove her tucking-gaff "thong from hell." She touched the smooth elasticized fabric and glanced at her image in the three-way mirror. It never ceased to amaze her that when she was wearing this "magic" garment, the bulge at her crotch was no more obvious than a woman's pubic bone. Maybe it was perverse, but at that moment she made a decision: She would not remove the tucking-gaff. She would leave it on for a reason that also might be perverse: to reserve a huge surprise for the President until the very last moment tonight.

She removed her hand from her crotch. Then, as if for old time's sake, she posed seductively, evocatively narrowing her eyes, forcing a fish-gape smile, and gracefully brushing her hair from her face, 100 percent Natalia. At her Cross Queen show in South Beach, the pose sent the audience onto their feet every time.

The Cross Queen show image in her mind stimulated an idea. It was an idea that was so off-the-wall, brazen, and shameless, she pictured the Cross Queen audience not just applauding her, but going ape-shit bonkers, whooping and cheering like never before. She vowed to clutch that image during her last moments in the President's bedroom tonight. When Rex Funck realized that the person in his bed was not his wife, but a trans woman, would he shoot her, strangle her, or have her dragged off to prison? Whatever he did, she knew she wouldn't find it amusing. *Unless...*

Suddenly, Moon's fear dissipated; she didn't give a shit about what the Funck fucker would do to her. She focused on what she would do to *him* first. *Shock?* Check. *Humiliation?* Check. Maybe she would even give the bastard a well-deserved stroke, or, more painful, a heart attack. Emboldened, she expanded the image beyond the Cross Queen audience. Tonight, Moon thought, I'm going to picture the whole world watching me when I go out in a blaze of Funck-fucking glory.

Chapter 26

Between Jackson and Memphis, TN

December 18, 3:30 a.m.

Natalia's face glowed with joy in the dim light from the Mustang dashboard, like a kid playing with a Christmas gift, thought Angel. She put the pedal to the metal and the car varoomed ahead. "Chica, you're crushing it," he said.

"No big deal!" Natalia glanced over at him and turned her hands on the steering wheel at the same time. The Mustang veered right and screeched onto the gravel shoulder. He reached out and twisted the wheel back to the left, just in time. "Sorry about that!" she said.

"*Ojos en el camino!*"

"Eyes on the road! Got it!" She chuckled. "I think this whole driving lesson thing is an excuse to teach me Spanish."

"You're gonna live in Baja, you gotta learn Spanish."

"Hey, I learned French in Paris." She turned to him again, realized she was turning the wheel too, and quickly corrected herself.

"Chica, before I sign off and catch some zzzs, there's one thing I gotta make sure you can do."

"Name it?"

"See that tanker?" He pointed to a truck up ahead, its shiny metal tailgate reflecting the Mustang's headlights.

"I see it."

"There might be a time, like when I'm asleep, that the highway narrows to only one lane each way."

"So?"

"If this was any other night, I'd say stay behind the slow-ass truck, don't risk trying to pass, but—"

"This isn't any other night," she said, as if reading his mind.

"We've got to kick butt to make it to Tijuana before—"

"The shit hits the White House fan."

"Right."

"So I need you to show me you can pass a truck like that pinche monster ahead of us even if there's only two lanes." He pointed to a yellow road sign that indicated the road was narrowing. "Like what's about to happen right pinche now."

"I can do that." Natalia hunched closer to the wheel and pressed the pedal until the Mustang crept up close behind the tanker. She steered the car to the left, pulled slightly into the oncoming lane and flicked on her brights. No sign of oncoming headlights. "Now?"

Angel nodded. "Now!"

Natalia twisted the wheel until their car was in the center of the oncoming lane, then floored it. The Mustang lurched forward, the speedometer shooting from 60 to 70, then 80. They pulled up next to the tanker, the Mustang's red reflection like a garish smear of lipstick on its shiny metal side.

"What do they carry in tankers?" she asked, her eyes on the road.

"Sometimes *leche,* milk, but mostly..." He shut up when he spotted the headlights of an oncoming truck. It was moving fast. There wasn't a lot of time left for Natalia to finish passing before it would be on top of them.

She strangled the wheel, pressing harder on the pedal. *"Hovvvvvvno!"*

The Mustang hurtled out in front of the tanker, then swerved to the right, safely in front of the tanker and back into their own lane. Seconds afterward, the truck roared past. A flurry of white feathers plastered their windshield, then blew away, like snowflakes.

"Pinche chickens!" said Angel.

Natalia focused on her breathing, slowing it down as she had learned in yoga. "So what was the 'mostly'?"

"What 'mostly'?"

She nodded toward the receding image of the tanker in the rear-view mirror. "What do tanker trucks carry most of time, instead of leche?"

"*Gasolina.*"

"Gasoline. I knew that." She eased up on the pedal. She turned to Angel with a big grin, this time without turning the wheel at the same time. "I sure hope Moon is having as much fun right now as we are."

Chapter 27

The White House

December 18, 3:00 a.m.

Moon eyed the box of latex gloves on the side table outside the President's bedroom. So *this* is what Natalia meant about her acrylic nails breaking when she had sex with him, she thought. The germophobic ghoul makes her wear latex gloves. Moon was more than willing to sacrifice her own acrylics for her grand-finale performance tonight. She slipped her left hand into a glove. The 15-karat diamond on Natalia's engagement ring punched a hole in the latex. She peeled off the glove, trashed it, and tried again, this time more delicately. All good.

She nodded to Agent Pricker that she was ready to enter Rex's bedroom. He shook his head and nodded toward another box on the table by the door. It held a stack of sanitary face masks. Moon was surprised that Natalia hadn't mentioned them. She felt a twinge of disappointment as she put one on. The mask would keep her cooties off the President, but it would hide part of her *unable-to-tell-its-not-really-Natalia* face from him.

Pricker touched the coiled-plastic tubing on his radio earpiece: "Trophy is ready, sir." He took a seat outside the President's bedroom door. She supposed that it was a signal she could knock. She slipped her fingers under her black-satin robe and adjusted the straps of her black-silk negligée underneath. She was glad that she had ditched peach for black.

Taking a deep breath to fortify herself, Moon yanked open the bedroom door and walked inside. Blinking in the bright light from the crystal chandeliers, she lowered the dimmer switch on the wall until they glowed softly. She saw that Funck was wearing a terrycloth bathrobe and sitting in the red-velvet "throne" that Natalia had mentioned. He was sipping Diet Coke and watching FOX News, just as she had said. Moon slammed the door behind her. Funck didn't flinch.

"Rex, darling, first I'm going to suck you," she said in her softest, sexiest Natalia voice. "And then you're going to fuck me once to make a baby, and once, just for fun, in the ass."

That did it. The President turned around and gaped at her. *"Huh?"*

She untied her robe and let it fall to the white carpet. In her black-silk negligée, she struck her best sexy Natalia pose, complete with fish-gape smile. "You heard me. Now turn off fucking FOX News! I can't wait to put my lips around your stiff, swollen dick!"

He stood up and stared at her, his mouth hanging open. She wondered if he had ever been speechless like this before.

"Take off your fucking bathrobe!" she commanded.

He fumbled with the belt, finally untied it, and pulled off the bathrobe.

Seeing the President naked, Moon forced herself to keep a straight face. His man-breasts sagged like an old woman's. Folds of fat padded his waist and hips, like skinfolds on a rhino, and drooped over his crotch. His pecker looked like a thumbs-up poking up from a sparse tangle of dyed-orange pubic hair.

"Natalia, baby, is this really *you*?" For a moment she feared that he had seen through her ruse. Until a lascivious smirk erupted on his face. "You never talk dirty to me like that." He reached for her. "Tell me more!"

She shoved his hand aside—the President's fingers really *do* look like pencil stubs, she thought—and leaned into him. She sucked his flaccid turkey neck and gave it a few quick love bites. It tasted foul, like a combination of man sweat, rancid cologne, and hamburger grease.

Funck reached inside her nightie, grabbed her left breast, and squeezed. She held her breath, hoping her "Natalia breast" would stand the test. He made a sound that was half squeal, half snort, like a horny bulldog.

She pushed him back down into his chair. In a sitting position, his dork disappeared under his belly flesh, like a snail hiding in its shell. He reached down and fumbled around for it. Moon realized that this could go on for hours. She wasn't sure how long she could continue without laughing. She reached under her nightie, pulled off her "thong from hell," and kicked it aside. She checked that the tape was still in place, securing her "Mr. Happy" to her ass crack.

Hips swaying invitingly, she sashayed over to his bed. It was twice the size of a king-sized bed, its carved Baroque black-and-gold wooden headboard even tackier than Natalia had described. "Rex thinks he's the Sun King of France reincarnated," she had explained.

Moon climbed onto the bed, the satin bedspread slippery beneath her knees. She scanned the nightstand, located the red button that Natalia had mentioned, and pushed it. With a hum, the headboard sank below the bed, revealing a massive gold-tinted wall mirror. She positioned herself on her knees, her hands pressed against the mirror.

"Fuck me in the ass," she called over her shoulder.

"What about making a baby?"

"Later! Fuck me in the ass right fucking now!"

In the mirror, Moon could see Funck's face reddening, perspiration beading his forehead. He bent over with a groan and rummaged in a box under his chair. He picked out a small flesh-colored device and lowered it towards his private parts. It took Moon a moment, but she recognized it from a display she had seen at her favorite erotic-toy boutique in South Beach: a penis sheath. He awkwardly attempted to squeeze his flaccid, miniscule member into it. *Whoa,* she thought. *It's like trying to force toothpaste back into a tube.*

When the deed was finally accomplished, he walked over and climbed slowly onto the bed. He winced and rubbed his left knee. *Arthritis?* Moon thought she could hear his bones creak as he took up position behind her. He forced her head to the left so that he could see his own reflection in the giant mirror. Grabbing one of her breasts with his left hand and pulling up her black nightie with his right, he leaned closer to the mirror and peered dreamily into the reflection of his own watery blue eyes.

Moon felt a tickle at the moment when his penis sleeve came into contact with her taped-down "Mr. Happy," which was blocking the entrance to her only bodily orifice in that location. Rex grunted, attempting penetration. No go.

A rush that was part excitement, part fear, gripped Moon as she followed Funck's next move in the mirror: He grudgingly took his eyes off of his own reflection and glanced down at her ass, to help improve his aim. His eyes widened in horror.

"What the fuck?"

Moon had once used a mirror to see the image that she knew the President of the United States was gaping at right now: With her member taped to her butt-crack, it had reminded her of a hot dog nestled in a bun. She stifled a giggle, wishing that her Cross Queen fans were actually watching the horror and humiliation on Rex Funck's face right now, as they were in her imagination.

"What the shitass, motherfucking hell?"

Enraged, Funck backed away from her. He lurched off the bed...

Lost his balance...

Toppled...

Bashing his head on the sharp gilt-edged corner of the antique nightstand as he plunged to the floor.

Blood gushed from under his comb-over, like lava from a mini-volcano, onto the white carpet.

Moon scrambled off the bed. *"Ohmygod, ohmygod!"*

Rex struggled to his knees. "You *motherfucking...!*" Spotting the blood on the rug, he touched his head. When he saw that his fingers were wet with blood, his anger switched to panic and he collapsed on the floor. "Fuck me! I'm dying!"

Moon suddenly morphed into Registered Nurse mode. She knelt beside him. "You're going to be okay, Mr. President!" She grabbed a pillow from the bed and yanked off the pillowcase.

Funck wiped blood from his eyes. "Who the fuck *are* you?"

She hastily ripped the pillowcase into strips. "Stay calm, sir!" She wadded them up and pressed them against his head wound.

He shoved her away. "Don't fucking touch me!" He reached up and fumbled to open the nightstand drawer. With shaky fingers he groped inside and pulled out a .45 Magnum. "I'm gonna fucking kill you!"

Moon raised her hands. "Don't shoot! I'm an RN!"

"I'm gonna fucking blow you away!" Funck aimed the gun at her with one wobbly hand, wiped the blood streaming down his head into his eyes with the other.

Terrified, she scrambled backward on her knees across the carpet, away from him. "Sir, please! I need to apply pressure to that wound!"

Suddenly, a muscular forearm yanked Moon's neck back and a meaty hand shoved her head forward. "Got her!" She couldn't turn to look, but she knew it was Secret Service Agent Pricker.

"You're hurting me!"

"Good!" He tightened his chokehold on her.

Wild-eyed, Funck lay back on the rug, dropped his gun, and picked up the bloody wad of torn pillowcase. "Get my fucking doctor!" He pressed the wad to his wound, then removed it and checked again. It was soaked with more blood. "Fuck!"

"Sir, you must apply pressure!" called Moon.

"Fuck you!"

Pricker shoved Moon down onto the rug. Her wig slid off, taking her sanitary face mask along with it onto the floor. "Don't fucking move, pervert!" He pressed his gun against her shaved head, planted his boot on her back, and spoke into his radio walkie-talkie: "The King's down! Code red!"

"*King.*" So that's the Secret-Service code name for the President, she thought.

Woozy, Funck pressed the blood-soaked strips of cloth to his scalp wound and unsteadily climbed onto his bed. He propped a pillow under his head. "No ambulance!" he yelled at Pricker. "No fucking sirens!"

With the cold metal of the gun against her scalp, Moon glanced at Funck's bloated naked body sprawled on the bed, blood staining his pillow. It occurred to her that maybe he really was the reincarnation of Louis XIV, France's powerful, greedy Sun King. She had once read that Louis XIV died an agonizing death when he was seventy-seven. Funck was seventy-four. I hope he won't hang around for another three years, she thought, but that his death will be just as agonizing.

Chapter 28

The White House

December 18, 3:15 a.m.

"Get this son-of-a-bitch off of me!" Funck squirmed on his bed as Moon sat beside him pressing a sterile gauze pad to his head wound. "I want my doctor!"

"You made your doctor Secretary of Labor, Daddy," said Gretchen, walking over.

"I *did*?"

"Or maybe it was Secretary of Defense."

"Fuck!" He waved Moon away, but she wouldn't budge from the bed.

"We have to make sure the bleeding's completely stopped before I stitch you up, sir," she said softly.

"You're not touching me!"

"Daddy, please," said Gretchen. "This...*person*...is a registered nurse. He...*she* does stitches all the time."

"I don't give a shit! He's a freak!"

"Daddy, I don't know how many times I need to repeat—"

"What?"

"The only people who can know about what happened here tonight are the people in this room. That means me, this...*nurse*, and your bulldog." She glanced at Pricker, who was sitting on a sofa, hunched over his laptop.

Moon tuned out the argument between the President and his daughter. She was relieved that his head wound had stopped gushing blood before Gretchen arrived, five minutes after Pricker summoned her on his walkie-talkie. In the case of an emergency that involved the President's sex life, she had learned from eavesdropping, Gretchen was the first call. Funck feared leaks to the press even more than he feared germs. He didn't trust the Secret Service, the Attorney General, or the CIA. He trusted the FBI least of all. The only person he trusted, beside himself, was his favorite child.

The first thing Gretchen had done when she arrived in what she moaned looked like a combat zone was to turn to Moon and say: "I don't give a rat's ass right now who you are or what you are, or where the hell the real FLOTUS is. But swear on your mother's life you are a Registered Nurse."

"My mother's dead, olav ha sholom, but I swear on her grave," Moon said.

"And that you can stitch up Daddy's wound without assassinating him!"

Moon had sworn on her mother's grave that she could do that too. Given the circumstances, she wasn't about to admit that though she was an RN, her specialty was hospice care. She was skilled at dispensing morphine, whispering tender words of encouragement, and holding the frail hands of people who were dying of cancer or old age. She couldn't exactly tell Gretchen, "I'm the best hospice nurse in Miami, even though all my patients end up dead." The truth was this: The last time Moon had sutured a wound was when she was in nursing school.

The second thing Gretchen had done after she entered the bedroom, once she realized that her father was not going to croak, was to motion for Pricker to tighten his chokehold on Moon. Moon had claimed it was unnecessary, but he would not relax his hairy forearm pressing against her neck. "Go ahead, strangle me," she gasped. "I'm proud to admit the First Lady escaped by impersonating me and that her hairdresser and best friend, Angel Garcia, helped her."

Angel and Natalia had told Moon to say that if she were found out. She was relieved that they hadn't told her where they were headed. She happily swore to Gretchen on her mother's grave that she didn't know their destination. She didn't mention that Natalia had mistakenly said the name, "Vaclav," before they left, and that Angel had told Moon to forget she ever heard it. She wished she had forgotten it. She didn't know who Vaclav was, but she vowed that she would never reveal his name, even under pain of death.

Moon then had helped Gretchen dress Funck in a clean bathrobe and position him on the bed with his head raised on a fresh pillow. Gretchen had eyed her black-satin nightie and yelled, "That's obscene! Put something on over that! And put your fucking wig back on!" Moon had donned her wig and selected one of the dozen men's terrycloth bathrobes she found hanging on the mirrored walls in Funck's cavernous bathroom. His shower had mirrored walls too, she noticed, with windshield wipers to keep them clear during a shower and double the number of showerheads as in the First Lady's bathroom. She bet the President watched himself in the mirror when he beat off, or humped his mistresses, in the shower.

"Let's get this show on the road," said Gretchen.

"Yes, ma'am." Moon stood up from the bed and handed the gauze pad to her. "Keep this on the wound, but lightly. Don't press too hard."

"Don't tell me what to do," Gretchen grumbled.

Moon walked over to the first-aid kit on the coffee table. Pricker had rushed it into the bedroom from the first-aid station down the hall. She reached out to open it but realized that she was still wearing the latex gloves with which she'd started this evening's "adventure." They were speckled with Funck's dried blood. She walked toward the bedroom door, past where Pricker was sitting on a sofa. On Gretchen's orders, he was googling Angel Garcia and looking for a clue about where Angel took Natalia.

When the Secret Service agent saw Moon with her hand on the bedroom door, he pulled his gun. "Forgetabout it!"

She shrugged her shoulders and held up her blood-spattered latex gloves. Pricker grudgingly walked over to the bedroom door, opened it a crack, and peered out. Seeing the hall was empty, he grabbed the box of latex gloves from the side table, handed it to her, and closed the door.

"Thank you." She peeled off her soiled gloves and dumped them into a garbage can.

Moon cleaned her hands with the Purell hand sanitizer on the coffee table, one of many bottles of it in the room, then shoved her left hand into a new sanitary glove. Natalia's 15-karat diamond snagged on the latex. For an instant, the glimmer on the mega-diamond, a reflection from the chandelier, looked to her like a smile. The diamond ring is laughing at me, she thought.

Moon put her finger into her mouth and sucked hard on the rings, saliva oozing onto her lips. She walked over to the bed, where Funck and Gretchen were talking quietly. "You better take these," she mumbled.

Gretchen noticed that she had something in her mouth and was sucking on her finger. "What the fuck are you doing?"

Moon spat the rings into her hand.

Gretchen gagged. *"Eeeewww!"*

Funck stared at the rings, which glistened with Moon's spittle. "You stole Natalia's rings!"

"She gave them to me." Moon pulled a handful of tissues from a Kleenex box on the nightstand and nestled the rings in them. "And now I'm giving them to you." She reached out to hand him the package.

Gretchen intercepted and stowed it in the pocket of her sporty black-leather jacket. "Stitch up Daddy's head so he can get some sleep and you can go to hell!"

"Yes, ma'am." Moon walked back to the coffee table. Donning fresh latex gloves, she put on a face mask and unwrapped the sterilized items in the first-aid kit. One by one, she laid them out on the sterile tray that Pricker also had fetched from the first-aid station: first, the suture pad, then suture needles, nylon monofilament sutures, two scalpels, a mayo suture holder/

driver and forceps/pickups and scissors, plus a dozen packages of hydrogen-peroxide-soaked cloths. She had only a vague memory of what to do with each. Too bad I can't watch a how-to-suture You Tube video, she thought. She noticed a plastic-wrapped sterilized syringe and a bottle of Lidocaine. Y'know what's really too bad? she added to herself. That I can't skip the painkiller before sewing him up.

"I got the security-area video footage," Pricker called to Gretchen and Funck. "It shows FLOTUS's hairdresser leaving the White House with this trans woman in a pink-streaked black wig. Like, dude, it's unbelievable! You'd never guess the trans was FLOTUS."

"That's not the point!" Gretchen said. "Save the video footage on your laptop but delete it from the security monitors. No one else can see it!"

"Yes, ma'am."

"Sew him up, whatever your name is!" Gretchen got up from the bed and walked over to a desk.

"Moon Kusnetsov," she said, but Gretchen was oblivious, tapping on her phone. She walked back to the bed and set the tray of sterile instruments on the nightstand. As she leaned over to inspect the dried blood caked on Funck's hair, he squeezed his eyes closed, as if her gaze sickened him. "I'm afraid I'll have to cut away some of the Presidential locks to get to the wound," she said.

"You will not touch a hair on my head," he muttered with closed eyes.

"But, it's unsanitary to—"

"Not one fucking hair!"

"Got it, not one hair." She used forceps to carefully lift strands of hair on Funck's head. Despite all the dried blood, she saw that she was holding his comb-over. It reminded her of the two-days-dead pet hamster that she had discovered in its cage when she was a little boy; she had wept over it.

She could see that Funck's head wound was on a large bald spot. Unable to resist teasing him, she lifted up her wig and patted her own bald head. "See?"

"What?"

"We're twins!"

He opened his eyes and glowered at her. "Shut the fuck up!"

"The good news is, you only need three or four stitches."

"Then how come there was so much blood?"

"You were hot to trot, Mr. President. Sexual arousal can raise your blood pressure."

"I was *not* sexually aroused!"

Moon struggled to keep a straight face.

Gretchen walked over, her cell phone to her ear. "I'm putting you on speaker, Ingrid, so Daddy can hear," she said into the phone. She motioned for Moon to get up, then sat on the bed beside her father.

Natalia's mother's voice was shrill on the phone: "Mr. President, it's the middle of the night! Is my daughter *okay?*"

"You tell me," he sneered. "She's gone."

"What?" Ingrid paused, then blurted out, "Hovno! That stupid suka! Ó môj bože! I'll strangle her myself!"

Gretchen's voice sharpened. "Ingrid, you know the house in Palm Beach Daddy bought you? And your $250,000-a-year membership to Beau Rivage? Not to mention the first-class airplane tickets every time you go visit your loser son in Slovakia!"

"I'm very grateful for everything my beloved son-in-law has given me and Papa, may he rest in peace," said Ingrid. "I'm sure Natalia is very grateful too!"

"You're sure, huh?" Funck's face reddened with such fury that Moon worried his head wound would start bleeding again.

"You can tell no one about this, Ingrid, but you better help us find your whore of a daughter," said Gretchen. "Where did she go? Is she cheating on Daddy?"

"My daughter is not the cheating spouse!"

"Watch your tone, bitch!" yelled Funck.

"Think hard, Ingrid," said Gretchen. "I know Slovak women are better known for their beauty than their brains, but think about where Natalia went or you will be on the next flight to Slovakia. And you won't be flying first class!"

"Wait," said Ingrid. "There was an old boyfriend. Natalia got..." She stopped herself. "He was her first love."

"'First love?'" Gretchen snorted. "What does 'first love' mean in Slovakia? They fucked when they were ten?"

"Fourteen."

"Close enough. We're going to track his ass down. What's his name?"

Moon's heart dropped. She knew Natalia's mother would say "Vaclav." She hoped that Natalia would find Vaclav before the White House did.

Chapter 29

Dallas, TX

December 18, 10:00 a.m.

Angel pulled the Mustang up in front of a gleaming white-marble, high-rise building. Natalia nervously twisted the bangs on her wig. "Can't we stop at a Hilton? Or a Sheraton?"

"Chica, this is one place we know they've got FOX News blasting in every bar, restaurant, and bathroom twenty-four/seven," he said. "We gotta make sure that Moon got away from the White House last night and see what the fuck they're doing about it."

A young parking attendant ran over to the car and opened Natalia's door. "Welcome to Funck Hotel Dallas," he said.

She climbed out of the car and stretched in the blazing sunshine. The valet parker stared at her, his eyes sweeping from her ample cleavage down to her bulging crotch. His smile faded. "Uh...have a nice stay."

"Glad to be here." Glad you can't tell who I really am, she thought. She also was glad she hadn't totaled the car last night while Angel took a siesta. After he woke up, he had driven here from Memphis while she napped. If they kept up this pace, she would be with Vaclav in Rosarito Beach on schedule.

She followed Angel through the ornate portico into the hotel. Because the Funck International Hotel in Washington, D.C., was set in an historic government building, Rex's interior design team had been forced to keep the style historic. In this new hotel, the look was modern/flashy, with gold-trimmed contemporary furniture and garish gold chandeliers. Rex sure loves gold, she thought.

Angel nodded to a restroom sign. "Gotta take a piss."

"Me too." Her footsteps echoed after his down a marble

corridor. He entered the men's room; she walked into the ladies' room.

She glimpsed herself in the gold-trimmed wall mirror. It startled her to see that she was looking at a trans woman with a pink-streaked black wig, false eyelashes, and glittery purple eye shadow. Above her reflection, a TV screen was set into the mirror. What Natalia saw on TV was even more startling:

On FOX News, Shana Wiley, a voluptuous blonde anchor, was sitting with Darren Roberts, a graying White House correspondent. They were discussing the official First Family Christmas photo that had been released to the public minutes ago. The photo was blown up on-screen behind them.

In the picture, President Funck was standing in front of the White House Christmas tree flanked on both sides by his children, their spouses, and his grandchildren. His arm was around the First Lady, who was clad in the red-beaded Valentino gown, a red-choker scarf around her neck. She was gazing admiringly at the President, smiling broadly.

"It certainly looks like POTUS and FLOTUS are getting into the Christmas spirit," said Shana. "They look as happy as newlyweds!"

Roberts chimed in. "I'd say she is giving the President his best Christmas present ever. Forgiveness!"

In the hotel ladies' room, Natalia trembled. Moon was still in the White House, impersonating her. How was that *possible*? She stared at the photo on TV: The First Lady looked exactly like her, but she knew in her head and her heart that it was Moon. *And yet...*

Suddenly dizzy, her heart pounding, she braced herself against the sink. Her eyes darted back and forth between FLOTUS in the White House photo and her face in the mirror. The person in the mirror wasn't her, but the FLOTUS in the photo wasn't her either.

She gasped. This is what it must feel like to have an out-of-body experience, she thought.

She burst out of the ladies' room just as Angel burst out of the men's room. "You saw it?"

"*Chingados!* Fuck me!"

"Me too!"

"We're outta!" He hustled her toward the hotel exit. "We gotta move!"

Chapter 30

Azusa, CA

December 18, 11:00 a.m.

"Mom? I'm home!" Phil called out, the way he had done when he was a teenager living with his mother in an historic Greene and Greene craftsman house in Pasadena, two blocks from the Rose Bowl. He pictured the sprawling, six-bedroom, redwood-and-brick mansion shaded by ancient California oak trees. It wasn't really their house. Betty, Phil's mother, whose grandparents had come to California as impoverished migrant Oakies during the 1930s Dust Bowl, was the maid and cook. She and Phil lived in the servants' quarters above the garage. But when the Hendersons, the Pasadena banker and his wife who owned the house, were at their condo on Maui, Phil would burst into the kitchen after a day at Pasadena High School. "I'm home," he would call out to his mother, as if the place were theirs.

Sometimes she was in the butler's pantry, polishing the family silverware, or upstairs in the master bathroom, scrubbing the tiles. At the sound of his voice, Betty would cheerfully call back, "Did you have a good day at school, dear?" Phil never did. At Pasadena High, he was one of the nerdy losers who played Nintendo alone during lunch and was last picked for the baseball team. But he always answered, "Yes."

"Philip, dear, you don't have to scream! I'm right here!" His mother's voice wrenched him back to the present. She opened the squeaky door to her mobile home. Phil walked in. Betty had lived in this $250-a-month rental ever since the banker retired in Maui. It galled him that the Hendersons didn't pay his mother Social Security all those years. The mobile home was all she could afford now on what she made as an aide in an Azusa nursing home. Phil never told his mother what he really thought of Azusa, a motley collection of strip malls, mobile-home parks, and nursing homes, fifteen minutes east of Pasadena. Someone had come up with the name "Azusa" because it was a town with "everything from A to Z in the USA." What a joke, he thought.

"Mom, you look great!" He embraced her, inhaling her familiar sweet Dove soap scent and feeling her brittle gray hair against his cheek. She seemed smaller and more fragile in his arms than the last time he saw her. Had it been a year? Two? He felt a twinge of guilt, as if her deterioration was his fault. "Are you okay?"

"I'm fine. Just older." Betty took the box of See's candy he pulled from his backpack. "Thank you." She eyed him suspiciously. "What do you want?"

"C'mon, Mom, I just wanted to see you."

"That's great. I'm happy to see *you*. What do you want?"

Phil noted the wariness in his mother's eyes, as if she knew the next thing out of his mouth would disappoint her. He had seen that look the day he dropped out of Pasadena City College, and a few years later when he brought her clippings of three *National Enquirer* articles featuring the paparazzi photos that had earned him a total of $15,000. He assured her that they would be the first of many lucrative celebrity photos in his paparazzo career.

On his mother's refrigerator, Phil eyed two yellowed *Pasadena Daily* clippings. One was from 1976: his then seventeen-year-old mother in a white drum-majorette uniform, with tasseled white boots and shiny baton, as she led the Pasadena High School marching band in the Rose Parade. The other newspaper clipping was from 2004: Phil at seventeen in his Eagle Scout uniform, holding the scout badge he'd won for taking photos of Pasadena's famous historic buildings and landmarks, including the Craftsman house where they had lived. When Phil won the scout badge, his mother told Mr. Henderson, who gave them to his friend, the publisher of the *Pasadena Daily*. The newspaper ran two of Phil's old Pasadena photos, including the one of the banker's Craftsman house, and paid Phil $50. His mother never posted the *National Enquirer* clippings on her refrigerator in the place of honor, next to these. He wondered if she had saved them in a drawer or trashed them.

"Okay, I do want something, Mom," he said. "It's really important and it could help both of us. I promise." He sat down at the kitchen table.

Betty sat down guardedly, across from him. She placed the box of See's candy on the table between them. "Both of us?"

Phil opened the box of candy and offered her one. "I have the chance to take a picture that will be beyond incredible. It will run in newspapers, magazines and on websites around the world."

"Really, Phillip?"

He saw the wariness in her eyes again. "Cross my heart and hope to die!" He realized he hadn't said that since he was a little boy. At the time his mother had scolded him. "It's bad luck to say that, Phillip. Never say it again! Your father said, 'Cross my heart and hope to die' whenever he lied to me. He ended up dying in a car wreck on the Pasadena Freeway. He had promised me he stopped drinking, but he was driving drunk!"

"Mom, listen to me, please," said Phil. "I've discovered something that no one else knows. At least, not yet. It has to do with one of the most famous celebrities in the world. And if I get a great picture of her, or him—I can't give away the celebrity's gender—I can sell it for hundreds of thousands of dollars, maybe more! You won't have to live in this dump!"

"This is not a dump!" she said. "It's perfectly fine, and I can walk to work."

"You won't have to *work*!"

The paper wrappers of the See's candies rustled as his mother selected a chocolate. He remembered the rustling sound, like a mouse making a nest, from the New Year's Day mornings in their servants' quarters when they treated themselves to See's candy while watching the Rose Parade on TV.

"So, about this photo that's going to make you a millionaire." Betty took a delicate bite of her chocolate. "What do you need from *me*?"

As if he were making a chess move, he selected a white-chocolate See's candy with lumps that he knew from experience were salted peanuts. As he chewed it, he pulled out his camera. "Okay, so this is the Nikon digital SLR camera I bought with the money I made thanks to my George Clooney photo."

"I remember you telling me," she said.

"I love this camera." He reached into his camera bag and pulled out a lens. "This is the 70-200 millimeter zoom lens I bought with the money I made from the Beyoncé photo."

"You told me about that, too."

He attached the lens to the camera. "With this, I can shoot a close-up of someone 350 feet away. He held out the camera for her inspection.

She shook her head. "I haven't got a clue about cameras, Philip. Or about what you're getting at."

He dug into the pocket of his jeans and pulled out a wadded-up brochure. He smoothed it out and laid it on the table. It featured a picture of a lens that was at least twice the length of his own. "Mom, this is the newest Nikon lens on the market. Talk about next gen. It's got four extra-low dispersion elements that reduce aberrations in the aperture range, and nano-crystal and super-integrated coatings to suppress flare. Mom, the most amazing thing is it's 600 millimeters, but it's much lighter than your traditional 600-millimeter lens. You can get a great close-up of someone 700 feet away or more!"

A mouse-nest rustling made Phil realize that his mother was burrowing in the See's box. "Mom, you're not listening."

"I am listening, but I don't understand. What do you want?"

He slapped his palm on the brochure. "I want this lens! I need this lens!"

"How much does it cost?"

Phil hesitated, debating how truthful to be. He had spent most of his meager savings on the plane ticket from Washington to L.A. and he needed whatever was left to rent a car and pay expenses on his trip to Tijuana. "It retails for between $8,000 and $11,000," he blurted out. His mother stopped chewing. "Mom, they know me at Samy's Camera. I've been going there since I was a kid. I'm pretty sure I can get a discount."

"*How* sure?" Before Phil could answer, his mother shook her head and stood up from the table, brushing her palms together to get rid of the candy crumbs. "Never mind. If you are half as convincing with the guys at Samy's as you are with me, I'm sure you'll get a great deal!"

"Mom, thank you, thank you, thank you!" He stood up and came around to her side of the table, reaching out to grab her in a bear hug.

"Jeez, Philip, you want the money or what?" She avoided his arms and headed into the bedroom.

"You keep $11,000 in *cash*?"

"Bankers are cheats!"

Phil followed her into the tiny bedroom. The single bed was impeccably made, with not a wrinkle in the bedspread. He remembered that it was the way the banker's wife liked it. The bedspread was embroidered with red roses surrounding a red banner with the words, "Rose Parade 1976."

Betty pulled aside a makeshift curtain and rummaged on a shelf above a pole where her clothes hung. He had never seen the black cardboard box that she pulled down and placed on her bed. She opened the box slowly, as if afraid the memories it held would escape. Inside were her white drum-majorette boots from high school, their white tassels now yellowed. His mother had often told him that the day she led the marching band in the Rose Parade was the happiest day of her life. She reached into one boot, dug out a wad of cash that was secured with a rubber band and handed it to him. "Take what you need."

He hugged her. "Mom, I want to make you proud of me."

"I know you do, Philip." She slowly and softly petted the back of his head, the way she did when he was a little boy home from school and sick in bed with a fever. "And I want you to have a chance, like I did, to do something very special," she continued. "Something you will always remember."

Chapter 31

El Paso, TX

December 18, 12:00 p.m.

The blazing sky turned the front window of Cody's Pawn Shop into a mirror. Natalia regarded her reflection: She was wearing Moon's fuchsia polyester nurses' scrubs and skid-resistant plastic nurses' clogs; they were white with little fuchsia hearts. She had discovered them under Moon's FLOTUS-impersonator dresses in the garment bag. Natalia had also discovered half a dozen bandanas that Moon used to hide her Adam's apple. She had tied a few together to bind her breasts. It wasn't comfortable, but she didn't want her big boobs to give her away. Glimpsing her size B bosom, she chuckled to herself. Now I know how Moon feels when she wears that thong from hell to hide her vták, she thought.

Natalia also had shed Moon's nose and ear studs, Buddha tattoo, and false eyelashes, and the wadded-up Frette washcloth with which she had created the man bulge at her crotch. Thanks to Angel's artistry, her makeup was subtle: a little lipstick and a touch of blush, what a flat-chested RN, not an over-the-top trans woman trying to make a statement, would wear. She had ditched Moon's pink-streaked black wig too. To hide her baldness, she was wearing an old gray-knit winter cap that Angel had found in his trunk.

Angel climbed out of the Mustang and walked toward the pawn shop. It was too bad they had found nothing in Moon's garment bag to help him change his appearance, she thought. He had shaved his stubble, cut his hair short, and removed the silver studs from his left ear. Still, she wasn't certain that what she had worn leaving the White House now worked on him: Moon's white wife-beater T-shirt was so big that it sagged on his chest, revealing his nipples. "No way am I wearing Moon's ginormous motorcycle boots," Angel had said. "With my *camarón* feet, I'll trip and fall on my ass." She suspected that Angel refused to wear them because he was obsessed with his red-alligator cowboy boots. He claimed Moon's jeans were so long on him, that they would droop down and cover them.

She sized him up as he joined her in front of the pawn shop. "Moon's jeans are definitely too long and I hate to break it to you, Angel. They don't totally conceal your cowboy boots." She pointed to the red boot tips that were sticking out.

Ignoring her, he said, "Okay, so what's the plan?"

"Well, we know Moon didn't escape from the White House last night. She was there this morning, impersonating me in the White House Christmas photo."

"Which means they caught her ass and now Rex Funck is forcing her to impersonate you until they find *your* ass."

"Or *Gretchen* is forcing Moon."

"Either way, if they know Moon's the First Lady in the White House, they know you walked outta there yesterday looking like the tranny Moon *really* is and I was the pinche dude with you," he said. "We gotta, like, dump our IDs, my credit cards, and my Mustang, and get to TJ looking like people the Secret Service and FBI aren't expecting."

"Rex won't get the FBI involved. He thinks they're out to get him. They probably are," she said. "As for the Secret Service, he can't send them all after us. Too many moving parts. The press could find out."

"Can you see the pinche headlines? 'FLOTUS Flees the White House!'"

"The only Secret Service agent Rex trusts is his personal bodyguard, a guy with a last name..." She tried to remember. "It sounds obscene... 'Pricker.' Rex's got, like, a 'bromance' going with Pricker."

"So that leaves just Pricker the prick looking for us," he said.

"That's, like, a good thing, right?"

"Don't forget Gretchen."

"Shit, Gretchen will be all over this, like a pit bull on a rooster!"

"That's a bad thing." Natalia sighed. "I'm glad we didn't tell Moon where we were going. They'd pull out her fingernails to get the info from her. Not her acrylics, her real ones!"

"Doesn't matter. They can trace my credit card records," he said. "I've been using my VISA for gas and food since we left D.C. They will see we drove through the south and into Texas. It's an easy guess that from Texas we're heading to, like, New Mexico, Arizona, and California, and from there, why not Mexico, where I'm from? FLOTUS will be safe there. The Mexican government has no love for Funck. They won't build his pinche border wall. They sure as hell won't return his wife!"

"So, what do we do now?" She glanced at the pistols, rifles, and machine guns mounted in the pawn-shop window. "Don't tell me we're buying guns to hold them off."

"No pinche way!"

"Angel, I was kidding."

He gently touched her arm. "Chica, I know we are both freaked out about this thing with Moon being stuck in the White House and them knowing—"

"We didn't see it coming."

"We're gonna be okay. We're gonna make it to TJ."

"Promise?"

"Promise. I've got, like, $20 left." He pulled up his pant leg and braced his foot against the bottom rim of the store window. "Let's see how much we can get for these babies." He used his car key to wedge open the secret compartment in the silver heel of his cowboy boot. He carefully retrieved the six unset diamonds. "Vamanos!"

Angel opened the door to the pawn shop for Natalia, then followed her inside.

Behind the counter was a middle-aged cowboy-wannabe wearing a Stetson hat and a faded plaid cowboy shirt, his bloated belly resting on the top of the glass case, like a sleeping cat. "What can I do you for?"

"I've got a few stones," Angel said. "I'd like to know what they're worth."

"You betcha." The pawnbroker looked Natalia up and down. She saw his eyes glaze over. How refreshing to be checked out by a man and see he has no desire to jump my bones, she thought, relieved that her flat-chested nurse disguise was working.

The pawnbroker reached under the counter and retrieved a blue-velvet-lined tray. Angel carefully let the diamonds fall from his palm onto the velvet, as if he were throwing dice in a game he had to win.

Pulling a jeweler's eyepiece from his shirt pocket, the pawnbroker extended his hand. "I'm Cody, by the way. This is my place."

Angel shook Cody's hand, but didn't offer his name. "Pleased to meet you."

"No worries. I'll give you the best price." He picked up one of the diamonds and looked at it through his loupe.

Cody must deal with people like us all the time, thought Natalia. No-name losers on the run. She stared at the floor while he examined the diamonds.

Cody removed the loupe from his eye and moved the smallest diamond to the edge of the tray. "Five of your diamonds are fake," he said. "Sorry about that." He tapped the small diamond. "This one's real. I can give you fifty bucks for it."

Natalia saw Angel's jaw tighten. She forced herself to stay calm.

"Let me talk to my, like, partner," Angel said. He led her to a corner.

"Take your time," Cody called after them.

"Is he telling truth?" she whispered.

"Maybe. If the dude thinks he can only sell one small-ass diamond to the trailer trash that comes in here, he'll only buy one. And he'll say the others are, like, fake, so we'll think we won the lottery to get $50 for it because the others aren't worth jack shit." He thought for a moment. "Unless—"

"What?"

"Unless one of Funck's first three wives scammed him after their divorce, returned fake diamonds to him, and kept the real ones."

"Maybe Rex scammed his wives and gave them fake diamonds to begin with." She laughed. "I wouldn't put it past him."

Angel led her back to the counter and scooped up the rejected diamonds. "Okay, Cody, we'll take the $50. We appreciate your generosity."

"Sure thing." The pawnbroker put the velvet tray with the diamond on the back counter, unlocked a cash drawer and counted out $50 in tens. He handed it to Angel. "I can see you folks are disappointed not to leave here with more. Tell you what, how about I give you another fifty bucks for your boots?"

Angel glanced down. The red tips of his cowboy boots were sticking out from under his drooping cuffs. He hitched up his jeans. It didn't help. "Dude, I can't part with my boots." He flashed the Rolex watch that Natalia had given him for Christmas. "But how much for this?"

Cody pondered Angel's question, then burped. "The thing is, there are a lot of fake Rolexes out there. Diamonds I can tell, but how do I know that Rolex's not fake?"

"It's not fake!" said Natalia. "I paid $9,000 for it!"

Cody looked from her to Angel. "The truth is, the folks who come in here can't afford a Rolex, even if it's fake. I've got no use for it. But them red boots. I can sell them in a heartbeat."

Angel looked down at his boots and sighed. "$150."

Cody held out his hand. "$100." Angel reluctantly shook it.

Chapter 32

The White House

December 18, 3:00 p.m.

"Christmas came early for President Funck today!" gushed Brandon Brighton on FOX TV. "His approval ratings soared fifteen points!"

"Amazing," said co-anchor Shana Wiley, pointing to the official Christmas photo of the President, his admiring First Lady and his family.

"All because of this picture!" Brighton said. "And this picture says POTUS and FLOTUS are lovebirds once again!"

In Natalia's White House bedroom, Moon clicked off the TV, disgruntled about the news and feeling guilty about her part in it. She rubbed her hand over her bald head, as if brushing back unruly hair, and slumped against the pile of goose-down pillows on the bed. She reached under the terrycloth bathrobe she was wearing—Natalia's peach Prada—and scratched her balls.

"Way to go, Moon. Daddy and I can't thank you enough!" she said in a high voice and accent that imitated the First Daughter's. Then, in her own voice: "Oh, it was my pleasure, Gretchen. Anything to keep you and Big Daddy in the White House for another four years."

She leaned toward a crystal bowl of fresh fruit on the nightstand and selected a strawberry. She popped it into her mouth, then frowned. She had no appetite. She was about to take another bite anyway, but noticed Hilda peering out at her from the servant's alcove. A cautious smile creased the Slovak maid's square face.

Moon tossed the half-eaten strawberry across the room, toward the wastebasket. It missed by inches, landing on the thick white carpet. Hilda scurried over, with a sound that reminded

Moon of rustling leaves. It was the sound of Hilda's support-panty-hosed thighs rubbing together as she walked. The lardo nurses at Good Samaritan Hospital in Miami sounded like that. Hilda stiffly bent over, grunting, and scooped up the offending strawberry.

"You thought what I said was funny," said Moon. As if she hadn't heard her, Hilda ducked back into the servant's pantry alcove. "Girlfriend, you understand what I'm saying, don't you?"

Hilda returned with a wet towel. "No speak English," she said in a thick Slovak accent. With another grunt, she hunkered down on her hands and knees, her enormous ass in the air, and delicately patted the strawberry stain with the towel.

"Bullshit!"

Hilda stopped patting the stain and nervously pushed her wire-rimmed glasses up on her nose.

"C'mon, Hilda. You understand every word that is said in the First Lady's bedroom, Slovak or English. You pretend you only speak Slovak, but the First Daughter got you this job so you could play 'dumb Slovak maid' and spy on Natalia." Hilda didn't look up, focused on patting the stain. "It's okay, Hilda. You can tell me," she said. "By tomorrow this time, FLOTUS will be back in the White House, or the White House will announce she went to Slovakia to visit her ailing babika. Either way, I'll be counting geckos on the ceiling in Git-mo."

Hilda looked up at Moon. "They will send you to prison? Not fair. You do more for President's ratings than real First Lady."

"Tell me about it." She flopped back against the pillows.

Hilda nervously pushed her glasses up on her nose. "Can I ask—?"

"What?"

"What's it like?"

"What's what like? Guantanamo prison? Ask me in a week."

"No. You are man who wants to be woman." She pushed her

glasses up again and took a cautious step closer. "What's it like?"

Moon hadn't been this close to Hilda before. She saw that the maid wore no makeup and that her wire-rimmed glasses were men's glasses, a size too big. Her short brown hair was shaggy, as if she had cut it herself. The "moustache" of black hair on her upper lip could easily have been wiped off with Nair. And why didn't she wax off the bear fur on her stubby arms?

"You know what you really want, Hilda?"

"What?"

"You want to know if a woman can become a man."

Hilda's chubby cheeks reddened. "I love woman, but I would like to be man loving woman. Is it possible?"

"You mean, can you get your very own one-eyed trouser snake?

"One-eyed trouser snake?"

"A Mr. Winky, a tallywhacker, a shlong!"

Hilda still didn't get it.

"Girlfriend, would you like to have a penis?"

"A vták?" She thought a moment, then nodded, her cheeks turning purple. "Do you still have vták, or did they cut it off?

"First of all, they do not cut off a man's...*vták*...when he is transitioning to female," said Moon. "There's a surgical procedure where they sort of turn it inside out to create a vagina."

"Do you have vagina?"

"No!" said Moon. "I still have my vták and I intend to keep it."

Hilda thought that over. "But you want to be woman."

"I want other people to look at me and *see* a woman. I need more surgery on my face for that," said Moon. "If all goes well, people will be looking at my face, not my *vták*. So I'll keep it, thank you very much. I need it to have sex with my girlfriend."

"You have *girlfriend*?"

Moon nodded. "She's a nurse, like me. Eliza. She's from Trinidad. Eliza loves me whether I'm a man *or* a woman."

Hilda smiled for the first time. "I have girlfriend in Slovakia," she said wistfully. "Kveta loves me whether I'm woman or man. But if I have vták, when I go back to Slovakia I can fuck Kveta with it."

Moon chuckled. "I think you're asking me to recommend a good gender-reassignment doctor." Hilda nodded.

"How about this? I will personally take you to see mine in Miami. She is the best gender-reassignment surgeon in the world. In return, you do something for me."

"What?"

"Help me escape from this bedroom, from the goddamn White House!"

To her surprise, Hilda didn't flinch at the offer. She was about to push her wire-rimmed glasses up on her nose again. She touched her finger to her lip instead. Moon hoped that it meant she was seriously considering it.

Chapter 33

Tucson, AZ

December 18, 6:00 p.m.

Elegant in her red Valentino gown, Natalia nervously descended the grand staircase of the White House, feeling for the carpet beneath the toe of her red Manolos before taking each step. Rex and the entire Funck family were watching from the foyer below, as if waiting for her to stumble. She focused on the moment so that she wouldn't lose her balance, remembering her yoga teacher's calming routine: "What do you smell?" The pine scent of the Christmas tree. "What do you feel?" The smoothness of the polished-oak banister. "What do you hear?" The whisper of my silk gown.

Suddenly the whisper of silk was coming from an identical red Valentino gown worn by an identical First Lady. Natalia's doppelganger was stepping toward Rex and the line-up of Funcks posing in front of the Christmas tree. Natalia hastened down the steps so that she could get to them first.

"Hey, wait! I'm the real First Lady," she called.

The photographer motioned to everyone to move closer together. "Smile like you really mean it," he said. That was hard for this family, but Natalia realized it shouldn't be. When Rex was elected President, they got exactly what they dreamed of: the opportunity to quadruple their riches and to make Rex's self-centered worldview real, with his bloated ego at the top. The thought made her stop just short of them. Did she really want to be part of the Funck dynasty? Did she really want to bring another Funck child into the world?

She turned to leave, but a foot shot out and tripped her.

As Natalia fell, in the flare of the photographer's lights she looked up at the culprit: Gretchen.

* * *

Natalia startled awake from her dream and squinted into an overpowering radiance. She straightened up in the Mustang passenger seat and shielded her eyes. The sunset was pouring in through the windshield; bands of red, orange, and purple hovering over the stark desert, like a mirage. "You've got to see this!"

No answer from the driver's seat. Angel was gone.

Panicking, she climbed out of the car. The parking lot was empty except for a few dirty pickup trucks. Where am I? she thought. The last thing she remembered before falling asleep was Angel cruising past a "Welcome to Arizona" sign and pointing out the window to a lone, towering cactus. "That's a saguaro," he had said, pointing to its uplifted arm. "It's saying 'Hi,' to you."

There were more saguaros surrounding the parking lot, some with one, others with two or more "arms." They looked like giants. She noticed sharp spines on the cactus closest to her. Dangerous giants.

Where was Angel?

As the dusk deepened, a light flashed on over a sign: "Home Depot." To her relief, she spotted Angel by the store entrance. He was talking with a group of Latino men in dusty jeans, T-shirts, and work boots, some wearing faded camouflage jackets and either baseball caps or straw cowboy hats. They huddled under the torn canvas awning of a taco stand made from nailed-together two-by-fours.

A weathered Latina woman in a patched cowboy shirt, a torn apron over her faded jeans, was cooking tortillas over a rusty barrel that Natalia guessed held dried-out brush. She remembered seeing poor women in Slovakia cooking flattened potato dough over stoves like that on the banks of the Váh River in Žilina. Sometimes, on schooldays, if her brother Franc hadn't come home for dinner, her mother would send her out to find him. Natalia knew he spent Sundays smoking dope on the riverbank with his friends, so she always looked there first. The sunsets in Žilina are not as beautiful as they are here in the desert, she thought. In Žilina, usually the sun sinks quickly behind a cold gray cloudbank, as if swallowed whole by the darkness.

Angel walked over to the Mustang, the hems of Moon's too-long jeans dragging on the ground now that he was wearing flip-flops instead of his beloved red-alligator cowboy boots. Cody, the pawnbroker, had generously thrown in the flip-flops as part of the deal.

"Want me to roll up your cuffs for you?" Natalia asked.

"No, but thanks," he said. "I tried. They rolled right back down. Maybe they like the taste of dirt. Here, have a taco." He handed her one of the two newspaper-wrapped packets he was carrying.

"Thanks." She unwrapped the greasy taco. It was scantily filled with beans, rice, and salsa.

"I hope you like your salsa on fire."

Natalia took a bite. "*Ooooeeee,*" she gasped. "That's spicier than Slovak paprika!" The mouth-searing peppers didn't stop her from scarfing down the taco.

"The poorer the Mexican, the hotter the sauce," he said between bites. "You forget that all you're eating is rice, beans, and corn, that you can't afford meat." He nodded towards the taco stand. "See that woman? That used to be my mom."

"Your mom?"

"She had a taco stand like this at Home Depot in Tijuana. Every Home Depot where there are Mexicans has one. *Trabajadores,* workers, who need a job, show up before the store opens at six. They need something to eat so they'll have energy to grind all day working, like, construction, landscaping, or painting houses. If they're lucky enough to get a gig."

"'Lucky enough?'"

"These are guys with, like, no jobs, no money. At the U.S. Home Depots, most of them are illegal. They live in some shack with dozens of family members whose mouths gotta get fed. So they walk to the nearest Home Depot in the dark before sunrise, so they'll arrive before the pickups start showing up. They know the drivers are looking for a work crew. Most of the time the drivers are Chicanos, guys who are legal. They're, like, the *jefes*, the bosses of the workers. They report to the gringos who own the trucks. The jefes look for guys who are *fuerte*, strong, to do a tough day's work. If you're small, or old, *olvídalo*, forget it. The 'lucky' guys go off with the jefe in his truck. At the end of the day, right about now, when the sun is setting so it's too dark to work anymore, the jefe drops them back off in the Home Depot parking lot. If they're lucky, the jefe pays them for the work they did.

"Sometimes they *don't* pay them?"

"Yeah, like, sometimes the redneck boss tells the jefe, 'Stiff 'em! What the fuck are they gonna do? Come after me?' Sometimes the jefe keeps the money himself."

"That's terrible!"

"My mom always saved a few tortillas for the guys who got stiffed, so they didn't go to sleep that night hungry."

"That was so generous of her."

"Pretty soon, she got to know which jefes were *pendejos*, motherfuckers, and wouldn't pay a dude for an honest day's work. In the morning, if a worker got picked for a job, he'd look over at my mom at the taco stand. If my mom nodded her head, that meant the jefe was honest. If the worker did a good job that day, he'd get paid. If my mom shook her head, it meant don't get on the pinche truck. You're gonna work your pinche ass off all day and get pinche *nada*, nothing!"

A banged-up gray Chevy Sierra pickup pulled into the parking lot, its wheels spitting gravel. Eight Latino workmen were huddled in the truck bed. The driver climbed out, walked around to the back, and unhitched the tailgate. The men jumped down. The jefe pulled a wad of cash from his back pocket and paid them, one at a time.

"I think we got an honest one," said Angel. He glanced over at the woman behind the taco stand. The woman nodded her head. "Be right back!"

* * *

A faint purple stain, the last trace of sunset, lingered in the sky. Sitting in the passenger seat of the Chevy Sierra pickup, Natalia stretched out her legs. A lot more room than Angel's Mustang. She wore the dusty work boots, jeans, and a "Corona" T-shirt of one of the workmen they'd met in the Home Depot parking lot. Over it, his ragged camouflage jacket. His faded camouflage hat hid her bald head. She pulled the brim low and studied her reflection in the mirror on the sun visor. "How do I look?"

Angel glanced at her from the driver's seat. "Chica, I'd pick you for a construction crew anytime." He laughed. "But I'm not sure I'd pay you at the end of the day. I mean, dude, you'd have to really crush it!"

"I *would* crush it!" She looked Angel up and down. He was wearing a nearly identical "Mexican worker" outfit, taken from another one of the men at the taco stand. "I'm not sure I'd hire you for construction. Painting a bathroom, maybe."

"Yo, I'm a pinche great painter."

"I'm sure you are." She laughed. "I'm picturing the guy who traded clothes with you. He's wearing Moon's stuff right now. I hope his jeans aren't dragging in the dirt! And the guy who traded clothes with me is wearing Moon's nurse's scrubs and clogs. What will his wife say?"

"His wife will go nuts for Moon's fancy female-impersonator gown. She'll shorten it so her daughter can wear it for her *fiestas de quince años*."

"What's a fiestas de quince años?"

"When girls in Mexico turn fifteen, their families throw a big party. The quince girls dress up in these long pink dresses and wear tiaras, like little crowns."

"I would have loved that when I was fifteen!"

"Can I tell you a secret?"

"Of course."

"When I was fifteen, I, like, really wanted a fiesta de quince años. I wanted to wear one of those dresses."

"Did you?"

"It was before I came out to my parents. Raphael and I were fooling around, but we kept it secret. He knew how much it meant to me, so he, like, stole his sister's quince años dress and brought it to this little casita we sometimes met at, near the mayor's big-ass hacienda. I think I told you, Raphael's dad was, like, deputy mayor. He discovered where his dad hid the key to the mayor's casita. Raphael figured the mayor met his *sancha,* his mistress, there. That maybe his dad met, like, his sancha there too. So when the mayor and Raphael's father left town for government business, we'd sneak into the casita for, y'know... Then, on my fifteenth birthday, I show up at the casita and Raphael surprises me with his sister's pink fiesta de quince años dress. I looked pretty pinche good in it!"

"I bet!"

He turned on the truck's headlights, piercing the darkness of the empty highway ahead of them.

"Y'know, I'm still not sure why the jefe traded his truck for your Mustang," she said. "I mean, what's his boss going to say? You can't fit a lot of $5-an-hour Mexican workers in a Mustang."

"I figure the jefe's got, like, two choices. Either he gives his boss the Mustang cuz he knows the dude will be totally psyched and that he's got enough cash from all the times he stiffed his workers to buy another truck."

"What's his other choice?"

"The jefe sells the Mustang to a drug dealer who's totally psyched. The jefe takes the money and moves back to Mexico.

Yo, either way it's not our problem."

"Right. Our only problem is getting into Mexico ourselves."

"It's gonna happen, chica," he said. "Sooner than you think!"

Chapter 34

The White House

December 18, 7:00 p.m.

I'm having a déjà vu, thought Moon. She looked at the President, who was wearing his bathrobe and sitting on his throne in his bedroom, his eyes glued to FOX TV. It was the same scenario that last night had launched her descent into the lower depths of First Lady Hell.

Wait. Tonight was worse: On FOX TV, the commentators were as gleeful as flies on shit because the President's ratings had soared today thanks to this morning's "happy couple" Christmas photo. Gretchen was standing behind her father with her hands on his shoulders, as if he were her ventriloquist's dummy. "We'll set up another photo shoot for tomorrow, Daddy," she said. "Your ratings will go through the roof!"

Moon squirmed on the sofa, wishing that she was *not* wearing Funck's required latex gloves and sanitary face mask, and that she was wearing her own clothes instead of Natalia's damn peach-terrycloth Frette bathrobe that she'd worn all day. This isn't a déjà vu, she thought. It's a fucking nightmare.

"Sally-Ann, you will attend the next and every photo shoot, got that?" Gretchen turned to Natalia's social secretary, who moments before had been sworn to secrecy as part of the "Find FLOTUS" command team.

"Yes, ma'am," Sally-Ann said quietly. Obviously still in shock to be here, she raised her hand to her mouth, as if to nervously bite a fingernail. When her latex-glove-covered finger bumped into her sanitary-mask-covered mouth, she sheepishly glanced around the room, as if hoping no one had noticed. Her eyes met Moon's. Moon winked at her. She quickly dipped her hand into her Tory Burch tote bag and rummaged around, as if hunting for something.

God knows what the First Daughter threatened the former Dixie deb with if she spills the beans, thought Moon. No more African hunting safaris with her big-bucks Republican daddy and Gretchen's macho brothers? More likely, no career in Washington or anywhere else in the whole wide world for the rest of her whole pathetic life.

"Sally-Ann, set up a visit for the First Couple to Georgetown University Hospital tomorrow morning," said Gretchen. "The children's ward."

"Yes, ma'am," said Sally-Ann, her voice muffled by her face mask. She pulled her iPad out of the tote bag and punched the "On" button.

"Oh good," said Moon. "I feel right at home in hospitals!"

"Shut up! This isn't about you!" Gretchen adjusted her own face mask. Moon found it amusing that even the First Daughter now was required by the President to wear one in his presence. The "pecker-as-hot-dog-in-a-bun" incident last night must have spooked him big time, she thought. Funck's popularity ratings may have soared today, but his germ phobia did too.

While Gretchen and Sally-Ann discussed tomorrow's hospital visit, Moon felt a twinge in her gut. Maybe there was a way she could use the President's germ phobia, at this point a secret from everyone except the people in this room, to torpedo his popularity. It would ease her guilt for helping increase it.

"Okay, I just got the info you wanted," said Pricker, who was sitting on the sofa across from Moon, hunched over his laptop.

"Speak to me," said Gretchen. "Sally-Ann, take notes!"

"Vaclav Szabo went through immigration at the San Diego Airport at 12:45 p.m. after arriving on American Airlines flight #1543 from Prague via Chicago," Pricker said. "At 2:06 p.m., he departed from the U.S. by car, a Honda Civic rented from Enterprise, at the Cruce Peatonal Hacia, and crossed the border into Mexico."

"Excellent, Pricker," said Gretchen. "I want you on the next flight to San Diego. Rent a car and drive across the border. If you find Natalia's Slovak lover boy in Tijuana, you'll find Natalia."

"Agent Pricker is not going anywhere!" It was President Funck, his eyes on the TV.

"But Daddy!" She stepped in front of his chair, blocking his view of the screen. "We need him in TJ! We can't give this job to anyone else! It's not like we can send the Secret Service or the fucking army after FLOTUS! If this gets out to the—"

"Pricker is my *personal* Secret Service agent!" Funck glared at her, his lower lip thrusting out even farther than usual. "I do not loan out Special Agent Pricker like a copy of my book, *The Art of the Con*. Pricker's job description entails staying no more than twenty feet away from me at all times unless he's asleep for the five hours he is allowed each night, or in the can. You want someone to go get FLOTUS, give the job to the U.D. officer on duty when she walked right fucking past him out of the fucking staff-entrance security area. Tell the son-of-a-bitch that he's dead meat if he doesn't find her. And that if anything about this leaks to the press, he's more than dead meat. He's a handful of ashes that I will dump in the toilet, fucking shit on, and fucking flush down into the sewer!"

"That's good, Daddy. You are right, as always! I will do that!"

Moon could see that Gretchen was clenching her jaw in anger. The First Daughter doesn't like to be crossed, just like her dad, she thought.

"Sir, there were two U.D. officers on duty when FLOTUS walked," said Pricker, checking his laptop. "A James Conner and a Tallisha Jones."

"'Tallisha Jones?'" Rex snickered. "She's black, right?"

"I believe so, Mr. President."

"You '*believe*' so? A person is either fucking black or white."

"No, sir, I mean, yes, sir," said Pricker, rattled. "I'm looking at her ID photo on my laptop, and yes, affirmative, Tallisha Jones is African-American."

"Then send Officer Conner to Tijuana to find Natalia's ass."

"What about U.D. Officer Jones?"

"Demote her. Assign her to the staff cafeteria. No, make that the staff-cafeteria kitchen, in the basement. The night shift!"

"Yes, sir!"

Moon chuckled to herself. She conjured up an image of Tallisha Jones hanging out at 1:30 a.m. in the staff-cafeteria kitchen with Stella. Stella is punching dough and Tallisha is reading aloud from Michelle Obama's memoir, just as they were doing last night. Only now, thanks to her demotion, it is Tallisha's job to be in the staff kitchen. The U.D. officer no longer has to sneak down there in her off hours. She can spend time with her true love as part of her job description. And in the morning, when their shifts end, they can leave the White House together, hand in hand, and go home to the apartment they will soon share as wife and wife.

Chapter 35

Near the Mexican Border, CA

December 18, 10:00 p.m.

Natalia shivered in the cold desert wind that whipped the tumbleweeds, like battered soccer balls, across the parking lot. She was wearing Angel's wool-knit cap under her camouflage hat, but still she was chilled to the bone. "I thought deserts were hot," she said as Angel jumped out of the pickup truck.

"Not at night in December." He walked a few feet away from the truck and flicked on his flashlight, panning the beam in a slow circle around them. "It's gotta be here somewhere."

"What are we looking for?

His flashlight beam picked up a wooden sign in the distance. "C'mon!" His boots crunched on the gravel as he trudged across the parking lot and onto a trail. Natalia followed him.

Above, with no moon, the sky shimmered with stars. It reminded her of the sky above her babika's farm in Slovakia when she was a child. On moonless nights, even if it was past her bedtime, her babika would take her outside to show her the constellations, like the *Veľký voz*. She said it was the soup ladle that Zlatorog, the mythical Slovak mountain-goat god, used to eat his Slovak sauerkraut soup. She looked up and spotted it in the sky, wondering if Vaclav, her very own Zlatorog, was looking at the Big Dipper right now. She pictured him walking alone on the beach in Rosarito; he should have arrived there today. She hoped that he was as excited about their reunion there tomorrow as she was. She crossed herself and said a silent prayer that all would go well.

She caught up with Angel in front of the sign. In the glow of his flashlight beam, she read it: "*The Pacific Crest National Scenic Trail (PCT) is a treasured pathway through some of the most*

205

outstanding scenic terrain in the United States. Beginning in southern California at the Mexican border, the PCT travels a total distance of 2,650 miles through California, Oregon, and Washington, before reaching the Canadian border."

"I saw a movie about this," she said. "Reese Witherspoon plays this woman, Cheryl, who really did hike the PCT, over one thousand miles, all by herself. She was trying to get over a bad marriage and prove she could do something on her own. What she did was really difficult, really amazing. It helped her find herself."

"Great," said Angel. "Now we gotta find the tunnel where I proved I didn't have to be a poor dumb maricón in Mexico for the rest of my life."

"I don't get it," said Natalia. "This is the start of a trail that goes north to Canada, not south to Mexico."

"Yo, the tunnel I took from Mexico comes out exactly five miles due south of this sign," he said. "So paid coyotes, or family, or, like, whoever's waiting for an illegal burrito to sneak through the tunnel knows to meet him here." He pulled a metal compass out of his pocket. "I used this to find my way here from the tunnel the night I came through." He led Natalia back to the truck. "Some Mexicans got, like, a St. Christopher medal in their car to watch over them. I keep this in my pocket for the same reason."

They climbed into the truck. Angel started the engine and kept one eye on the compass as he drove south.

"Was someone waiting for you?"

"Huh?"

"That night at the Pacific Crest Trail sign?"

"My tio Claudio, my mom's brother," he said. "Claudio escaped through the tunnel himself a few times. He was what they call a 'sandbeaner.' The plan was, if the border Nazis showed up, we'd hit the PCT and head north."

"What happened?"

"ICE shows up. Claudio takes off to the west. They go after him. He planned it so I could get away on the trail. I followed it north a mile or so, then used my compass to head east. The first Greyhound station I hit, I bought a ticket to Miami."

"What about your uncle?"

"They caught him, detained him a few months, then sent him back to Mexico. But he hopped the border again."

"Where is he now?"

"Phoenix. He manages a car wash and has two kids in college."

"Awesome!"

* * *

In the pitch dark, Natalia pulled down her jeans and squatted behind a rock. Hoping she wasn't aiming at a sleeping rattlesnake, she peed. She figured she'd better go now—and boy, did she need to go—before they entered the tunnel. Angel had said it was two miles long and only three-feet high. They would have to crawl on their bellies. "So many poor fucks escape through that tunnel, it stinks of piss and shit," he warned her. "You might even see *un muerto*, a dead body, or smell one." Angel explained that illegals died in the tunnel from lack of food or dehydration. "Chica, I hope you can deal with it." She hoped she could too.

Natalia knew all about the importance of staying hydrated. Since Paris, she always carried a bottle of natural spring water with her, like Evian, San Pellegrino, or Perrier. She hadn't drunk, or seen, any of what she called "the big three" since leaving the White House. At the Golden Acorn Casino, where she and Angel had stopped for a break on the drive here tonight from Tucson, the only bottled water they sold was a generic brand. She worried that someone had filled the bottle with tap water and passed it off as purified. Then it hit her: What did it matter whether she drank bottled whatever water or tap water? Where she was going, she wouldn't be riding in the back of a limo stocked with designer water. At the Indian casino, as a test, she had forced herself to drink four bottles of a generic brand. It didn't give her cramps, gas, or diarrhea, as she feared. All it did was make her need to pee.

"*La puta!*" Angel shouted. "Shit!"

Natalia hurriedly zipped up. She spotted Angel's flashlight beam and rushed over to him. "What happened? Are you all right?"

He was standing near a saguaro cactus that looked worse than the dangerous giants she had seen earlier. Its arm had rotted off, leaving a festering hole where a lizard perched, a wriggling centipede in its mouth. The reptile skittered away. Muttering in Spanish, Angel was staring at an uneven circle on the ground of what looked like rocks, pebbles, and tar, about five feet in diameter.

"What's that?"

"Dude, how could I be so pinche stupid?" His voice was trembling with rage.

"Stupid about what?"

"Like, how could I *not* get that the minute Rex Funck became President, he'd fill in every pinche gopher hole, every pinche crack in the earth, where wetback drug dealers and rapists... and...and pinches cannibals...could sneak into the good old U.S. of A!"

Natalia gaped at the mound of rocks and tar. "This was the hole for the *tunnel*?"

"They plugged it with pinche asphalt!" Angel threw his compass on the ground. "We're fucked!"

Angel raised his foot to stomp on it, but Natalia hastily scooped it up. "No!"

Suddenly it hit her: If she couldn't get into Mexico, she wouldn't see Vaclav tomorrow.

"*NO!*" she screamed.

"Shhhh!" Angel clapped his hand over her mouth. "I bet they

got, like, mics out here, and radar and drones with night-vision cameras. And...and pinches robots!" He hustled her back to the pickup. They climbed in. He flicked on the lights and the engine.

She spotted searchlights flashing on along the horizon. "Look!" The searchlight beams grew brighter, moving closer.

"Computerized searchlights." He flicked off the headlights. "They're like those sprinkler systems mounted on wheels that roll through farm fields. Only the searchlights aren't watering strawberries. I bet they're equipped with, like, video cameras. Anyone caught in the glare of the searchlights gets picked up by them. ICE sees them on a monitor and sends guys in cars, trucks, and ATVs after them." He handed her the compass and shoved the truck into gear. "Point me north, dead north."

Natalia was too upset to focus on the compass. Her dream for a life with Vaclav was crumbling, rotting away like the arm on that cactus.

"Mexico won't build a pinche brick-and-mortar wall, so Funck builds a wall of American technology!" It was pitch dark. With the headlights off, Angel was driving blind, jolting over rocks and sideswiping cacti. "Are we heading north?"

When she didn't answer, he looked over and saw the tears on her face. "Look, I'm as sorry about this as you are, but I'll get you to TJ, I swear." He read the doubt on her face. "Chica, have I ever let you down?"

She wasn't angry at Angel. Right now, she was too disappointed, too sad, to feel any emotion. "If my mother wasn't such a suka, a bitch, y'know what I'd say right now?"

"What?"

"I want my mamina," she whimpered.

Angel's eyes suddenly widened, as if he was seeing a vision. A smile erupted on his face.

"What's so funny? I didn't mean it as a joke."

"You want your mamina? Your *mommy*?"

Natalia shook her head. "No, forget it. I don't. I definitely do *not* want my mother right now. My mother is a world-class suka! She will be overjoyed when I go back to the White House because I can't get into Mexico. She will kiss Rex's feet. She will kiss his fat disgusting ass!"

"Chica, you're not going back to the White House!"

"Oh, really? *What?* We're going to drive over the Mexican border, like we're tourists? What do we use for passports?"

"We won't need passports cuz we're going to see *my* mommy."

"*Your* mother?"

"*Mi mamacita* is NOT a bitch. She's a wonderful, kind, generous, and sweet woman I love even more than I love you. Sorry, chica, but, like, she's my mom. She's also brave. So brave she is going to drive us across the pinche border herself!"

Part IV

Chapter 36

San Diego, CA

December 18, 10:30 p.m.

U.D. Officer James Conner walked off Delta flight #1345 from Washington, D.C. with a swagger in his step. He wore his only newish pair of jeans, his only button-down white shirt without a frayed collar, and over it a black North Face puffer vest he had "borrowed" from the U.D. staff locker room at the White House. He had been too amped up to sleep on the plane and he was too amped up to sleep now. Tomorrow my life will change forever, he thought.

Conner had no doubt in his mind that he would pull off his assignment from the First Daughter, a mission straight from POTUS himself. After his success, he was certain that he would be promoted to the rank of Secret Service special agent. No more wimpy U.D. uniform, complete with ASP aluminum tactical baton and pepper spray; it made him look like a goddamn flatfoot. No more tedious days checking IDs at the White House staff entrance. He pictured himself as a babe magnet in a sleek black suit and tie, packing a Sig Sauer P229 handgun, on his dream assignment: striding alongside the President's limo in a Presidential motorcade, one hand on the shiny black metal skin of the "Beast," one hand on his 12-gauge Remington 870 shotgun. Or wait... What I really want to do is *drive* the Beast, he thought.

As he walked through San Diego International Airport, Conner spotted a Sunglass Hut kiosk. The vendor, a young Chicana, was locking up. He hustled over and persuaded her to stay open so that he could buy a pair. "It won't take long. I know the shades I want," he assured her. He zeroed in on a pair of Ray-Ban Aviators with polarized lenses and slipped them on. At $180, they were the most expensive sunglasses he had ever bought. I don't give a shit, he thought. All special agents wear Ray-Bans.

"Do I look cool?" he asked her as he admired himself in the mirror.

"Absolutely."

He thought of asking the chick to have a drink with him in the airport bar. Maybe after renting his car, he could fuck her in it before heading to TJ. He checked her out and decided against it. She wasn't that hot; her tits were the size of marshmallows. Besides, he had a job to do. He thanked her and walked in the direction of the sign: "Rental Cars."

Chapter 37

Rosarito Beach, MX

December 19, 2:00 a.m.

Conner checked the GPS on his rental car. He'd been on the ground for nearly three hours since his plane landed in San Diego, but he was still a few blocks away from his destination. It had taken a shitload of time just to rent this piece of garbage at the airport. Thrifty had charged him so much for extra insurance to drive into Mexico, that he could have bought the damn car. Not that I'd ever want to own a Ford Fiesta, he thought. No class.

According to the rental-agent nerd, the cost of insurance for a Ford Fiesta was half of what it was for a Mustang or an SUV, cars that drug dealers love, because the chances those cars will get ripped off in TJ are twice as high. Conner sure wished he could have afforded the one black Escalade on the rental lot. It would have been good practice for driving the "Beast" in a Presidential motorcade. "Sorry, sir," the Thrifty asshole had said. "We can't rent you an Escalade if you're driving to Mexico."

At 1:30 a.m., the border crossing itself had been a piece of cake. The line was mostly trucks. Conner's was one of the few cars and the border agent didn't even ask his purpose of entry. The dude must have taken one look at me—a stud wearing Ray-Bans, even in the middle of the night—and figured I'm going to TJ to get drunk and get laid, he thought. Don't I wish.

As he drove through Tijuana, he was surprised to find that it was a big modern city with eight-lane freeways, high-rise buildings, and shopping malls. It was the slums in the city outskirts that blew his mind: thousands of shacks made of cardboard boxes, old tires, and scraps of tin. Conner had never seen such wretched shantytowns. It sucks, big-time, to be poor in Mexico, he thought. But better the poor sons-of-bitches stay and rot in Mexican slums than come to pollute America.

"Turn left on Calle Cantil," said the GPS voice. As Conner hung a louie, he had to admit that the neighborhood was getting nicer. A road sign indicated that he was leaving the Tijuana city limits and entering Rosarito Beach. According to the GPS, he was a mile from the ocean. The houses here were made of stucco painted white or pastel colors. Some had two stories, windows covered with decorative iron grates, and satellite dishes on the tiled roofs. All were surrounded by cinderblock fences topped with shards of broken Coke bottles, or steel fences topped with sharp-pointed pickets. Either would nail the ass of a crook attempting to break in, he thought.

Conner reached the address he was looking for, 434 Calle El Toro, parked in front, and rummaged in his backpack. He pulled out the copy of an old *People* article that Gretchen had given him, *FLOTUS Is Besties with her Barber*, and reread it. It was about Angel Garcia's rise to fame as the First Lady's hairdresser and how when Angel made enough money, he moved his family out of the Tijuana slums into this very house. Conner looked out the window at it. "Shit," he grumbled. It pissed him off that the greaser homo's family was living in a three-story stucco house with a satellite dish big enough to get TV channels from Mars. His headlights revealed what he considered the only consolation: The house was painted pink. I may live in a shithole, he thought, but at least it's not pussy pink.

The house lights were off, so he climbed out of the car and walked over to the steel gate to check out the driveway. A security sensor light over the garage flashed on. As he feared, an alarm blared. He knew he had only a few seconds to ascertain a positive ID on the Garcia house. He glimpsed what he was looking for: a food truck parked alongside it. He took off his Ray-Bans so that he could ID the name on the truck: "Mama G's Tacos." Even without his sunglasses, it was too dark to make out the food truck's decorations. All he could see was that whoever painted them had used a lot of Pepto-Bismol pink.

With the house-alarm blaring, Conner took off in the rental car. He drove with the lights off until he was three blocks away. He heard no sirens. So much for Mexican home security, he thought, then turned on his headlights and cruised through the neighborhood. His plan was to return and stake out the house before sunrise. If Angel Garcia was in Tijuana with the First Lady, he figured that there was a 50-50 chance that he had brought her to his family's house. If Angel and the First Lady were inside, asleep, he would spot them there in the morning. If he didn't, he would follow Angel's mother when she left in the food truck. According to the *People* article, the Mama G's Tacos food truck that Angel bought his mother had made her rich and famous — at least for a Mexican in TJ. "Follow his mother," Gretchen Funck had instructed him. "She'll know where they are." Conner hated his own mother and had never done shit for her, so he had to take the First Daughter's word for it.

He drove west, following the GPS route to the beach. In a few blocks, the houses gave way to sand dunes and the pot-holed asphalt road dwindled to a gravel trail. He pulled over, climbed out of the car, and walked in the chilly night air to the edge of an ocean bluff.

The beach below was shrouded in fog, but he could hear the *thump* of what he guessed were motherfucking-big waves slamming the sand. The thump reminded him of the sound his regulation ASP aluminum tactical baton had made on the back of a crazy Indian with a butcher knife who tried to break into the White House one time on Conner's watch. It had been his most exciting day on the job. Once he was promoted to special agent, he knew his job would be much more exciting. I won't be stuck pacifying nut jobs with a stick, he thought. I'll do it with a SIG V-Crown nickel-case, stacked hollow-point bullet.

Through the fog, Conner could make out the blinking "Vacancy" signs on a few beach hotels in the distance. No one wants to stay overnight at the beach in the fog, he thought. He was more interested in the colored lights on the beach directly below him. From the canned salsa music and the shrill laughter of what he hoped were shit-faced señoritas, he figured there was a beach bar that was still open, maybe one with a thatched roof and palm trees, like in a Corona commercial. He checked his watch. Three hours until sunrise. Why not make the most of it?

As if in response to his question, the fog dissipated, revealing a steep path to the sand. He climbed down it, his hands getting pricked by the needles of cacti he carelessly grabbed to keep from slipping. At the bottom was an open-air shack of a drinking hole, its thatched roof as scruffy as a half-plucked chicken. Okay, so it wasn't the beach party in a Corona commercial, but two hot young Mexican babes were sitting on stools and drinking, *yep*, Coronas. They wore short shorts and low-cut T-shirts that revealed the biggest boobs he'd seen in a long time that he could swear were real. He was glad that he had consulted Grandpa Google and discovered that the age of consent in Mexico is seventeen. The bimbos looked just this side of legal.

He slipped his Ray-Bans back on and strode toward them. "*Muchachas,*" he called, using one of the only words he remembered from ninth-grade Spanish. He held out his scratched-up hands, and in what he determined was an enticing come-on, said, "I got stuck with cactus needles. Which of you ladies wants to suck them out?"

They smiled coyly. As he stepped closer, he was surprised to see that they had attractive faces and naturally plump lips. He was already imagining how good it would feel to have them wrapped around his dick.

Twenty minutes, three Coronas, and one killer reefer later, Conner was leading the girls back up the rocky path to his car. Or, rather, they were leading him. One of his hands was tucked into the ripped back pocket of the short shorts worn by Rosa, the hotter of the two. His other hand was parked in the back pocket of her friend Maria. Neither hottie was wearing undies. Instead of cactus needles, his fingers were squeezing soft warm bootie. He felt like the luckiest white dude in TJ, except for one thing. I sure wish I had that black Escalade from the car-rental lot, instead of a piece-of-shit Ford Fiesta, to fuck them in, he thought.

They reached the bluff and walked toward his car. He squinted into a bank of security lights beaming from an ocean cliff to the north of them. He realized that he hadn't noticed the lights before because they were hidden by fog. As his eyes adjusted to the glare, he saw that they were positioned atop a wrought-iron fence enclosing a white-marble mansion that was ten times larger than any he had ever seen in D.C. It pissed him off that some rich greaser dared to build a house that big.

"Who the hell lives there?" he asked. Suddenly, his head was spinning. He saw stars. He'd drunk three beers and shared a joint with women plenty of times before, but *this*...

Dark tentacles engulfed his brain and his legs gave out.

"I'm fucked," Conner whispered before all went black.

Chapter 38

Washington, D.C.

December 19, 9 a.m.

"Welcome to Georgetown University Hospital, Mr. President, Madame First Lady," said the willowy young Asian woman with a flawless ivory complexion. Moon thought she couldn't possibly be older than sixteen. Was she really a doctor? She was wearing a white medical jacket and a stethoscope dangled from her neck. Moon read the woman's nametag: "Dr. Yvonne Chang." Note to self, she thought. Google what Chinese women put on their skin to look so goddamned young.

Dr. Chang bowed slightly. "We are honored to have you visit our children today, Mr. President."

"It's our pleasure," replied Funck, but Moon could see that he was lying: He neither smiled nor made eye contact with the doctor. As they followed Dr. Chang down the spotlessly clean hospital corridor, the President's neck remained rigid, but Moon could see his eyes dancing around, as if he were searching for an emergency exit. For a man who always swung his arms forcefully when he walked, it was unusual to see his hands plunged deep into his overcoat pockets. And why was he wearing an overcoat anyway? It was a good 75 degrees in here. The minute they had walked into the hospital, Moon had taken off her prim blue-wool Dior coat and slung it over her arm. She noticed beads of sweat shimmering on Funck's nose. He is creeped out by all the germs he imagines in here, she thought. Bad for the President; good for me.

They entered what looked like a playroom at a rich-kids' nursery school. It was packed with a dozen members of the press corps, whose cameras clicked away at them. The walls were decorated with Disney posters; the shelves were filled with kids' books and games; and kid-height tables were piled with colorful puzzles and toys. But the children playing in the room were not those you'd see at an upscale nursery school. Wearing hospital gowns decorated with cartoon characters, some of them were rail-thin, others were unnaturally bloated. All had silicone ports implanted in their arms for administering intravenous drugs and taking blood samples. A few wore over-the-ear nasal cannulas attached to portable oxygen tanks, while several were propped up by blankets in oversized Radio Flyer Red Wagons. Moon knew from her nursing experience that in hospital children's wards, the wagons were often used as a kid-friendly alternative to wheelchairs.

She glanced over at Funck. He grabbed a handkerchief held out by Special Agent Pricker and wiped the sweat from his face, his jaw flexing. She guessed that he was grinding his teeth, counting the minutes until he could get the hell out of here.

"Would you like to read to the children, Mr. President?" said Sally-Ann, who had accompanied the First Couple to the hospital.

"Let's have the First Lady do it." Funck plunged his hands deeper into his pockets. "She's great at reading to kids."

Moon glimpsed the terror on Sally-Ann's face. Sally-Ann thinks I'll blow my cover when I open my mouth, she thought. "I'd be delighted to read to the children," she said in her best Natalia voice.

The photographers frantically snapped away as Moon picked a book from the shelf— *Where the Wild Things Are*. It had been her favorite kids' book when she was a little boy. The nurses gathered the children together. She adjusted the white-silk scarf she wore around her neck to hide her bulbous Adam's apple, reminding herself not to let the press get a possibly revealing profile shot.

She looked around for a place to sit. Dr. Chang brought over a kids-sized chair. "I'm afraid this is all we've got."

Moon saw Sally-Ann turn pale as she lowered herself down onto the mini-chair, the hem of her tight blue dress threatening to hike up above her knees. A few of the photographers were smirking, as if waiting for the chance to "upskirt" the First Lady. To prevent one of them from getting a shot up her dress, Moon squeezed her thighs together and slung her coat over them.

She rested the book on top of the coat and began to read: *"The night Max wore his wolf suit and made mischief of one kind... and another."*

* * *

"Thank you so much for coming today," said Dr. Chang, shaking hands with the President and the First Lady as they walked out of the children's ward. "It meant so much to the kids!"

"Our pleasure." Funck forced a smile for the cameras, then steered Moon toward the hospital exit. Agent Pricker was waiting to open the door for them.

"Wait!" Moon turned back to the doctor. "Does the hospital have a hospice ward, Dr. Chang? Rex and I take a particular interest in end-of-life hospice care."

"Of course," she said. "How wonderful! I'm sure the hospice patients will be thrilled to see you." She pulled the cell phone from the pocket of her medical jacket. "Just give me one minute."

As Dr. Chang made a call, Funck moved closer to Moon. "What the fuck?" he whispered. "No way am I visiting a ward where people are fucking dying!"

Moon savored the panic on his face. "I thought it would be a kind gesture."

Rex nodded to Sally-Ann. "Call Gretchen."

Sally-Ann hurriedly stepped into a corner and made a call. She talked, listened, nodded, and hung up. She walked back to the First Couple. "Gretchen says nobody wants to see dying people," she whispered. "She says it's a, uh, fucking downer. A shit photo op."

Funck sneered at Moon. "What did I fucking *tell*—?"

"The hospice patients are so excited to meet you, President Funck, Madame First Lady!" Dr. Chang pocketed her cell phone.

"Too late," Moon whispered to Rex and Sally-Ann, feeling as mischievous as Max in *Where the Wild Things Are.* She eagerly followed Dr. Chang down the hall and into an elevator. A reluctant Sally-Ann, and an even more reluctant President Funck, followed.

The elevator doors opened on the fourth floor. A dozen hospice patients had been lined up in wheelchairs along one wall. Their faces were gaunt, their skin was pallid, and their bodies were frail. A few smiled weakly. Moon recognized the look of the dying and thought of her patients at the Good Samaritan Hospital in Miami. As soon as my White House prison term ends, I'm hanging up my Natalia wig for good, she thought. My work with hospice patients is what makes life worth living.

Moon walked graciously down the unlikely receiving line. She warmly greeted each patient with a few words— *"What a beautiful smile!" "I'm so happy to meet you!" "You look nice today!"* — and shook their hands. The bones of their fingers felt as light as the hollow bones of birds. With the patients that she sensed had only a few days more to live, she bent down and gently kissed their delicate cheeks. She was too caught up in the poignant moment to notice the chatter of cameras around her.

Until the chatter stopped.

She turned and saw that Funck was standing at the beginning of the "reception line." His hands were buried in his pockets, his jaw was thrust out, and his lips were pressed tightly together. All eyes were on him, but he was in vapor lock.

"Rex, darling!" Moon walked over to him. "I want you to meet my friends." She discretely pulled his right hand out of his pocket and nudged him toward the first patient in the line. She judged that the man was in his early thirties, but with his head bald and gray pallor, no doubt from chemo, he looked ancient. He was hunched over in his wheelchair, his hands on his lap. They were covered with scaly-red patches of psoriasis.

"You're Oliver, right?" she said, remembering his name. The man nodded weakly. Moon turned to Funck. "Mr. President, meet my friend, Oliver."

Oliver weakly lifted one of his scabby hands. Rex looked at it with ill-concealed disgust, then at the photographers. Their cameras were poised to catch the moment. He shot Moon a look that said, "I'll kill you for this," and shook the dying man's hand. The cameras clicked away.

As if he had been jolted with electricity, Funck jerked back his hand.

"Sorry, got to go!" He waved at the photographers and turned to leave. They continued snapping photos as Pricker escorted Funck, and then Moon and Sally-Ann, into the elevator. He waved again as the doors closed.

The photo of Rex waving isn't the photo that will end up on TV tonight, thought Moon, satisfied that she had accomplished her mission. It will be the photo of a horrified President Funck getting his hand zapped by a dying man in the hospice ward.

Chapter 39

Rosarito Beach, MX

December 19, 6:00 a.m.

Conner's eyes were glued shut. He willed them to open. Nothing happened. I'm a fucking Secret Service special agent, he told himself. Special Agent Conner, open your fucking eyes!

* * *

Conner awoke slowly from a dream about crawling out of a tunnel lined with prickly cactus needles. They were painfully jabbing him in his arms, his legs, his ass. It took him a few minutes to comprehend that his sweaty, six-foot-tall body was uncomfortably wedged into the back seat of a very small car, his head jammed against a scorching-hot window. Then, like exploding shrapnel, the memory hit him all at once: the steep rocky path to the beach last night; the Latinas with the great tits and killer weed.

Shit, he thought, did I get *rolled*?

Conner had an old high-school buddy, Chuck, who tended bar at his favorite neighborhood joint in D.C. Chuck had warned him again and again: "Don't fucking pick up sluts in bars! You think you're hooking up with a ho for some fast fun, a bitch too scuzzy even for Tinder. Before you can whip out your cock, she slips you something — maybe in your beer, maybe in a capsule she shoves down your throat with a sloppy French kiss. You wake up with your pants around your knees, your wallet missing, and your car off somewhere getting repainted to ship to Nicaragua!"

Despite Chuck's warnings, Conner had picked up plenty of sluts at plenty of bars, including Chuck's, and the dude's sluts-from-hell horror story had never happened to him. "I guess they love my dick too much," he had boasted to Chuck. He swore he would never tell Chuck that the sluts in TJ didn't give a shit about his dick. The last words he whispered before passing out last night came back to him. This time he screamed them: "I'm fucked!"

Conner scrambled out of the back seat and onto the passenger seat of the Ford Fiesta. Not even TJ whores had bothered stealing this piece-of-shit car, he thought. He spotted his wallet wedged under the gas pedal and snatched it. The bitches had taken the $100 in twenties he got from an airport ATM, but they had left his driver's license and passport. Thank you, Lord Jesus, he thought.

He discovered his backpack squashed under the driver's seat and emptied out the contents. The intel items that Gretchen gave him had been tossed like a bad hand of poker. He scooped them up and laid them out on the dashboard. Present and accounted for were the ID photos of Angel and the First Lady, and a printout of the Facebook page for a band in Prague called Zlatorog and the Dragons. The rockers in the profile picture looked scuzzy—long hair, tattoos, earrings—but he had to admit that the guitarist was hot. Gretchen had told Conner his name was Vaclav and alerted him to be on the lookout. She suspected that Natalia might be meeting up with him. After seeing photos of the First Lady with the President, he couldn't picture her with this lowlife, no matter how hot he was.

Conner was relieved that the printout of the *People* article was still there too. Once more, he told himself, I'm one lucky white dude. The hookers may have taken my money, but they didn't touch what's much more valuable—if you want to blackmail the President of the United States. He figured that even if the señoritas could speak some English, they had been too stupid to read the article. And that they were no doubt too poor to own a TV. If they hadn't watched Funck's inauguration, they might never have seen the First Lady. And why would a Mexican bimbo watch the inauguration or care about the First Lady of the United States, anyway?

To his surprise, the hos had not taken the black-steel tactical handcuffs that Pricker issued him. Conner figured the girls might have wanted them for S&M, but oh well. Another lucky-white-dude point for me, he thought. His instructions were that once he found the First Lady, he was to cuff her gently and call the White House ASAP.

Call the White House?

Panicking, he checked his pants pocket. Lordy, Lordy! His iPhone was still there.

He was about to check the pocket of his North Face puffer vest for his Ray-Bans, when he realized that he wasn't wearing the vest or the sunglasses, and that they were not in the car. *Shit.* The boss vest that he had "borrowed" from the White House staff locker room and the awesome shades that he had shelled out $180 for were gone.

He remembered letting Rosa, the whore with the biggest tits, wear his Ray-Bans last night. "I want to look cool, like you," she said flirtatiously as she ran her fingers over his crotch. She *had* looked foxy in them, the bitch. He realized that he would never be able to wear Ray-Bans without picturing that moment. I definitely got fucking rolled, he thought.

Conner drove back at high speed to the Garcia family house. He made it there by 6:05 a.m., but he saw no lights on or people inside, and Mama G's food truck was gone. Still groggy from whatever had hit him last night, he sat in the car with the engine off for an hour, staking out the house. The lights stayed off and no people appeared to be inside—and it was getting fucking hot in his car.

I'm a smart soon-to-be Secret Service special agent even if I did blow it last night, he told himself, as he fumbled to figure out his next move. His stomach growled. It reminded him that he had read in the *People* article that Mama G's Tacos were such a hit, every day Angel's mom drove the food truck around TJ, making stops where fans lined up for her tacos.

That's it! he thought. I'll hit every street in TJ where foodies go!

He turned on the car's engine and then the AC. All that spewed out of the vents was hot air. He sighed. On top of all the other bad shit that had come down on him, he refused to let the broken AC piss him off. He focused on finding Mama G's food truck, trying to picture what it had looked like in the shadowy driveway of the Garcia house last night. All he remembered was that there were a lot of decorations painted on it, in a lot of pink.

"Follow the pink," he said out loud as he gunned it to downtown Tijuana.

Chapter 40

San Diego, CA

December 19, 11:30 a.m.

"You painted it?" Natalia asked Angel. Sitting beside him on a wrought-iron bench across the street, she was admiring the decorations covering every inch of Mama G's Tacos food truck: swirls of pinks, reds, and purples, like interlocking rainbows; pink-and-green butterflies; and lush pink tropical flowers. Mama G's was the most colorful of the food trucks parked nose-to-tail around a cobblestone square in San Diego's Old Town, beating out Bitchin' Burgers, Haad Sai Thai Food, and Groovy Greek. Mama G's also has the longest line of customers waiting for them to open, she thought.

"Mexican plus gay equals 'artistic,'" Angel joked. "Like I told you, bright colors make you happy even when there's nada to be happy about. It's, like, a Mexican thing. A gay thing too."

"In Slovakia, everything is gray, brown, or...gray," she said. "People are depressed and they stay depressed."

"You like my Frida Kahlo touch?" He pointed to replicas of the famous artist's self-portraits on the truck. He had added bluebird's wings to one, angel's wings to another.

"Love them!"

"Y'know, Frida was almost killed in a bus accident. She spent the rest of her life in, like, a body cast, sometimes in a wheelchair, or in bed." He read an inscription above the truck's service window: *"Feet, what do I need you for when I have wings to fly?"*

"That's beautiful."

"Frida said that. It's my mom's favorite quote."

"Is that your mother?" Natalia nodded toward a small Mexican woman sliding open the service window from inside the Mama G's food truck. She was wearing a hot-pink Mama G's logo cap and apron.

He nodded. "Oralia Garcia. I think I told you, she's stuck in a wheelchair. When I was a kid and we lived in the *barrios bajos*, the slums, she was caught in the crossfire of a gang fight."

Natalia gently touched his hand, then watched as Oralia smiled and waved to the customers lining up outside the truck. They waved back. "Her customers sure love her."

"Me too," said Angel.

The back doors of the food truck opened. A Mexican man maybe in his fifties, but looking older, lowered a ramp to the street and stepped down it. He couldn't have been more than five-feet four, like Angel, and he had Angel's bushy eyebrows. Definitely Angel's father, she thought. Wearing a hot-pink Mama G's Tacos baseball cap and apron, like his wife Oralia, he walked around to the side of the truck and flipped up a portable counter under the service window.

"Your dad looks like you!" she said.

"You mean he's a camarón!"

"A guapo camarón, like his son! What's his name?"

"Armando."

She watched as Oralia handed bottles of El Pato and La Victoria hot sauce and bowls of fresh salsa to Armando through the opening. He placed them on the counter.

"Seeing your mom in action, you'd never guess she was in a wheelchair."

"When I got her the food truck I had it retrofitted. Then that story about you and me came out in *People*. It kinda put her on the map. Some gringo foodies got so psyched about her fish tacos in TJ, they invited her to join the food-truck gathering here in San Diego on Fridays. Mama G's is the only food truck that comes all the way up from TJ for it. They got her, like, a special border pass."

"Now I'm beginning to understand why we're sitting here,

disguised as Mexican workers." The only item from what Angel called his "old life" was his red Gucci satchel. It was stuffed into a brown paper Walmart shopping bag at his feet.

"So how exactly is your mom going to sneak us into Mexico?" she asked.

"The retrofitters put, like, a false floor in the food truck," he said. "That way, when my mom is in her wheelchair, she is up high enough to cook on the grill and talk out the window to customers. My dad is so short it helps him too. Anyway, under the false floor is another space. It's three feet tall and runs half the length of the truck. It's refrigerated. My mom and dad store, like, fresh tuna, snapper, and shrimp for their tacos in there."

"We're going to hide with the *fish*?"

"Depends how many fish tacos they sell today," he said. "If you're lucky, they'll sell out."

Natalia watched as Armando joined Oralia inside the food truck. They worked as an efficient team as he took orders and she prepared food. "They look much sweeter than my parents," she said. "Mine were always fighting. Mamina knew Papa cheated on her. Instead of leaving him, she used it as her excuse to bitch at him nonstop."

"Lots of Mexicans cheat on their wives. It's, like, a macho thing," said Angel. "But my dad never did. I'd bet my life on it. They really love each other."

"They're lucky," she said wistfully. "So when do we eat? I'm dying for a fish taco."

Angel put his fingers in his mouth and whistled to a couple of Chicano boys who were kicking a soccer ball around the square. They looked over at him. He held up a twenty-dollar bill. They grabbed their ball, crossed the street, and ran over.

"Yo, want a couple of free fish tacos from Mama G's?" Angel said.

The boy in a San Diego Padres T-shirt reached out to grab the money. Angel pulled it away.

"For real?" asked the boy wearing a Xolos of TJ T-shirt.

"For real if you do me a favor." He chatted with the boys in Spanish, took a pen from his pocket, and wrote something on the twenty-dollar bill. Natalia watched as the boys grabbed it, crossed the street, and waited in line at the Mama G's food truck. When it was their turn at the window, the Chicano in the Xolos T-shirt gave the bill to Angel's mother. Oralia read the words on it and glanced up. Natalia saw her eyes meet Angel's, but her face didn't give away that she recognized him.

Minutes later, the boys jogged back to Angel and Natalia with pink Mama G's caps on their heads and a carton full of fish tacos. Angel kept two tacos for him and Natalia and gave the rest to the boys.

"Gracias," they said, and scampered away.

Natalia savored her taco. "*Úžasný!* Fantastic!"

Chapter 41

The White House

December 19, 2:00 p.m.

In the bathroom of the First Lady's bedroom, Moon turned on all six showerheads and raised the water temperature to the maximum. She took a quick pee, then stepped over the blue Dior dress, underwear, and white Adam's-apple-hiding scarf that she had dropped on the floor the moment she and Rex had returned from the hospital. She was glad that she had tricked the President into revealing his germ phobia in front of photographers. She hoped it would make the news tonight and torpedo his ratings. Before then, she planned to take an extremely hot shower, order something beyond delicious to eat from the White House kitchen, and take a long nap in Natalia's heavenly bed.

Scratch that, she thought. Only Gretchen, Rex, Agent Pricker, Sally-Ann, and Hilda know the truth about who I am. The kitchen will continue to send up the real First Lady's inedible health food until Hilda...

Hilda!

Where was Hilda? The Slovak maid was usually poking around in the First Lady's bedroom around this time of day, arranging flowers, straightening clothes in the closet, spying. She wondered if the maid had thought about her proposed bargain yesterday: Hilda helps Moon escape from the White House; Moon takes Hilda to the best sex-reassignment surgeon in the world.

She stepped into the shower, enjoying the blast of hot water on her body from so many angles. This would be a perfect time and place to have a wank, she thought. The problem was, she couldn't talk herself into feeling sexy. All she could think about was getting out of here and going home. She wondered if Eliza, her girlfriend in Miami, was worrying about her. She hoped that dear, sweet Eliza hadn't forgotten her.

After ten minutes, Moon stepped out of the shower and grabbed a towel. Drying herself off, she made her way through the steamy bathroom into the bedroom. Hilda had made the bed while she was away from the White House this morning. She walked over, dropped the towel, and pulled back the downy-soft Frette comforter. She climbed between the sheets, then reached up to adjust the dozens of goose-down-filled pillows, from very small to ridiculously large in size. She realized that the incredible array of soft pillows had become the amenity she most appreciated in the First Lady's bedroom.

Her fingers touched something under the pillows that was not as luxurious as 1000-count-cotton pillowcases. She pulled it out: a white polyester maid's uniform with a "White House" logo embroidered over the breast pocket. A yellow post-it stuck out of the pocket. She read the scrawl: "Under bed." Yay! Hilda heard my plea, she thought.

She climbed out of bed, got down on all fours, her penis and balls brushing against her thighs, and retrieved the items lined up under it: thick-rubber-soled white maids' shoes in her size; a white bra; white panties; and support pantyhose. There was even a pair of men's glasses that looked just like Hilda's. Moon scooped everything up onto the bed and tried on the glasses. Suddenly everything was a blur. Definitely Hilda's. She wondered if the clothes were Hilda's too, or if she had borrowed them from the housekeeping laundry room. She took a sniff. They smelled clean and fresh, as if they'd just come out of a dryer sweetened with strips of Springtime Bounce.

Moon checked to make sure that there was nothing left under the bed, stretching her arm as far out as she could and groping around on the carpet.

"*Yikes!*"

She yanked her arm back, certain that her fingers had touched a dead rat. Realizing that was impossible—there cannot be rats in the White House other than the President, she thought—she reached back in and snatched the furry item. It was a short brown wig, the same "no style" style as Hilda's hair. She slapped the wig onto her bald head, vowing to kiss the maid's feet the next time she saw her. She wondered where and when that would be? Hilda was obviously resourceful. She trusted that Hilda would figure it out.

Moon rushed into the bathroom and hurriedly dressed into her "escape" clothes. She checked herself out in the mirror. She looked like Hilda, but a slimmer Hilda. She returned to the bedroom and grabbed a small pillow from the bed. She stuffed it under her maid's uniform, positioned it over her stomach and tightened the belt to keep the pillow from dropping onto the floor. She rechecked her image in the mirror. The pillow gave her a gut, but not as big as Hilda's. If anyone asks, I'll say I went on a diet, she thought.

There was only one thing about her Hilda imitation that wasn't quite convincing. When Moon walked across the room in her control pantyhose, she didn't make Hilda's "rustling leaves" sound. Her thighs simply weren't fat enough to rub together, like Hilda's did. She pressed her thighs tighter together and walked across the room again. It sounded *sort of* like rustling leaves, very *small* rustling leaves. Close enough. She spotted the discarded white-silk scarf on the bathroom floor and tied it around her Adam's apple. Voila! A jaunty new look for Hilda.

As Moon hastened to the bathroom door, she reminded herself that she had no ID, no money, no iPhone. She had given them to Natalia and Angel. Once she stepped out of the White House, she had no idea how she would get home to Miami. She thought of stopping in the staff-cafeteria kitchen and borrowing money from Stella. But Stella worked the night shift; she wouldn't be there yet. She decided to hang out in the staff cafeteria until Stella showed up.

Moon's musings about exit details were cut short when she walked out of the bathroom. Gretchen was standing in the doorway to the First Lady's bedroom, Sally-Ann one step behind her, like a Secret Service agent.

The First Daughter's face was a mask of anger. In fact, her chin was jutting out the way Rex's had when he threatened to shoot her the other night. The evil daughter is more like the evil father every day, Moon thought. She considered imitating Hilda's voice and saying something like, "I thought I'd go down for fresh towels," or, "Can I get you some afternoon tea, Madam First Daughter?" She knew it was useless.

"You really fucked things up for Daddy this morning," Gretchen said, twisting the pen in her hand as if it were Moon's neck. "If it weren't for the fact that the First Lady came across as a *star* at the hospital, and that we have no alternative, I would have you executed!" She turned to Sally-Ann. "You are not to let our pseudo, *psycho*, FLOTUS out of your sight until we figure out next steps."

"Yes, ma'am," said the social secretary, without a hint of enthusiasm.

"And you…" Gretchen said to Moon. "Take off Hilda's fucking uniform, not that Hilda can use it."

"You fired Hilda?" She felt sad, but only a little guilty.

Without answering, Gretchen walked out the door and locked it noisily from outside.

Moon turned to Sally-Ann. "So, do you like the *Ellen DeGeneres Show*?"

Sally-Ann sighed, defeated.

Chapter 42

San Diego, CA

December 19, 2:00 p.m.

In the unseasonably record-high temperature for December, 80 degrees F, the ice cubes in Phil's iced latte had melted, but he sipped the tepid drink anyway. He didn't want to spend $4.95 for another fruit-and-nut protein bar that would disappear in three bites. He intended to stretch the two hundred dollars in cash he had brought from Los Angeles for travel expenses. Who knew how many more days he would be on the road? I'll get my daily requirement of protein from what's left of the latte milk, he thought.

Phil had been sitting on the Starbucks patio in San Diego's Old Town for the past three hours, his laptop open as if he were working on a screenplay, like other poor souls who hung out at Starbucks in Southern California. But he wasn't writing a screenplay. He was taking advantage of the free Wi-Fi to do additional research on the topic that obsessed him: the First Lady's escape from the White House. "Be prepared" was the Boy Scout motto. Phil had never forgotten it. For the first time, he was glad that he had excelled in the Boy Scouts. It was just about the only organization in which he did.

He certainly had done a thorough investigation. Googling Angel Garcia had led him to the *People* article about the Mexican hairdresser and the First Lady and how Angel bought his mom a food truck. Googling Mama G's Tacos had led him to San Diego Yelp. That's where Phil learned that Angel's mother's taco truck was now part of the lunchtime food-truck gathering in San Diego's Old Town on Fridays, which, his good luck, was today.

Phil knew that his theory about the First Lady escaping from the White House bordered on bat-shit crazy. There had been no mention about it in the press, but still he believed that his assumption was correct. His photos of Angel Garcia leaving the White House with a tall trans woman had led him on Google to a trans woman named Moon Kusnetzov, who did an amazingly realistic impersonation of the First Lady at the Cross Queen nightclub in South Beach. When he called the club, he learned that Moon hadn't shown up for work for the past two nights and hadn't called to explain.

Then there was the official White House Christmas photo on TV yesterday, in which the First Lady was standing next to the President. Since following Natalia on the First Lady paparazzi trail, Phil had taken hundreds of photos of her. He might be the only person in the world who believed it, but he was convinced that the First Lady in the official White House Christmas photo was not the *real* First Lady. Phil was certain that it was Moon Kusnetzov.

Today, he had hit the jackpot. Or at least he was certain that he would before the day ended. He had been sitting across the street from the Mama G's Tacos truck since 11:30 a.m., watching a diminutive Mexican lady and her husband, no doubt Angel Garcia's parents, selling tacos to happy customers. He also was keeping his eye on a couple of unkempt Mexican workmen sitting on a bench across the street, a rumpled brown-paper Walmart bag at their feet. The men had been there when he arrived this morning; they hadn't moved since. Why would Mexican workers hang out on a park bench in San Diego's Old Town, a tourist destination? Were they waiting until it got dark enough to rob tourists?

Phil had thought it was a possibility until he saw the smaller of the two workmen give $20 to some Chicano kids for tacos at Mama G's. When the boys gave her the twenty-dollar bill, Angel's mother glanced at the workers. Phil noticed that the look on her face wasn't his own mother's usual "I'm expecting to be disappointed" wariness. It was as if Señora Garcia were fighting back her elation at seeing someone she loved, so as not to give it away.

He had a hunch that the short Mexican worker in the ratty clothes was Angel Garcia, and that the tall Mexican worker was Natalia, the First Lady of the United States. There was one way to prove it. It would happen momentarily, when lunch ended and the food trucks left.

He reached into his camera bag and stroked his new 600-mm Nikon telephoto lens. Some paparazzi had little dogs that they carried around with them for security, friendship, and good luck. Phil's new state-of-the-art lens did it for him. He was grateful that his mother had given him the money for it and proud of himself for talking the guys at Samy's Camera into selling it to him for $6,500, nearly $4,000 off retail. Soon this lens will make me a fortune and my mother will finally be proud of me, he thought.

By 2:15 p.m., the lunch customers were drifting away and the food-truck owners were closing up. He watched as Angel's father stepped out of the back of the Mama G's truck and walked around to the side window. He removed the dishes of salsa and hot sauce on the portable serving counter and handed them up through the service window to his wife inside the truck. Then he secured the service counter against the side of the truck. Inside it, Mrs. Garcia closed the serving window and pulled down a window shade with the Mrs. G's Tacos logo on it.

Phil wiped the sweat from his brow, took out his camera and slung the strap around his neck. He turned his attention to the Mexican workers on the park bench. As Angel's father walked up the ramp at the back of the truck, the short worker picked up the grubby Walmart bag, and the two workers got up and started toward the truck. He clicked a few photos of them. From so far away, he was astounded at how much detail his new telephoto lens captured. It even caught something red poking out of the Walmart bag.

He had planned to compare these new photos to the photos he had taken of Angel and the trans woman leaving the White House. He realized that he didn't need to. As he watched the two workers cross the street and climb into the food truck, he felt certain that the difference between their heights was the same as that between Angel and the trans woman in the earlier photo. The tall Mexican workman was the First Lady in disguise; he would swear it on his mother's life.

He got a few more shots off before the food-truck doors closed behind the workers. He heard an excited cry from inside: A mother greeting a son she hadn't seen in a long time? Señor Garcia climbed behind the wheel, turned on the engine, and pulled out from the curb.

Phil hustled across the street, over to his rented Chevy. He jumped into the car and raced to catch up with the food truck. The truck was so colorfully decorated, it was easy to tail, even in heavy traffic.

As he expected, soon the food truck merged onto Interstate Highway 5, heading south in the direction of the U.S.–Mexico Border Crossing. According to his GPS, it would take twenty-five minutes. Today would be the first time Phil traveled outside the borders of the United States. He was excited, yet nervous. He shoved the Nikon camera and mega-lens back into his camera bag, pulled out his passport, and laid it on the passenger seat. He put his hand into his backpack to reassure himself that he had brought along a manila file folder.

He had done his research about crossing the border too. He discovered that sometimes border guards ask a lot of questions, such as "What is the purpose of your visit to Mexico?" They did it to see if they can psych you out and get you to reveal some secret, illegal motive. Maybe he was being paranoid, but he had decided to do the Boy Scout thing and come prepared. The file folder held eight-by-ten-inch black-and-white photos of Pasadena's historical buildings and landmarks that he took when he was in high school. If questioned about why he was going to Mexico, he planned to show them to the border guards and say that he was going to take photos of Tijuana's historical buildings and landmarks. He would flatter them about how marvelous they were: the Avenida Revolucion, with its dramatic peace arch; the beautiful Catedral de Nuestra Señora de Guadalupe; and Caesar's, the 1924 art-deco restaurant where the famous Caesar salad was invented.

As he rehearsed the names in his head, an idea occurred to Phil: After taking the big-bucks photos of the First Lady, why not stop at Caesar's Restaurant to celebrate before he returned to the United States? If he got the goods on her, and whomever she was with, he would be able to afford a lot more than a Caesar salad.

Chapter 43

Mexico–U.S. Border Crossing, CA

December 19, 3:30 p.m.

The twenty-five-lane southbound highway from the United States into Mexico was packed with cars and trucks, but at least they were moving. It could be worse, thought Oralia Garcia. The thirty-four-lane highway northbound from Tijuana into the United States was in gridlock. She surveyed the bleak sight through the windshield of the Mama G's Tacos food truck, where she sat in her wheelchair in the passenger space that had been retrofitted to hold it safely. Her husband Armando was at the wheel beside her.

Oralia was always happy to be driving home on Friday afternoon after a good day at the food-truck gathering in San Diego. Today she was even happier. She didn't understand exactly why—Angel hadn't had time to explain—but hidden under the false floor in the back of the truck with her son was a disguised, but very important, passenger. She hoped that they weren't freezing in the refrigerated compartment. She also hoped that the truck wouldn't be stopped at the border. In the year that she and Armando had been driving their food truck to San Diego and back on Fridays, the U.S. border patrols going either way had never searched their vehicle. She was somewhat of a local legend thanks to her son's renown as the hairdresser to the First Lady of the United States and the media coverage of her food truck. She always prepared half-a-dozen fish tacos to give the border-patrol officers when they went through passport control into the United States in the morning, and another batch for when they returned to Mexico in the afternoon. The guards on both sides of the border appreciated them. It worried her that today they had sold all their tacos in San Diego. Maybe it was the unseasonably warm weather for December, but there had been as many customers as on a summer day.

There were only two vehicles in front of them. Soon it would be Armando's turn to drive up to the booth and show their passports and the special U.S. visa that they had been issued to sell tacos at the Friday food-truck gathering in San Diego. She hoped the U.S. border patrol officer on duty today was Raul Vallejo, the young bilingual Chicano who was usually stationed at Booth 24 on Friday afternoons. In fact, it was because they liked Raul so much that they always tried to drive through border control in the twenty-fourth lane.

But as the truck crept closer, Oralia could see that the duty officer at Booth 24 was not Raul. It was an older man who was definitely not Chicano. His neck was bigger than her waistline; it was red and sweaty from the heat. His face was red and sweaty too, and it was contorted in a scowl. Oralia and Armando had heard rumors that President Funck had begun sending stricter, and meaner, border-patrol officers to the San Ysidro Port of Entry, one of the busiest border crossings on the entire U.S.–Mexico border. Their instructions were to harass anyone Hispanic, whether or not they were U.S. citizens and whether they were heading north from Mexico into the United States, or south from the United States into Mexico.

The officer was shouting at the driver of a pickup truck driven by an elderly Mexican man in a green gardener's uniform, a tattered straw hat on his head. Oralia couldn't hear their conversation, but the officer was stabbing his finger at a nearby inspection station, no doubt commanding the gardener to drive his truck over to it for a search. The truck started toward it, smoke trailing from its crooked exhaust pipe. What if the gringo sent them to the inspection station too? She looked over at her husband. His eyes were wide and sweat was dripping down his forehead. Armando is as terrified as I am, she thought.

The officer glared at the food truck as they pulled up to his booth, shaking his head and snickering, as if disgusted with the bright colors and fanciful Frida paintings. Just as he stepped toward Armando's window, a phone rang in his booth. He walked into the booth and answered it. They watched as he rolled his eyes and gritted his teeth, seemingly resenting whatever instructions he was getting from his boss. He slammed down the phone and sauntered back out to the food truck. Grumbling to himself, he grabbed their passports and visas from Armando. Oralia held her breath as he studied the documents.

To her relief, the officer wiped his brow on his sleeve and slapped them back into Armando's hand. "Move it," he yelled. "It's like a goddamn cattle drive today! Gotta keep moving!"

* * *

Hidden under the plywood false floor of the food truck, Natalia and Angel heard the officer shouting, though they couldn't make out his words. They held their breaths. Then they heard two stomps of Armando's foot on the floor of the driver's compartment. It was the signal that they had been waiting for: They were safely through U.S. passport control. The gears groaned as the truck lurched forward.

"Welcome to Mexico, mi amor," whispered Angel. They were lying on their sides like spoons, Angel in front of Natalia, his head pressed against her breasts, his butt nestled against her crotch. It was the only way the two of them had been able to fit into the cramped space. Oralia had turned off the refrigerator, but it was still cold. Natalia held Angel tightly in her arms, as if she were protecting a child from the chill.

"No fish in here, but it sure smells like fish," she said.

"It's me," he said. "I farted."

She kneed him in the butt.

"Yo, chica, you trying to, like, hump me?"

"Want me to?"

"I'm saving it for Raphael."

"Yeah, well, I'm saving it for Vaclav!"

Natalia sensed that the truck was moving faster, as if it were roaring down a highway. Or maybe the illusion of speed was because now that they were in Mexico, she was free. "I love you, my angel," she said.

"I love you too, chica."

Chapter 44

Mexico–U.S. Border Crossing, Mexico

December 19, 3:32 p.m.

Conner was proud of himself for resisting the urge to lean on his horn. Why bother? he thought. His Ford Fiesta was trapped in thirty-four lanes of bumper-to-bumper traffic, among the thousands of cars and trucks that had been waiting for over an hour to cross the border from Tijuana into the United States. If he honked, in fact, it might have the opposite effect of soothing his rage. He could see that most of the drivers around him were poor Mexicans, seedy dudes who must be as pissed off as he was about being stuck here. If he blasted his horn, they might jump out of their banged-up vehicles and beat the shit out of him.

He felt a massive burp coming on and opened his mouth. It escaped with a loud *"blllarrrgh"* that burned his throat and reeked of hot sauce. How many tacos had he scarfed down while he drove around Tijuana today, moving from one street to the next in search of the Mama G's Tacos truck? Follow the pink, my ass, he thought.

Conner had felt like a doofus when he stumbled across what they called the Tijuana Gastropark because it had over two-dozen food trucks jammed into one big parking lot. The place was full of hipsters with tattoos, man buns, and nose rings, many of them American. They acted like they'd died and gone to foodie heaven because the trucks sold everything from Baja fish tacos to sushi tacos, Korean BBQ tacos, and even vegan-gluten-free tacos. Plus stuff like hamburgers, pizza, and beer. Thank God they sold beer, he thought. He'd downed a couple of Coronas.

Conner hated hipsters. He hated anyone who was cooler than he was. And he really, *really* hated the hipster at the gastropark he asked about Mama G's Tacos. "Sure, dude, I know Mama

G's," the guy had said to him. "Mama G's is here every day but Fridays. That's when she sells tacos in San Diego's Old Town." He flashed him a thumbs-down—"Too bad, dude"—followed by a thumbs-up: "Mama G's is *the* best."

From the gastropark, Conner had driven to the border, eager to make it to San Diego and find Mama G and her son. It wasn't until he had been stuck in this gridlock for an hour that he checked his phone, googled around, and learned that Mama G's only sold tacos in San Diego on Fridays until 2:30 p.m. Now it was 3:32 p.m., but there was no way he could pull out of the northbound lane. He would have to cross the border into the United States before he could turn around and return to Tijuana. Another two hours down the crapper.

He killed the bottle of water that he had bought at the gastropark. He was about to crumple the cheap plastic bottle in his fist but came up with a better idea. He didn't give a shit if the drivers around him could see what he was doing. They probably did it themselves when they were stuck here. He unzipped his fly, stuck his pecker into the bottle, and peed. What a relief. That's the smartest thing I've done all day, he thought.

He turned off his motor—no reason to use up gas—and opened his window. The air was hot and stank of diesel. He climbed out of the car and glanced over at the southbound traffic entering Mexico. If that line was moving, he knew it would piss him off even more. It was.

But that's not what made Conner want to scream with road rage. He glimpsed the hot-pink, wildly decorated Mama G's Tacos truck pulling away from the Border Patrol Booth 24. Mama G was going south, entering Mexico. He was going north, to the United States.

I'm totally screwed, he thought.

Chapter 45

Tijuana, MX

December 19, 4:00 p.m.

Natalia and Angel waved goodbye to Angel's parents as they pulled away in the food truck, its tires spitting grit on the unpaved road. "They're so sweet. Just like you!" said Natalia. She saw that they had been left off at the top of a stark hillside that was crammed with tin-roofed shacks made of cardboard boxes and tires. She noticed women in rags cooking over rusty oil cans spewing smoke and barefoot children playing in the dirt. In the distance, the high-rises of downtown Tijuana were barely visible through a wall of smog. Angel had told her in the truck that his parents were dropping them off at the school his sister ran in the slum where they grew up, a school that he and his sister had attended once themselves.

Angel rushed over to an attractive young Latina standing in the open gate of a wrought-iron fence. She was petite and had his bushy eyebrows and radiant smile. They looked so alike that they could be twins, though Angel had told Natalia that his sister was two years older. He warmly embraced the woman and called to her: "Come meet *mi hermana*, Claudia!"

"Hola, Claudia!" She walked over to them, surprised to see through the fence that the school was striking, a series of white-stucco buildings with sensually curved lines, boldly asymmetrical windows, and colorful mosaic-tile decorations. The design reminded her of the remarkable buildings by the famous Spanish architect Antoni Gaudi that she and Yvonne, her flat-mate in Paris, had seen on their one trip to Barcelona.

"I know what you're thinking," said Claudia, hugging her warmly, as if she were an old friend. "How can such a beautiful school exist in a place so *not* beautiful?"

"It's thanks to a very generous American woman," said Angel. "Leila believes that even kids in a Mexican slum deserve an education in a place that will, like, inspire them and give them joy. That's why she named it 'Escuela de Alegría!' It means 'School of Joy!'"

"Amazing," said Natalia.

"Take your friend to the studio," said Claudia. "It's all yours."

"Thanks, hermana!" Angel led Natalia across a playground where boys around seven or eight years old, in blue pants and white shirts, kicked soccer balls around. A few girls the same age, wearing similar uniforms, rehearsed dance routines. They all waved to Angel. Some came over and hugged him. "I love these kids," he said. "I come see them every time I visit my family."

"It's so late," she said. "When do they go home?"

"These are kids whose parents work at night. They stay here overnight during the week. Claudia's got, like, a little dorm next to her bedroom."

"She lives at the school?"

"She's really dedicated. She got that from Leila, the founder. Leila was like a second mom to me and Claudia. The government doesn't give Leila money for the school. She raises it all herself. I'm now one of her biggest donors. That's another thing in my life that would have been impossible without you, chica. If you didn't have faith in me, I'd still be broke!"

"Y'know what, Angel?"

"What?"

"I have even more faith in you now. I mean, you got me to Tijuana, just like you promised!"

She took his arm as they walked toward a white-stucco building emblazoned with a bold mural glittering with patches of broken-tile mosaics. The mural depicted students dancing, the boys in traditional Mexican sombreros, the girls in full-skirted, embroidered ranchero dresses.

"I worked on this mural when I was a student here," he said. "Now, every year, new students add onto it."

Inside the dance studio, three walls were mirrored floor-to-ceiling. Pouring through the windows on the fourth wall, the sun's rays made the polished wood floor glisten as if it were wet.

"Wow," she said.

"At Escuela de Alegría, Leila wanted all the students, even the boys, to learn how to dance!" He stretched his arms into a ballet position and pirouetted around the room.

"Angel, you paint, you dance, you create with hair and makeup," she said, admiring his moves. "Is there anything you *can't* do?"

He danced over, took her in his arms, and waltzed her around the room. Towering over him, she laughed. She broke away and began to dance a Slovak polka, hands on hips, her feet kicking in the air.

"I can't do *that*!" He plunked down on the floor.

"Yes, you can!" She pulled him to his feet and danced around the room with him, "*la la la-ing*" to an old Slovak folk tune she remembered. "After being sardines in a taco truck, this feels great!"

"Bravo!" Claudia walked into the dance studio with the Walmart shopping bag. "You forgot this in the truck, Angel. Papa dropped it off for you!" The paper tore as she set the bag down on the floor. Angel's red Gucci satchel flopped out.

"*Ohmygod, ohmygod*," he said in an imitation of Moon. He broke away from Natalia, ran over and playfully hugged it. "Without this, I can't turn you into a princess for your prince!"

* * *

Natalia sat on a folding chair in front of the dance-studio mirror. Angel flitted around her as he put the finishing touches on her makeup. He had showered and changed into jeans and a *guayabera*, a traditional short-sleeved white cotton shirt that he said Mexican men wear to parties. His mother had found them among the clothes that Angel left at her house when he went to the United States. Oralia had also brought over a pair of Angel's old cowboy boots for him to wear. They were black, and Natalia was sure that they had three-inch elevator insoles, but he had grumbled when he put them on. "Yo, first thing I do tomorrow after you're, like, safe and sound with your dude, is go out and buy myself a pair of red-alligator cowboy boots with silver heels."

Oralia had also brought clothes to the school for Natalia to wear, some from her own and some from Claudia's closet: a white Mexican peasant skirt that was supposed to be ankle-length, but which came only to Natalia's knees; and a white Mexican peasant blouse with vivid orange, yellow, and pink-embroidered flowers bordering the scooped neckline. On her feet Natalia wore black-rubber flip-flops, which Angel jokingly called "Mexican Manolos."

Angel had given Natalia a quick mani-pedi, using nail polish loaned by Claudia. It was shocking pink and sparkling with pink glitter. She was grateful that Angel had sent Claudia to Target to buy her a black nightie, some bras and undies, plus a toothbrush, toothpaste, and makeup.

She studied herself in the mirror and patted her hair. "I'm sure glad Moon kept an extra Natalia wig in his garment bag and that you remembered to bring it."

"You're welcome." Angel was brushing blusher on her cheekbones.

"And I love the way you do my makeup."

"You're welcome again."

She sighed deeply. "I guess I look pretty much like I did before we started our little adventure."

Sensing her disappointment, he studied her face in the mirror. "It's the jutting eyebrow ridge, right?"

She nodded. "The caveman look works if you want masculine. But feminine? Not so much."

Getting an idea, he rummaged in his satchel. He pulled out a roll of duct tape, then removed Natalia's wig.

She saw that the hair was starting to grow in on her bald head. "I'm as fuzzy as a teddy bear. It's a start!"

Angel ripped off a four-inch length of tape. "This goes on your finger for now." She held up her finger. He attached the tape lightly to the tip. He did the same thing with another piece of tape. "Watch this."

Studying her face in the mirror, he pressed his thumb just above Natalia's right eyebrow and pulled the drooping skin of her forehead upward, toward her scalp. He quickly attached the tape to the top of her head—it held the raised forehead skin in place—then repeated the process with the skin above her left eyebrow. He carefully replaced the wig on her head. Her drooping forehead had all but disappeared and neither piece of tape showed. "Magic!" he said.

"Magic?" Without moving her head, Natalia looked up and down, then right and left. The skin on her forehead drooped again and the end of both strips of tape showed below her wig hairline. "I wish."

Angel rested the wig in Natalia's lap, tore off fresh pieces of tape, and repeated the eyebrow-lifting process. She did her eye-movement thing and got the same result: Both eyebrows drooped and both pieces of tape showed. He sighed, removed the wig and started over again.

"Stop," she said.

"Dude, I'm just getting the hang of it."

"No." She put the wig back on. "I don't need it. I'm fine like this."

"Don't you want to look, like, perfect?"

She met his eyes in the mirror. "Aren't you the guy who said, 'You're out of the White House, out of the public eye, Natalia?

You don't have to look perfect anymore?'"

"You're right. I said that. But what about Prince Vaclav?"

"Y'know, in the past few days, I've eaten whatever I want: ribs; onion rings; and tacos loaded with carbs, processed sugar, and saturated fat. The only exercise I've gotten is walking around in the desert at midnight, trying not to step on a rattlesnake. Am I fat?"

"No."

"I haven't had a sip of Evian, San Pellegrino, or Perrier in three days. Have I died of dehydration?"

"No."

"Right. In fact, I feel pretty damn good!" She stood up from the chair and groaned. "Except for right here." She put her hand on her lower back. "That's from spooning with you in the taco truck."

"I'll give you a massage." He stepped behind her and started to rub her back. She brushed his hands away.

"Vamanos!" From the floor, she grabbed the plastic Target shopping bag holding her new clothes and sundries. "It's almost sunset. My dream was to run into Vaclav's arms on the beach as the sun sinks into the ocean. I don't want to miss it!"

"Okay, okay!" Angel scooped the makeup and other beautifying gear into his satchel. As he zipped it up, he noticed that Natalia was staring at herself in the mirror, her eyes wide with what looked like terror.

"Chica, you look great! You look beautiful! He's gonna take one look at you and, like, come in his pants!"

"*Eeeeewwww*! Gross!" She playfully slapped his arm, then softly said, "Are you sure?"

Angel stood on his tiptoes and kissed the tip of her nose. "Yes, mi amor, I promise."

Chapter 46

Rosarito Beach, MX

December 19, 5:00 p.m.

Fog wrapped the beach in a gray shroud. No romantic ocean sunset tonight, Natalia thought. She reminded herself to stay positive. Sitting in Claudia's beat-up old Escuela de Alegría VW van, she could see Angel talking to the receptionist in the glassed-in lobby of the Hotel Paraiso. "Paradise" is definitely not the best name for this place, she thought, noticing the fountain with broken tiles and a trickle of dirty water, the anemic palm trees whose fronds had been snapped off by the wind, and the neon "Vacancy" sign that randomly blinked on and off, as if rats were chewing on the wires.

Stay positive, she repeated to herself, taking a deep yoga breath.

She caught a glimpse of herself in the rear-view mirror: She was wearing oversized sunglasses and a ridiculously large sombrero that Angel had dug out of a costume box at the school. "It's a perfect disguise," he had said playfully. She nervously toyed with a tiny plastic Ronald McDonald figure that she had dug out of a hole in the plastic seat cover. On the floor she spotted a crumpled Happy Meal carton, no doubt left over from one of Claudia's excursions with her students to the local Golden Arches. The sight triggered a memory of Rex: His mouth opening wide, like a shark's, as he took an obnoxiously big bite of a Big Mac, his chin dripping with grease, his eyes glued to his own image on FOX News.

"I must not think of Rex," she said aloud. "Rex is zlý, bad! I must think of Vaclav. Vaclav is dobrý, good!"

Except, where was Vaclav?

Because Angel's tunnel plan had bombed last night, it was

257

now hours later than when he had told Vaclav they would meet him here. She hoped that Vaclav didn't think that she had chickened out, or that Rex had sent Secret Service men who tracked her down and whisked her back to the White House. If he did, she wouldn't blame him if he had climbed into his rental car, driven back across the border, and hopped on the first flight to Prague.

"He's around here somewhere." Angel said, walking over to the van. "The dude at the desk says a guest with a Slovak passport and, like, a weird accent, hasn't checked out." He pointed to a dusty Honda Civic with an Enterprise Car Rental sticker in the half-empty parking lot. "That's his car."

"Vd'aka Bohu," sighed Natalia. "Thank God!" She grabbed her Target shopping bag and climbed out of the van, determined to find him. She walked around the outside of the three-story hotel, its white paint blistered in patches that revealed the cinderblocks beneath. On the ocean-side of the building, a patio with a swimming pool extended to a steep bluff overlooking the beach. The wind was so strong, it rippled the surface of the water in the pool and nudged the empty chaise lounges on the patio, their aluminum legs scraping the cement like cats' claws.

Natalia saw a few joggers and people walking dogs on the beach below. Along the shoreline, two blonde American teenagers in shorts were galloping on horses, the horses' hooves kicking up spray. The riders were laughing and screaming, "Yee-haw! Yee-haw!" An old Mexican man in a straw hat straggled behind them on a donkey, his shouts swallowed by the wind. She figured that he had rented the horses to the girls and now was terrified that because of their recklessness, either they or his animals would end up dead.

Natalia remembered how she had dreamed as a child of owning a horse, but for a poor Slovak girl it seemed no more achievable than becoming a fashion model. When she married Rex and her modeling career ended, she took a few riding lessons in Central Park. She enjoyed it so much that she asked him if he would buy her a horse so that she could compete in dressage. Rex said no: "The only horses I like are the ones you can bet on."

"Natalia?" Angel's voice pulled her out of her reverie.

She turned around. He was walking toward her with a handsome Mexican man about his age, a backpack with a Four Seasons Hotels logo slung over one shoulder. He was tall and lean and he towered over Angel, but with their arms around each other she thought they made a cute couple.

"Raphael?"

"Si Señora!" He greeted her with a warm Latino two-cheek kiss. "Mucho gusto!"

"I'm pleased to meet you too!" She could see that Angel and Raphael were nervous as they talked quietly in Spanish, their fingers touching lightly. She wondered if it would be like that for her and Vaclav when they met.

If they met.

She searched the beach again, her eyes suddenly squinting into the rays of a sunset that emerged from under a fog bank, a narrow band of gold shimmering on the horizon. The sunset backlit a figure jogging on the beach about a half mile away. She hadn't noticed him before. He was tall and lanky and took long strides, his ponytail flopping against his neck each time his foot hit the sand. Was it Vaclav?

Natalia took off her sunglasses and shielded her eyes so that she could see him more clearly.

"Ohmygod, ohmygod, it's Vaclav!"

"I told you!" Angel put up his hand to slap her high-five, but she was too excited to notice.

"I can't believe this is happening!" She grabbed him in a bear hug. "Oh, Angel, my angel, I can't thank you enough for all you've done for me!" She stepped back and looked into his eyes. "You're my best friend ever. How can I live without you?" She felt tears on her face and noticed that his eyes were moist.

"Hovno, I'll ruin my makeup!"

"You look beautiful. Nothing can ruin that!" He grabbed her hands. "See you, like, soon, okay? You and your prince will come to Todos Santos. Me and Raphael will be waiting for you." He nodded toward the beach. Vaclav was still running, unaware of them. "You better get your butt down there, or he'll run away!"

She wouldn't let go of Angel's hands. "What if I don't love him? What if I hate Vaclav and he hates me? How will I find you?"

Raphael pulled a couple of shiny new Google Pixel 2SL smartphones from his backpack. "Angel asked me to get these for you. I already keyed in your phone numbers." He gave one to her, the other to Angel.

"Wow, this is, like, state-of-the-art," said Angel. "Thanks!" He pocketed his phone.

"Thank you, Raphael." With no pockets on her white Mexican peasant skirt, Natalia stowed her new smartphone in the plastic Target shopping bag filled with her belongings.

"So, we're, like, good to go, right?" Angel looked at her intently and nodded, as if urging her to nod too.

She tried to think of something else to say, to stretch out their goodbye. It hit her that she couldn't bear saying farewell to him because she was terrified about saying hello to Vaclav. She spotted him running on the beach. He was so far away now, that he was just a speck. "I can do this." She took a deep breath, as if preparing to dive into ice-cold water.

She turned back to Angel and kissed the top of his head. "Be safe, be good, and don't forget me, okay?"

He looked up at her, his lips trembling. "I won't, if you won't."

"Deal." She hugged him tightly, then clutched the Target shopping bag and climbed down a narrow wooden stairway from the bluff to the beach. When she reached the sand, she discovered that it was too soft and deep to run wearing flip-flops. She kicked them off. She turned and looked up at the bluff, to give a last wave to Angel. He and Raphael stood with their arms around each other, watching her. They waved back.

She broke into a run. As she jounced across the sand, her sombrero and sunglasses flew off. She dumped the Target shopping bag so that she could use both hands to hold her wig down and keep it from flying off too.

As she drew closer to him, she saw that Vaclav had stopped running and was cooling down. He was walking back and forth along the shoreline, breathing hard and gazing at the sunset.

"*Vaclav!*"

He turned and spotted her. "*Natalia!*" He waved, then began running toward her.

Natalia needed to stop and catch her breath, but a sudden burst of exhilaration forced her lungs to open wider and her heart to beat faster...

She raced toward Vaclav, dizzy with joy and hope and love.

* * *

On the ocean bluff, Angel watched Natalia run into Vaclav's arms. He and Raphael were too far away from the couple and it was getting too dark to see the looks on their faces, but he could hear their shrieks of joy and laughter. The lovers on the beach spun around, as if dancing to music as beautiful as the lavender hues of the waning ocean sunset. Natalia's wig fell off, but Vaclav didn't seem to care. He cupped her face in his hands and kissed every inch of her fuzzy head. His kisses moved to her neck and then to her face. Embracing fervently, they sank down onto the sand.

First Natalia was on top of Vaclav, then Vaclav was on top of her. Suddenly Vaclav flipped her over onto her stomach. On his knees, he crouched over her. Angel and Raphael saw a flash of white as Vaclav pulled up Natalia's Mexican peasant skirt.

"Uh-oh," said Raphael. "I think this is where we stop watching."

"Wait," Angel said. "He's not going to hump her. He's, like, IDing her."

"Huh?"

"She's got a mole shaped like a heart on her butt."

"How the hell do *you* know?"

"Long story."

Raphael looked at him suspiciously, as if wondering whether he had had sex with her.

"Yo, it's not what you think."

In the gathering darkness, from what he could see so far away, it appeared that Vaclav found Natalia's identifying mole. He kissed it lovingly, then with more fervor.

"Uh, this is where we stop watching," he said.

At that moment, the last sliver of sun dipped below the horizon. Angel took Raphael's arm. They walked south, along the bluff.

* * *

With his new 600-mm telephoto lens, Phil took photo after photo of Natalia's reunion with the man he guessed was her old lover, as if it were in dramatic, movie-screen-worthy close-up: their first passionate kiss; their twirling with joy on the beach; their collapsing into each other's arms on the sand. He even captured the moment when the man flipped her over and pulled up her skirt. The lens was so powerful, that it picked up the mole shaped like a heart on Natalia's butt cheek. If he sold that photo to the *National Enquirer*, he imagined earning not only thousands of dollars for himself, but that thousands of women would run out to their nearest tattoo shop and request the exact same valentine-shape tattooed on their own butt.

Phil was breathless with excitement about the amazing shots

he was getting, grateful that he had been able to tail the Mama G's Tacos truck through the Mexico border crossing, all the way to the surprisingly beautiful school in the shantytown. He had parked his car under the one eucalyptus tree that he could find nearby and staked out the school for nearly an hour. Finally, a tall woman in a traditional Mexican skirt and blouse, but with a Natalia wig, sunglasses, and an over-the-top Mexican sombrero, had stepped outside the school gate. In Phil's opinion, there was no way that she was *not* Natalia, the First Lady of the United States.

As if to confirm his hunch, Angel, the First Lady's gay Mexican hairdresser, had then driven up in the rickety school van. Sitting beside him was a young Mexican woman who could have been Angel's twin. He watched as Natalia climbed inside the van. At that moment, Phil wished he could high-five himself. All his research had paid off. His targets were within his crosshairs.

Phil had tailed the school van to the Hotel Paraiso. When the van arrived, he could see from the frown on Natalia's face that it was far from her idea of paradise. He parked his car in the Chevron station across the street. From there he shot photos of Natalia nervously sitting in the van while Angel checked with the receptionist at the desk in the lobby. When they walked around the hotel to the swimming pool, he climbed out of his car and tailed them to a bluff overlooking the beach. He stayed far enough behind so that if either Natalia or Angel turned around they wouldn't be able to ID him. Natalia had seemed preoccupied, searching the beach below for someone that he could only imagine. Angel was looking around nervously too, perhaps for a mystery person of his own. Phil hid behind a stack of aluminum chaise lounges south of the pool. From there he had a clear view of Angel and Natalia and the beach below.

From his hiding place, he had snapped photos of Natalia's beautiful face—he saw anguish, fear, and disappointment—as she searched the beach for someone. Then Angel joined her on the bluff with a tall, thin Mexican man about his age. From their warm, but tentative, body language, he guessed that the two men once had been lovers.

Soon Phil had captured Natalia's face lighting up as she spotted her "someone" on the beach below. From that point on, he had clicked shot after shot of Natalia: climbing down the rickety wooden stairway to the beach; ditching her sunglasses, sombrero, and Target bag to dash across the sand; and falling into the arms of a tall, handsome man about her age in jogging shorts.

After taking photos of Natalia's heart-mole shot, Phil realized that she and her ponytailed lover were about to have sex on the beach. He squirmed. He had only had sex with women a few times. The encounters occurred because his paparazzi pals dared him to try Tinder. He considered them embarrassing "accidents" that he preferred to forget.

In the mounting darkness, he knew that his telephoto lens soon would lose its clarity. He quickly snapped more photos: the creamy flesh of Natalia's breasts as her lover unbuttoned her blouse; his muscular back as she pulled off his shirt. Phil hesitated. Could he really photograph the woman who had enchanted him, the woman with whom he was obsessed, in the act of love?

I'm not a pornographer, he told himself. This is beyond the realm of a paparazzo. This is filth.

He clicked off his camera and climbed back up to the bluff. That's when he spotted Angel and his friend walking his way. He scrambled back down the cliff to the beach before they could see him. He would decide what to do next, and shoot next, tomorrow.

* * *

High on a cliff, just north of El Paraiso Hotel, Rosa stood on a white-marble terrace looking through night-vision binoculars. For the past thirty minutes, she had been watching the First Lady and a hunky guy with a ponytail make passionate love on the beach below.

"He's so hot!" she said.

"So's the First Lady," said Maria, who was watching them through night-vision binoculars beside her. "Too bad they don't seem in the mood for a threesome."

"Or a foursome."

The last wisps of purple on the horizon were fading to black. Through her night-vision binoculars, Rosa watched as the couple got dressed and walked hand-in-hand across the beach to the hotel. She put her night-vision binoculars on a patio table, buttoned the black North Face puffer vest she was wearing over her T-shirt, and picked up her iPhone. She checked the photo she had taken of the *People* article that she and Maria found in the backpack of the gringo moron they had robbed last night. She also checked the iPhone photos that she had taken of the pictures they found in his backpack: the gay Mexican hairdresser; the First Lady of the United States; and the Facebook page for a rock band in Prague called Zlatorog and the Dragons. It was hard to tell for sure—seeing a man through night-vision binoculars wasn't as accurate as seeing him in the flesh—but Rosa had a hunch that the hot guitarist was the guy the First Lady was fucking on the beach.

This morning, Rosa and Maria had showed the photos they took last night to their boss-slash-pimp, Fernando. He didn't get it. At six-foot-three, the tallest Mexican Rosa had ever seen, Fernando was as strong as a bull, but as dumb as a jackass. Too much cocaine, one of the dangers of the biz, she thought. Once they explained the situation to him, and what it could mean for their boss, Fernando was stoked. He let them keep the hundred dollars, puffer vest, and Ray-Bans that they had ripped off from the gringo. "Keep watching the beach," Fernando told them.

"When you find something more about the maricón hairdresser and his famous client, then we'll tell Dionisio."

Sensing the darkness, the security lights along the perimeter of the white mansion that Dionisio had built for himself automatically switched on. Too bad Dio isn't here so we can tell him in person what we saw tonight, she thought. But Dionissio was in hiding. It wasn't just the Mexican government that was after his ass. The Gulf Cartel, the Juarez Cartel, and every other powerful Mexican drug cartel wanted him dead so that they could move in on his Baja Cartel territory. But Rosa fucked Dio from time to time. She knew that he was smarter than they were. Okay, he sucked in bed, but he had TVs in his bedroom tuned to CNBC. To get a hard-on, he watched the stock market. She wondered how big a reward he would give her and Maria for their information. And what he would do with it.

"Chica," she said to Maria, who was wearing the gringo's Ray-Bans and watching a Beyoncé music video on her iPhone. Maria pulled out one of her earbuds and looked at her. "We gotta be checking the beach when the sun comes up tomorrow. Let's hit the sack." Maria nodded.

They walked across the terrace and into the mansion. Fernando and three Baja Cartel toughs as big as he was were lounging on red leather sofas in what Dionisio called the "play room." It had black marble floors and shiny black-lacquered walls, two pool tables, and a wall full of video-game machines. She knew that their job was to hang out here and make sure none of Dio's rivals broke in. They were smoking Cuban cigars and watching *The Godfather* on a theater-sized video screen, as if they owned the place. They ignored the girls as they walked past.

"Fernando said we could sleep in Dio's room tonight," whispered Maria. "Sort of a reward."

"Que chido!" She followed her down a hall and into a room that was big as the play room, but white from top to bottom. They flopped down on the round waterbed covered with a white sheepskin bedspread.

"Y'know the best part about sleeping in Dio's bed tonight?" said Rosa. "No Dio!"

"No pendejos, period! Fernando promised." Maria got up and walked over to the door. "Another reward for last night," she said, locking it.

Chapter 47

Rosarito Beach, MX

December 19, 8:00 p.m.

Phil walked into the musty motel room and flicked on the light switch. Nothing happened. Leaving the door open to let in the glow of a streetlight outside, he made his way over to the nightstand and turned on the lamp. With its threadbare carpeting and peeling paint, the room was so shabby that Phil realized the dim yellow light was all he wanted. He dumped his camera bag and backpack on the bed and sprawled beside them.

The mattress sagged under his weight and the springs creaked. For $15 a night, what did he expect? He couldn't exactly afford a room with an ocean view and he didn't need a TV. El Mar Azul had what he needed most tonight: It was located across the street from El Paraiso, where Natalia and her lover were spending the night. He had watched them through his 600mm lens as they entered their room. They were kissing passionately and tearing at each other's clothes before they even closed the door.

All Phil wanted to do now was upload today's photos to his laptop, recharge his camera, and get a burger to eat in the dingy cafe downstairs. Then he'd scrub off the dust and the sweat in the mold-stained shower and crash. He hoped this wasn't one of those cheap TJ motels he'd seen in movies where hookers scam johns. The last thing he wanted tonight was to be kept awake by the sound of the bed next door slamming against his wall and fake female screams of pleasure. He needed to be rested in the morning so that he could snap more photos of the First Lady and her lover. He didn't think that they would be up and at 'em at the crack of dawn. Just in case, he planned to be.

Phil reached into his backpack and pulled out the plastic water bottle he bought this morning at Starbuck's. No surprise that it was empty. He was lightheaded from dehydration, but he didn't dare refill the bottle with tap water. His googling had yielded the fact that drinking tap water in Mexico can lead to a case of the runs. Another "never in Mexico" warning on Google said not to leave valuables in your hotel room. Impulsively, he stood up, slung his backpack and camera case over his shoulder, and walked out.

The cafe downstairs didn't have an ocean view, but it had a TV. Phil took a seat on a bar stool within viewing distance. He was surprised to see that it was tuned to FOX News. With all the bad blood that Rex Funck had stirred up between the United States and Mexico, he couldn't imagine why Mexicans would watch the American President's favorite TV channel. The bartender, a young Mexican with slicked-back hair and a gold earring, explained the reason: "Most of our customers are gringos and FOX is the only station we get because our satellite dish was ripped off."

Phil ordered a burger, well done, no lettuce or tomato. Undercooked meat and fresh vegetables were additional Mexican "no-no's" on his Google list. He didn't trust Coke from a dispenser, but the bartender had Coke in a can, along with a bottle of Coke-owned Dasani purified water. Phil asked the bartender to let him pop the Coke can and open the Dasani bottle himself. From his raised eyebrow, the bartender no doubt had received this request from other wary Americans. Phil bought an extra six-pack of Dasani water for tomorrow.

On FOX News, a young blonde newscaster was talking to Gus Banks, a balding newscaster Phil had seen in a *Washington Post* photo of the President golfing with friends. They were discussing the First Couple's visit today to the hospice ward of Georgetown Hospital. "The way the President reacted to shaking hands with a young hospice patient today has become a hot meme on the internet," said the blonde. "Let's take a look."

The camera focused in on a short, speeded-up video of

President Funck, his eyes wide in seeming panic, shaking hands with a sick, slumped-over bald patient, then quickly pulling his hand back, as if it had been zapped with electricity. The video repeated, forward and then backward, so that it looked as if the President's hand was jerking first into, and then out of, the patient's hand. Standing beside him in the video, the First Lady broke into a grin, and then out of it, and then into it again, as the meme repeated. Phil noticed that the First Lady grinned when the President pulled his hand away from the patient, not when he shook hands with him. It was as if the "zapped hand" part of President Funck's handshake was the one she liked best.

Phil knew that the First Lady was really Moon Kusnetzov. He wondered if the President had figured it out. If he knew about Moon, the President also knew that the real First Lady was missing. But there was no mention of it on FOX News.

Phil watched as Gus Banks proceeded to explain away the President's unease at the hospital. "President Funck has been under a lot of pressure lately," he said. The newscaster licked his lips, a sure sign, Phil had read, that the next thing out of his mouth would be a lie. "I'm sure that jerky movement was just an involuntary muscle spasm. It happened one time when we were playing golf at Beau Rivage. And y'know what? Right after that, the President hit a hole in one!"

"Yo, I heard you talking to the bartender in English." A tall man in his mid-thirties, with a buzz cut, a sweat-stained white shirt, and a backpack, was nursing a Corona a few stools away. "You're American, right?"

"Yes."

"Mind if I ask you something?"

"I guess not." Phil didn't want to deal with questions tonight. He hoped the guy would make it quick.

The man took his Corona bottle with him as he slid onto the bar stool next to Phil's. "So, my name's..." —he licked his lips— "John." He extended his hand. Phil shook it, figuring that the lip licking meant "John" wasn't his real name. Two can play at this game, he thought.

"Nice to meet you. I'm Bob," said Phil.

"So, like, I'm kinda looking for this dude, and I wonder if you seen him." John leaned closer to Phil, so close that Phil could smell his bar breath. The Corona was definitely not the first beer John had drunk tonight. Looking at John close up, Phil felt a cold awareness creep over him: He had seen him before.

"It's like, y'see, well, I mean, you look like a nice guy, Bob, an honest guy, so I'm just gonna tell you…" He licked his lips twice, like a dog eying a steak. "I think this dude is fucking my wife."

"Oh," said Phil. He wasn't sure whether to say, "I'm sorry" or not. His mind was scrambling to figure out where he had seen John before.

"Yeah, the truth is… I might as well just say it, right?" More lip licking. "I think maybe this asshole and my wife took off together. I mean, she told me she was going to her sister's, but she fucking hates her sister, so, like, I think she's with this guy. She knows him from work. Dude, I just want to catch up with them. It's not like I'm out to hurt them or nothing. Seriously. All I want is to know for sure."

Phil guessed that the guy's story was pure bullshit, but he wondered where it would lead. "You got a picture of the guy?"

"Yeah, maybe you seen him today. I think she said she and her sister were going to Rosarito Beach, so like, y'know…" John rummaged in his backpack and pulled out a printout of a Facebook page. Before Phil could see all of it, John carefully ripped the paper and handed Phil the photo of a guitarist with a ponytail. In mid-song, his mouth was wide and his eyes were closed. Phil didn't need to see the color of his eyes to know who it was.

"That's the guy who's screwing your wife?"

"You seen him?" John's eyes widened and he climbed off the

bar stool, as if expecting good news. He hitched up his jeans, put his hand on his crotch, and hastily rearranged his balls. At that moment, it hit Phil where he had seen John. He was a U.D. officer at the White House. Phil had seen him do this same gesture, playing Macho Cop, when he interrogated visitors in the staff-entrance security area.

Phil wished he could open his laptop and check the photos he took of Moon and Angel leaving the security checkpoint. He bet if he looked closely, he would see this U.D. officer in the background. He wondered: Did the White House send him after the First Lady because he fucked up and let her walk out on his watch?

"So, like, did you see this guy or not?" John impatiently drummed his fingers on the bar.

Phil knew he had to get the U.D. officer away from Rosarito Beach ASAP. If John were here tomorrow morning, he would spot Natalia and her lover. The Secret Service would be all over them and Phil would never get his million-dollar shot.

"Yeah, come to think of it, I did see him." He handed the photo back to John.

"All right!" He pounded his fist on the bar. "I'm gonna get that fucker's ass. Where'd you see him?"

"Uh, he was checking out when I was checking in, an hour or so ago."

John's face froze. "He was *leaving*?"

"Before he left, he was on his phone. He had an accent—"

"Do you know who he was talking to?"

"Definitely a woman. He called her 'babe.' I think I heard him say, 'I love you!'" Phil stopped and pretended to think for a moment. He knew John would be happy about what he said next. He blurted it out: "He arranged to meet her in Ensenada. Yeah! He told her he would see her tonight, at the..." He fumbled for a name that would sound believable. "I think it was the Ensenada Hotel. Yeah, the Hotel Ensenada in Ensenada."

John pumped Phil's hand. Phil worried for a moment that this sweaty guy was going to hug him.

"Look, man… Sorry, what's your name again?"

Phil hoped he remembered it right, then he realized that it wouldn't matter because John didn't. "Bob."

"Yeah, Bob. I can't thank you enough. You saved my life!" John motioned to the bartender, who was walking over with Phil's hamburger. "Hey, dude, let me pay for this guy's tab."

"You don't have to do that," said Phil.

"No, seriously, you're saving my fucking life here." John opened his wallet, realized he had no cash. "Actually, the thing is, I, uh, didn't get a chance to hit an ATM today. I'll buy you a drink next time!"

"No problem, dude." He was starting to enjoy the "dude this" and "dude that" patter. Like learning a foreign language. Hell, he was starting to enjoy *lying*. He'd never told a whopper like this before. I get why the President loves telling lies, he thought. It makes me feel…*strong.*

John shook Phil's hand again. "So, you said Hotel Ensenada, right? Wait. Where the hell is Ensenada? You know where Ensenada is?"

"Uh, south of here somewhere?"

The bartender put down Phil's fries and a bottle of ketchup. "Ensenada's south on Highway 1 about two hours from TJ," he said. "That'll be $7 for the Coronas."

John started to take out his credit card, but hesitated. Phil figured it was because John didn't want him to see his real name on it. He wondered what bullshit excuse John would come up with now.

"Dude, you mind adding my beers to your bill?" He licked his lips one time too many; spittle oozed from the corners of his mouth. "Like, in case I don't find my wife, I don't want her to see my credit-card bill and realize I've been in TJ on her tail."

"Sure, no problem," said Phil. He was impressed by John's

bullshit level. I could learn something from it, he thought. In fact, suddenly he felt emboldened enough by John's bravado to do something only self-confident macho guys do. He slipped off his bar stool and gave John a hug, clapping him hard on the back. "Dude, I sure hope you find your man," he said. "And hey, if he is with your wife, it's okay with me if you fuck him up a little. I won't tell."

John looked surprised. "Thanks, man." He ran for the door.

Phil felt like he was on a roll. He hitched up his jeans and for the first time in his life put his hand on his crotch and hastily rearranged his privates. Climbing back on his bar stool, he waved to the bartender. "Dude, get me a beer!"

Chapter 48

Ensenada, MX

December 19, 10:00 p.m.

Angel kicked off his new red-alligator cowboy boots, laid his new Google Pixel 2SL smartphone on the nightstand, and sprawled on the king-size bed. He was grateful that Raphael had bought new phones for him and Natalia and had insisted on buying Angel new boots the minute they arrived in Ensenada. The shops were open late on Friday night and the streets were filled with tourists. It seemed like a good time for shopping. Angel knew that the real, unspoken reason they agreed to stop in a few stores was to delay the moment ahead that made them both nervous. It was one thing to reminisce about old times, to laugh at old jokes, and to discuss plans for their life after they settled in Todos Santos. But Angel didn't feel ready emotionally to be intimate with Raphael. He sensed his old friend felt the same way. Perhaps witnessing the passion between Natalia and Vaclav had made them feel insecure, as if they feared their own love wouldn't pass the test of time, as Natalia and Vaclav's apparently did.

Angel also was grateful that Raphael had made them a reservation at the best hotel in Ensenada. Tomorrow they would continue driving south to Todos Santos. Their suite at the Playa Bonita was a far cry from one at the Funck Hotel Washington, D.C.: no Jacuzzi tub, no terrycloth bathrobes, no flat-screen TV. But it was spacious and clean; it had a king-size bed; and there were a few vibrant modern Mexican paintings on the walls.

Angel stood up and opened the sliding-glass door to the terrace, to let in the ocean air and the crash of the waves. The chill helped clear his mind. He was glad to be alone in the suite for a few minutes to assess his feelings. Raphael had gone down the hall to fill the ice bucket to chill the bottle of Veuve Clicquot that he had brought. Raphael had also brought an ice chest filled with gourmet treats for a candlelight dinner on the terrace: fresh Baja oysters; shrimp ceviche; and a salad of baby micro-greens and herbs from Raphael's own garden topped with thin-sliced ahi tuna. Angel was delighted that Raphael was excited to show off his new culinary skills, but neither of them was hungry for dinner yet. Angel hoped that a glass of champagne would relax them enough to talk about why, after Raphael was disowned by his father and left TJ, he had cut off all contact with Angel. It had hurt him deeply. Once that was out in the open, an old wound could mend. Then, just maybe, a second glass of champagne would relax them enough to make love.

Since talking to Raphael on Facetime, Angel had felt intense longing for Raphael, like he did when they were fifteen and crazy about each other. But would it last? So much time had passed. After Raphael, Angel's relationships had never lasted more than nine or ten months, maybe because he still loved Raphael. He hoped to discover if that was true. Right now, he wished he could discuss his feelings with Natalia. He wondered how she was getting along with her true love right now.

Angel grabbed his new Google Pixel 2SL from the nightstand and lay down on the bed. Raphael had programmed Natalia's number into the phone, but he figured that she and Vaclav were having a romantic dinner about now or making love. He didn't want to disturb them. He opened Google instead. He wondered if there was any news about the missing FLOTUS.

When he googled "First Lady of the United States," what popped up was a meme of President Funck looking like he was being shocked by electricity while shaking hands with a hospice patient. Standing beside Funck was Natalia/Moon. Angel relished the grin on her face at the moment Funck made a fool of himself. He hoped that Moon wouldn't have to continue pretending to be FLOTUS much longer, now that Natalia was safely with Vaclav.

"Hola!" Raphael entered the room with a bucket sparkling with ice cubes. He plunged the champagne bottle into it and put the bucket on the table. He nodded to Angel, who was smiling as he watched the meme on his phone. "What's so funny?"

"You've gotta see this." Angel patted the bed.

Raphael lay down beside him and watched the meme on Angel's screen. "Humiliating for the President of the United States, but hilarious!"

Angel felt Raphael's arm warm against his and breathed in the scent of his body: dust after a rain, boy sweat, and a hint of Gillette shaving cream. "Yo, remember the first time we shaved?" he said. "We both had, like, three whiskers on our chins and decided to shave them off together." As if it were second nature, he nestled closer to Raphael.

"Then we got in a shaving cream fight!" Raphael tickled Angel and rolled on top of him. They looked into each other's eyes for a long moment. "Hola, mi angel," Raphael said softly. *"Lo siento mucho."*

"I accept your apology, mi amor." Angel tenderly kissed Raphael for the first time in how many years? It felt as if had been only a minute since their last kiss.

Part V

Chapter 49

Rosarito Beach, MX

December 20, 3:00 a.m.

Natalia was fifteen years old, making love with young Vaclav on the bank of the Váh River in Žilina. She knew it was a dream because the air was hot, not icy, like it was in Slovakia in December. And instead of feeling the prick of frozen grass blades under her back, she felt the softness of warm sand. A shrill whistle, like that of the train to Bratislava chugging toward the railroad bridge, awakened her.

* * *

For a split second, Natalia was startled to see grown-up Vaclav lying beside her in bed. He was naked, sprawled on sheets that were crumpled from their lovemaking and gritty from the sand they had tracked in from the beach. The memory of their reunion, their passion, and their joy last night came back to her. It seemed more like a dream than her dream moments ago of them as teenagers in Žilina.

Vaclav was sleeping on his side, facing away from her. She sat up and studied his body, then touched his shoulder as if to convince herself that he was really here. She gently brushed his hair from his brow, remembering how he used to do that when he was young and couldn't afford haircuts. Now his hair was deliberately long. "It's part of my rock-star image, like my tattoos," he had told her last night with a laugh. She was glad that Vaclav didn't take the whole rocker thing too seriously. Pop musicians are narcissistic, she thought, showing off on stage and craving the attention of fans. "I play in a band because I love music, not for the glory," he said last night. "All because of you! You became a model. You inspired me to follow my dream!"

Natalia was relieved that Vaclav was so different from Rex. She was grateful that she would never have to deal with a man's narcissistic selfishness, swollen ego, and dick-measuring machismo again. She traced the letters of "Natalia" tattooed on Vaclav's toned bicep, the only word among dozens of tattooed pictures that he had added to his body over the years: surreal guitars, warped musical notes, the moon in various phases, and zigzag lightning bolts. "The lightning was my rage over losing you," he said.

Natalia was not a fan of tattoos—she had never been the least bit tempted to get one—but she was touched that Vaclav had imprinted her name on his body. She smiled, remembering how last night on the beach he had playfully exposed her right butt cheek to check that her heart-shaped mole was still there. "Hey, I gotta make sure it's you!" he joked. After smothering her mole with kisses, he showed her the heart that he had tattooed on his own right butt cheek, the same size and shape as her mole. She impulsively bent over and kissed Vaclav's heart tattoo now. He stirred in his sleep. She hoped he was dreaming about her.

While he slept, she admired Vaclav's high cheekbones, thick eyebrows, and long eyelashes. She remembered that in high school she called his sexy eyes "bedroom eyes." When, after so many years, she looked into them last night, the term still made sense. She found it amazing that Vaclav showed few signs of aging, unlike most men in their late forties. There wasn't a trace of gray in his hair and his only wrinkles were the crows' feet that appeared when he smiled. She loved his smile; it was so natural, so genuine, the opposite of Rex's.

It struck her that last night they had barely mentioned their new life together and where it would lead. Instead, they spoke of old times: the happy ones, like when they made love in secret places after school, some of which left splinters in their backsides, and in her babika's barn. They spoke of sad times too, like the day her father told Vaclav he could never see her again.

She confided something in Vaclav that she had never mentioned to anyone other than Yvonne one night in Paris when they were drinking cheap Beaujolais and sharing secrets: the pain of giving birth to Vaclav's son and having him ripped from her arms. Last night, she burst into tears as the story spilled out of her. Vaclav cried too and held her tightly. "I hope we will have children together now," he said.

Natalia leaned over his sleeping body. His skin smelled of sweat, his sweat and hers, and of sex. She found it intoxicating. Her body warmed as she recalled the details of their lovemaking last night. He had given her pleasure, what was it? Five times? *Six?* Miraculous. His vták was as long, thick, and beautiful as she remembered, and it still perked up, stiff, like a young man's, the moment he saw her. For a split second she pictured Rex sitting on his throne in the White House, his stubby vták stuffed in a silicone sleeve. The image revolted her. She vowed never to describe it to Vaclav. She vowed never to mention anything about her life with Rex to Vaclav. Everything about it seemed obscene now.

Vaclav rolled over in his sleep, bringing her back to the reality of their musty hotel room. Feeling thirsty, Natalia got up from bed, careful not to wake him, and walked over to a table by the window. He had been thoughtful enough to stock up on bottled water. He had somehow managed to get a bottle of Russian vodka and a tin of Russian caviar too. Last night he had surprised her with them. "Where did you get these?" she asked. Vaclav just smiled. "Connections."

When Natalia lived in Paris, Russian caviar had been just about the only perk of going on escort dates with rich men. Rex never ate caviar. "How can you eat fish eggs?" he said. "They come out of the same hole as fish shit!"

Last night Vaclav and Natalia had scooped caviar out of the tin with their fingers and toasted each other with vodka. She hadn't drunk hard liquor since Paris. One shot and she was buzzing. Vaclav managed to down half the bottle without seeming sloshed. It certainly didn't impede his lovemaking, she thought.

She wondered if Angel and Raphael's lovemaking had been as passionate as hers and Vaclav's. She realized that she hadn't thought about Angel since her reunion with Vaclav. Now it struck her that their reunion would never have happened without Angel, that her whole life wouldn't have been transformed if it hadn't been for him. She wanted to thank him again. Plus, she missed him. It was too late to call, but she decided to text him.

Natalia searched the room for her plastic Target shopping bag. She had tossed her new phone into it yesterday. She looked under the clothes scattered on the floor, but it wasn't there. Then she remembered that she had dumped the bag on the sand when she ran across the beach to Vaclav last night. Her new thong undies, nighties, toothbrush, and toothpaste, not to mention her makeup, were in the bag too.

Natalia put on her white Mexican skirt and blouse so that she could run down to the beach and retrieve the bag. She was certain that she had dropped it near the bottom of the staircase down the bluff to the sand.

As she opened the door to leave, the hinges squeaked.

Vaclav sat up in bed. "Hey, are you running out on me already?" he said sleepily.

"I forgot my stuff on the beach. My new phone—"

"We'll get it tomorrow. Come back to bed."

"What if someone steals it?"

"In the middle of the night? C'mon, I want you." He climbed off of the bed and padded toward her, naked. The lights were off, but her eyes were adjusted enough to the dark that she could see his erection. She felt lightheaded in anticipation.

"Are you sure? Again?"

Vaclav scooped her up in his arms and carried her back to the bed. "Again and again and again!" He kissed her. She parted her lips, inviting his tongue into her mouth.

Chapter 50

Ensenada, MX

December 20, 3:30 a.m.

Conner leaned drunkenly on the withers of a donkey with a bushy mane, like an overgrown crew cut, a red sombrero on its head. He placed the sombrero on his own head, downed all but the last sip from his glass of beer and then offered it to the donkey. The animal's thick pink tongue darted into and out of the glass, quickly replacing the dregs of the beer with donkey drool.

"Okay, mi amigo," Conner said, slurring his words. After three beers and four tequila shots at this shithole tourist bar in Ensenada, he was blotto. "I shared my booze with you, now talk." He leaned over and whispered into the donkey's ear, standing so close that its fur tickled his nose: "Where the fuck are the Slovak dude and the First Lady?" The donkey opened its mouth and belched. He put the sombrero back on its head. "Thank you and fuck you."

Conner unsteadily carried his empty glass over to the bar. "Yo, dude, hit me again," he said to the bartender, an old Mexican with a waxed mustache. Without looking up from his smartphone, as if he could do this in his sleep, the bartender refilled Conner's glass from the tap. He chuckled as he handed it to him.

"What's so funny?"

"You seen this?" The bartender showed him his smartphone screen: the meme of President Funck getting "zapped" by the dying patient in the hospital. "Is your President as loco as he looks?"

Conner was about to launch into a defense of President Funck, but guessed that the greaser wouldn't buy it after the whole Mexican border-wall thing. Besides, he was thinking about the American guy who had been watching this meme in the bar in TJ. What was his name? *"Bob?"* The dude had sent him to Ensenada on what turned out to be a wild goose chase.

When he arrived, Conner had searched his GPS for a Hotel Ensenada and an Ensenada Hotel, but found neither. There was an Ensenada Inn, but when he drove up, he discovered the charred ruins of boarded-up motel. From the number of broken windows he figured it had been closed for years. He wondered if Bob had lied to him, or if the dude wasn't really Bob at all. Maybe "Bob" was looking for the First Lady himself, he thought.

Conner had called the First Daughter on the drive from TJ to Ensenada. "I'm on their tail," he said to Gretchen, oozing excitement and self-confidence. "I'll have her in cuffs within an hour!" When he hit a dead end, he ended up in this bar. He had been drinking for a couple of hours now, trying to figure out what to do next. Instead of feeling excited, he was scared shitless.

He paid his bar tab. "I don't suppose you know a Hotel Ensenada or an Ensenada Hotel in town," he said to the bartender.

"I live here fifty years and the only place I know with name 'Ensenada' is an old inn that was a whore house." The bartender scratched his head. "Funny, right? You'd think a town named Ensenada would have a hotel named Ensenada."

"Right." Conner drained the last of his beer. He didn't stop to pat the donkey on his way out.

Outside the bar, the darkened streets were deserted. Even the wildest ravers in this party town have hit the sack, he thought. He tried to remember where he had parked his rental car. What was it again? A Chevy? A Ford? He rummaged in his pocket and clicked the button on his car key. A block away, the lights of a Ford Fiesta lit up. He trudged along the shadowy unpaved street toward it.

Footsteps echoed behind him. He turned and saw three young

Latino thugs with bandannas around their foreheads. They wore white T-shirts and low-slung, baggy chinos. Gangbangers. What did they want? he wondered. The twenty bucks in his wallet? His piece-of-shit car? Right now, Conner's vision of himself in Ray-Bans and a black suit, strutting alongside the "Beast," was a bad joke. They could have his life for all he cared.

Chapter 51

The White House

December 20, 6:30 a.m.

"Fuck! I look like a fucking spooked wimp, a candy-ass fucking nut job!"

Rex Funck paced his bedroom, the "zapped hand" meme of him in the hospice ward playing over and over on his giant TV screen. His blue terrycloth bathrobe had sprung open, revealing his hairless chest and Big-Mac gut, but not his dork. All Gretchen could see below his sagging paunch was a scant tangle of pubes. She was so fed up with her father that she dared sneer to herself that he was in such a snit, his dork had gone into hiding. She pulled off her sanitary face mask and trashed it.

"Daddy, c'mon, you've got to get some sleep, *I've* got to get some sleep! I've been here all night. My kids need me."

"*What* kids?" He shook his head, as if trying to remember if Gretchen had any. "Baby, you are not going anywhere until we make this go away!" He gestured to the meme on TV.

"Daddy, it's all going to happen. It's all good! Conner said last night on the phone he was on his way to Ensenada. He got an ID on the Slovak guy from a reliable witness in Tijuana. Once the real FLOTUS is back in the White House, you'll be more relaxed. These things won't happen."

"I want Moon whatever-his-or-her-name-is shot! No, I want her electrocuted!" He grabbed the remote and switched from CNN to FOX News. The "President zapped" meme was running there too. "Fuck! FOX threw me under the bus for ratings!"

"Daddy, it's yesterday's news cycle. Today's news cycle starts any minute!" Desperate, she grabbed her cell phone from the coffee table. She pushed "Call Back" on the phone number from which Conner called her at 1.00 a.m. Eastern, which was 10:00

p.m. Pacific time. That was more than eight hours ago. Where the hell was he?

"Digame," said a man's deep voice on the phone. *"Quien es?"*

Gretchen quickly hung up the phone. What if Conner got mugged? she thought. What if a Mexican low-life had ripped off his cell phone with a private White House number on it? As if it were burning her fingers, she pressed the "Off" button and threw the phone into the wastebasket. She didn't know what to do next. At least the press hadn't bagged a shot of her trashing her phone. If a photo like that ended up a meme on the Internet, she knew it would make her look as whacked out as her father.

Chapter 52

Rosarito Beach, MX

December 20, 7:00 a.m.

Natalia awoke to the roar of a helicopter. She sat up in bed with a start, terrified that it was Marine One. Had the Secret Service found her?

Vaclav wasn't in the motel room. Where was he? She ran over to the window: A helicopter was circling above the beach. It was much smaller than Marine One, she realized. Maybe it was taking tourists on a scenic flight over the ocean, like she had seen helicopters do in Palm Beach. It straightened out and flew north along the coast.

She noticed a lone figure on the beach. Vaclav. He was watching the helicopter disappear into the brightening sky. Wearing his jogging clothes, he launched into a series of post-run leg stretches. She wondered how far he had run this morning. She had slept so soundly—she was exhausted from their marathon lovemaking—that she had no idea when he had left their room. She admired his tall, lean, muscular body as he continued to stretch. She was thrilled that Vaclav was into exercise. It was something they could share. She pictured them running together on the beach in Todos Santos.

Natalia longed to join Vaclav, but she had no workout clothes. She didn't even have clean underwear. She saw him turn and walk toward the bluff. She hoped that he would spot her plastic Target shopping bag on the sand and bring it up to their room.

As she awaited his arrival, she picked up their discarded clothes on the floor, swept the sand off the bed, and straightened the tangle of sheets. Her body was still buzzing from last night's sex. The sheets were coarse, maybe not even cotton, let alone 1000-count, 100-percent Egyptian cotton. Instead of Italy, where her soft Frette sheets at the White House came from, they were probably made in China. Still, she had a crazy notion to steal the sheets and take them when they drove to Todos Santos, a souvenir of their momentous reunion.

She could hear Vaclav's footsteps on the second-floor landing, walking toward their room. He was singing a rock song in Slovak, one that she didn't recognize. It sounded like a cross between the Rolling Stones and... Natalia realized that she hadn't listened to pop music in the past fourteen years. I have so much to experience in my new life with Vaclav, she thought.

He walked in carrying a box of Dunkin' Donuts. A cardboard carrier balanced on top held two paper cups of coffee. "The coffee might be cold," he said. "I drove over and picked up breakfast before my run, then left it on the porch."

"No problem," she said, though she couldn't remember the last time she ate a doughnut—empty calories—and she hated drinking coffee out of a paper cup. "Thank you."

"Since it's already cold..." He put down the box and walked over to her. "Good morning, my love." She could see the outline of his erection against his nylon jogging shorts. It reminded her of the first time they kissed in the Žilnia Catholic School gym. He fondled her naked breasts, and then thrust his tongue into her mouth. Feeling unprepared, even slightly offended, she broke away from him.

"Shouldn't we get going? Angel said it's a whole day's drive to Todos Santos."

He drew her closer, pressing his erection against her naked body. "We have time."

Natalia felt aroused, but she sensed it would take more foreplay than he might have in mind to get up to his level. Besides, there were practical matters to attend to. "We must leave. We must disappear before Rex finds out where we are."

With a sigh of frustration, he stepped back, pulled off his shirt, and then his shorts, socks, and thong underwear. Seeing this naked Adonis in front of her, his vták erect, Natalia felt a sudden urge to wrestle him to the floor and climb on top of him.

As if to punish her for rejecting him, he walked into the bathroom. She heard the shower turn on and Vaclav singing the Slovak rock song again. Hovno, she thought. How can I pass up a chance for ecstasy? I haven't experienced bliss in so many years, as my mamina would say, "I'm entitled." She followed him into the bathroom. She giggled, knowing that her mother would have a stroke if she saw her with Vaclav right now.

He was peeing into the toilet, his back to her. She was tempted to bend down and kiss the heart tattoo on his right butt cheek. Before she could, he flushed the toilet, pulled back the torn opaque shower curtain, and stepped into the shower. It was tiny, barely large enough for one person. For a moment, she remembered the image that still flashed in her dreams from time to time: her father, who was as large a man as Vaclav, taking a shower when she was a little girl in their apartment bathroom in Žilnia. In order to catch the bus in time to get to school in the morning, on her mother's instructions she peed and washed up while her father was showering. The shower was so small and the cheap shower curtain so thin, that the curtain stuck to his skin. While she was brushing her teeth, in the mirror she could see the outline of her father behind her in the shower, washing his balls as carefully as if they were jewels. When she told her mother it disgusted her to see this, she made light of it: "Papa's balls *are* jewels," she said, chuckling. "The family jewels."

Natalia could see Vaclav washing his balls through the shower curtain now. She felt a pang of disgust, as she did when she had watched her father.

"Come in and join me," he called.

"The shower's too small."

"I'll make room." He pulled back the curtain, as if the shower were a stage and his erection was the star of the show. He pulled her into the shower, turning her so that they were face-to-face.

He thrust his vták between her thighs. Natalia felt aroused, but she was also uncomfortable. The water was tepid and came down in rivulets, and she glimpsed dark patches of mold staining the tiles. This was not the romantic shower-for-two she had envisioned. "Uncomfortable" won.

She stepped out of the shower. "Vaclav, we really need to get going. We need to talk about our life in Todos Santos too."

"Natalia, are you sure you want to live in Baja for the rest of your life?"

There was an undercurrent to his voice that troubled her. "Angel says Baja is beautiful," she replied. "Laid-back. You can play music at clubs in Cabo and go surfing. I can raise goats."

"*Goats?* Goats stink!"

"And children. I want to have your children."

He climbed out of the shower and gestured for her to take a turn. She reluctantly stepped under the lukewarm spray. He picked up the miniscule bar of soap and washed her body, scrubbing hard, as if she were a child covered in mud.

"Natalia, I don't want to live in Todos Santos."

"*What?* When did you decide this? Why didn't you tell me?"

There was a long pause. Then he replied, "I wanted to tell you now, when we are together."

She stepped out of the shower, grabbed the one flimsy towel off the rack, and hurriedly dried herself off. "What's wrong with Todos Santos?"

"It's fucking hot in Mexico and everyone's poor as fuck. And I don't speak Spanish. Do you?"

"No, but I can learn. *We* can learn."

"I don't give a shit about Spanish." Vaclav grabbed the towel away from her and dried himself off.

Even though the bathroom was steaming, she felt a chill. "Where do you want to live if not Todos Santos?"

He playfully swatted her with the towel and walked out of the bathroom. "Get dressed and I will tell you. It will be a surprise, like the caviar and vodka!"

She felt the blood rushing to her cheeks. It was as if she and Vaclav were driving in a car, trying to pass a gasoline truck on the highway, but they didn't have the time or the space to make it alive.

As she finished drying herself off, she saw Vaclav pulling on a green velour tracksuit, like those that Rex's Russian oligarch friends wore on the Beau Rivage golf course. All he needs to look like one of those thugs is a heavy gold chain around his neck, she thought. When he grabbed one out of his backpack and put it on, she winced. He took his mobile phone from his pocket and began texting.

"Did you find my Target bag on the beach?" she asked, trying to control her mounting panic.

"No," he said, without looking up at her. "Someone must have ripped it off."

"We should have searched for it last night."

"I'll get you a new phone. It's all good. Get dressed." He finished his text and pushed "Send."

"I don't have clean underwear."

"Then wear dirty. Let's go." He looked out the window and searched the sky.

Her stomach clenching, Natalia hurriedly dressed in yesterday's panties and bra, and the Mexican peasant outfit. She caught her reflection in the window: she wasn't wearing a wig. She had lost it on the beach and completely forgotten about it. "Hovno!"

Vaclav put his arms around her and kissed her fuzzy head. "No worries. You look beautiful!" He escorted her out of the room.

"Where are we going?"

"You'll see." He led her down the steps from the second-floor landing to the pool patio.

In the sky, she spotted the helicopter she had seen earlier. It was flying in their direction. "Vaclav, I don't like this. I don't understand where we're going." She stopped cold. "Tell me where you want us to go."

He rolled his eyes, as if she were a little girl questioning her father's authority. "Okay, you really want to know?" He glanced at the helicopter. It was hovering over the beach, preparing to land.

She fought the panic rising in her throat. "Vaclav, please! Tell me!"

"Okay, so I have this Russian friend, Sergei, in Prague. Sergei owns the club where my band plays. His brother, Ivan, lives in Moscow. Ivan has lots of money, lots of influence. He's like this with President Popovich." Vaclav held up his hand and pressed his index and middle fingers tightly together.

Natalia's heart was pounding. "So?"

"So Ivan has a club in Moscow. He wants us to become partners. He'll get us a big apartment. My band will play in the club. You'll be, like, the hostess. We'll make big bucks. Can you picture it? The former First Lady of the United States running a club in Moscow? It will be *huuuuge...*"

The way Vaclav prolonged the word "huge," he sounded like Rex!

Fuming, she grabbed Vaclav's raised fingers. "You know what I think of your plan to live in Moscow and make big bucks?" She wrenched his index finger aside, so that only his middle finger was pointing to the sky. She bit it hard, tasting blood, then ran down the rickety staircase to the beach.

"Suka!" he yelled, shaking his hand to stop the pain. He hustled down the staircase and ran after her down the beach. He quickly caught up with her. He grabbed her roughly from behind and spun her around to face him. "It's happening, Natalia!"

His eyes glowed with wrath, like Rex's eyes when he was angry. On impulse, she did what she had long wanted to do to Rex, but never dared: She spit in his face.

Vaclav shook her hard. "You fucking bitch! It's fucking happening!"

The helicopter was descending rapidly toward the beach, its rotors whirring up a gale. When he glanced over at it, Natalia wrenched free of his grasp. She turned and ran.

"It is *not* fucking happening, you *maniak!*"

"Natalia, wait! I will give you good life! Great life!" He charged after her.

"You are not going to use me, Vaclav! I will not be used!"

"But I love you!"

"Bullshit!"

Vaclav started shouting in Russian at the top of his lungs.

Natalia turned around to see who he was shouting to: Two hulking men in red velour tracksuits, gold chains around their necks, jumped down from the helicopter. They ran toward Vaclav.

"I love you, Natalia!" Vaclav yelled. "I've always loved you!" The Russians caught up with him. The three men conferred and then took off after her together.

"I don't love *you*, Vaclav!" she screamed. "You are a self-centered, egotistical asshole, just like Rex! *Worse* than Rex! I hate you!"

She ran faster down the beach, not knowing where she was going, not knowing what her choices were. All she knew was that she had to escape the ogres behind her. She pictured the glee on Boris Popovich's pinched face as he greeted her in Moscow. The "First Lady of Russia," *Izvestia* would label her. It made her run faster.

"Madame First Lady!"

The voice she heard behind her wasn't Vaclav's. There was no trace of a Slovak or Russian accent. She turned around. Behind her, and behind Vaclav and the Russians, a man was galloping down the beach on horseback, the backpack slung over his shoulder jolting against his body each time the horse's hooves hit the sand.

Riding a bony dappled-gray horse with a scraggly tail, the man galloped past Vaclav and the Russians. They shouted at him to stop. He kicked his mount, urging it forward. As he neared her, Natalia saw that he clenched the pommel of his saddle with one hand, hanging on for dear life. With the other hand he clutched the reins of an equally skinny brown horse without a rider. The horse was following the dappled-gray's lead. They may be scrawny, she thought, but they sure can run!

Far behind the horses and the thugs, she spotted an old Mexican man trotting after them on a donkey. She remembered seeing him yesterday on the beach when two blonde teenagers were riding the same two horses. She assumed that the horses were his.

Natalia had no idea who her rescuer was. She didn't care. She ran toward him. He pulled back on his reins, yelling "Whoa!" No use. The dappled-gray was running away with him. He dropped the reins of the brown horse that he was leading and pulled back with both hands on his horse's reins.

"Whoa!" he screamed. *"Whoa!"*

Maybe it was because the dappled-gray horse saw Natalia running toward it, or that the rider was pulling back on the reins so hard that the bit hurt its mouth, but it slowed down. Behind it, the brown horse slowed too.

"Whoa, you motherfucker!"

The man's voice was stronger now, more self-confident, as if he were gaining control over his mount. Natalia didn't know for sure, but she guessed that it was his commanding tone of voice that made the dappled-gray, and then the brown horse, slow to a halt.

She could see that Vaclav and his Russian thugs were running toward them. She had only a few seconds before they would catch up. She forced her mind to remember everything she had learned from her short-lived riding lessons in Central Park. She walked calmly over to the brown horse, speaking to it in a soft, high, feminine voice: "You're so beautiful, horsey! I'm not going to hurt you, beautiful horsey!" The animal snorted and shook its head, as if eager to break into a run again.

Natalia scooped the horse's reins up from the sand, threw them over its neck, and hoisted herself up into the saddle. She wished she were wearing jeans instead of a Mexican peasant skirt. The good news was that the horse was a lot shorter than the thoroughbreds she rode in Central Park. If it threw her, she wouldn't have far to fall, and the sand was soft.

She made the clucking sound that her riding teacher had taught her and kicked the horse with her bare heels. Her heart pounded as the animal heaved its body forward, jolting into a gallop. She was both terrified and elated as the horse raced down the beach. "Elated" won.

"Yee-haw!" she couldn't stop herself from screaming. "Yee-haw!"

The dappled-gray took off after her mount. "Yee-haw!" the rider shouted.

Natalia looked behind her: Vaclav and the Russians were far behind. The men stopped running and leaned over, hands on knees, to catch their breath.

As she urged her horse on, out of the corner of her eye she caught a glimpse of the dappled-gray catching up with it. For the first time, she was close enough to see the rider's face. To her amazement, it was Phil, the creepy paparazzo she called her "shadow."

"Well, fuck me," she said out loud, because she knew that's what Angel would say right now. "He really *is* my fucking shadow!"

Suddenly Phil didn't look so creepy to her. He pointed to a sand dune up ahead. "That way!" Clucking and kicking, she pressed her horse to climb the dune. Its hooves sank into the deep sand, but it barreled upward. She urged it forward, clucking louder and kicking harder. Finally, nostrils flaring, it reached the top.

Below, Phil struggled to force his horse to follow.

"Kick him!" she shouted. "You're the boss!"

Phil kicked and clucked. Finally, the horse got the message. It lurched, hooves sinking into the sand, toward the top of the dune.

From the top, Natalia had a view of the whole beach. In the distance, she spotted Vaclav and the Russians scrambling into the helicopter. It lifted off, rotors whirring.

"Yee-haw!" she shouted, triumphant. "Yee-haw!"

Her moment of relief disappeared when she saw the helicopter turn and swoop their way. She feared that the Russians had guns, and that they would shoot her. As it bore down on them, she spotted Vaclav leaning out of the open side.

Was he holding a *pistol?*

As it drew closer, she saw that he was giving her the finger. She could see his lips moving. Over the roar of the engine, she couldn't hear what he was saying or even whether he was speaking Slovak, Russian, or English. But in any language, she was sure that Vaclav was shouting, "Fuck you!"

Natalia didn't bother to flip him the bird in return. Instead, she turned to her rescuer as his horse caught up with hers. "Phil, right?" He gaped at her, as if amazed that she knew his name. Breathless from the exertion, he simply nodded. She reached out and shook his hand. "Thank you, Phil!"

Chapter 53

Rosarito Beach, MX

December 20, 8:00 a.m.

Natalia jumped down from her horse, patted its bony, sweat-stained haunches, and led it toward a weathered shack with a sign: "Establos de Playa." She tied its reins to a post in front. Spotting a rusty bucket of water beside the shack, she hauled it over. The horse plunged its head into the bucket and sucked noisily.

Phil rode over on his dappled-gray horse. She watched as he dismounted awkwardly, as if he'd never done it before. "Are you okay?" she asked. He nodded.

"Gringo cocksuckers!"

The old Mexican man on the donkey caught up with them. "You kill my horses!"

Natalia's emotions were in turmoil: She felt rage at Vaclav and a creeping despair over the loss of her dream of true love. But she also felt jubilant from her unexpected, exhilarating escape on horseback.

"C'mon, your horses had as much fun as we did! How much do we owe you?"

The Mexican seemed surprised that she was eager to pay. "$60! Double cuz you kill my horses!"

She turned to Phil. "I'm afraid FLOTUS doesn't carry cash."

Phil dipped into his backpack, pulled out his wallet, and checked inside. "I've only got a twenty."

"No problem." She snatched the bill from him and walked over to the Mexican. He dismounted slowly, groaning, as if every bone in his body ached. "Señor?" She handed him the money. He looked at it and frowned. "Do you have a mobile phone?" she asked.

"Que?"

"A cell phone? A mobile phone with a camera?" She mimed taking a photo. "I will take a selfie with you."

Wrinkling his brow in confusion, the Mexican pulled a cell phone from the pocket of his dusty jeans. Natalia grabbed it and set it to take a selfie. She held the phone out at arm's length, slung her other arm around the man, and gave him an affectionate squeeze. He flinched, surprised. She checked the framing. "You're not smiling," she said to him. "Smile!" He managed a toothless grin.

Natalia snapped a few selfies and handed him the phone. "Show your amigos. One of them will know who I am. You can sell the picture for *mucho dinero!*"

She walked back over to her horse and patted him. "You did good. Thank you," she said. With a wave to Phil, she walked toward a gravel road that wound through the sand dunes.

"Wait!" He ran to catch up with her. They walked along for a few minutes in silence. She stepped over a dead rattlesnake that had been flattened by a tire. The glare of the morning sun bore down on her fuzz-covered head. She put her hand over it, feeling more vulnerable than ever.

"Here." Phil rummaged in his backpack and pulled out a battered blue L.A. Dodgers baseball cap. "You need this."

"That, and a lot more," she said. From his blank expression, she gathered that he didn't get her irony. She put on the hat. "Thanks."

"You're welcome."

They continued walking on the dusty road.

"So, Phil, why did you do that?"

"Give you the hat?"

"No. Why did you rescue me?"

He stopped to think about it, as if the question hadn't occurred to him. "I was a Boy Scout?" He said it tentatively, as if unsure whether that explained it or not. Natalia remembered when her brother, Franc, joined the Boy Scouts in Slovakia. "Do a Good Turn Daily," was their slogan. Franc didn't do a "good turn" even once. They kicked him out.

"How did you know I was in Baja?"

Phil lowered his eyes, gazing shyly at the ground. "I've taken a lot of pictures of you, Madame First Lady."

"I know that."

"It makes me feel that I know you at least a little bit, Madame First Lady."

"Please don't call me Madame First Lady. It makes me sound like a dictator's wife." She chuckled. "Which I guess, in a way, I am. Anyway, my name's Natalia."

"I know, er, Natalia."

"So, okay, you take pictures of me. How did that lead you to find me?"

"Well, I studied my photos of you and your hairdresser leaving the White House."

"How did you know that was *me*? Do you work for the CIA?"

He smiled nervously, as if unsure if she was joking. "Then, on the beach this morning, it looked like your, er, *boyfriend*, or whatever, like he was trying to make you do something you didn't want to. I mean, I was far away, but I have this very long telephoto lens. I could see your face like I was right next to you. You sure were angry!"

"You got that right!"

"So that Mexican guy was walking his horses on the beach—"

"And you borrowed a couple?"

"Yeah, I borrowed them."

"First time on a horse?"

"You got that right!"

"Fun, right? *Yee-haw!*"

He nodded. *"Yee-haw!"*

"I'm glad you did it. Thank you."

Natalia spotted a bus stop across the street and hurried

toward it. He kept up with her. She frowned. "So what are you going to do now? Sell your best shots of me and my boyfriend to the *National Enquirer*? Make enough money to put your kids through college?"

"I don't have kids. I don't have a family, except for my mom in Pasadena."

She sat down on the bus-stop bench. "Can I see the pictures you took of me?" She snatched his backpack and rummaged inside it.

He sat down beside her. "The pictures are on my laptop and in my camera."

"Really?" She pulled out a file folder. "What's in here?" She opened it and looked through the photos of Pasadena's famous buildings and landmarks. "These are nice! Beautiful! How come you don't take serious photos, like these? I mean, what kind of life is it lurking around the White House for a chance to get one cheap shot of me?" She put the folder back in the backpack. "No money in historic buildings, right?"

He hesitated, unsure what to say next. "Y'know, I'm sorry I took all those pictures of you and...that *guy*," he said softly. "I mean, I could see how much he meant to you and that stuff you did together last night was pretty private."

"You took pictures of us last *night*?"

He nodded guiltily. "And of you fighting on the beach today. It must be hard for you. I can only imagine how you feel."

"I feel like hovno, like shit, Phil. And disappointed. I'm sad it didn't work out with the man I thought was my true love. Most of all, I'm angry at myself for being so goddamned *hlúpy*, stupid!" She fought back tears.

A horn blasted. Natalia looked up, expecting a bus. Instead, a dusty Range Rover screeched up. Two brawny Mexicans barreled out of it. They pointed pistols at them. "Vamanos!"

Natalia's heart jumped. Phil raised his hands. "Don't hurt us, please!"

One thug opened the rear door to the Range Rover and motioned for them to climb in. The last thing Natalia saw before a gunnysack was shoved over her head was a striking Mexican teenager in cutoffs in the back seat. Clutching the plastic Target shopping bag that Natalia had lost on the beach, she was smiling broadly, as if she had just won the lottery.

Chapter 54

The White House

December 20, 12:00 p.m.

Repulsive. The President of the United States is repulsive, thought Moon.

Across from where she sat primly on a sofa in the Oval Office, a smile pasted on her First Lady face, Funck was hunched forward in an armchair. He was holding a coffee cup, his legs spread wide, his gut lolling over his belt, his long red tie dangling below his crotch like a wayward testicle. Cookie crumbs flew out of his mouth as he pontificated to his honored guests from Bangladesh about the future of the planet. Amazing how Rex can avoid the use of words like "global warming" and "climate change" when talking to statesmen from a country that will be underwater in ten years, she thought. Not one of the three short, dark-skinned Bangladeshi men could get a word in edgewise. But Moon had quickly learned that this was how it always went during diplomatic meet-and-greets with the President.

Her only job was to sit still, nod politely, and say nothing more than, "Pleased to meet you," and "So happy you could join us" in her best Natalia voice. No more visits to hospitals for *this* First Lady. Gretchen had decreed that Moon was only allowed to join meetings and events *within* the White House, where she, Sally-Ann, and Special Agent Pricker could keep a close eye on her. Sally-Ann sat in a chair behind Moon, hugging her Tory Burch tote bag as if it were a lap dog. Moon had dubbed her "Sally-Ann the Minder."

At least Gretchen had allowed Moon to buy a few items of designer clothing for her First Lady public appearances. It kept her from going stir-crazy. She smoothed down the bodice of the $3,000 yellow Victoria Beckham maxi-dress that she had selected for today's Oval Office meeting. It fit in with the yellow-and-cream-striped upholstered sofa.

Tuning out Funck's monologue, Moon fantasized about lying in bed this afternoon and googling "expensive designer women's clothing" on the heavily monitored iPad that Gretchen had given her. Suddenly, the First Daughter walked into the Oval Office. Teetering in her five-inch-high Manolo stilettos, she rushed over to the President.

"You all know the First Daughter and future President," he said proudly, putting his arm around her. "What is it, baby?" Moon cringed that he called his thirty-six-year-old daughter "baby" and fondled her in public. Gretchen whispered into his ear. Handing off his coffee cup to her, he lurched to his feet. "Everyone out!" He clapped his hands, as if his distinguished foreign guests were the hired help. "President Popovich is calling on Skype!"

The Bangladeshis bowed low as they backed out of the Oval Office, as if Rex were the king of England. Moon stayed put, hoping that Gretchen wouldn't notice her. Rex never did. She was curious to watch a call between these two world leaders. She wondered which was worse? Funck or Popovich?

Rex walked over and sat down behind his antique mahogany desk, putting his feet up. Moon noticed flattened lavender bubble gum on the sole of his left shoe. She wondered if he had fucked a teeny-bopper at the Funck Hotel last night. Who else would chew lavender bubble gum?

Rex fiddled with the computer on his desk. "How the hell do you get Skype?"

"Oh, Daddy. You're so silly!" Gretchen walked over, grabbed the mouse, and deftly clicked on Skype. She stood behind her father, her face out of range of his Skype video camera. Moon stealthily stepped around the side of Rex's desk so that she could watch without being noticed. Sally-Ann quietly parked her tote bag on the chair and followed.

Boris Popovich's pale, haggard face filled the computer screen.

"Hey, how's it going, Boris?" said Rex. "I'm hoping you can come spend a weekend with us at Beau Rivage in Palm Beach!" Eying his own small video image in the upper right-hand corner of the screen, Rex smoothed down his comb-over and checked his teeth for gunk. "We'll play some golf, hang out in the sauna. I want to talk to you about this deal that's great for Russia, great for the U.S. You're gonna love it." He came out with it, flashing a pitchman smile: "How about building a Funck International Hotel in Kiev?"

"Kiev is in Ukraine, not in Russia," said Popovich.

"Oh. Well, I bet Kiev won't always be in Ukraine, not if you have your way, right, Boris?" On-screen, Popovich didn't move a muscle. "Anyway, Natalia and I would love to get you down to Beau Rivage. How about this weekend?"

A sly smile crept across the Russian President's face. "Natalia will be back in U.S. by then?"

"Huh?"

"You did not know? Natalia is in Rosarito Beach, Mexico."

"*What?*"

"My sources spotted your First Lady on the beach. Want to see?" Popovich showed a screen beside him that projected a photo taken from a helicopter: a fuzzy-headed Natalia galloping across the sand on a skinny brown horse, her Mexican peasant skirt flapping in the wind. "Natalia is good rider," he said. "I will take her riding at my *dacha* sometime. She will ride Cossack stallion!"

Tongue-tied, Rex glanced over his shoulder at Gretchen. She whispered in his ear. "Yeah, Natalia loves to ride," he said to Popovich, doing his best to recover. "That's why she went to Mexico. She's on a little horseback-riding vacation."

"Really? With *this* guy?" Popovich pushed a button and a selfie flashed on his screen: a handsome Slavic-looking man with a ponytail sitting on a bed beside a sleeping Natalia. They were both naked.

Holy shit, thought Moon. That must be Vaclav.

"Okay, Popovich, what do you want?" Rex's eyes narrowed, his mouth forming that fish "O" that reminded Moon of a big fleshy koi. "How about I build you that Funck International Hotel in Kiev at my own expense?"

"I told you: Kiev is not in Russia. How about you cancel the economic sanctions you slapped on my Russian colleagues, especially our mutual friends Igor, Arkady, and Oleg? You play golf with them, no? How could you do that to golf—?"

"I had to do sanctions on them. The press was up my ass, saying you fucked around with our Presidential election."

"You think you'd be sitting where you are right now if we hadn't?"

"That's fake news!"

"Whatever you say." Popovich's face hardened. "So you 'had to do sanctions?'" He flashed another selfie on his screen: Vaclav beaming at the camera while making love to Natalia from behind, her face to the wall. "I 'had to do' pretty pictures."

Moon saw that Rex was sweating profusely and his face was turning red, warning signs of a stroke. She tensed, her RN persona kicking in.

"You motherfucker!" yelled Rex. "I'm not taking this shit from you, Popovich! Who do you think you're fucking talking to?" He looked around on the computer for a button to turn off Skype. He was clueless. As if ready to explode, he stood up from his desk and stormed across the room. "Go fuck yourself!" he shouted. "You and your fucking oligarchs!"

On Skype, Moon saw Popovich reach for the button to turn off his own computer. Before he could, Gretchen slipped into Rex's desk chair and smiled. "President Popovich? Hi, I'm Gretchen Funck. We met at the summit meeting, remember?" Popovich didn't respond.

Moon heard a *ffft* and glanced over at Rex. Guzzling from a newly opened can of Diet Coke, he slumped down onto a sofa. He grabbed the remote and aimed it at the TV: FOX News clicked on.

"Anyway, I want you to know I just talked to Daddy," continued Gretchen. "Good news! He's more than happy to lift the economic sanctions against your distinguished Russian colleagues."

"Yes?" Popovich was scowling, unconvinced.

"Absolutely! Consider it done! So, like, can you kill any fake news about the First Lady being in Mexico? And, I mean, can Daddy trust you to burn those photos?"

"He doesn't trust President of Russia?"

"Of course he does. It's just, y'know... Okay, the truth? It's really me, President Popovich. I'm pretty new at this politics thing, so I just need, like, your reassurance."

Popovich narrowed his eyes into slits. "I hear someday you are running for President of United States."

"I sure hope so, President Popovich! And I bet you'll still be ruling Russia when I do!"

"You can count on that!" Offscreen, an aide handed him a shot glass brimming with a clear liquid that Moon guessed was vodka. "And you can trust me." He lifted his glass. "*Na zdorovye!*" He chugged the shot.

"Cheers to you, too, President Popovich! And thanks so much! I hope we'll see you down at Beau Rivage soon!" Gretchen clicked on the Skype "Off" button. Popovich's face disappeared.

With a sigh of relief, she sank back in her father's chair. "I hope that bastard *is* still in office when I'm President! I'll nuke his ass!" Rex didn't respond, allowing FOX News to wash over him.

Her iPhone buzzed, throbbing on top of Rex's desk. She looked at the screen to see who was calling. "Fuck." She scooped up the phone and punched the "On" button. "Conner? This better be good!" She listened. "You saw Natalia riding a horse on the—?" She listened another beat. "She disappeared?"

"Tell Conner his ass is fired!" Rex shouted from the sofa.

"No, Conner, you are definitely *not* fired," Gretchen said into her phone. "Daddy was overreacting. He does that sometimes, don't you? In fact, Daddy is promoting you to special agent! Is that cool, or what?" She listened again. "Of course you can drive the Beast in the Presidential motorcade. President Funck would love that!" She listened again. "You're welcome, but Conner, there is only one caveat." She listened, rolling her eyes. "What's a 'caveat?' It's, like, a thing, a condition. You only get to drive the Beast if you do it." She listened again. "You can't guess the 'thing,' Conner? The 'condition?' Well, then listen to me and listen good: If you tell anyone, and I mean *anyone*, the fake news about the First Lady in Mexico, you will not be *driving* the fucking Beast. I will personally throw you *under* the fucking Beast! Now get your ass back to Washington!"

She pressed the "Off" button and threw the phone onto the desk. "Fuck me," she murmured. Then, with a sudden sweep of her arm, she knocked the phone onto the floor and put her head on the desk, face-first. "Fuck, fuck, *fuck* me!" she mumbled into the burnished mahogany.

Moon and Sally-Ann stealthily returned to the sofa across from the President's. Moon didn't know what amazed her more: that the conversations she had just heard actually took place, or that neither the President nor the First Daughter realized she was in the room.

Chapter 55

Helicopter over Baja, MX

December 20, 1:00 p.m.

Phil sat in the rear of the cramped four-seat helicopter, shoulder-to-shoulder with Natalia. He glanced down at the mountainous desert landscape far below them. He was relieved that before the helicopter had lifted off, the Mexican teenager in the Range Rover removed the gunnysacks from their heads and the ropes binding their wrists. "I'm Rosa," she said. "I wanna make sure you catch the awesome view. Baja at its best!"

In the distance, he glimpsed the glittering water that hugged the narrow Baja Peninsula: the ink-blue Pacific to the west, and to the east the Gulf of California, its water the blue-green hue of Navajo turquoise. He resisted the urge to tug his camera out of his backpack and snap some beauty shots. A hot desert wind buffeted the helicopter. Shooting the view through an ordinary lens might result in blurry photos caused by the movement, but he knew that if he took pictures with his new 600mm lens, they would be as clear as if he had taken them on solid ground. My new lens was made for panoramas like this, he thought.

This was his first ride in a helicopter. He realized that he would have considered it exhilarating if it weren't for two facts: 1.) The sides of the chopper were open, essentially making his seat belt the only thing between him and oblivion; and 2.) When he arrived at his destination, he guessed that there was a 99 percent chance he would be killed. He didn't know whether to laugh or cry. Why should I fear plunging out of a helicopter to my death, he thought, if I'm going to die from a bullet later anyway?

Everyone in the helicopter was wearing headsets so that they could communicate over the drone of the engine. Rosa sat in front, next to the pilot. "Can you hear me back there?" she said, her voice through his earphones muffled by static. "If you can, raise your hand." Phil raised his. Natalia didn't respond. She was staring down out of the open cockpit, her expression flat with despair. I hope she isn't thinking about jumping, he thought. He nudged her gently. She slowly raised her hand halfway.

"Good, so I'm sure you're wondering where we're heading," said Rosa. "Here's the deal: We're on our way to meet Dionisio Reyes. *The* Dionisio Reyes. You heard of him, right? Nod if you heard of him."

Phil didn't respond. He wasn't sure if the reason Natalia didn't respond was because she hadn't heard of the name either, or that she had zoned out.

"Shit! You never heard of Dionisio Reyes?!"

"Not really," Phil said.

"What planet do you live on? Dio runs the Baja drug cartel. He's, like, one of the richest, most wanted men in Mexico. Make that the world!" She shook her head. "Whatever you do, when you meet him, act like you heard of him, like he's a big fucking deal! It'll kill him if you don't and then he might..." She stopped herself. "Nod if you got that."

Phil nodded and nudged Natalia. She nodded too.

"So the reason I'm taking you to Dio is cuz me and my amiga, Maria, discovered that one of you sitting back there, okay, the lady with the bald head, was getting it on with a guy who was not her husband—who just happens to be the President of the United States."

Phil debated whether or not to ask Rosa how she found out. Before he could decide...

"I won't reveal the details of how we made our discovery," she said. "I'm not exactly proud of our research methods. But, I mean, like, *whoa*... Madam First Lady, your guy was a hunk, a total stud!" When Natalia didn't respond, she continued, "Movie-star handsome, y'know? I don't blame you for dumping your pendejo husband for him."

"Too bad my movie star turned out to be as big an asshole as my husband," Natalia murmured.

"Yeah, that really sucks, right?"

"May they both rot in hell!"

It surprised Phil that Natalia was so straightforward with Rosa. Maybe it was a woman thing. Or maybe it was because she was so angry with both her husband and her lover, and herself, that she didn't care what she said or to whom she said it. He saw that her eyes brimmed with tears. He reached into his backpack, pulled out a half-used package of Wash 'n Dry towelettes and held it out to her. She didn't take it, as if she were too numb to notice.

"Anyway, you don't need to sweat that Dio is gonna, like, y'know, whack you, ma'am," continued Rosa. "He's gonna contact President Funck and make a trade for you. Y'see, his baby brother, Pancho, is in a U.S. prison awaiting trial. The poor fuck's been rotting in there for six months. Pancho's a lot better looking than Dionisio, but Dio's the brother with the brains. I bet he's smarter than President Funck too, and that he's got a shitload more money!"

Phil was surprised that Rosa was such a motor mouth. Since he could see that Natalia was lost in thought, he felt an impulse to keep the conversation going with Rosa. She had said that her boss wouldn't kill Natalia, but she hadn't mentioned what Dio would do to him. Maybe if she gets to like me, I'll have a better chance of staying alive, he thought.

"How'd you learn to speak such good English?" he asked.

"Dude, I spent a summer at my sister's in San Diego," Rosa said. "Carla's married to a Chicano. He's the lemur keeper at the San Diego Zoo. I spent the whole time watching reruns of *Seinfeld*, *Friends*, and *Mad Men*. By the time I got off their couch and went home to TJ, I could pass for a gringo."

"Do you know where the name 'Dionisio' comes from?" he

said, remembering the *D'Aulaire's Greek Myths* book that he had pored over at the library when he was a kid. "It's Spanish for 'Dionysus.'"

"What's Dionysus?"

"In Greek mythology, Dionysus is the god of wine and drunken revelry."

"I never heard about Greek gods, but Dionysus sure sounds like Dio! He makes his own wine—he's got, like, this secret vineyard—and he sure as fuck loves to party!" She laughed. "He also loves playing the stock market and building houses. Wait 'til you see the house he put on top of a pinche mountain. He calls it his 'fortress.' He's totally into design porn."

"Design *porn*?"

"He creams over magazines about beautiful houses. I always bring him some when I visit." She rustled in the plastic Target bag on her lap, pulled out a magazine, and held it up for Phil to see: *Architectural Digest*. "He's got this dream to someday get his fortress on the cover of *A.D.*"

Phil was surprised when Natalia spoke up. "Rosa, you should see Phil's architectural pictures. They're amazing!" She nudged him. "Show her the photos you took of famous buildings."

"Really?"

"Yes, Phil," Natalia said firmly, like a command. "They're in that file folder I saw." She leaned toward him, opened her eyes wide, and stared into his, as if trying to tell him something.

He didn't have a clue what Natalia was getting at, but he dug the file folder out of his backpack. It wasn't easy; the wind was buffeting the helicopter more powerfully now. With an unsteady hand, he handed the folder over the seat to Rosa. "Here you go."

She opened the folder and leafed through the historic photos. "Awesome," she said, "for pictures of buildings."

"That's my true love," he said. "Why I became a photographer."

"You like buildings more than people?"

"No, but beautiful buildings are works of art," he said. "Plus, y'know what? They don't move!"

Rosa laughed at Phil's sort-of-joke. He told himself that he was on the right track, to keep talking. "I took those pictures in Pasadena, home of the Rose Bowl. Have you ever watched the Rose Bowl?"

"The what?"

"It's a football game on New Year's Day."

"Mexicans only watch soccer, and on New Year's Day I'm too hungover to watch anything." She looked at a few more pictures. "Yeah, these are pretty damn good."

"Aren't they?" said Natalia. "If Phil takes pictures of Dio's house, I can get them into *Architectural Digest*."

"No shit?"

"I'm best friends with the magazine editor. We do lunch whenever I'm in New York. She'll love Phil's photos. You think *A.D.* wouldn't want photos of a house owned by one of the most famous men in the world?"

"Que chido! That would be way cool," said Rosa. "I'll tell Dio."

Natalia winked at Phil. He finally understood the point of her sudden enthusiasm for his architectural photos. If he took photos of Dionisio's house, pictures guaranteed to end up in *Architectural Digest*, his chances of getting "whacked" would drop to 50 percent, or maybe, if he was really lucky, zero. He touched Natalia's hand and mouthed the words: "Thank you."

Rosa returned the file to him. "Photo guy, what's your name again?"

"Phil," he said.

"So, Phil, how about you show me the pictures you took of the lovebirds. I mean, me and Maria watched them going at it on the beach through night-vision binocs, but I spotted you down there with your camera. If you got some hot pictures, I'd sure love to check them out."

Phil stiffened. It hit him that he didn't want to show his

pictures of Natalia and her lover to Rosa or to anyone. Now that he had rescued her from him, he felt overwhelmed with guilt about invading her privacy. He knew that he could get hundreds of thousands of dollars for the shots he took of the romantic couple. Maybe even a million. He pictured a bidding war with the *National Enquirer, People, Us* and perhaps even the *New York Post* or—okay, it was a stretch—the *Washington Post,* all competing for an exclusive. He had waited his entire career for an opportunity like this. He wanted more than anything to make his mother proud of him.

Suddenly he felt stupid for not realizing it earlier: Would photos that people snicker at and gossip about, photos that some men would masturbate over, make his mother proud? No way.

Disgusted with himself, he closed his eyes and shook his head, as if hoping to erase the images in the photos from his mind.

"Hey, photo dude, Phil, we're gonna land soon," said Rosa. "Show me the pinche pictures!"

He pulled his Dell laptop out of his backpack and turned it on. Every photo he had ever taken lived on this laptop. He caressed its smooth metal skin, as if saying goodbye to a dear friend who was on his deathbed. You've been good to me, and I'm really sorry about what I must do, but it's the right thing, he thought.

"Let me upload the pictures I took this morning from my camera first," he said to Rosa. "It'll just take a minute." He grabbed his Nikon, removed the photo disk, and slotted it into his laptop. "Then every single picture will be on my computer. It's easier to view them there than on my camera."

"Just pinche hurry. We'll be there in ten minutes." The wind shook the helicopter. "If we don't crash first." She elbowed the pilot and bitched at him in Spanish, as if the strong gusts were his fault.

A *ding* indicated that the photos on his camera had uploaded to his laptop. He sucked in his breath and hit the key to delete all the photos on the photo disk. When it was completed, he removed the empty disk and inserted it back into his camera.

The helicopter jolted in the stiff wind. He clutched the computer on his lap. On the screen, he glanced at the photos of Natalia and Vaclav that he had taken last night: Dozens of beautiful shots of the loving couple on the beach at sunset that captured the joy in their eyes and their passion. In some of the photos they were kissing. In others they were pulling off each other's clothes and embracing on the sand. He was ashamed to admit that several of the photos bordered on soft porn.

He turned to the new photos from this morning. Among the shots he took of them leaving the hotel, some revealed the anger on Natalia's face as she confronted Vaclav. The shots he took on the beach captured Vaclav fiercely grabbing and shaking her. He remembered when he took them; that was the moment he decided to help her. He knew it was lame, but one of the three Boy Scout Promises had flashed in his mind: "Duty to Other People."

He studied the next photo, of Natalia wrenching away from Vaclav. After he took that picture was when he stuffed his camera into his backpack and hurried over to the old man walking horses on the beach. Phil had never been on a horse—he was scared of horses as a child—but he grabbed the reins of the brown horse and then hoisted himself up onto the back of the dappled-gray horse. He kicked the horse as he had seen it done in old Western movies on TCM and took off after Natalia.

Thinking back on that moment now, he realized: In my whole life, I've never done anything so brave. The wind pummeled the helicopter again. He knew that what he was about to do next required even more bravery.

"Rosa," he called. "I think I'm going to barf!"

"I don't blame you!" As the helicopter lurched in the wind, she grabbed the metal safety bar above the cockpit window.

"Just don't barf in the chopper!"

With one hand, Phil grabbed the railing on the back of her seat. He tightly held the laptop with his other hand and leaned out of the open side of the chopper. Looking down at the ground, thousands of feet below, made his head spin.

He felt a hand grab the back of his waistband. "I've got you," said Natalia.

Phil waited until another gust of wind slammed the helicopter. He leaned farther out over the side, made a loud barfing sound, and then let go of his laptop. It dropped like a rock.

"Fuck!" he yelled. "My whole life is on that laptop! Fuck!" He wiped his mouth, as if cleaning up vomit.

But Rosa wasn't watching. In the front seat, she was puking out of the helicopter.

"I'm so sorry, Phil," said Natalia, letting go of his waistband.

"That sucks big-time!" Rosa said, wiping her mouth and groaning. "Wait! Shit! Does that mean you lost all your pinches photos of Natalia and pinche lover boy?"

"Fuck, fuck, fuck!" cried Phil, playing it for all it was worth. "I'm totally fucked!"

Feeling Natalia's warm hand on his arm, he met her eyes. She mouthed the words: "Thank you."

Chapter 56

Middle of Nowhere, Baja, MX

December 20, 4:00 p.m.

"Try my Tempranillo, Señora Funck."

Natalia wasn't accustomed to drinking wine, certainly not in the afternoon, but her host had insisted that she sample the latest vintages from his secret vineyard in the Valle de la something in Baja. She was lightheaded after sipping what she had considered a bitter Zinfandel, but she sensed that if she turned down another glass, he would be hurt, or worse, pissed off at her. She forced a smile. "If you insist."

As Dionisio Reyes handed her a Baccarat crystal glass of ruby wine, she sized him up. He was a heavy-set man about her height and age, with obviously dyed black hair and miniscule strands bordering his hairline, the telltale sign of a hair weave. His face was badly pocked with the vestiges of teenage acne and scarred from knife fights. I doubt that a good plastic surgeon, or even a great one, could turn this toad into a prince, she thought.

An hour ago, she didn't know what to expect when the helicopter landed on the mountaintop and three husky men in white-linen suits escorted her and Phil into the drug lord's fortress. She certainly couldn't have predicted Dionisio Reyes' warm greeting. She had the sense that his sociability was less because of her status as First Lady than his loneliness. Rosa had mentioned that since both the U.S. and Mexican feds, plus every rival Mexican drug cartel, were out to catch or kill him, Dio was stuck here in hiding.

He nodded for her to take a sip of wine. "You know, it's a miracle that anyone can grow wine grapes in Mexico because it's below the 30th parallel, the theoretical boundary of successful grape growing," he said. "Fortunately, my vineyard is arid—grapes hate humidity—and located at a high altitude. That's why my wine is so great, so terrific!"

"Great" and "terrific" were two of Rex's favorite adjectives. Rex and Dio would probably get along like old friends, she thought. They both believe their own bullshit. With Dio's eyes on her, she took a sip. "Delicious," she said, wishing there was a potted plant nearby where she could dump the rest of the wine in her glass.

Grinning with pride, he walked over to Phil, who was setting up bottles of Dio wine on a massive oak table. Natalia was relieved that the two men had bonded. *Architectural Digest* had been the two magic words out of her mouth. It didn't take long for Dio to promise to spare Phil's life as a thank-you for Phil photographing Dio's home for the magazine. Phil suggested placing Dio's wine bottles in some of the shots, even though the wine wasn't for sale. "They'll know what a multi-talented man you are," he said. "That you are not just a, er, businessman."

"My editor friend at *Architectural Digest* will love your house, Señor Reyes," said Natalia, taking in the vast, circular great room.

Dio beamed. "You really think so?"

"Absolutely!" In truth, she didn't know the editor of *A.D.* It would be her secret.

She had to admit that Dio's house was one of the most magnificent she had ever set foot in. From the air, as the helicopter had swooped closer to the craggy desert mountain, it was impossible to see that there was a dwelling on the summit. "Dio has a super-high-tech camouflage system," Rosa explained to her and Phil. "It uses computer-generated imaging to prevent anyone from spotting the house from the air unless he gives the go-ahead." She coaxed Phil to aim his camera at where her finger pointed, to capture the moment the system was turned off so that they could land. A flash of light and suddenly they could see a massive glass and sandstone structure poised on what moments before had looked like a rugged mountaintop.

Inside, the sense that the house was an extension of the mountain played out through boulders that seemingly erupted out of the polished-granite floors, rough sandstone walls, and soaring, cantilevered windows that overlooked the steep mountainside. The natural style was definitely more to Natalia's liking than the antique-and-crystal-chandelier-French-whorehouse style that Rex favored. Though sunlight poured inside, the temperature was comfortable thanks to a state-of-the-art solar-powered cooling system. "We are off the grid," Dio had explained with pride.

She walked over and sat down on a supple latte-colored leather armchair, gazing out at a terrace. Rosa, their strangely friendly teenage "escort," was splashing in a swimming pool with her three-year-old daughter, Conchita.

After they had landed, Rosa introduced Conchita to her, explaining that her daughter lived here with Rosa's mother, who was Dio's cook. The little girl shook Natalia's hand softly, gazing at her with dark eyes fringed with long eyelashes, and welcomed her politely in perfect English. Natalia was enchanted. Rosa said that Dio enjoyed having a child in the house, especially one that was essentially a prison for him. "His own children...there are too many to count," she joked, "live with his numerous ex-wives and ex-mistresses in secret compounds of their own, scattered across Mexico."

The first thing out of Dio's mouth when Natalia had met him was, "Do not worry, Señora Funck. I do not have sex with women over the age of eighteen." Then he looked her up and down and added, "If I ever made an exception, it would be you." She sensed from the leaden tone of his voice that he had only said it to flatter her, not because he really meant it. At least that's what she told herself.

Natalia heard the jingle of what sounded to her practiced

ear like 14-karat gold. An elderly woman wearing bangles on both arms, no doubt to hide her loose, crepe-like skin, and a short yellow sundress that was much too young for her, approached. "Greetings, Madame Funck," the woman said in a gravely smoker's voice that reminded her of her mother's. Her Juvedermed, Botoxed, and plastic-surgery-planed face also reminded her of Ingrid.

Natalia guessed: "Señora Reyes?"

Dionisio's mother held out her hand. The emerald-cut diamond on her ring was larger than Natalia's, perhaps 20 karats, and she wore it on her middle finger. As the mother of a drug lord, perhaps it is appropriate that she wear it on her "fuck-you" finger, she thought.

"Welcome to our beautiful home. Please call me Isabella."

Natalia shook Isabella's hand, trying to decide what to say next: Not happy to be here? Please don't let your son kill me? She glanced down at the glass of wine she was holding. "Your son makes excellent wine," she said. In her mind, she added: But it's weird to drink wine here that's the color of blood.

Isabella attempted to smile, but her lips barely moved. Natalia recognized it as a sign of too much Botox on her upper lip. She had once had that problem herself. Seeing it now on this woman made her vow never to get Botox again.

"Are we ready?" Across the room, Dio drained his wineglass and handed it to a white-uniformed Mexican butler. "I want to contact your husband, Señora Funck, and settle the business I have with him. I am eager to get down to business I find much more exciting: helping Señor Smith photograph my house for *Architectural Digest*."

Natalia was about to join Dio, but Isabella stopped her. "Before you go, there's a favor I must ask."

"Certainly," she said.

"I'll be in Miami next week." Isabella touched her cheek lightly. "Time for a little touchup, you know how it is," she said in a conspiratorial whisper. She waited for a response. Natalia just smiled. "Anyway, it has always been my dream to visit Beau Rivage. Is that something you can arrange? I know your husband may have a problem with my son, but I have many aliases, many passports."

"Do you?"

As if eager to close the deal, Isabella added, "You can tell your husband that I am willing to make a substantial donation to his favorite cause."

"I'm sure he'll appreciate that," she said. Especially because his favorite cause is himself, she thought. She turned to go, then remembered something and turned back to Isabella. "My mother is a member of Beau Rivage. She has lunch there five days a week. If you'd like, I'm happy to ask her to take you to lunch there as her guest."

Isabella clasped her hands together gratefully. "How lovely! Thank you!"

"You two will love each other."

Chapter 57

The White House

December 20, 9:00 p.m.

"This is a fucking disgrace! A total fucking disaster!"

Pacing his bedroom, Rex Funck hurled his can of Diet Coke at the TV screen. It bounced off, leaving droplets of brown liquid, like dirty tears, on Christian Anderson's face. The CNN anchor was interviewing a psychiatrist about the President's decision to lift the economic sanctions on the Russian oligarchs.

"Dr. Frankenberg, do you agree with *The New York Times*'s implication that President Funck's latest decision reveals an unsound mental capacity?" asked Anderson.

The bald, elderly psychiatrist twisted the tip of his waxed gray moustache. "POTUS's abrupt about-face on a far-reaching economic decision, combined with his recent episode of apparent mysophobia, germ phobia, is more than worrying." He shook his head. "Worst-case scenario, the President could be on the verge of losing contact with reality!"

Rex muted the sound. He pointed his stubby finger at Gretchen, who was sitting on a sofa next to Pricker, both their faces hidden behind sanitary masks. "This is all your fault, First Daughter. I should spank your ass!"

Sitting with Sally-Ann on the sofa across the room, their faces also masked, Moon snickered. I bet POTUS and the First Daughter would both get off on that, she thought.

"Oh, calm your body down, Daddy," said Gretchen, as if scolding one of her children. "What choice did we have? I mean, even if President Popovich doesn't make public the photos he's got of Natalia and her hottie, now we've got this selfie to explain away." She pointed to the TV screen: Christian Anderson was commenting on a selfie of an unidentified old Mexican man in

329

a straw hat posing with a bald woman in a Mexican peasant blouse who looked uncannily like the First Lady.

"Tell them it's fake!"

"At least I'm doing something that's getting good ratings," said Moon, her voice muffled by the face mask. She nodded to the TV screen. CNN was running a video shot this afternoon: *The First Lady walking into a Breast Cancer charity fashion show, Sally-Ann trailing behind her. FLOTUS looks glamorous in a long, sweeping Dolce and Gabbana dress imprinted with portraits of famous women from Joan of Arc to Frida Kahlo. The audience, including celebs Sarah Jessica Parker and Cindy Crawford, gives her a standing ovation. Sarah urges Natalia to model her outfit on the runway. Natalia hesitates, but Cindy brings over a small stepladder and helps her up onto the runway. Like the famous fashion model that she once was, FLOTUS does the "walk" down the runway. She is poised, elegant, a smash. The crowd goes wild.*

"They loved me!" said Moon, tears in her eyes.

Sitting beside her, Sally-Ann checked that Gretchen wasn't watching, then pulled down her face mask, revealing her wide grin. "You rocked!" She stealthily high-fived Moon.

The Skype tone *wah-wahed* on Rex's desk computer.

"If that's Popovich again, tell him to shove it," he said to Gretchen. He grabbed another Diet Coke from the mini-fridge behind his desk. Gretchen hustled over to the computer. "It's from someone named 'Dionisio' in Baja California," she said, reading the screen as she sank into his desk chair. "Isn't that some Greek god?"

"Don't answer!" He cracked open the can and swigged the soda.

"He's texting." Gretchen read his words on the screen, her eyes widening. "Holy shit! He says he's got Natalia! She's his hostage!"

"I don't believe it! It's fake! Hang up!" He flopped down into an armchair and put his stockinged feet up onto the coffee table, knocking off a bottle of Purell. Sally-Ann hastily put it back.

"Daddy, wait! He wants to trade Natalia for his brother, Pancho Reyes. He says Pancho's in a federal supermax prison in Colorado."

"Pricker, check to see if we've got a greaser named Pancho Reyes in supermax," said Rex.

Pricker googled on his laptop. "Yeah, we do."

"What's he in for?"

Pricker scanned his screen and summarized: "He's awaiting trial for killing twelve undercover DEA agents in Baja. His brother is Dionisio Reyes, head of the Baja cartel. Listen to this: Talk about a dufus. Pancho Reyes was nabbed by the feds when he was partying with some bimbos on a yacht off Cabo." He chuckled. "They were all bare-assed!"

"Got any photos of that?"

"Nope. Here's all I got." Pricker turned his laptop around to show his screen to Rex: a photo of Dionisio Reyes snapped on the sly in an airport, and a mug shot of Pancho Reyes. "Dio—that's what they call the older brother—is the ugly one. But you can see his younger brother Pancho's kinda hot. At least he thinks so." He enlarged Pancho's photo. "Looks like he plucks his eyebrows and does Botox and filler. Must be gay."

"That's not just for homos," said Rex. "Lots of heteros do it."

Yeah, like you and your sons, fucking Funck fucker, thought Moon. She winked at Sally-Ann, who winked back.

"Check one more thing for me," Funck said. "How much is this cartel boss, Dionysus, or whatever the fuck his name is, worth?"

Pricker googled again. "According to the FBI, $53 billion."

"Fuck the FBI. They're morons. I bet he's worth more." Rex walked over to his desk, yanked his daughter out of his chair, and sat down. "Gretchen, baby, take the call." She leaned over and clicked the mouse on the prompt.

Moon crept from the sofa to a spot behind the desk so that

she could see the computer screen. Sally-Ann joined her. Neither Rex nor Gretchen noticed.

On-screen: A man with a scarred face standing beside a bald-headed Natalia.

"Shit," said Rex, surveying their faces. "Looks like we need a couple of paper bags for you two. Honey, what the fuck happened to your *hair*?"

"Hi, Rex. And how are *you*?"

"I wish I could say 'happier' now that I see you."

"But you can't, right?"

"You said it, sweetheart, not me!"

"What the fuck?" Dio scowled. "I thought you were one happy family. Let's make this quick. You give me my brother, Pancho. I give you back your wife."

"What if I don't want her?"

"Daddy, you don't mean that," whispered Gretchen.

Moon would have laughed, but she feared for Natalia's life.

"So Dio *whatever*, how about I build a Funck International Hotel in Cabo? Funck is a much bigger brand than Four Seasons, Rosewood, or Hilton. My son just went to Cabo to check them out. He says they're shit. A total disgrace!"

"*A disgrace*? I own the Four Seasons, Rosewood, and Hilton in Cabo! They're not a disgrace! They're great! They're terrific! Do you want your wife back or not?"

"Look, I...I need to think about this," said Rex. "I have my trusted advisors here in the room. Go get a drink, or take some drugs. Hell, it's okay with me if you want to fuck my wife. I'll Skype you right back."

Rex nodded to Gretchen; she clicked off Skype. Moon and Sally-Ann crept quietly back to their places on the sofa.

"Daddy, you have to make this deal," Gretchen said. "We need FLOTUS here. People love Natalia!"

"People don't love Natalia." He pointed to Moon. "*There's* the FLOTUS everyone loves." He beckoned her over to his desk.

Moon reluctantly stood up and walked over. "What's your price, Moon?"

"For what?"

"What will it take for you to stick around and be FLOTUS forever?"

She didn't know whether to laugh or scream. "You've got to be kidding!"

"What do you want? You'll have your own bedroom, of course. And you can be damn sure I will never, *ever* set foot in there, or make you come to mine. You can buy all the designer clothes, all the diamonds and expensive jewelry you want. How about a house on St. Barts? I have one there I'll give you. I hate St. Barts. Too many goddamn gays!"

Moon flinched. "I'm not gay, I'm a trans."

"Whatever. How about a million dollars? *Two* million?"

"Don't forget the girlfriend from Trinidad," piped in Pricker.

"Right, I forgot. I hear you've got a black girlfriend from Trinidad."

"Moon's got a *girlfriend*?" Sally-Ann shook her head, confused.

"Her name's Eliza," added Pricker. "Like in *Hamilton*."

"What's *Hamilton*?" asked Rex.

"Keep Eliza out of this," said Moon.

"I hear she's got visa problems. I could make them disappear, just like this." Rex tried to snap his fingers. They were so short, the snap sounded to Moon like a *ffft*.

"Y'know what, Mr. President?" She bristled with indignation. "Living here in the White House with you has been a truly unique experience. I am grateful for that, really. It has even been a smidgen, and I mean a *teeny-tiny* smidgen, fun. But you know what's astonished me the most?"

"That I'm so great?" Rex put his stockinged feet up on his desk, in Moon's face. "Great enough to be king of the world?"

"Are you *joking*?"

"Not really."

"Mr. President, what has amazed me most is that you, and also your beloved daughter, are ten times... No, make that *1,000 times* crueler, stupider, and more incompetent than any piece-of-shit human being I ever could imagine!" She turned abruptly and started toward the door.

Gretchen nodded to Pricker, who hustled over and grabbed Moon's arm. Gretchen walked over until she was nose-to-nose with her. "How about Daddy pays for your complete transformation?"

"What?"

"From a man to a woman. I mean, I know you've already got the tits, the nose, and the ass, but there's more work to be done, right? I hear the operation takes all day and you hurt like hell for weeks, but they'll get rid of that hideous Neanderthal ridge..." She tapped her finger on Moon's brow, then the lump covered by Moon's neck bandanna. "And your golf ball of an Adam's apple."

"Don't touch me!" Moon swatted her hand away.

Gretchen grabbed Moon's crotch and squeezed until she yelped. "Best of all, they will cut off your balls and take your beloved penis and turn it into a pulsating pink pussy!"

Chapter 58

Middle of Nowhere, Baja MX

December 20, 7:00 p.m.

"So the lovely little girl grew up into a kind, generous, and beautiful lady. One day her grandmother said, 'My darling granddaughter, it is time for you to climb up to the top of the mountain and marry Zlatorog.'"

"*Zlatorog?*" Conchita looked up at Natalia from where she lay in a pink, canopied, four-poster bed right out of a fairy tale. She was clutching a small pink-piglet plush toy. "But you said Zlatorog was a mean, selfish mountain-goat god who kept all his gold in a cave, and that he was guarded by a dragon with a hundred heads."

"He was," said Natalia, sitting beside her.

She had asked Rosa if she could tell Conchita a bedtime story to take her mind off the question haunting her: What would Rex say when he Skyped back? Dio was expecting his call any minute. If Rex refused to trade Dio's brother for her, would he kill her? If Dio was as evil as her own husband, she knew it was entirely possible.

Conchita wrinkled her brow. "If Zlatorog was so bad, why would the beautiful lady's *abuela*, her grandmother, want her to marry him?"

"Because her grandma said that if Zlatorog met a beautiful lady who was kind and generous, that he would change from a hideous monster into a handsome prince as kind and generous as she was."

"And then he would slay the dragon?"

"That's right. And he would invite all the people in the valley to climb up the mountain and take whatever gold they needed to live a happy life."

"So what did the beautiful lady do?"

Natalia brushed strands of Conchita's dark hair off her cheek. "What do you think she should do?"

The child stroked her small pink-piglet plush toy, thinking. "Do what her abuela said and marry Zlatorog?"

Natalia read the confusion on Conchita's face. "You know what, darling? When you grow up, sometimes it's okay *not* to do what your abuela, or your mother, says."

"It is?"

"Grandmothers and mothers are usually right, but not always. Sometimes they think something is true because they *hope* it is true. But hoping it's true is not the same as something *really* being true. So someday, when you are all grown up, no matter what anyone else tells you, even your mother or grandmother, you have to do what you know in your own heart is right."

"You mean the beautiful lady did *not* follow her abuela's advice?"

"In her heart, she didn't believe that an evil, selfish monster could ever change into a kind and generous prince, even if she married him. She thought once a monster is a monster, he can't change and become good, not even with a loving wife."

"So what did she do?"

"She didn't climb the mountain to Zlatorog's cave, that's for sure! She ran back to the little village where she grew up and lived her own happy life. A good life. One in which she helped other people and—"

"The White House is on Skype."

Rosa stood in the doorway of Conchita's bedroom.

Natalia tucked the little girl's pink covers under her chin. "I really enjoyed telling you that story, Conchita. I hope you will always remember it."

"I will." She tucked her little pink-piglet plush toy under the covers beside her.

"Good." She kissed her on the forehead and stood up from

the bed.

Rosa came over and kissed her daughter. "I love you, Conchita. Sleep tight." She followed Natalia to the door.

"I love you, Mama. I love you, Natalia," said the little girl as Rosa dimmed the lights and closed the door.

As they walked down the hallway toward Dio's office, Natalia noticed that Rosa was crying softly. "I'm the one who should be crying," she said. "Rex is going to have me—"

"You will be safe. I feel it in here." Rosa touched her heart. "And I want you to take Conchita with you."

"What?"

Rosa looked behind them to make sure no one was listening. "My sister Carla and her husband in San Diego don't have kids. They tried, but nothing worked. They'd love to take Conchita. They'll be good parents. Better than I could ever be."

"Can't they come to Mexico and adopt her?"

"Dio's lonely. He loves having Conchita here. He won't let her go. I mean, he thinks he's giving her a good life. He got her an English tutor and he gives her toys and books. But it scares the shit out of me to think what her life will be like if she grows up here. It's one thing now, when she's little. But once she gets *tits*? I don't trust Dio."

"What about Conchita's father? Can't he help?"

"I had Conchita when I was fourteen."

"You're only *seventeen*?"

"In six months, I'll be eighteen. Then I won't have to worry anymore about Dio jumping my ass. He really meant what he said. He never touches females over the age of eighteen. It's like he thinks if he does, he'll grow old, like them."

"Wait," she said, thinking. "Is Dio Conchita's *father*?"

Rosa laughed. "Dio got fixed after his tenth kid. Conchita's father was my boyfriend when I was fourteen. We thought we were in love. You know how it is."

"I know how it is," Natalia said wistfully.

"I didn't want to get an abortion. The whole Catholic thing." She made the sign of the cross. "Her dad's never seen Conchita, which is fine with me. My mom's a good grandma. I come to visit as often as I can. But I'm hoping you can do something." She touched her arm. "It's too late for me, but not for Conchita. It's like that fairy tale you told her... I was the pretty sister. I listened to my mom and got mixed up with bad men. Monsters with money. Men like that don't change. They stay bad."

"Where the fuck are you? The President is on Skype!" Dio was yelling from down the hall. "Get your ass here right now!"

"You are a good woman. You will be okay. I know it in here." She touched her chest, then grabbed Natalia's hand. They ran down the hall toward Dio's office.

Chapter 59

The White House

December 20, 10:30 p.m.

"She's bringing a *kid* with her? No way! She either comes home and gets knocked up with *my* kid in time for the convention, or no deal!"

Rex lay on a sofa in his bedroom, his shoes off, eating French fries from a McDonald's bag balanced on his stomach and watching FOX News with the sound off. Moon wasn't surprised that he had turned over the negotiating to Gretchen, who was seated at Rex's computer talking to Natalia on Skype. Moon couldn't see the computer screen from where she sat, but she had heard enough to know that the hostage exchange had been set up for tomorrow in Baja: FLOTUS for Dio's brother. Only one detail remained unsettled: Natalia refused to return unless she could bring along a three-year-old Mexican girl named Conchita Gonzales and an American photographer named Phillip Smith.

Across from the President, Moon sat on a sofa beside Sally-Ann, who was now her BFF. After Moon's scathing putdown of Rex, Gretchen had ordered her to plant herself beside her minder and keep her mouth shut. Sally-Ann had whispered into Moon's ear: "You blew him out of the water!" and squeezed her hand.

"Natalia says she's not adopting the little Mexican, Daddy," said Gretchen. "The kid's got an aunt and uncle in San Diego. They're U.S. citizens. All you have to do is get her a U.S. passport. They will adopt her."

"Fine! Done! Now who the fuck is this photographer?"

"I just googled Phillip Smith," said Pricker, who was sitting on the floor, hunched over his laptop. "He's a paparazzi."

"She's bringing home a fucking *paparazzi*? We don't have

enough of those vermin hanging around the White House?"

"Phillip Smith is not a paparazzo." Natalia's voice boomed over the computer speaker. "He is an architectural documentarian. And one more thing. I want you to hire him to photograph the most historic government buildings in Washington."

"Sounds fucking boring, but whatever," said Rex. "Just get your bootie back here!"

"I will. Tomorrow."

"How about tonight?"

"You miss me, Rex?" When he didn't answer, she continued. "Tomorrow. Philip has some photos he's got to shoot tonight for Dio."

With a *whoop* sound, Skype flicked off.

Gretchen stood up from Rex's desk and moved over to where he was sprawled on the sofa. She picked up her father's stretched-out legs, sat down, and cradled them on her lap.

"Scratch," he said.

Gretchen inserted both her hands up his right pant leg and scratched his leg with her long nails.

"*Mmmm.* Feels so fucking good," he murmured, closing his eyes.

Moon glanced over at Sally-Ann and made a finger-down-the-throat "barf" sign. Sally-Ann stifled a laugh.

"Daddy?" Gretchen cooed.

"What, baby?"

"I foresee a minor problem about tomorrow's hostage exchange. Actually, it's more of a major problem."

"What?"

"I mean, I'll be thrilled to get the real FLOTUS home tomorrow and kick out this fake." She shot Moon a dirty look. "But Pancho Reyes killed twelve DEA agents. You can't just let him go free."

"Why the fuck not? I'm the President."

"I know, Daddy, but we have to keep this whole hostage exchange top-secret. If we let Pancho out of prison, there are too many prison guards and officials, not to mention the grieving families of the victims, who will find out. And you know who will find out next!"

"The fake *New York Times*!" He pulled up his left pant cuff. "Scratch." She began scratching his left leg. "What's your solution?"

"I don't have one, Daddy," she said. "Do you?"

"Hey, don't look at me. I'm just the President!" He snickered. "Wait, I know."

He swung his legs off of Gretchen's lap and onto the floor. "In this very room, we are honored to have a man, whoops, I mean a woman, or *sort* of a woman, who just convinced the whole fucking world that she is FLOTUS." He stood up and walked over to Moon. "Moon, sweetheart, you're the world's greatest female impersonator. But you've still got balls and a pecker. I know cuz, fuck, I saw them myself! How about we pay you to impersonate Pancho Reyes? I mean, that would make you the world's greatest *male* impersonator, right?"

Moon glared up at him from the sofa. "*Forgetaboutit!*"

"C'mon," pressed Funck. "From what Pricker says, Pancho Reyes is hot. You do a little filler, a little Botox. It'll be a cake walk."

Before she could tell Rex to go to hell, Pricker looked up from his laptop. "Cancel that. It says here that Pancho Reyes is five-foot-four inches tall."

"How tall are you?" Rex asked Moon.

"Five eleven and a half. Same as Natalia."

"Too bad," he said. "If we can't make this work tomorrow, she'll be the loser." He walked back over to his sofa, lay down, and put his legs back up on Gretchen's lap. "Scratch."

Moon sat there a moment, fighting mounting panic. The bastard was right. If Dio didn't get his brother back, he would kill Natalia. She felt a hand on hers. Sally-Ann beckoned her closer and whispered in her ear. Moon brightened.

"No worries, I have the perfect solution," she announced to Rex and Gretchen. *Ohmygod, ohmygod, ohmygod!* she thought. Natalia is coming home!

Chapter 60

Middle of Nowhere, Baja MX

December 21, 12:00 p.m.

The Baja sun at noon was unforgiving. Natalia took off her blue L.A. Dodgers baseball hat, grateful that Phil had given it to her, and wiped the sweat from her head. Her hair was growing in fast. It felt as if she were petting a wet cat.

She walked over and sat down on a canvas folding chair under the enormous sun canopy, complete with solar-powered air-conditioning fans, that Dio's butlers had set up in the middle of what looked like flat, endless desert. Guarding the perimeter were six barrel-chested Mexican men in white-linen suits and sunglasses. Natalia noted that the walkie-talkie radio devices on their ears looked identical to those worn by U.S. Secret Service agents. So did the bulges of their handguns under their jackets.

She smoothed down the pink, red, and yellow YSL caftan that she was wearing, courtesy of Dio's mother. The loose, flowing gown was the only garment in Isabella's closet that had fit her. Like Cinderella's stepsisters, she had tried to squeeze into the tiny woman's shoes, but they were all too small. Isabella had given her a pair of Dio's hand-sewn leather huaraches to wear today. "You cannot walk on the desert at midday in your bare feet," she warned Natalia. "Your soles will be scorched, as if you'd stepped on hot coals."

Wearing a similar pair of huaraches, Dio was sitting with Phil at a nearby table. He was wearing a Panama hat, sunglasses, and a white-linen suit. Except for the scars on his face, he looks like a distinguished Mexican businessman, she thought. The two men were reviewing the photos that Phil had taken last night of Dio's house. They were displayed on a new Mac Book Pro that he had given Phil to take home with him. Natalia was thrilled that Dio was bananas over Phil's pictures. She could see from where she sat that they were worthy of *Architectural Digest.*

Wearing earbuds, Isabella was slouched on a sofa, glued to a Mexican telenovela on an iPad and smoking a cigarette. Natalia wondered if Isabella could really show up at Beau Rivage under an alias and not be revealed as the mother of one of the most notorious criminals in the world. With her ostentatious jewelry and over-the-top plastic surgery, she would fit in with the wives of some of the billionaires who belonged to Rex's club. Come to think of it, more than a few of those men made their money in ways that were as suspect as dealing drugs. The only difference is that they don't kill people, thought Natalia, at least not that we know of.

Rosa was sitting on another canvas sofa with Conchita on her lap, reading aloud from a book. Natalia was pleased to see that it was *Rosie Revere, Engineer.* Conchita stroked her small pink-piglet plush toy, riveted by the story. Too bad I wasn't exposed to books like that when I was Conchita's age, she thought. All she knew were the fairy tales that her babika told her, about princesses who married princes and lived happily ever after.

Natalia had convinced Dio to let Conchita go to the United States with her today by threatening to cancel her offer to take Phil's house photos to *Architectural Digest.* It had been a no-brainer for Dio: He loved Conchita, but he loved his house more.

Last night, while Dio supervised Phil's photo shoot, Natalia and Rosa had talked for hours on the terrace. They lay on their backs on chaise lounges, looking up at the stars. Rosa mentioned that someday, if she could figure out a way, she wanted to finish high school and go to college. She revealed that over the past year or so, during her visits here with Conchita, Dio had taught her about the stock market. "He likes having company when he's parked in front of CNBC," she said. "Sometimes he lets me pick stocks for him. If they make money, he lets me keep half. Guess what? I've earned enough to start a college fund for Conchita, and for me!" Rosa said she wanted to study finance and maybe go to business school. Natalia hoped that she would accomplish her dream. In fact, it hit her that there might be a way for her to help Rosa, like she was helping her daughter.

Before they went to bed, Natalia had glimpsed the Big Dipper and remembered the night—was it only two nights ago?—that she wondered if her "true love" was looking at the Big Dipper too. *Vaclav.* How could I have been so stupid? she thought.

She remembered what Angel always said: "Never look at what was. Focus on what will be." She wasn't sure what "will be" was for her. Maybe figuring it out would require a journey like the one on the Pacific Crest Trail that the Cheryl character took in that movie. Or maybe I already took that journey, she thought. Maybe my journey was escaping from the White House with Angel, meeting with Vaclav, and ending up here. Maybe all I need to do now is figure out what I learned from it.

"*Aquí vienen!* Here they come!"

Dio's helicopter pilot was pointing to an aircraft in the distance. Looking into the sun, Natalia couldn't make out much detail, but she was certain that it was the U.S. Army helicopter that Rex was sending for her and her two guests. Dio had deliberately selected this flat desolate patch of desert for their rendezvous, a wide-open space where both sides could see that there were no hidden gunmen. She hoped that all would go well, that both sides would play fair, and that she would be back at the White House with Conchita and Phil by tomorrow morning.

Dio's butlers hastily laid down a red carpet on the spot that was halfway between where Dio's Sikorsky had landed and where the U.S. helicopter was to land shortly. Rex had said that he wouldn't be on board because he had an important meeting at the White House. She pictured him sitting in his bedroom with his feet up, drinking a Diet Coke and watching FOX News. Or maybe he was frolicking under the covers with his latest piece of ass in the Presidential suite at the Washington Funck Hotel. She tried to picture it, but no image came to her.

Images of Rex with other women had haunted her like bad dreams since she met him. She tried to conjure one up now, but nothing appeared in her mind. She suddenly realized that the thought of Rex in bed with a bimbo didn't stab her in the heart, like it always did before she fled the White House. Maybe my journey here has taught me that Rex can't hurt me anymore, she thought. That I won't *let* him hurt me. Before she could ponder it further, Dio walked over.

"Señora Funck, it has been my pleasure to have you as a guest in my home," he said. He extended his hand and helped her up out of her chair.

"I hope someday you will meet my husband," she said. "You two have a lot in common."

Isabella joined them as they walked over to Dio's helicopter. She had traded her iPad and earphones for a pair of binoculars, which she was aiming eagerly at the sky.

His backpack slung over his shoulder, Phil strode over with Rosa, who was carrying Conchita tightly in her arms. Conchita clutched the book, *Rosie Revere, Engineer,* and her small pink-piglet plush toy. Natalia could see that both mother and daughter were fighting back tears.

The pilot jumped into the cockpit of Dio's helicopter. Natalia, Dio, and their entourage, and one of Dio's guards, stood in its shade and watched as the U.S. army helicopter swooped lower, the camouflaged colors on its cabin merging with the desert. The helicopter landed so gently—no jolting, no screeching brakes, as with an airplane landing—that it reminded Natalia of a grasshopper alighting on a potato plant in her babika's garden. If her babika saw it, the old woman would hobble over, grab the insect, and snap off its head. She cringed at the grisly memory.

The pilot cut his engine and the spinning rotors slowed. The hatch opened. From the shadowy interior, a short heavy-set man in the loose orange shirt and boxy pants of a prison uniform emerged. Pancho Reyes also wore a brimmed khaki cap that threw a shadow over his face. His hands were handcuffed behind his back. A Secret Service agent wearing a black T-shirt, black combat pants, and boots, nudged him from behind. Pancho climbed down a few portable steps from the helicopter to the ground. The agent followed and unlocked Pancho's handcuffs. Pancho stretched his arms and rubbed his wrists.

Natalia was surprised by how short he was: no more than five-feet-four, a lot shorter than his brother, Dio. Pancho was pudgy, his eyebrows were carefully plucked, and his pronounced lips, cheekbones, and jaw screamed Juvederm. A narcissist, like Rex, she thought.

"Mi hijo! Mi hijo!"

Isabella was peering at the prisoner through binoculars, wiping back tears. "They fed him well, *Dios mio!*"

Dio took the binoculars to see for himself. *"Muy bien,"* he said.

Dio handed the binoculars back to Isabella, then motioned for a guard to come forward. Natalia turned to Rosa and held out her arms. "I will take good care of you, Conchita, I promise," she said gently. "I will keep you safe."

Biting her lip, Rosa settled Conchita into Natalia's arms. "You are a brave little girl, mi amor, and very strong and very smart, like Rosie Revere." She kissed her cheek.

Natalia knew the plan. The Secret Service agent would escort Pancho Reyes from the U.S. helicopter to the red carpet. At the same time, Dio's guard would escort her, Conchita, and Phil over to it. The moment that Pancho and she passed each other on the red carpet, both pilots would switch on their engines. Passengers would proceed quickly to their respective helicopters, which would lift off at the same moment.

Dio's guard squeezed her arm as he escorted her toward the red carpet, leaning so close that she could smell his stale sweat. It was deadly still in the desert; she could hear the crunch of her huaraches on the sand.

She could see the prisoner more clearly as he approached. Though his cheekbones and lips were grotesquely thick from dermal filler, there was something about Pancho that looked familiar. Could she possibly have seen this Mexican man before?

They stepped onto the red carpet at the same time. Their eyes met. Pancho winked so quickly that she thought his eye had twitched. He did it again. A chill ran through her...

Ohmygod, it's Angel!

As he swept pass her, she clutched Conchita tighter and continued toward the helicopter.

"*No es mi hijo!*" Isabella shrieked.

Natalia glanced behind her: Dio grabbed the binoculars from his mother and aimed them at Angel. "Gringo motherfuckers! That is not my brother!" He called to the guard holding Natalia's arm: "*Mátalo!* Kill him!"

The guard dropped Natalia's arm. As he pulled a Walther from under his jacket, Angel's guard shot him in the stomach. The Mexican dropped to the ground.

Four Secret Service agents piled out of the U.S. helicopter, guns drawn. Two of Dio's guards traded fire with them.

Angel's guard let go of him and grabbed Natalia. Another one ran over and took Conchita. The men shielded them with their bodies as they raced toward the helicopter. Phil trailed behind them. As more shots were fired, the guards piled them all into the helicopter.

Natalia took Conchita from the agent's arms and sat down on a bench. The little girl wrapped her arms tightly around her neck, burying her head against her shoulder. "We're safe now," she murmured into Conchita's hair. "We're safe." Through the open side of the aircraft she watched Dio's helicopter lift into the air. Dio was leaning out of it, shaking his fist at them.

Phil pulled his camera from his backpack and aimed it at Dio. A Secret Service agent swatted at it. "No photos!" Phil sheepishly stowed away the camera.

Outside the helicopter, two of Dio's guards were down, blood seeping off the red carpet onto the sand. A Secret Service agent was helping a wounded colleague. Where was Angel? Natalia feared that Dio's men had forced him into their helicopter, which was rising into the sky. She dreaded that they would kill him.

A swath of bright orange on the pallid desert caught her eye: Angel in his prison uniform. With bullets flying, a hulking Secret Service agent hoisted his limp body into his arms and rushed him over to the helicopter. Reaching down from it, two others hoisted him inside. The agent jumped in and the helicopter lifted off.

As the chopper careened into the sky, Natalia kissed Conchita. "You were very brave," she said, brushing the little girl's dark hair out of her wide, terrified eyes.

"I didn't cry," she murmured.

"Your mother will be so proud." She hugged her. "I'll be right back." She handed Conchita to Phil and nodded to the book under the child's arm. "Read her *Rosie Revere*."

"Sure thing," he said.

She made her way over to where Angel was sprawled on the floor behind the pilot's seat. His eyes closed, he was motionless. A woman in a nurse's uniform crouched over his body.

Her heart sinking, Natalia whispered, "Is he *dead*?"

"I think he fainted."

At the sound of the nurse's familiar low feminine voice, Natalia looked at her. She took in the pink-streaked black wig under her nurse's cap, her glittering purple eye shadow, and the pink hearts on her white nurses' clogs. *"Moon?"*

Moon blew her an air-kiss, then turned back to Angel. She carefully ripped away his orange prison garb. Underneath it he was wearing a thick Kevlar bulletproof body suit. A slug was wedged into the extra-thick metal padding over his chest. She pulled it out with difficulty. "He is one lucky angel."

One of his eyelids flickered, as if he were winking in a dream.

"Angel," Natalia whispered. *"Angel?"*

He opened his eyes, blinked a few times, and looked up into her face. "Que chido," he said weakly, smiling. "Did I die and go to heaven?"

"Yes, my angel." She kissed him on the forehead.

Chapter 61

The White House

January 21, 8:00 a.m.

Natalia watched in the mirror as Angel put the finishing touches on her new hairstyle. She knew that millions of Americans would judge it tonight when she stood behind her husband as he gave his State of the Union address in the Capitol. Some people will be shocked by my hair, so expect a tweet storm, she thought, but I love it. The style was shorter than any she had worn before, making the most of the hair that had grown in since she returned a month ago from what she referred to as her "Baja Adventure." Angel and she had debated about whether or not to allow the few strands of gray that had appeared among her natural ash-blonde strands. "They're natural, they're mine, they stay," she decided.

Angel unsnapped the plastic beauty-salon cape she was wearing over her Lululemon workout clothes and whipped it off. He studied her face in the mirror.

"Chica, I'd call your hairstyle a cross between Audrey Hepburn and...*well*, Natalia."

"Once again, you've worked a miracle!"

"It's way cool, even the whisper of gray. It adds *gravitas*, dignity!" He adjusted a curl near her ear. "The new you!"

She swung the styling chair around so that she faced him. "I kind of do feel like a new person since, y'know —"

"Does it feel good?"

"Definitely. I don't feel the old anger, or the fear. I guess you could say I feel in control."

"I don't!" He examined his face in the mirror, patting his pumped-up cheekbones and bulbous lips, fingering the space that remained between his plucked eyebrows. "I can't wait to *not* look like Pancho Reyes! How many more pinches weeks—?"

"You're still guapo!"

He tossed his comb onto the counter. "So what are you wearing tonight to go with my new hairdo?"

"I hope you like it!" She stood up and walked into the closet, Angel one step behind her. She checked the number "438" that she had scrawled in ink on her palm and punched it into the keypad on the garment-rack system. The clothes whirred by for a few seconds and stopped at slot 438. Angel removed the hanger holding a red garment that was nestled in tissue and plastic, then led her over to the alcove with a three-way mirror. As he removed the garment from the hanger, she stripped down to her bra and thong undies and stepped up onto the pedestal in front of the mirror.

He glanced at her right butt cheek. "I see your heart mole made it home intact."

"I'm glad." She laughed. "It got quite a workout."

He handed her the short red-wool suit skirt first, which she stepped into and pulled up, then the suit jacket. He buttoned it. The form-fitting jacket had a V-neck, but it wasn't so low-cut that it revealed her cleavage. "No boob show, huh? Pretty conservative for Dolce and Gabbana."

"Think it's too Republican?"

He tugged the jacket down so that there was a discrete glimpse of cleavage. "That's better." He stood back and admired her. "*Elegante*, and red's definitely your color."

"Zip me up please?" She turned around and Angel pulled up the back zipper on her skirt. It wouldn't close.

"Are alterations scheduled?"

"I had it altered last week!" She giggled. "I guess I need to have it taken out again."

"Yo, you are growing fast, mama!"

She punched an intercom button on the wall. "Sally-Ann? Can you come in here? And call the new maid, what's her name?"

"Kim Yi," said Sally-Ann over the intercom.

"I need Kim Yi to make some quick alterations on my suit for tonight."

"Yo, what happened to Hilda?" asked Angel.

"Gretchen fired her while I was gone."

"The bitch!"

"I know. I tried to hire her back, but guess what?"

"What?"

"She went to Miami."

"Miami?"

"Moon is taking her to her sex-change surgeon there. Hilda wants to transition to a man, vták and all!"

"Good for her!"

Natalia put her hands on her belly and looked at herself in the three-way mirror. "Am I showing yet?"

"In your head, yes. In the mirror, no."

"I can't wait until I do. The whole thing... I mean, I still can't believe Rex went along with my terms."

"You drove a hard bargain."

The cell phone in his pocket rang. Natalia was glad that she had convinced Rex to allow Angel to carry a phone in the White House.

"It's Raphael. He arrives tomorrow from Cabo to start his new gig!" Angel answered the phone, listened, then spoke rapidly in Spanish. "Raphael says, 'hola!'" he called to her on his way out of the room.

Natalia was delighted that Raphael was taking a job as head chef at Lafayette, one of the best restaurants in D.C. He was moving in with Angel; they would be her family. As she waited for him to return from taking the call with Raphael, she thought back to the events of the past month. When she returned from Baja, she had carried through on the condition that Rex demanded for rescuing her: She met with Dr. Steinberg to start a new series of hormone shots so that Rex could get her pregnant in time for the Republican Convention in August. To her surprise, the doctor had discovered that she didn't need more hormone shots.

"I have good news!" she told Rex after her doctor's examination. "I'm pregnant!"

"Terrific," he said. "All that fucking we did before you, y'know, worked!"

Then she told Rex the bad news, for him. "Dr. Steinberg did a DNA test. The baby isn't yours."

"It's that Slovak fuck's?"

"Couldn't be anyone else's."

"You're getting a goddamn abortion!" Rex roared.

"No, I am not," she said. "You either let me have my baby or I will let the world know that you, yes, *you*, Mr. "pro-life" President, wanted it aborted."

Of course, Rex couldn't let the press find that out, so he caved. It gave her the courage to make a deal with him: Rex could have as many affairs as he wished as long as he kept them secret and they didn't take place inside the White House. In return, she would show up at the Republican Convention with her baby bump to make Rex look like a stud and help him get reelected. If he won, she would stay with him in the White House, raising "their" child, for another four years. If he lost, she would divorce him after the new President was inaugurated and take the baby to live in San Diego. She planned to open a school there for the children of newly arrived Mexican immigrants. It would be a sister school to the Escuela de Alegría that she had visited in Tijuana. If Rex didn't want to pay for it, she was sure that she could raise the money herself.

It seemed like a great deal, but Natalia was troubled. With the new self-confidence that she had gained on her journey, she had pressed Rex to ease up on immigration and anti-abortion laws, and to propose new laws supporting the LGBTQ community and the environment. "Are you fucking crazy?" he screamed. "My base will kick me in the balls!" And if Rex won the election, as was predicted, she would be stuck living with him for another four years.

I can't do it, she thought. There's got to be a way out...

Angel returned to the closet. "Yo, it's all good," he said, as if reading the concern on her face.

Sally-Ann was a few steps behind Angel, her iPad at the ready, her tote bag slung over her shoulder. "Ma'am, are you okay?"

"I'm fine, thanks," she said. Sally-Ann had been warmer since her return, as if whatever had transpired between Moon and her during Moon's "tenure" as FLOTUS had changed her for the better. Natalia now considered her social secretary a friend.

Sally-Ann turned on her iPad. "What can I help you with?"

"Can you please check on the status of the immigration petitions the President requested for Rosa Gonzales and her daughter, Conchita?" Natalia had insisted in her deal with Rex that he guarantee U.S. citizenship for both the daughter and the mother. Rosa had been thrilled when she told her the news: Once their legal status was confirmed, Rosa would be free to live with Conchita at her sister's in San Diego and finish school.

"I checked this morning. Good news! Their papers have been approved!"

"Fantastic!"

"It's amazing what you can accomplish when you get tough with your husband."

Natalia stared at her social secretary. Before she fled the White House, Sally-Ann had been meek and obedient. "Excuse me. Did you really just *say* that?"

Sally-Ann stood there nervously, as if not sure what to say next.

"Dude, go for it." Angel wink/twitched at Sally-Ann.

She walked over and closed the closet door, then returned to them. "Ma'am, there's something I need to tell you."

Sally-Ann's enunciation and Southern accent were more

pronounced than usual, as if what she was about to say was important. "Whatever it is, you can say it in front of Angel. We're all family here."

"I know," she said, blushing. "That's what I feel too. That's why I'm telling you this."

Natalia beckoned Sally-Ann and Angel to follow her over to a sitting area in a corner of the vast closet. They sank down onto a white-leather sofa. "What is it?"

"I have a confession to make." She hugged the enormous tote bag on her lap.

"A confession?"

"I know the reason I was hired to be your social secretary was because my daddy was a big Funck supporter."

"No worries. That's the way it works," she said. "We all know that."

"But then Gretchen told me what was required in the job. I should have said 'no' to her, but I wanted—"

"'No' to what?"

"Gretchen gave me this." Sally-Ann reached into her tote bag and pulled out a small digital tape recorder.

Natalia shook her head. "Why am I not surprised?"

"She told me to keep it secret, but that whenever I was with you, I was to record your conversations: in your bedroom, your salon, your office. I brought her the diskettes once a week and we would sit down and listen to them. If Gretchen didn't know who you were talking to on a tape, I'd explain. I mean, most of your conversations were with your mom, or your yoga and Pilates teachers."

"Or me?" said Angel.

"Sometimes, but Natalia usually kicked me out when you showed up. Anyway, Gretchen got bored. I don't know what she was hoping for—"

"That I was cheating on Rex?" Natalia laughed. "That I was conspiring to have her assassinated?"

"I'm not sure, but after a couple of months, she said, 'I don't have time to listen to this shit.'"

"A long attention span was never one of Gretchen's strong points."

"She told me to keep recording the First Lady's conversations, but only to come to her if there was something incriminating on the tapes, something she should know about. So since she didn't tell me otherwise, I kept taping your conversations. And then, when Moon became First Lady, I continued. She didn't say *not* to. Believe me, once Gretchen made me Moon's minder, the conversations I recorded got a lot more, er, interesting!"

"Wow, that's, well, I appreciate that you told me this, Sally-Ann," said Natalia, stunned. "I appreciate your honesty, and your loyalty."

"You're the best, ma'am!" Her cheeks reddened, as if she were about to cry. "I sure wish you were President, instead of your husband!"

"That's so sweet of—"

"Ask Sally-Ann if she still has them," Angel blurted out.

"What?"

"The tapes."

"I assume Gretchen has them." Natalia turned to Sally-Ann, suddenly hoping that she didn't. "Do you—?"

"Gretchen told me to destroy them, but I have this thing about trashing stuff. My mom calls me 'Harriet Hoarder' cuz I can't throw things away. Back home in Alabama, I've still got every doll I ever played with, every dress I ever wore as a—"

"You've got the *tapes*?" Natalia took a deep breath of anticipation.

Sally-Ann rummaged in her tote bag and pulled out a Neiman-Marcus shopping bag. She opened it.

Natalia peered inside: dozens of mini-tape-recorder diskettes. "*Seriously?*"

"These are just the conversations I taped after you left for, er, wherever. Some of them are so unbelievable they don't sound real, but, trust me, they are." She held out the bag.

Natalia flexed her fingers, wondering if she had the strength to do what she imagined might be possible.

"Chica, you proved you got cajones," said Angel. "Take 'em!"

Natalia turned to him, unsure. He grabbed the Neiman-Marcus bag from Sally-Ann. With a rustle of plastic, he plopped it onto her lap.

The bag felt light, but her mind raced with how *weighty* the tapes could be, not just for strengthening her deal with Rex. Her heart pounded as she considered the possibilities.

As if worried that Natalia was zoning out, Sally-Ann said, "I know you don't want to do anything to hurt your husband. I mean, I was raised to respect whatever my husband says or does, if I ever find one. It's the Southern way. But ma'am, like, you are—"

"FLOTUS!" Natalia rubbed her index finger over the wedding band on her left finger. "You didn't notice. I'm not wearing the locomotive headlight."

"The *what*?" said Angel.

"My 15-karat diamond engagement ring."

"Someone *stole* it?" said Sally-Ann.

She shook her head. "It's in the safe. I told Rex I wouldn't wear it anymore. It's ostentatious, flashy. It sends the wrong message to the public. I took a stand about that ring. I can take a stand about a lot more!" She gripped the Neiman-Marcus shopping bag and stood up. "The tapes are going in the safe too."

"Que chido!" said Angel.

Natalia took a deep yoga breath to clear her head and give her courage. "Thank you, Sally-Ann." She gently took her hand. "Thanks to both of you!" She took Angel's hand too. Then she beckoned them into a group hug.

EPILOGUE

Los Angeles Convention Center

August 5, 8:00 p.m.

Phil made his way through the mob of revelers in the vast auditorium of the Los Angeles Convention Center. The delegates at the GOP Convention ranged from stuffy, white-haired, old-timers, and shorthaired, clean-cut Yuppies, to what he considered an alarming number of rednecks wearing "Funck More Years" baseball hats and carrying "Funck Forever" signs. Above them, a net stretched across the ceiling sagged under what he had read in the *L.A. Times* were more than two million balloons, like a giant red, white, and blue storm cloud.

Phil's special press pass gained him entry to the VIP area in front of the gigantic stage. Natalia had arranged for it, of course. Since returning to the White House, the First Lady had helped him jumpstart a new life. She introduced him to the editor-in-chief of *Architectural Digest*, who promptly bought his photos of Dio's house. When the story of the drug king's fortress ran in the June issue with Phil's photos on the cover, it was the biggest-selling issue in *A.D.* history and the editor-in-chief made him a contributing photographer. He looked forward to shooting other remarkable houses around the world for the magazine. He was also working on a coffee-table book featuring historic government buildings for *National Geographic*, a dream gig that Natalia helped get him.

He was glad that this year's Republican Convention was in Los Angeles. It was giving him a chance to spend time with his mother. She was so proud of his recent accomplishments, that she had plastered his *A.D.* photos on the refrigerator in her new house, a California Craftsman bungalow with a river-rock façade and redwood trim. He had put a down payment on it for her with the money he earned from the article and the book advance.

Phil was carrying his camera and super-long lens tonight

because he wanted to get a photo of Natalia when she appeared on stage with her husband. He checked his watch. The First Couple was due to arrive any minute.

Funck had won most of the Republican primaries. Phil had heard rumors that Joe Gertz, an old-line conservative from Oklahoma who came in second, was paid from GOP coffers to go up against Funck so that it would appear that Republicans had a choice. But everyone knew that Funck's hard-core base held all the cards. According to the latest polls, this fall's race between Funck and Denzel Epstein, the Democratic nominee, was a toss-up. Epstein was a rookie Congressman from California, a brilliant Rhodes Scholar who was half-Jewish, half-black. Phil had voted for him in the California Democratic Primary and believed he would make a great President, but he didn't dare contemplate Epstein's chances against the President in November. Phil despised everything about Rex Funck: his politics, his personality, his... He could go on and on. It only made him angry. He decided to stop thinking and take photos.

"Ladies and gentlemen!"

The Republican Party Chairman's voice rang out in the cavernous arena. "It is my honor to introduce the next President of the United States, who just happens to be the *current* President of the United States. And with him tonight is his amazing First Lady! Please join me in a warm welcome!"

The crowd went wild as President Funck and Natalia, flanked by Secret Service agents, made their way through the throng on the stage, holding hands and waving. Trailing behind them were Funck's children and grandchildren, waving as if they were the stars tonight themselves. The First Couple's approach to the podium was slow going. Politicos stepped up to pump Rex's hand and admire the prominent baby bump that Natalia carried with what Phil considered her usual grace.

He raised his camera and began snapping photos. Through his long lens, he could see her clearly, as if she were three feet away. Looking elegant in a red maternity dress, she had a glow to her skin and her eyes were bright. He saw none of the fear, sadness, and anxiety that he had captured in his earlier coverage of her. For the first time in the years he had photographed Natalia, she looked genuinely happy.

"Ladies and gentlemen, tonight it is our honor to witness the moment when President Rex Funck accepts the nomination as the Republican Candidate for President of the United States!"

The crowd screamed and yelled, "Four more years," for what seemed like an hour. Phil hated being stuck in the middle of an unruly crowd. It seemed as if every person here was either smashed, stoned, or caught up in a frenzy of mob hysteria. Their fervor rattled him. He took a deep yoga breath to calm himself.

Yoga was another new thing in his life for which he thanked Natalia. She had invited him to join the yoga class that she now taught once a week for White House employees in the staff cafeteria. Everyone was welcome, from butlers, maids, and cooks, to Secret Service agents. Phil had made friends with students in the yoga class, including a junior White House historian. He wished that Min Linh, the granddaughter of Vietnamese refugees, could be here with him now.

Rex Funck stepped up to the podium. Natalia positioned herself a few steps to the left and behind him. The Secret Service agents moved off to the sides of the stage. Phil noted that another team of Secret Service agents was positioned in front of it, warily scanning the audience.

When the crowd finally stopped cheering, Rex cleared his throat and began to speak. "Ladies and gentlemen, friends, family and my lovely First Lady—who, as you can see, is soon to be the mother of my newest daughter!" The crowd roared. He turned and kissed Natalia on the cheek, then waited for the cheers to die down.

"Okay, so I have good news. Yours truly crushed it in every single Republican primary but one." Applause and whistles in the audience. Phil knew that Rex was incorrect, that he had won all but five of the primaries, but what he did expect from this world-class liar?

"Campaigning was terrific! It was just great! I had so much fun on the campaign trail!" He put his thumb and index finger in an "o" shape that matched his lips, a gesture of his that Phil loathed. "Out there in the heartland, I got to meet so many wonderful people, terrific people, salt-of-the earth *American* people! Thank you so much for that opportunity! I will never ever forget it!"

The cheers and applause went on and on. Funck raised his hands. "I know, I know! I've done a great job as President, a tremendous job, and you love me, you really love me! I love you too, I really do, but tonight I've also got some bad news."

The crowd gasped as one.

Phil could see that Rex was ignoring the words on the teleprompter as he continued. "As much as I would love to—and, trust me, I would really, really love to—I have decided *not* to accept the Republican nomination for President of the United States!"

There was a moment of stunned silence, then groans and sobs erupted in the crowd.

"I know, you're sad about it. Trust me, I'm even sadder! But Natalia and I discussed it for weeks and I made my decision," he said. "By the way, she only let me run again because she knows how much I get off on campaigning. I mean, I've been running for reelection since the day I got elected the first time, right?" He turned to her. "Thank you, sweetie, for letting me have so much fun the past six months." He kissed her cheek, then turned back to the audience.

"WTF!" someone yelled from the crowd. "What the fuck!?"

An angry chant started: "*What the fuck? What the fuck? What the—?*"

"Okay, I know you want to know why I made this decision,

and you're entitled, believe me, you're entitled!" The crowd simmered down. "Is it because I'm too old? I'm seventy-five. Okay, I could stand to lose a few pounds, but I'm in great shape for seventy-five. I don't have high blood pressure, a heart condition, or cancer. I sure as hell don't have Alzheimer's and I can still get it up, big time! Ask my wife!"

Natalia blushed with embarrassment. Phil could see that on stage and in the audience, even the President's diehard fans squirmed.

"But seventy-five is seventy-five," Funck continued. "At my age, enough is enough, right? And I have another kid coming. I've got to get back to my business in New York and focus on my family. I turned my company over to my kids four years ago and now it's a mess, a complete fucking disaster!"

Behind him, Funck's children cringed. Phil shot some photos of them, then swung around to capture shots of the audience: Young, old, and redneck alike were glaring at the President. This turn of events will ruin the election for the Republicans, he thought. Suddenly euphoric, he kept shooting.

Rex turned to his children. "Just kidding, guys! You've done a great job with my business! Just terrific!" They didn't smile, as if terrified of what he'd say next.

"We've got Funck International Hotels going up in all the countries that I or my kids have visited while I've been President. That's thirty-four new Funck International Hotels! Rex Funck will not only go down as the best leader, but also as the best businessman in the history of our great country!" He applauded, each clap of his hands echoing in the growing silence of the cavernous room.

Through his long lens, Phil focused in on the Republican Party Chairman as he approached Funck at the podium, angrily motioning for him to wrap it up. Funck ignored him. Though no one was applauding, he kept clapping and waving to the crowd, as if he had just won the election in November.

"So, you folks out there are now stuck with Joe Gertz as your candidate, even though I beat the bastard by, like, millions and millions of votes!" It was another lie on Rex's part, Phil knew. "But I have another solution," he said. "If you don't want Joe Gertz—and who the fuck would?—how's this for an alternative? How about giving the nomination to the First Daughter?"

He beckoned Gretchen to join him. Her eyes and mouth were wide with astonishment. "C'mon, baby! Come to papa!" He motioned for the crowd to join him in applause, but no one did. Gretchen hesitated, then broke into a fake smile and started toward him. Her husband grabbed her arm to stop her, but she batted his hand away and stepped up to the podium beside her father.

"I mean, you gotta hand it to her," said Funck, slipping his arm around her. "These past four years, Gretchen has not only been my trusted White House advisor, but she has built her designer brand all over the world. You've got Gretchen Funck perfume, Gretchen Funck purses, and Gretchen Funck pantyhose, you name it! And how about this? Gretchen Funck tampons are now the best-selling tampons in China!"

Phil could hear "boos" rippling through the crowd. Rex kissed her on the lips and the "boos" grew thunderous. As if her father were the Grim Reaper, Gretchen pulled away and ran off stage.

"Well, if you don't want my baby girl, how about my smart-ass son, James?" Funck turned around, looking at where his oldest son had been standing. James and his siblings were hustling their families off stage. Some of the GOP VIPs were exiting as well. Others just stood there, unsure what to do.

The Republican Party Chairman frantically beckoned to the Secret Service agents flanking the stage. They hustled toward Funck.

A chant in the crowd, growing louder. *"Natalia! Natalia! Natalia!"*

Rex looked stunned. "You want my *wife*?"

"*Yesssssss!*" and whistles from the crowd.

"You can have the bitch! She's fucking leaving me after the inauguration!"

Phil snapped a photo of the mortification on Natalia's face.

The Secret Service agents reached Funck and grabbed his arms. As they wrestled him off the stage, Natalia boldly stepped up to the mic. "Ladies and gentleman, I know you wanted Rex Funck as your candidate. I know his rejection of that honor comes as a shock. I am genuinely sorry."

"*Natalia! Natalia! Natalia!*" the crowd roared.

Phil joined in. "*Natalia for President! Natalia for President!*"

"Believe me, I would like to serve you, but I was not born in America," she continued. "I cannot run for President. Maybe that rule in the Constitution will change some day." The GOP Chairman whispered in her ear, but she ignored him. "But for now, I promise I will serve my adopted country in other ways, like with my new school for immigrant children in San Diego."

The chairman beckoned to the Secret Service agents below the stage. They leaped up onto it and moved in on Natalia.

Suddenly, like a storm cloud bursting, the net hanging from the ceiling gave way and millions of balloons deluged the auditorium. Phil snapped a barrage of photos as Natalia was whisked off stage in a blur of red, white, and blue.

The audience exploded in mayhem. At the mic, the GOP chairman was trying to calm everyone down, but he didn't stand a chance. Jostled by the crowd and batting away balloons, Phil made his way slowly through the throng, away from the stage.

Suddenly, he heard what sounded like a gunshot and froze. More "shots" rang out and he realized that they were the sounds of balloons popping: Angry delegates were stabbing at them with pins, pens, and whatever sharp objects they could find as they rained down. The mob of irate balloon poppers swelled.

Phil forced his way through the mob, but soon found himself

wedged between two sweaty guys wearing "Dixie Digs Funck" hats who towered over him. Instead of popping balloons, they were swigging beer.

"Someone's got deep dirt on the old guy," one said in a thick Southern accent. "Why else would he back out?"

"Bet it's a sex thing," drawled his friend.

"Or money, or god knows what!"

"Think it's China?"

"How 'bout the Russians?" said his companion.

Phil had had enough. He flicked on his camera's "flash" button and snapped a salvo of photos in the big guys' faces. They shielded their eyes from the light. He seized the moment to slip away from them.

"Motherfucker!" one shouted after him as he elbowed his way through the balloon-popping crowd.

He spotted an exit sign up ahead and pressed toward it. Finally, he burst out of the convention-center doors.

Outside, the sidewalk was brimming with enraged Republicans and over-the-moon Democratic protesters. Screaming matches and fistfights were breaking out, spilling into the street. Phil snapped a few photos, but he could see the red lights and hear the sirens of police cars approaching. I'm fucking outta here, he thought.

He skirted the throng and slowly made his way down a couple of long city blocks. When the crowd around him thinned, he hoisted his camera. Before he stowed it in his backpack, he wanted to check out the last photos he had snapped of Natalia. He stepped into a deserted alley and clicked through them. Captured with his super-long lens, the shots were remarkably clear, revealing every nuance of her expression: Natalia approaching the mic; Natalia speaking to the crowd; Natalia being escorted off stage in a tempest of balloons. In all of the photos, she looked calm and self-confident, smiling and happy. "Natalia, you crushed it!" he said to himself. He shoved his camera into his backpack and jogged down the alley.

When he emerged, he spotted a Metro sign up ahead and broke into a run. As he dashed across a busy street, zigzagging through traffic, he threw his arms into the air, as if he were crossing a finish line at the Olympics. "You rocked, Natalia!" he shouted. "You go, girl!"

Feeling the wind on his face, he was jolted back to the memory of galloping down the beach with her on their feisty little horses in Baja. "*Yee-haw*, Natalia!" he yelled, laughing.

"*Yee-fucking-haw!*"

About the Author

Verity Speeks was inspired to write *The First Lady Escapes: FLOTUS Flees the White House* because of the outrage, frustration, and helplessness she has felt since November 8, 2016, when a meteor with a bad comb-over struck the earth and caused devastating consequences that continue to wreak havoc.

Email: Verity.Speeks@gmail.com

Twitter: @verityspeeks

Facebook: @Firstladyescapes

FICTION

Put simply, we publish great stories. Whether it's literary or popular, a gentle tale or a pulsating thriller, the connecting theme in all Roundfire fiction titles is that once you pick them up you won't want to put them down.

If you have enjoyed this book, why not tell other readers by posting a review on your preferred book site.

Recent bestsellers in the JHP Fiction range are:

The Bookseller's Sonnets
Andi Rosenthal
The Bookseller's Sonnets intertwines three love stories with a tale of religious identity and mystery spanning five hundred years and three countries.
Paperback: 978-1-84694-342-3 ebook: 978-184694-626-4

Birds of the Nile
An Egyptian Adventure
N.E. David
Ex-diplomat Michael Blake wanted a quiet birding trip up the Nile – he wasn't expecting a revolution.
Paperback: 978-1-78279-158-4 ebook: 978-1-78279-157-7

Blood Profit$
The Lithium Conspiracy
J. Victor Tomaszek, James N. Patrick, Sr.
The blood of the many for the profits of the few... *Blood Profit$* will take you into the cigar-smoke-filled room where American policy and laws are really made.
Paperback: 978-1-78279-483-7 ebook: 978-1-78279-277-2

The Burden
A Family Saga
N.E. David
Frank will do anything to keep his mother and father apart. But he's carrying baggage – and it might just weigh him down ...
Paperback: 978-1-78279-936-8 ebook: 978-1-78279-937-5

The Cause
Roderick Vincent
The second American Revolution will be a fire lit from an internal spark.
Paperback: 978-1-78279-763-0 ebook: 978-1-78279-762-3

Don't Drink and Fly
The Story of Bernice O'Hanlon: Part One
Cathie Devitt
Bernice is a witch living in Glasgow. She loses her way in her life and wanders off the beaten track looking for the garden of enlightenment.
Paperback: 978-1-78279-016-7 ebook: 978-1-78279-015-0

Gag
Melissa Unger
One rainy afternoon in a Brooklyn diner, Peter Howland punctures an egg with his fork. Repulsed, Peter pushes the plate away and never eats again.
Paperback: 978-1-78279-564-3 ebook: 978-1-78279-563-6

The Master Yeshua
The Undiscovered Gospel of Joseph
Joyce Luck
Jesus is not who you think he is. The year is 75 CE. Joseph ben Jude is frail and ailing, but he has a prophecy to fulfil ...
Paperback: 978-1-78279-974-0 ebook: 978-1-78279-975-7

Tuareg
Alberto Vazquez-Figueroa
With over 5 million copies sold worldwide, *Tuareg* is a classic adventure story from best-selling author Alberto Vazquez-Figueroa, about honour, revenge and a clash of cultures.
Paperback: 978-1-84694-192-4

On the Far Side, There's a Boy
Paula Coston

Martine Haslett, a thirty-something 1980s woman, plays hard on the fringes of the London drag club scene until one night which prompts her to sign up to a charity. She writes to a young Sri Lankan boy, with consequences far and long.

Paperback: 978-1-78279-574-2 ebook: 978-1-78279-573-5

David and the Philistine Woman
Paul Boorstin

Young David's destiny collides with the wife of Goliath in this suspenseful re-imagining of a crucial turning point in the Bible.

Paperback: 978-1-78535-537-0 ebook: 978-1-78535-538-7

Kill All Normies
Angela Nagle

How internet subcultures are conquering the mainstream, from from 4chan and Tumblr to Trump and the alt-right.

Paperback: 978-1-78535-543-1 ebook: 978-1-78535-544-8

The Coming Revolution: Capitalism in the 21st Century
Ben Reynolds

A technological revolution is driving capitalism toward crisis and collapse – can our society evolve in time to rescue the future?

Paperback: 978-1-78535-709-1 ebook: 978-1-78535-710-7

The Meaning of Trump
Brian Francis Culkin

An ideological critique of Donald Trump in which his election is seen as only a natural progression of the logic that is innate to neoliberal globalization.

Paperback: 978-1-78904-046-3 ebook: 978-1-78904-047-0

Readers of ebooks can buy or view any of these bestsellers by clicking on the live link in the title. Most titles are published in paperback and as an ebook. Paperbacks are available in traditional bookshops. Both print and ebook formats are available online.

Find more titles and sign up to our readers' newsletter at
http://www.johnhuntpublishing.com/fiction

Follow us on Facebook at
https://www.facebook.com/JHPfiction
and Twitter at https://twitter.com/JHPFiction